OF LORDS AND COMMONERS

BOOK 1

THE LORDS AND COMMONERS SERIES

LYNNE HILL

Third Edition: 2019

❀ Created with Vellum

OTHER BOOKS BY LYNNE

<u>The Lords and Commoners Series</u>

Of Lords and Commoners Book 1

Of Princes and Dragons Book 2

Of Gods and Goddesses Book 3

A Gods and Goddesses Novelette

<u>A Woman's World Series</u>

A Woman's World Book 1

Lost Powers Book 2

A Collision of Worlds Book 3

This book is dedicated, with much love, to Steve. Thank you for everything!

Thee, whom the Angels desire to look into, may my heart ever hunger after and feed upon; and may my soul be filled with thy sweetness.

Saint Augustine's Prayer Book (1947)

PROLOGUE

We ran swiftly through the forest. Teller was on my left and a familiar young man was on my right — though I did not know his name. Odd — why could I not place him? I cared deeply for him. A dear friend, a lover? Surely not.

My home came into view in a small meadow. Sunlight filtered down through the surrounding tall trees, illuminating the small house. As we entered my home I looked to Teller, only he was no longer human; he was a large gray wolf. A brief glance around confirmed my suspicion — we were all wolves. Behind us were many others — my pack. I would die for them, as they would for me. We were in full hunting mode. Teller crouched down and stealthily headed for the common room, where I knew my father would be. The familiar wolf on my right headed up the stairs after my brother, no doubt. Yet I did not care — I was hungry.

Father sat sleeping in his favorite chair. He had been waiting up for someone, probably me. Just as Teller lunged for Father's throat, I bit into Father's leg. The iron-sweet taste of blood flooded into my mouth.

I woke with a start, sitting straight up in bed. I spat to get the taste of blood out of my mouth and used my sleeve to try to wipe away the imaginary substance. It was not the first time I had had that awful dream. I slowly lay back down. *Just a dream, it is not real,* I tried to comfort myself. Yet the nightmare was becoming more and more vivid as the years passed. *Don't be a fool, Vallachia — the dream does not even make sense,* my voice of reason argued. *Teller and I would never kill my father and I would not let someone harm my brother!*

It was the middle of the night. As tired as I was, I did not allow my eyes to close. I feared falling back into that nightmare. I stared across the hall to my brother's room, resisting the urge to crawl into bed with him, as I would have done when I was a child.

CHAPTER 1 LUDUS 1260 AD

As I washed dishes in the tavern, something suddenly jabbed me in the ribs. I let out a scream and jumped. When I turned around, Teller was laughing heartily.

He stopped laughing long enough to say, "I can't believe you are still fooled by that. You are easy to scare."

He had always enjoyed startling me, much to my dislike. One would think I would have become accustomed to it but I had not. "Teller! Why must you always do that?" I yelled. My heart was pounding; I had nearly jumped out of my skin. I took the dishrag from over my shoulder and tried to hit him with it but he easily dodged it.

This brought a fresh round of laughter from him.

"I'm glad I amuse you."

"You always have." His voice was full of affection, which lessened my irritation.

He looked different; he had grown a beard! Well, most of a beard. I marched up to him and scratched his furry chin with my fingertips. "What is this?"

"My little brother and I have been in the mountains for the past week, gathering wood for your uncle."

"So that is where you have been?" I tilted my head and studied him for a moment. He was no longer a little boy. *How had that happened?* He was now a handsome man. With dark hair and olive skin, he looked quite unlike my brother and me, with our flaxen hair and fair complexions. Teller was the oldest of the local smithy's sons. Like me, he had a lot of responsibility. He had to help provide for his five younger brothers.

Teller shifted uncomfortably under my stare. "What is it? Do I have something on my face?"

I smiled. "No. Well, not apart from that awful hair." I preferred him looking younger, more like my childhood friend.

"Then I will be sure to get rid of it." His eyes were a dark green. Sometimes they could appear almost black but now they sparkled like emeralds.

Uncle Ezekiel approached and looked between us for a moment. With a frown he said to Teller, "Back already?"

"Yes, sir. We have a full load of wood on the cart outside."

"Good, then you had best get to work unloading it."

Teller nodded to Ezekiel and shot me a dashing smile before turning to leave.

I did not want Teller to go. "Wait. Are you hungry? I could make something up for you and your brother."

"We have already eaten but thank you anyway." Teller's smile was warm. It was a smile that changed everything.

A new and strange feeling came over me. Though I had no name for it, it was wonderful! I shook my head and returned to the washing. The washing was easy; it made sense, unlike this odd and unfamiliar emotion.

Uncle Ezekiel watched me thoughtfully for a moment then went back to repairing one of the tables in the dining area. He clearly had something on his mind. As I worked, I could see Teller and his brother through the window as they unloaded the wood from the horse-drawn cart behind the tavern. I noticed for the first time that Teller was more muscular. *He is no longer the skinny boy I grew up with.* He was starting to resemble his father, Ivan, who was a giant of a man. This thought made me frown, as I had never cared for Ivan. Hopefully,

Teller would inherit only his father's physique and not take on the man's despotic and even, at times, violent personality.

Mari walked by outside, interrupting my thoughts. She greeted Teller and changed her previous course to approach him. Teller returned her greeting cheerfully. She brushed the palm of her hand across his jaw. Though I could not make out what they were saying, it was surely about his new facial hair. As I watched this scene, my spirits fell. The ugliest feeling rose up inside me. Whatever it was, it was alarming. Their greeting was nothing new or odd. The three of us had been friends our whole lives. Yet for the second time that morning, I was suddenly overtaken with a strange new emotion. Only this time it felt horrible.

I grabbed the dishrag from over my shoulder and stopped washing to wipe off the tables. It was watching Teller and Mari together that had brought this feeling on. Perhaps if I stopped watching them, the unwanted feeling would go away — it did not. Ezekiel stopped working on the table when he saw my face. He moved to survey the scene outside.

I continued to busy myself.

"How old are you, Vallachia?" Ezekiel asked. "About seventeen?"

I thought about it for a moment. "That is about right. Maybe eighteen, as it is spring." The only reason I knew which season I had been born in was because Father had always referred to me as his spring flower. That was what truly mattered, not a precise age.

Spring was the greatest of seasons, not only because it signaled the end of the cold but because it was our holiest season — the Paschal. Our religious rituals lasted throughout the entire spring, with many feasts and fasts.

"Most girls would have been married for a couple of years by now. They might even have children of their own. Don't you think it is time you married?" Ezekiel asked.

This stopped my table scrubbing, as I paused to ponder marriage — something I had not done very often. Father seemed to be in no hurry for me to marry. Once a girl came of age, she was viewed as a burden on a large family. Girls were often betrothed at a young age and married off as soon as it was deemed appropriate. This way their husbands could take over the responsibility of providing for them. Marrying off one's daughters while young also lessened the chance that they could become pregnant out of wedlock. This was a sin — the greatest of taboos — and rarely happened.

Usually I was so busy that there was little time to ponder marriage. I finally said, "Uncle, I have my hands full tending to Father and Brother, not to mention that you need me here. I could not possibly take care of a husband, let alone children as well." Marriage had seemed like an extra obligation — one I did not need. Most girls did not have responsibilities outside the home but my uncle's children were too young to help in the tavern. Since I was the only other suitable relative for the job, it fell to me.

Ezekiel frowned. "Perhaps we expect too much of you. You should be allowed to marry and start your own family. I could manage here without you ... somehow." He said this last word quietly, as if to himself.

That settled the debate about marriage in my mind. My family needed me. "Don't fret, Uncle. I enjoy taking care of my father and brother and helping you."

CHAPTER 2 LUDUS 1260 AD

I could hardly sleep that night. *Why did seeing Mari and Teller talking cause me to feel so miserable?* Normally, I would have retired momentarily from the endless tavern chores to join my friends. Mari and I would have proceeded to tease Teller about his new facial hair. That would have been normal. This emotion was not. I did not want Mari touching him. *Why? What did it matter?* I could not understand what was happening. Something was wrong with me. I hated the feeling and prayed for it to go away.

The only one to whom I could turn was my wise father, Adam. He was a gentle man — which I supposed was where the term *gentleman* came from. Pleasing him was my life.

Father was gifted in working with wood. After he married my mother he added a small kitchen on to his one-room house for her. The kitchen was partially partitioned off from the common room. After I was born, Father added the second story onto our small home. Above the common room and kitchen were three small bedrooms.

Our mother had died shortly after my brother, Josiah, was born, so we had never really known her. All I recalled of her was a soft voice singing me to sleep. Her face was blurry in my mind's eye. Father claims she was the most beautiful woman in the village, which meant the entire world, as people did not travel much — not common people anyway. Josiah and I must have gotten our blond hair from her, yet we had Father's blue eyes. Father would tell us stories of his precious Valentina; he still missed her very much. I had always hoped that the memory of her made it easier for him to remain unmarried. As a deacon of the Holy Orthodox Church he was only allowed to marry once. Since he had outlived his wife, marrying another was forbidden. He would never give up his place in the church for a second wife. In fact, once my brother and I were grown he might choose to take the vow of celibacy and be ordained as a bishop. This would bestow on him a higher rank in the church.

Father was tall and lean with dark wavy hair. He had been taken with the words of the New Testament at a young age and happily became the religious leader of Ludus. He was the voice of reason and peace in our village. He preached about concepts that many men had difficulty understanding, such as "turning the other cheek" and "loving your enemies." After all, men were valued for their bravery and idolized for their willingness to take up arms. Loathing one's enemy was a more intuitive notion than the teachings of Christ.

"What is the matter, my dear?" Father asked over the modest breakfast I had prepared. "You haven't touched your gruel and you look as if you hardly slept."

I stood to take my bowl still full of porridge to the kitchen. "I don't know what is wrong with me, Father. There is this horrible feeling that will not go away. All I can think about is Teller and Mari together in the tavern yard yesterday. Perhaps some evil, or a demon, has possessed me."

"Ah, I see what is going on."

I looked to Father with anticipation.

After a thoughtful pause, he continued, "Well, yes and no, my spring flower. It is a demon of sorts that has possessed you. What you are feeling is jealousy and jealousy is the work of the devil. You see, you care for Teller."

"Yes, of course. He is one of my dearest friends."

"No, my dear, that was not a question. What I am saying is you *love* him."

I almost dropped the clay bowl from my hand. I shook my head. *This could not be!* I did not like the grin on Father's face — it was unsettling.

"Aye, my spring flower is growing up."

I mulled over Father's words for days. I was so embarrassed and confused by these new feelings that I avoided Teller completely. Of course, Father was right. After a couple of weeks, I reluctantly accepted that there was no other explanation. Now the question was, how did Teller feel about me? Would he always view me as the knock-kneed tomboy who used to out-climb him up trees? I had always been lighter, so I could usually go higher and perch on branches that would have swayed under his weight. I will always remember the time I fell out of a tall tree and broke my arm.

CHAPTER 3 LUDUS 1260 AD

Our small village of Ludus was almost entirely surrounded by the Carpathian Mountains. We were quietly nestled in the lush green lands of the valley and largely isolated from the outside world by the glorious peaks surrounding us.

Every Sunday evening was spent in church. Josiah and I would listen to our Father deliver his orations. On occasion I would have to give Mari a nudge to wake her but my little brother and I hung onto every word. We listened earnestly, eager to understand. Our father had taught us to read so that we too could know the words of Christ firsthand. We had no other books to read at that time; the Bible was it. In fact, the only book in our entire village was Father's lone Bible. It was invaluable to us. The three of us would take turns reading it aloud by the fire on long, cold winter nights.

A wealthy noble who went by the title of Lord Chastellain had recently moved to Ludus. His estate was on a large piece of land outside of town. The lord seemed particularly old and sinister. His son was a debonair and supercilious young man named Elijah. Aside from his appearance in church, Elijah was only seen occasionally, riding a magnificent charger through town with his head held high.

Since they'd moved to Ludus, Lord Chastellain and his son had faithfully attended Father's Sunday services. The lord had befriended Father and they often took afternoon walks — endlessly discussing theology. One morning, the lord and his son paid us an unexpected visit.

"To what do we owe the pleasure of your company?" Father queried as he gestured for them to enter.

"Surely we do not need a reason to visit the village deacon?" Lord Chastellain replied.

"I am not sure our humble abode is quite up to the standards of nobles."

"Nonsense, my dear man. It is good to be reminded of how the common folk live."

The tone of the conversation was one of jest, yet I had the feeling that things could go wrong quickly, so I decided to change the subject and be a proper hostess.

"My Lord." I gave a slight bow. "I made a fresh batch of jam tarts. May I offer you both some?"

"That would be wonderful, child," replied the lord.

His critical gaze was disconcerting. It was a relief to head to the kitchen, which I did quickly.

After serving my famous pastries, I returned once again to the kitchen. It was customary that women should not concern themselves with men's conversations or be present with unrelated men in the home. Nevertheless, our home was small, so as I busied myself with cleaning, I could hear their conversation.

More niceties were exchanged before Lord Chastellain stated, "Of course, my dear friend, we have come today with a proposition for you. You see, my son here is quite taken with your lovely daughter. He has decided to offer her his hand in marriage."

My only thought was, *Can't the poor boy speak for himself?*

"Ah, I see," Father said. After a thoughtful pause, he continued, "I am afraid my daughter may not agree to such an arrangement. Yet I shall speak with her about the matter."

It was silent for a moment. "You will *speak* to your daughter?" the lord replied. His voice was deep and stern. "Are you not her father? Is it not your responsibility to find a suitable companion for her? There is no other who could provide for her as we can."

I did not like the way he used the word *we*, as if I would be married to him as well. The thought sent a chill down my spine.

"Of course, My Lord. I will see if I can talk some sense into the girl but I will not sentence her to a marriage to which she does not agree. I desire my daughter's happiness beyond all the riches in the world. In the end, the choice is hers, as it is her life."

"You..." Lord Chastellain paused, as if lost for words — which most likely did not happen very often. "You are unlike any other man I have ever met. I admire you."

Something told me that his "kind" words came with an underlying threat.

With that, Father stood. "If that is all, my friends, let me show you to the door. It is getting late."

I had never been more grateful to my father. It was easy to see what an extraordinary man he was.

After our company had safely departed, I said, "Oh, Father, what shall we do? I have the feeling that Lord Chastellain will not take no for an answer. I hardly know Elijah and his father is ... frightening."

"Now, now, my dear. Lord Chastellain is a friend." A concerned expression passed over his face. "However, there is something about this meeting that worries me. I can't quite place it — an uneasy feeling. For now, you can take your time in deciding. I presume we can put them off for a bit. Do not fret too much, as no immediate answer is required. Perhaps it would do no harm to get to know the boy a bit."

"As you wish, Father." The thought troubled me and Father looked as concerned as I felt.

Shortly after, I headed to the tavern. There were meals to prepare and rooms to clean. This kept me from thinking about my predicament too much. I did not make eye contact with Teller. When he approached me, I told him there was much to be done and that I did not have time to talk. I did not even slow down to see his reaction. Later, in the kitchen, he grabbed my arm to stop me.

"Did I do something to offend you?" he asked.

"No, not at all. What makes you say that?"

"Oh, I don't know," he said with derision. "Perhaps it is because you won't even say hello to me, like the time you were angry with me for lighting your hair on fire when we were nine years old."

I could not help smiling at the memory. Of course, at the time, I had been furious but now it seemed amusing. No permanent damage was done, as the hair had grown back nicely. My current behavior must seem odd to him. The red heat rushing to my cheeks would also seem odd. Fortunately, I was saved from further comment or embarrassment as Uncle Ezekiel came into the kitchen. He looked between us with the same down turned mouth that he had the last time he found Teller and me together. Teller quickly let go of my upper arm, which he had continued to hold to keep me from running away again.

"Did you retrieve the wine from the cellar for the guests?" Ezekiel asked.

"Not yet, Uncle. I will have it for them in an eye-blink." For the first time ever, I was relieved that he needed my help right away.

"I have to go," I stammered.

Teller gave me an irritated frown and turned to leave the tavern. My uncle followed him out, as if to speak with Teller in private. I wondered what that was about. Uncle clearly had a problem with us being alone. This was odd, as it had never been an issue before.

CHAPTER 4 LUDUS 1260 AD

Finally the work was done and it was time for me to head home for the night. That was when Mari entered the tavern to look for me.

"How are you?" Mari's voice was full of concern.

"Very well. Why? Do I not seem so?" I said.

"Teller asked me to come and walk you home. He is worried about your … unusual behavior lately."

"What unusual behavior?" I played ignorant.

She frowned at me. "You have hardly spoken to us lately."

"I see. He was hoping I would talk to you?"

"I suppose so."

"It would be nice to have the company." It was wonderful to see her. She was a true friend. Now that I better understood these strange new feelings, I was able to control them, or at least not let them control me. I was no longer jealous of Mari and Teller's friendship. However, I was ashamed about feeling jealous and discomfited by my new desire for Teller. Yet I would not allow the devil's work to harm my friendship with Mari. Father had raised me better than that.

I placed my arm in Mari's. She gave me a smile and we started walking home. Outside, it was pitch black, so we each carried a lantern as we walked in silence. This was unusual for us. We always spoke freely, as childhood friends do. Finally, she broke the awkward silence.

"So, what is going on with you?" Her large brown eyes were full of curiosity.

I did not want to tell her how I had recently discovered my feelings for Teller had changed, as this would be relayed directly to Teller. Nor did I wish to mention Elijah, for it would seem like boasting and that was *not* how I felt about the situation. *Would she understand my fears about Lord Chastellain and the complication of having to get to know Elijah?* I decided to try her.

"Do you swear not to tell a soul?" I started.

Mari looked displeased. "You know I despise secrets."

"Please. I do not want anyone to know yet, not even Teller." *Especially Teller,* I thought.

Mari reluctantly agreed.

"Do you know Lord Chastellain?" I began.

"You mean that sinister old man with the eccentric son?" Mari replied.

"Yes." I sighed. "That is to whom I'm referring. They visited our home and asked Father for my hand in marriage."

Mari's jaw dropped open. "That is ... unexpected. A nobleman and a deacon's daughter? That is virtually unheard of. Many folks assumed that the young lord would be betrothed to a foreign noble. Well, that is every girl's dream come true," she finished with excitement.

I remained silent.

By the light of the lantern, Mari studied the expression on my face. "And yet ... you're not happy about it, are you?"

Mari knew me well. I shook my head no in answer to her question. I was about to tear up. She put her arm around my shoulders. We walked in silence for a time and then, as if she had finally mustered up enough courage, she asked, "When will the wedding take place?"

That was when I realized I had not told her the whole story. Of course she thought that the arrangement had been sealed. Not many fathers would have been offered such an opportunity for a daughter to marry up in social status. The typical father would have quickly agreed to the arrangement and set a date for the near future in order to collect a hefty dowry for the rest of his family. This would also help to ensure that the young man did not have much time to change his mind. I suppose this was what the Chastellains had expected my father would do — gladly hand me over to them for an extravagant price.

"Oh, you know my beloved father. He is leaving the decision up to me."

Mari's eyes widened in surprise. "Your father is ... peculiar!" She laughed. I could not help joining her. With awe she asked, "What are you going to do?"

"Father asked that I at least get to know the young lord."

"You know, most women would love to be in your shoes. Not only to have such a solicitous father but to marry a future Lord. What an opportunity! And he is wondrously handsome. I cannot imagine anyone turning down such an offer."

Maybe I was peculiar as well because the thought of marrying Elijah only made my heart ache for Teller. Perhaps, like my father, I would rather be happy than wealthy. It appeared that I could not have both.

"It will be difficult to refuse Elijah. His father does not seem the type to take rejection well," I said.

"You are going to refuse him? You do realize this is a once-in-a-lifetime chance you are being given. Why would you possibly refuse?"

"I don't know." I did not want to tell her the main reason, so I gave her the secondary one. "Elijah's father is frightening."

She gave me a look as though I were being ridiculous.

Out of the darkness, a horrible tortured scream rang through the air. We exchanged a startled look and ran off the wagon trail toward the scream. While that may not have been the smartest thing to do, all I knew was that someone was in trouble and we had to help. We ran for quite a while, led by the faint sound of someone gasping for breath. The sound stopped yet we continued in the same direction. With my longer legs I was in the lead. I had always been able to outrun Mari. This time it was not to my advantage, as I fell over something that was covered in a warm, slimy liquid.

The fall caused me to drop the lantern and the candle went out. I slowly stood and tried to look around but there was no moonlight. Blackness was all around me, as if my eyes were closed when they were indeed wide open. Panic overtook me.

Thankfully, Mari came running up, bringing with her light to see by. She started screaming when she saw me — and the figure at my feet. We were both covered in blood. My heart raced even faster when I realized that it had been a person I had tripped over. Together we rolled the figure over. I recognized the face at once. He was the village baker.

"Emil!" I screamed. "No, no! What happened to you?" I shook him. Not knowing what else to do, I felt his face and chest; he was still warm. His neck and torso were covered in blood and there was a horrible wound on his neck. Once I had seen the town healer, Sofia, place an ear to an elderly man's nose to feel and listen for breath before pronouncing him dead. This was all I could think to do. I felt nothing. No breath.

Mari's face had gone pure white. "What do we do?" she whispered.

"Run and get help!"

Mari headed for town, leaving me, yet again, in compete darkness.

"Wait!" I fumbled for my lantern.

She used her candle to relight mine and I returned to Emil's side to wait with him, as Mari headed back to the village. Those were the longest moments of my life. It felt as if days had passed before Mari returned with help. All I could do was sit there by Emil, hoping he would wake — he did not. I was utterly useless and there was nothing I could do to save him.

CHAPTER 5 LUDUS 1260 AD

The next couple of days were a fog. I could scarcely get the blood off my hands and my dress was ruined. Eating was minimal, if at all. When I closed my eyes, all I could see was blood. This made sleep almost impossible. One night I woke to my brother shaking me. I had been dreaming that same nightmare about Teller killing our father.

"Shhh, you're not in danger," he was saying. "You are safe." After that I had to have my brother near in order to sleep. He started sleeping on the floor in my room.

Unfortunately, Emil was not the only victim. The following month, another person was found murdered and yet another had gone missing. The missing man was a farmer who lived outside of Ludus. The townspeople were in an uproar, which called for a village meeting. The only thing the villagers agreed on was that the villain must be captured. What to do with him once caught was a matter of debate.

Teller's father, Ivan and my own were often at odds. This particular village meeting proved to be no different. Ivan was a warrior; he'd fought against the Mongols before Teller and I were born. He enjoyed telling the story of heading off to war when his wife's belly was large with his first son. Thankfully, the Mongols did not stay long and Ivan was able to return home shortly after Teller was born.

Ivan was not one to "spare the rod" when it came to his children — or his wife, for that matter. He valued strength and stamina. Every summer, he organized a tournament of games designed to test a man's physical abilities. It had become the most anticipated community event in Ludus. Most men and boys aged fifteen and up participated — save the elders of the village, of course. Ivan competed and was often the winner of the games as well. All the villagers attended the tournament, just as they had turned out for this particular meeting. The summer tournament might be threatened this year if the killer was not caught.

"We need to set up a watch and men must be ready to form a hunting posse at a moment's notice," Ivan declared.

"A *hunting* posse?" Father asked. "What exactly will be done if someone suspected of the killings is caught?"

"If this is the work of one man, he will be hanged immediately. If this is the work of the Mongols provoking us to war, then all capable men must be ready to fight," Ivan proclaimed.

"Let us consider this for a moment," Father replied. "The first issue is that immediately hanging the man would be a sin. What if an innocent man is killed and the murders continue? He must be brought before the people of the village and detained until we can be sure the right man was caught. The people will decide his fate."

"Aye, Adam, ever the peacemaker," Ivan scoffed. He would do most anything to provoke my father. But Adam practiced what he believed and would never give Ivan the pleasure of an angry outburst.

Undeterred, Father continued, "Secondly, it is unlikely that these murders were committed by a foreign army. They are too few and they appear to be random, hence making them an unlikely prelude to war. The way the bodies are mutilated, the killings are most likely the work of a madman."

This sparked lots of murmuring in the crowd. Finally, one of the elders spoke over the villagers in a loud voice. Clamius was the unspoken leader of the village. He was not officially elected or even nominated by the people. He did not have a title of leadership. He was simply the oldest and wisest man amongst us. He was fair and the people trusted him.

"The killer is to be hanged only if he is caught in the act. If there is no doubt that he is the killer, then he will be hanged in the village square after all have heard the story of his guilt. If a man is suspected of the murders, without any witnesses, he is to be kept secured until we can be sure he is indeed the killer. Meanwhile, there will be a village curfew imposed. All men are to be safely indoors at home by dark, and women and children are to be home an hour prior to that."

This was disappointing, as I loved to go for walks on summer nights. Yet I had no desire to trip over another body on the dark forest floor — let alone to *become* one.

"Furthermore," Clamius continued, "we will set up a patrol — all able men must help to keep watch over the town at all times. Let us pray we catch the killer."

As folks filed out of the tavern, I overheard Ivan state that he would slay the killer on the spot if he was the one to find him. This concerned me. Ivan was out for blood and if he suspected someone, it would be over for him. Even if he had the wrong man, it wouldn't matter — the accused would be dead.

Father was handing out blessed amulets to each household. The amulets were Orthodox Patriarchal Crosses. Each one was hand carved and then blessed by Father. He greatly enjoyed working with wood and when he was not busy preparing orations, baptizing babies or visiting those who called on him for blessings, he often made furniture and created intricate woodcarvings.

As he handed the amulets to the head of each household he said, "May this protect you and yours from evil."

There were many replies of gratitude. "God bless you, Deacon," must have been stated fifty times over. Everyone gladly accepted this holy and powerful refuge from iniquity, that was, everyone aside from Ivan. He grabbed his wife's hand roughly as she reached eagerly for the amulet from Father.

"Such a small wooden thing is not capable of protecting us," Ivan's voice was deep and stern. "If you really want to give people something that will protect them, *Deacon,* then give every man a razor-sharp sword."

Father smiled with reassurance to Ivan's wife, who looked scared and desperate to have the protection of God. She was dragged out of the tavern by her husband.

Blasphemy! I thought. *Ivan claims to be Christian and yet he would forsake his family's safety simply to taunt my father — the Deacon, of all people — how dare he! Teller, as well as his family, are vulnerable to the crazed madman out there. They were naked without the blessed cross.*

Father turned toward me, handing me the cross that was meant for Ivan's household. He gave me a knowing nod and with a smile turned back to the next family awaiting a blessing. I knew exactly what he meant by this gesture; he wanted me to get the cross to Teller. Ivan would not take it from Father but Teller would take it from me. Though I was not sure how or when I would be able to do this surreptitiously. I quickly placed the cross in the front pouch of my dress.

The last one to accept an amulet was Lord Chastellain. He took the cross and examined it carefully. "Astounding craftsmanship. Did you carve this yourself?"

Father smiled and they walked out together, soon lost in conversation. Elijah gave me a beautiful smile and a nod before he joined our fathers.

CHAPTER 6 LUDUS 1260 AD

I stayed behind to clean up after the crowd. Bidding my uncle goodnight, I hurried out as soon as possible. I could not wait to get home, not only to make curfew but also to partake in Vespers, which I never missed. Sometimes my father and brother would have to wait until I returned from the tavern but we always lit candles and incense together. Father would read from the Book of Psalms. The informal services would end with silent individual prayers. On this particular day they would have been even more vehement than usual. This was a tradition Father learned while he studied in Targoviste to become a deacon. Bishops, deacons, monks and nuns would perform Vespers on a daily basis. The common person did not always conduct such a ceremony but in my house we were dogmatic about the evening prayer ritual.

As I stepped foot outside the tavern a male voice said, "How are you doing?" I spun around to find Teller leaning against the side of the tavern.

"Oh, thank God! It's you." I wanted to throw my arms around him but instead I settled for placing my arm in his.

"I'm glad to see you have stopped ignoring me." His green eyes sparkled as he gazed down at me. He was a welcome sight indeed. "I came by your house a couple of times but your father thought it best to leave you alone. You do know that I am here for you?"

I returned his smile and nodded; he had always been there and I hoped he always would be. We walked home arm in arm. "I was not avoiding you. Why would I avoid you?"

"I have no idea. I was hoping you would tell me why you would do such a thing."

"It is these murders and the disappearance —

"No, you stopped speaking to me before this whole ugly mess arose," Teller interrupted.

This was followed by too long of a pause from me. I had not thought about my trivial problems for a month or more — it seemed as if a year had passed since I was only a girl who had learned she was in love with her friend.

"Well, I suppose there was a lot on my mind."

"Like what?" he probed.

This was why avoiding Teller was easier, as I did not want to outright lie to him. I supposed I had to tell him. It was not likely to be a secret much longer anyway. Better he heard it from me. "Elijah, Lord Chastellain's son, has asked for my hand in marriage," I blurted out the words.

This stopped Teller in his tracks.

"And I do not know how to refuse him," I continued. I had stopped walking as well.

Either anger or concern crossed his face. Yet his voice remained indifferent as he replied, "Why would you refuse such a wealthy man?"

I hesitated again, not wanting to tell him the real reason, which was that I loved him and not Elijah. "I do not know Elijah and I cannot leave my father and brother with no woman to care for them." This was not lying, it was just not telling the entire truth. *There was a difference, wasn't there?*

Teller's expression lightened. "You're right; you should not leave your family so soon," he spoke with certainty.

"What do you mean, 'so soon'?"

"You are still young. Once your brother has married, then would be the time for you to consider such matters."

I pondered this. Would I have to wait to marry until my brother did so? Was it that my brother would have to have a wife to care for him, so my unwed father would not have to do so? Josiah was almost two years younger than I and boys tended to marry later than girls. Boys often needed more time to get settled into an occupation before marriage. It could be three or four years before my brother married. I would be an old maid by then. This made me uncomfortable, so I pushed the thought out of my head.

"Father wishes that I might at least become more familiar with Elijah before I give my answer."

"Certainly he does. He would probably be happy to marry you off to a noble." Teller retorted with irritation. "Better than someone like …"

"Like whom?"

"Well, rather than a … commoner."

I had hoped for a different answer — one that might give me an inkling as to how Teller felt about me. But everything he said could be the product of a brotherly concern. After all, he was my closest friend.

"Father says he values my happiness above riches."

"Your father is truly a good man. I wish my father were more like him. Perhaps then I could please him." Teller made this last statement quietly.

I had never been overly fond of Ivan. I could not imagine what it would be like to be his child, always on edge; nothing you did was ever good enough. My heart ached for Teller.

"I am truly blessed to have Adam for a father. He is more than I deserve." This reminded me of the cross in my pocket. It now felt heavy against my leg, as if it were prompting me to give it to Teller.

"Don't be so hard on yourself."

I placed my free hand in my pocket and held the cross. "Although your father might be like a lamb compared to having Lord Chastellain as a father-in-law."

Teller smiled. "You might be right about that. It is not only his wealth that makes him intimidating — with one look, he can command and control people."

That was the perfect description of Lord Chastellain. "I know precisely what you mean." I shivered.

Teller took his arm from mine and placed it around my shoulders. "Are you cold?"

"No, it is all this talk about Lord Chastellain that bothers me." Teller did not remove his arm, which was pleasant. I had missed him and now I fully realized how much. This was the way it should be, talking freely with each other and caring for each other — as we had always done. *Yet was it still only friendship?*

We were approaching my house, so it was now or never. I stopped walking and handed Father's amulet to Teller. He removed his arm from around me and took a step back. He looked at the object as if it were a snake.

"Please take this. I beg you."

He shook his head. "I can't. Father would be furious if I brought it home."

"Then don't let him see it. Please, for your family. It will keep them safe. You must take it!"

He looked into my eyes for a moment. A weary smile crossed his lips. "Your father knew I would take it from you, didn't he?" He wrapped his warm hand around mine that held the cross and slowly took it from me.

I exhaled, as relief flooded through me.

"I suppose it can't hurt," Teller said, as he studied the cross.

He walked me the rest of the way home. We were both quiet — thoughtfully reserved. Once we had reached the front door, he said, "This is goodnight. Stay safe inside and I hope you do not get to know the young lord too well."

What did that mean? I thought. "Goodnight, Tell," I said with a smile.

Once inside, I found Father seated in his favorite chair. He returned my smile and stood. "Did Teller accept the amulet?"

"Yes, Father."

"Good." He frowned. "Unfortunately, my dear, until you are married, you should not be seen alone with Teller. You are not children anymore and people will start to think poorly of you."

I put my head down. "Yes, Father." It was not fair that I could no longer be friends with Teller simply because we were older now. But I had to admit, things had changed. I no longer thought of Teller in the same way. The townspeople would be right to gossip. Grown men and women were not allowed to be close friends.

Father gently lifted my head, with his hand on my chin. "Don't lower your head. You have done nothing wrong, my spring flower. In fact, always keep your head raised high."

CHAPTER 7 LUDUS 1260 AD

My first chaperoned visit with Elijah was set for today. For an unknown reason I was nervous. Perhaps it was because I did not know what to expect. *It will probably be tedious, as I will have to listen to him talk endlessly about himself and how great and wealthy he is*, I thought.

Father and Lord Chastellain walked behind us, no doubt talking about theology and perhaps even some philosophy. They stayed out of earshot, yet within sight of Elijah and me, as was customary. At first it was silent and awkward. I did not understand how so many women could bear to marry men they did not know. Most marriages were arranged and women, who were in many respects still girls, were often thrown into marriage beds with men who were strangers. Again, a feeling of gratefulness overcame me at the knowledge that Father would not force me to marry.

"What are your thoughts about the meeting yesterday?" Elijah's voice was low and soft, gentle even, much unlike his father's.

I was taken aback. He wanted to know *my* thoughts. Women's thoughts and opinions were often not valued by men, especially when it came to politics. Yet he did not want to talk about himself. This was not the young man riding his splendid steed through town with his nose in the air, as if he were better than everyone else. Or perhaps asking for my thoughts was for show — his way of trying to win me over.

"It worries me that there is a dangerous killer lurking about and I worry that an innocent man could take the blame for it," I replied.

"Indeed, you are your father's daughter."

"Is that a bad thing?" My voice was full of accusation.

"Not in the least. Your father is an intelligent and kind man." There was sincerity in his voice. "In fact, there are not many men who can keep Father intrigued with scholarly conversation, as Adam does. It is fortunate that there is an educated man in the village to keep my father occupied." He glanced back briefly to our fathers behind us.

"Well then, thank you, My Lord."

"Please, no, do not call me that. Father relishes the title but I find it horrid. Titles like that are demeaning to the people who feel they must call me such."

"What, then, should I call you — simply Elijah?"

"That is my name," he said with a handsome crooked smile.

Once again, I was surprised. Most men would give anything for such a noble title as lord. I could not help smiling in return.

"Very well, *Elijah*." I tried out the informal title and it felt odd, almost disrespectful. After all, a strict decorum was required, in which people were ranked in clearly defined hierarchies. The hierarchy started with monarchs at the top, then lords or nobles, elders and clergy and then ordinary men. Women and children were at the bottom. Clear lines existed between these groups and such lines were not to be crossed.

There was silence again.

"What do you think happened to those people who were killed?" he asked.

My shoulders relaxed a bit as I was beginning to feel more comfortable. "It is unlikely that someone is trying to prompt us to war by slowly killing people from the village. I have the feeling that Ivan might be wishing for such. He appears to delight in the prospect of war."

"Very perceptive." Elijah sounded impressed. "Men like Ivan feel a sense of purpose when they are fighting for something bigger than themselves, like the protection of their village. It can be what drives them."

I nodded, knowing this to be true. Yet it was difficult to imagine that some people would consider war a good thing. "I suppose some men are keen on war?"

"Aye. And I am not sure it was a lone man who killed those people," he said.

"What do you think — that it was a group of men? Perhaps a youthful band of boys wreaking havoc for sport?" This was an appalling thought.

"No, though that is not entirely unrealistic. However, it may have been an animal or something ... not human anyway."

Why had I not thought of that? The way the bodies were covered in blood with the necks torn out, it could possibly have been a bear, although I had never heard of such attacks so close to the village. "Why did you not bring this up during the meeting? It seems plausible. Perhaps as plausible as a murderous man on the loose."

Elijah frowned, as if he had not liked the question. "I'm not entirely sure. The people, Ivan in particular, seem determined to blame a man for the killings. I was embarrassed to speak up. Such attacks this close to town are unheard of. Let's discuss something more lighthearted, shall we?"

I doubted he was afraid to speak up. The thought that it could be animal attacks comforted me a bit, for it was their nature, while humans should not kill randomly and for no reason. Perhaps there was not a lunatic on the loose after all. I felt the need to run to Father and tell him this new theory but I refrained. "Then what would you like to discuss?"

"I want to know about you."

Elijah was full of surprises, I thought. *He doesn't appear to want to talk about himself at all.* "Well, that won't take long and I'm afraid it will be quite boring."

"I'll be the judge of that." He smiled.

"Our mother died when my brother and I were young. I don't have many memories of her. Father is all we have so I do my best to take care of my family — filling my mother's shoes, I suppose. Surely I do a horrible job of it …

He appeared to be waiting for more.

"That is it," I said.

"I doubt that that is all and I doubt that you do a horrible job of taking your mother's place as the homemaker. The jam tarts you served us were delicious. If the rest of your cooking is that good, then I know your father and brother are well taken care of. Not to mention your home is well kept."

"You are kind to say such things." I found that I was now truly curious about him. "Where is your mother?"

His face was grim and he stared ahead without seeing the path or trees that surrounded us. "She died when I was about ten years old — murdered actually and I was the one who found her." His tone was flat — devoid of any emotion.

My heart sank. I stopped walking and Elijah did the same. *What on earth does someone say to something like that?* "I am sorry! I had no idea. If I had known, I would not have asked." I lowered my head in sorrow.

He gently lifted my chin with his index finger. His finger felt unusually cold for a warm summer day.

"It is fine that you asked. It's a legitimate question; besides, if we are to become familiar with each other, then you must know." Elijah gazed intently at me.

His eyes were a grayish blue and they were wise and gentle. There was a distinct sadness in them — too much sadness and too much intelligence for someone of only eighteen years. His eyes made him appear older. I shook my head to regain my focus from all that I saw in his stormy eyes.

"Who killed her?" I had a strong desire to know and he made me feel that I could ask.

He broke away from my stare and started walking again. Rather hastily, he stated, "I don't know. We never caught the culprit."

Again, I did not know what to say.

After a brief silence, he added, "There we go again, talking all doom and gloom. Tell me about your likes and dislikes and your friends."

Relieved to change the subject, I said, "I enjoy caring for my family. As we have already established — that is my life. I do like to read. The only book I have ever read is the Bible, as other books are impossible to come by. I have read the Bible too many times to count. As for my dislikes, I don't have many. I do not like an unkempt home, I suppose."

"And what about your friends; who are they?"

"My closest friend since childhood is Teller. There was a time when we were always together." I felt guilty for mentioning Teller. It made me feel that I was being unfaithful to Teller by talking to Elijah about him. *That is ridiculous,* I told myself and quickly went on, "Mari is also a wonderful friend. Now that we are older, we rely more and more on each other."

"This Teller fellow, is he only a friend?" Elijah asked.

"Yes, of course." My shoulders tensed. This was not entirely a lie, as he had not asked about my current feelings for Teller. He was indeed only a friend. "You know, it is getting late. I must head home to prepare dinner." I was feeling uncomfortable all over again. I did not like where the conversation had gone.

With a knowing look, Elijah replied, "Yes, of course."

We waited for our fathers to catch up to us.

"I'm truly sorry you were the one to find the baker." Elijah's expression was solemn.

I gave him a weak smile in return. "I appreciate your sincerity."

The four of us walked home together, making occasional idle conversation. Elijah turned into the boy I had seen before, falling silent and letting his father do the talking. He had the arrogant air about him again. I was truly curious about this mysterious pair and the power Elijah's father had over him.

Once inside, I collapsed into a chair. Things had gotten incredibly complicated. *Why couldn't Elijah be the pompous braggart most people assumed he was? That would have made things easier. Now how am I to reject him? On what grounds? Other than the fact that I want another, which would reflect poorly on me.* Women were not to have eyes for men whom their fathers had not chosen for them.

"Father, did you know that Elijah found his mother after she was murdered?"

"I had no idea. That is awful. Lord Chastellain mentioned, in passing, that she had died some years back. My dear, you know I would have warned you of this if I had known."

"Yes, Father, I know you would have. Elijah — I mean the young lord," remembering my formalities, "thinks that perhaps it was an animal who killed those people."

Father looked thoughtful for a moment. "It would be unusual, yet it could happen. I suppose such attacks are equally as rare as a murderer amongst us."

"Will you discuss this matter with the other village leaders to see what they think?" I asked.

"I will do just that. But first, what did you think of the young lord?"

I sighed. "It is difficult to say. He is not what I expected. There is a kindness and intelligence about him and he is … sad. It is confusing. I don't want to talk about it."

"Of course, my spring flower. Don't fret. It will work itself out in the end."

Father always knew how to comfort me. His words did just that, as there was always wisdom in them. *Everything will be fine. Will it not?*

Something was nagging at me. *What was it Elijah had said?* "It may have been an animal or something … not human." *If the killer is not human, then it would have to be an animal. There are no other options. Yet the way he said it suggested that "animal" and "not human" were two different things. If it is not a human and not an animal, then what was left? The devil, perhaps, or demons?* A chill went through me.

Busying myself with work was the best thing to do. That way, I would not dwell on this last unsettling thought. After all, no one, not even Elijah, knew for sure what had happened to the victims.

CHAPTER 8 LUDUS 1260 AD

I wanted my friend's opinions about the idea of animal attacks. After waiting for my chance at the tavern, I pulled Teller and Mari aside.

"It does make sense," Teller stated, "although I have never heard of animals attacking so close to Ludus."

"The thought of the killer being a predatory animal is better than the thought of a human killing people. Not to mention, an animal would be easier to hunt, would it not?" I asked.

"I suppose so," Teller said. "We have many good hunters in the village. Perhaps we should set up hunting parties to eliminate any big game around the village. We could send out a few of our best trackers and best hunters to see what they can find."

"Will you mention this to the village leaders?" I asked Teller. "It would be taken seriously coming from you, rather than from Mari or me."

"Yes, I will suggest it to them." Teller's bright eyes beamed at me.

I smiled warmly in return. "Thank you. Father has already mentioned the idea of animal attacks to them." I paused. "There is one more thing. What about the possibility of these murders being the work of something ... I don't know ... evil?"

Mari had been looking between Teller and me as if studying us but now fear flashed in her eyes. "Like what?"

"I'm not sure. The devil, demons or ... something evil." After saying it out loud, I felt uncomfortable. I knew Teller would disapprove.

Teller laughed and Mari frowned.

"Your father is filling your head with scary children's stories from that Bible of his," Teller said.

It was not the Bible that had given me the idea — it was Elijah but I could not bring myself to say so to Teller. I tried to brush it off as well. "Aye, maybe."

But Mari did not laugh. "I have heard many people talking about a curse on the village and demons amongst us."

Teller smiled at her as if she were a small child. "Father says there is no such thing as magic. You two should not worry yourselves with such silly notions."

Mari narrowed her eye's at Teller, clearly not convinced.

"I must be going." Teller turned to leave.

Once he was out of sight, Mari said, "I hope your last assumption is wrong. How would we ever fight against demons?"

"Yes, let us hope Teller is correct. All we can do is keep our amulets close and pray." I was feeling even more ill at ease. It was not surprising that folks were talking of the devil at play here. Ivan and Teller were the exception in their pragmatic view of the world. Of course, people would be talking of supernatural forces being behind such attacks.

When I returned home, Father informed me that we had been invited to take refreshments with the lord and his son at their estate. "Must we go, Father?"

"Well, it would be inconsiderate to refuse. What if I try to keep it a social affair and not a courting between you two youngsters?"

"That sounds better. Thank you, Father."

CHAPTER 9 LUDUS 1260 AD

I had never ridden in a carriage before. We lived close to town and had no need for horses, nor could we have afforded them. The ride was bouncy, yet comfortable enough. It seemed to take forever to reach the Chastellain estate. Once we arrived, I was sure my eyes deceived me. It was a *castle,* with expansive manicured grounds and gardens surrounding it. Servants opened doors for us and led us into a massive foyer to await our hosts. Father was smiling at the astonished look on my face.

"This cannot be real," I said. "How can one family have so much?"

"You may change your mind about this boy yet," Father teased.

I gathered my composure by closing my mouth and straightening my back. "Of course not, Father."

Our hosts greeted us warmly. After wine, cakes and customary niceties, Lord Chastellain offered for Elijah to show me around the fortress. Father, true to his word, suggested that we all go, as he would like to see the place as well.

The palace was cool and damp with endless wide halls that led to immense rooms with high ceilings. The walls were an impenetrable thick gray stone. It was difficult to imagine how such a place had ever been built. I was quickly lost in the maze. We passed several dining areas that contained tables that would not have fit in our entire home. Long tapestries hung from the walls.

The Great Hall had enough thick fabric curtains to clothe all the people in Ludus. They were the most beautiful red color with gold trim and fine gold ropes elegantly holding them open. An extremely intricate wrought iron chandelier hung from the center of the room. It was larger than a horse. The paintings were even more fascinating. They depicted scenes of people and places so foreign that I did not think they could possibly be fashioned after real people and places. The features of the people and the clothes they wore were entirely strange. Some of the paintings displayed images of enormous outlandish architecture. Father stopped to admire one such painting and Lord Chastellain explained that it depicted the Hagia Sophia in Constantinople.

"These buildings and people are real?" I asked, as Father and I stared at the painting of the large domed building with its golden roof. We had only heard of the grandeur of the Hagia Sophia, the heart of the Orthodox Church in the beloved Queen of Cities.

"Yes, of course, my dear. We acquired that masterpiece on one of our trips to Constantinople awhile back. Isn't that right, son?"

Elijah nodded slightly in reply and kept walking.

Multiple trips to Constantinople! That was uncanny but it seemed like nothing out of the ordinary to Elijah. The lord continued to carry on about how many of the paintings and furniture had been imported from far-off places, most of which I had never heard of.

Father was as overwhelmed as I was. He forgot his manners at this point and asked how the lord had made his fortune and how they had acquired such rare things from all over the world.

Chastellain was not offended in the least. In fact, he seemed to relish the chance to tell his story. "My grandfather was a self-made man. He accumulated his fortunes trading in France. He eventually reached his peak as a local merchant and decided to move his family east, in order to be closer to the heart of the trading industry. He became even more successful in Venice, where I was born. My father and grandfather would often travel to Constantinople for work. On one such trip they decided to take some time to explore the mountains of this region. My grandfather fell in love with this beautiful piece of land we now stand on. Being surrounded almost entirely by mountains, it was the ideal place for a summer home. Of course, we have continued to make improvements over the years, such as the installation of glass windows."

The lord was clearly proud of this rare luxury. He might as well have said, *Look how wealthy I am. I can afford the best.* I gave him an irritated scowl — to his back anyway.

"We maintain our lands in Venice as well as Denmark," the lord continued. "I still run some of the major trade routes from the Orient. This is where most of our fortunes were obtained and these treasures are things that have come across my family's path over the years."

"We saved the best room for last." Elijah took my arm in his. He whispered, "I knew all that would not impress you but ..." He opened two tall wooden doors to reveal an endless number of books. The walls were lined from the floor to the high ceiling with nothing but tightly packed shelves. So many books that a ladder was required to reach many of them. Overstuffed furniture surrounded a large fireplace, while tall glass windows on the far wall let in plenty of light for reading. Each book was a scarce and priceless hand-scribed treasure — well, priceless to me anyway. I did not know that there were this many books in the entire world, let alone in one room!

I'm sure my mouth was hanging open in awe, yet again. "If I had a room like this, I would never leave it," I exclaimed.

"Stay as long as you like," the lord replied.

Father and I read some of the titles on the book's spines. "Where does one start?" Father said.

Elijah chuckled.

We perused the books for a long time. Finally, the lord said, "Borrow whichever books you like and after you have read them, simply exchange them for some more."

This was too good to be true and Father and I graciously upheld the offer. When we each had a handful of these exquisite books, a servant informed us that the midday meal was ready. I was so excited to start reading that I did not have much of an appetite.

CHAPTER 10 LUDUS 1260 AD

Servants brought in a considerable spread of food – enough to feed the entire village. I had thought we were here for light refreshment. A servant came rushing in and spoke to the lord pointedly. They appeared to be talking in a normal tone but it was too quiet for me to make out what they said.

Lord Chastellain rested his elbow on the table and put his hand to his face, rubbing his forehead. Whatever urgent news had been brought to the lord, it worried or perhaps frustrated him. He stood and announced, "It appears I am needed back in Denmark. I must leave immediately. You will excuse me. My son will stay and tend to you." He turned to Elijah and said something so quietly I could not hear him.

Father and I exchanged a quick curious look as Elijah nodded in agreement to his father. With that, the lord swiftly exited the room with his servant.

"It is difficult for him to stay here for long, as there are often urgent matters to attend to in Copenhagen."

"That is a great deal of traveling. Will you eventually move back there?" Father asked.

"Yes, most likely when our business here is settled." Elijah smiled at me.

Is that what I am — business? It was all I could do not to glare at him.

"We find the weather much to our liking in Denmark," Elijah continued.

This was an odd reason to want to live in the north. I had heard the winters there were many times worse than ours. If people had the luxury to choose, they tended to prefer the warmer weather in southern regions.

After our repast, Elijah announced, "Before you go, allow me to show you some of the grounds and my personal favorite — the horse stables."

Just the mention of horses seemed to make his usually sad grey eyes brighten to a vibrant blue. *Who could resist that?* I thought. "It sounds as if we simply have to see the horses," I said.

As he led us out the back of the castle, he took my arm in his again. "Do you ride?"

I had to chuckle. "No, never! Horses are large and intimidating. Besides, why would I ever need to ride?"

He laughed. "It is not a matter of necessity. Don't you ever do something simply for the enjoyment of it?"

I thought about it a moment. "No, that would be a waste of time. There is usually too much work to be done." As we spoke, the work was piling up back at the tavern. Elijah and I clearly lived different lives.

"Well, My Lady, I will have to take you for a ride." Elijah gave me that handsome crooked smile of his.

I shook my head at him. There was no way he would get me on one of those beasts.

"I would like to stay here in this lovely rose garden." Father gave us a smile, one I knew well. It meant that he was up to something. "You two go ahead. I will keep an eye on you from here, Vallachia."

With uneasiness I nodded to Father; he was trying to give us some time "alone." *Why?* I did not know.

The horse stable — if one could call it that — was a colossal barn with many stalls and high ceilings. The Chastellains' horses lived better than we did in the village. They always had plenty of food and servants to clean up after them.

Elijah stopped at one of the stalls. "This is Hollis, named so because he was born in a grove of holly trees." The horse neighed a greeting to him and lumbered forward, placing his large head over the stall door for Elijah to rub. He spoke softly to the horse. I could not make out what he said. The horse jerked his head up and down once as if nodding in agreement.

"You see, they are not intimidating; they are graceful, powerful and simple. Horses are innocent, harmless creatures. They need only grass to survive." Elijah seemed to be envious of the beautiful beast. He ran his hand down Hollis's neck. Hollis closed his eyes as if enjoying the affection.

It was clear that Elijah would gladly trade places with the horse — if he could. This was curious. What about Elijah's life could possibly be so terrible that he would be envious of a horse?

"Go on; give him a pat," Elijah said.

"No!" I tried to soften my tone. "Thank you though. In fact, I should be getting back. My uncle will be needing me at the tavern." Besides, if I stayed much longer, Elijah would try to get me to ride that thing.

Father and I thanked Elijah for everything and on the way home, we had our noses buried in books, occasionally exchanging tidbits of information about what we were reading. The trip home flew by.

When we were almost home, Father stopped reading and looked out the window of the carriage. He was lost in thought.

"What is it, Father?"

"It appears that Lord Chastellain is a very important man." He held up the book he was reading and added, "And it seems they may know how to win us over yet." He smiled wearily.

It did appear that way. A hint of doubt entered into my mind. *Perhaps I could have wealth and happiness in this life.* I quickly pushed the thought out of my head. *It would take more than books to make me happy. In order to be truly content, I had no doubt that I needed Teller.*

It was my turn to peer out the window. "It is not fair how some can have so much."

"The Chastellains have worked hard for their wealth and even harder to maintain it."

"And we do not work hard?" I questioned.

Father sighed. "That, we do."

As soon as we returned, I hurried to Uncle's tavern. Just as predicted, there was plenty to do. Yet I longed to be reading. The work was not quite caught up when I had to stop in order to make curfew. As soon as I left the tavern, I heard someone call out behind me. I started. Spinning around I found Elijah stepping out of the late-evening shadows.

"Elijah, it's you — you scared me!" My heart fell even farther when I saw that he had Hollis in tow. *Oh no,* I thought.

"My apologies. I came to give you a ride home."

"That won't be necessary! I will do very well on my own."

"You cannot know for sure if you like horses or not if you have never ridden one."

"Honestly, I can't! I must be home well before dark."

"Never fear, I will have you home in no time and no one will know you were with me." With that, he surprised me by grabbing my waist with both hands. With impossible ease he lifted me onto the horse. Before I could protest, he swung himself up behind me in one swift motion and we were off at a gallop. My heart was pounding. It was terrifying to be up so high, moving so quickly. We sped through the woods behind the tavern.

Elijah placed his hands on my wrists and said, "Let go. You are pulling his mane."

"Oh, sorry," I said to the horse. Without realizing it, I had wrapped my fingers in Hollis's mane and was holding on for dear life. I eased my grip.

"Don't worry; I won't let you fall," Elijah whispered in my ear. I believed him; he knew what he was doing. I became acutely aware of his body against mine and his arms around me. This made me immensely uncomfortable, yet at the same time I did not want him to let go for fear of falling.

When we came to the meadow just outside of town, Elijah kicked Hollis's sides and the horse took off at a full run. I let out a scream and Elijah laughed. I lowered my torso to the horse's neck and tried to wrap my arms around him. Elijah put his hands on my waist again and raised me back to an upright position. He continued to run his hands along my arms, raising them out. He held my arms up as if we were spreading our wings.

"It's like soaring through the sky," he whispered in my ear.

The wind in my face, the ground moving quickly by — *we were flying!*

It was not long before we came galloping up in the woods behind my home. "That was marvelous!" I managed to say.

He wrapped one arm tightly around my waist and swiftly lowered me off the horse. "As promised, you are home in time to make curfew. Did I not say that horses could be enjoyable?" His smile was contagious.

"Thank you for the ride."

He nodded and was gone. With weak knees, I headed for the back door. I would have to pretend that the past exhilarating moments had not occurred. Father would be waiting for my safe return from the tavern. If I was not to be seen with Teller alone anymore, then I certainly should not be with Elijah unchaperoned, as Elijah was openly courting me. I would say nothing to anyone about the wonderful ride home this evening.

CHAPTER 11 LUDUS 1260 AD

As the summer tournament approached, Lord Chastellain announced that he would hold a gala as the opening ceremonies for the entire town. Usually the night before the tournament began, the villagers would gather for a dance at Uncle Ezekiel's tavern and local musicians would play late into the night. This year it appeared that Ludus Mures — so called because the village of Ludus was located on the Mures River — would have a proper dance.

"Father, is it appropriate to have an extravagant festival and the tournaments this year, with all that is going on?" I asked.

"You have a big heart, my dear. Your mother would be proud of the lady you are becoming. You are right to think of others and their losses. There are families in Ludus who will not have their dance partners this year." His expression was solemn, then it lightened. "On the other hand, life does go on. If we were to let this killer stop us from living, then he would win. We must carry on and find what joy we can. Otherwise, what is the point? We might as well all be dead."

How did Father always do that? He could make everything seem well — eliminating guilt with his wise words and effortlessly spreading comfort and reassurance. *If only I could be as wise.*

A knock came at the door. I smiled and shrugged at Father as he went to see who it was.

Two men stood at the door. One was carrying an enormous package. The other handed Father a note. "We are here on behalf of Lord Chastellain."

The man awkwardly placed the package on our table and quickly retreated.

Josiah came down from his room to see what was going on. "What on this good earth is that?" he asked, staring at the package that was as big as the table.

Another unknowing shrug was my only response to his question.

"The young lord is asking you to attend the gala with him," Father stated after reading the note.

This was not unexpected. When it had been announced that the Chastellains were to hold a celebration for the town, I had suspected it was Elijah and his father's plan to have me at their side.

"Open it!" Josiah said. We proceeded to unfold the linen wrapped package. It was most likely some type of gown. Though I could not imagine how to begin to put it on. It was brightly colored — of course. The fabric was of a texture I had never seen before. I did not have the words to describe it.

"What is it made of?" I asked.

"Never mind that — *what* is it?" Josiah questioned.

"It is a formal gown made from the finest silk," father answered with his usual patience. He ran his hand gently over the shiny smooth fabric as he examined it. "The entire garment is intricately embroidered, unlike the dyed linens we wear."

"Are you supposed to *wear* this?" Josiah looked baffled. He held up two of the five different pieces of clothing.

"That can't be, not all at once?" I must have looked confused as well because Father laughed at us. Soon all three of us were laughing heartily at the ridiculous thing strewn across our table. The only piece of clothing that was familiar was the white tunic that would be worn under the gown. I did not know how the other pieces of clothing would fit together.

That night at dinner, Father asked Josiah if he had someone to accompany him to the dance.

"Why do I have to ask someone to go with me?" Josiah wondered.

"This is not the normal impromptu Ludus gathering. This is a formal occasion," Father answered.

"Well, I prefer the old gathering." Yet Josiah looked thoughtful.

"At least you have a choice," I said to my brother.

"You *always* have a choice, my spring flower," Father said.

That night in bed, I thought about Father's words. *How did I have a choice? There was no choice.* I was starting to think of Elijah as a friend. *How can I refuse him? He has been gracious and kind. It was not as if I could go to the gala with Teller, even if he had asked me. Yet perhaps I could simply not go to the dance at all. Besides, being the only girl in a pretentious gown was not an appealing thought.*

That is it! I do have a choice! I can choose not to go at all! This put my mind at ease and made the following days more bearable. That was, until Elijah himself made a rare and unexpected visit to the tavern. He marched right up to me, not even trying to be discreet.

"It is not polite to keep a gentleman waiting for a response to an invitation," he said with no proper greeting.

"I do apologize; how rude of me. It is simply that I have decided ... well, I did not know how to tell you." My heart was racing. It was unclear as to why I felt nervous. I must have been afraid of his reaction.

"What is it? Do you not like the gown?"

"Oh, the gown is ... one of a kind. I do not even know how to put it on."

"That is not a problem. I will send servants to collect you before the festivities. They will see to it that you are ready."

"It is not the clothes. It is that I have decided not to attend the gala." This last part came out as quickly as possible. There, I said it. Relief. It was over.

Elijah stood even straighter than usual and narrowed his eyes. For the first time, I could see his father in him. More than a chill passed through me. For a moment I was actually afraid of him.

Elijah changed his expression by forcing a smile. "If you are concerned about being overdressed, don't be. We have invited foreign dignitaries and nobles, old friends of ours. They are visiting to see our refurbished place here and to celebrate. In the gown I gave you, you will fit right in. I will have you collected before the dance. See you then," he ended pointedly, spun gracefully on his heel and was gone.

This was good, as I had lost my nerve to deny him anyway. My thoughts were swirling. *What would foreign nobles have to celebrate in Ludus?* They would not care about our local tournament. There was a sinking feeling in my stomach. *Elijah and his father are up to something. Mari — I needed Mari.* As soon as the work for my uncle was done, I ran to Mari's house.

"How are you faring?" I asked Mari.

"Still trying to get back to normal after finding Emil's body. And you?"

"Even more confused and worried than usual," I answered.

She gave me a knowing smile and a chuckle.

"I need your help and it may be a good distraction for you."

"What is it now?" She looked skeptical.

"Elijah refuses to accept that I do not want to attend the celebration. Please come with me," I begged. "Wait until you see this preposterous thing he wants me to wear."

"I don't know. I do not have anything to wear to such an affair."

"Please! His father is intimidating, scary even but now I am concerned about Elijah as well."

"Why? What do you think they will do? And what can I do to help?"

"I'm not sure. The Chastellains are planning something. If you are there, then they will have to be on their best behavior. Your presence may … deter them. I need to have someone there I can trust."

She must have sensed my concern because she took my hands in hers. "Of course I will go with you."

CHAPTER 12 LUDUS 1260 AD

"Calm yourself. Everything is going to be fine. In fact, this will be exciting. Imagine, our very first proper gala!" Mari's large brown eyes were dancing.

I was so anxious about the gala that if it had not been for Mari, it would have been impossible for me to get into the lord's carriage. "Thank you for coming," I said.

A servant opened the carriage door and helped us out. I had to laugh at Mari's reaction when she saw the castle. Surely this was how Father and I had looked when we had seen this grand palace for the first time.

"Wait until you see the inside and the library," I said.

"They have their own library!" In the winter months, Father and I had been teaching Mari to read.

Elijah gave us a brief tour. We looked at the paintings for what seemed like a long while. Such artwork was our only way to glimpse what the outside world might be like.

"Come, ladies, you must go if you are to be ready for the festivities in time," Elijah said. "We have found a suitable gown for you as well, Mari. One of our guests from Adrianople offered its use."

Mari scarcely took notice of Elijah. "Do people honestly dress like that?" she asked in wonder as she stared at a painting of a group of noblewomen.

"Come, Mari, let us get ready. Then you will see that people do indeed dress in such nonsense," I replied. Though I was not sure why Elijah seemed to be in a hurry for us to get ready. It was only midday; the celebration would not start until this evening. Surely it would not take that long to put on a gown, even all five pieces of it. Elijah and I each had to take an arm of Mari's and drag her from the foreign artwork.

We followed Elijah to a large room full of maidservants, he quickly retreated. The room had a large four-poster bed with silky drapes cascading down around it. Before I could admire the rest of the room, the maidservants hurried us into a smaller room off the main bedchamber. There were two large tubs full of steaming water awaiting us.

"But I bathed this morning," I protested.

"Not like this," one of the maids declared.

Mari ran over to one of the tubs and inhaled. "You must smell the perfumed oils. I have only heard tales of such luxuries."

"Quickly, ladies. The water should be the perfect temperature and we have much to do."

Mari began to undress straightaway. She shared her one-room house with her entire family. She was used to changing in front of people but I was petrified. Father had added the upper level to our home, which allowed us privacy. No one had seen me undressed since I was a very small child. A maid started to lift up my dress to pull it over my head.

I shooed her away. "I can do it myself." Once my tunic was off I covered my chest with one arm and slowly slipped into the hot, smelly water. I supposed it smelled nice enough but it was too strong.

"Don't be prudish, Val. You are made no differently than anyone else in this room," Mari chastised. She was already at ease in the hot water, fully enjoying herself.

Soon I became used to the smell and my muscles began to loosen. I felt like a ragdoll helplessly floating in the water, unable to move.

Finally, when the water cooled, we were told we must be getting out for the next phase. I still did not want to move. As soon as I stepped out of the tub a maid wrapped a cloth around me and started to dry my skin. I took the cloth. "I can manage, thank you."

I quickly dried myself and reached eagerly for my tunic. A maid quickly snatched it away. "You will not be putting that old thing back on and you cannot dress until you have been properly oiled."

I looked to Mari, who was being rubbed down by three maids with more smelly oil. Soon there were slick hands all over me and I fought the urge to run from the room.

Mari laughed at the expression on my face.

Next, we were wrapped in unadorned silk robes and led back into the main bedchamber.

"I feel invigorated!" Mari exclaimed.

"I feel violated," I said. Even the maids laughed at this but I was not meaning to be funny.

Mari let the maids dress her but I chose to dress myself — well, mostly. It was a relief to put the new, white silk tunic on. It was longer and much softer than mine. Next came the main part of the gown. It was predominantly a blue brocade with a thick gold hem around the bottom. The upper arm was tightly fitted with armbands in a diamond-shaped pattern of green and blue. The sleeves opened up wide at the lower arm and hung below my knees. This was as far as I could get dressing myself. I had no idea what to do with the other pieces so the maids happily took over.

First they placed a long thin piece of fabric over my head. This resulted in a white strip running down my front and back. It had gold threads twisting elegantly, creating a spiral design down the front. The next piece was a loose belt that held up a portion of blue and green checkered silk. This hung diagonally across my legs. Finally, a large gold collar was placed over my shoulders. It had gold chains that held large teardrop shaped diamonds and emeralds; these hung down my chest.

"Lovely. Now for the hair," a maid announced.

Mari's gown was equally extravagant. It was mostly red with

yellow, with the same diamond patterned straps around the upper arm and running diagonally across her front legs. Mari and I were seated before one of two large dressing tables. There were full-length looking glasses, heavy oak wardrobes and chairs furnishing the room. Servants went straight to work on our hair and makeup. They were working feverishly and made comments to one another such as, "There is too much to do to get them ready." "Is it possible to have them looking suitable before the gala?" Mari and I chuckled to each other.

"Whose room is this?" I asked.

"For many years this was the Lady Chastellain's chambers," one of the maids answered.

"You said this 'was' her room. What happened to her?" I played ignorant — trying to get information. The servants exchanged concerned and knowing looks amongst one another.

"She died some years back. No one knows for sure what happened and besides, this is not the time for discussing the depressing past. You two young ladies should be focused on the upcoming festivities."

I decided to drop the subject, as it was doubtful that any more information would be divulged. Although ... this did not make sense. How could this have been Elijah's mother's room? She had died, or rather had been murdered, when he was ten. That had to be at least eight years ago. The Chastellains had only recently renovated this place. They moved to the area within the past three or four months. As far as we knew, Elijah and his father were new to the area. I had never heard of them living here for any length of time before.

I suppose this could have been Elijah's mother's room on brief summer visits during which the Chastellains sent servants to the market, while they themselves remained isolated from the villagers. This was possible. Yet the maidservant stated that it had been Lady Chastellain's room for many years. How could that have been, when no one in Ludus seemed to have known her? I certainly had never heard of the Chastellains until this spring and *everyone* in Ludus knows one another. Something was amiss.

CHAPTER 13 LUDUS 1260 AD

It seemed to take forever before we were finally ready. The finishing touches were the headdress and the shoes. My hair had been parted down the middle and curled around my face. It loosely came together at the back of my neck. Strands of pearls were braided into my hair as it fell down my back to my waist. A headband with a row of diamonds and emeralds partially crowned my head. The shoes were made of a gold fabric and had been embroidered with matching diamonds and emeralds. This was completely unnecessary, as one could not see them under the long brocade.

After five hours with six maids working frantically we were declared ready. Mari and I stood in front of one of the full-length mirrors.

"Well, at least no one from the village will recognize us," I exclaimed. Soon we were both laughing. This worried the servants.

"Stop that, girls; you will ruin all our hard work. You two must act like proper ladies." With one last effort to repair any damage our laughing may have caused, we were off to the celebration.

Apparently, everyone had already arrived. "We are fashionably late," Mari whispered. Her large eyes shone brighter than I had ever seen them before.

The Great Room was full. A lengthy table for the nobles ran along the far wall in front of the tall windows. Oddly, the curtains had been drawn shut, blocking out any evening sun that remained. Small round tables were placed along the outskirts of the room, most of them filled with people from the village. Another long table was full of food; two roasted pigs sat like bookends at either end of the table. Every type of food imaginable was on display: olives, chickens, apples, figs, pomegranates, dates, nuts, greens I had never seen before — enough food to feed our entire village for a week, maybe even a month.

Mari and I emerged at the top balcony and descended the stairs. The audience, one by one, stopped talking or dancing to stare at us. Elijah ascended the stairs and gave me his arm, which I took awkwardly because the overly long sleeves of my dress were in the way. His brocade matched mine, in color anyway. It too had a thick gold base, only instead of checkered green and blue fabric draped across the front of his legs it was wrapped elegantly across each shoulder. This formed a thick X across his chest, which accentuated his broad shoulders. He also wore a full golden crown inlaid with diamonds and emeralds. He looked like an emperor, not a nobleman. He was regal in his full splendor.

My stomach tightened at all the eyes on us. I did not like to be the center of attention.

A handsome young suitor approached and offered Mari his arm. She looked at me with wide questioning eyes. I shrugged — indicating that I had no idea who he was. By the looks of him, he was a noble. He did not wear a crown but was dressed in a red and yellow brocade in the same fashion as Elijah's, yet it was clearly a match to Mari's gown. *This was all carefully planned, every detail,* this thought worried me all the more.

Elijah appeared to be comfortable and confident. Perhaps he liked the attention. I suppose he was used to being the host of large gatherings with important people. It was all I could do to keep my hands from shaking. I was not used to all these layers of clothes. I missed a step and would have fallen down the stairs but Elijah easily kept me upright with his arm, which thankfully was hooked in mine.

"All is well; there is no need to be scared," Elijah whispered.

Once we were at the bottom of the stairs, people started to mingle and join in a circle dance again.

"There are many people to introduce you to," Elijah said. "Let us start with Samuel. He is from Denmark and a lord in our Court. Samuel, let me introduce you to Lady Mari and Lady Vallachia."

Samuel gave me a bow. He took Mari's hand, kissed it and said, "The pleasure is mine."

Mari's cheeks turned crimson.

"You came all the way from Denmark to attend this gala?" I was incredulous.

"Yes, of course. I have known Elijah for ... quite some time. When I received word that he had finally set his eyes upon a lady, I had to come and meet her. Now I see what all the fuss is about." Samuel smiled and nodded as if in farewell to Elijah and me. He held a bent arm out to Mari. "Shall we dance, My Lady?"

Before I knew it, Samuel had swept Mari away. *So much for my protection,* I thought.

"There are many more people I would like you to meet," Elijah exclaimed.

When we turned around, I found myself face to face with Father. He looked at me in disbelief, kissed my cheek and said in my ear, "You look like an empress, my dear." Then to everyone around, he added, "Look at my daughter, a true lady of nobility."

I gave him a curtsy. "Thank you, Father."

He wore his liturgical vestments, which consisted of a long white phelonion with a gold omophor wrapped carefully across his chest so that a red patriarchal cross rested at each shoulder as well as his knees. This was how he dressed every Sunday and for an occasion such as this, when he wished to make it known that he was a man of the Church.

"Ah. Deacon, please join us. There is someone I would like you to meet as well." Elijah led us to an older gentleman dressed in elaborate religious vestments like the ones I had seen in the art gallery, complete with a tall rounded white hat. The man stood as we approached.

"Bishop Constantain, allow me to introduce you to our local Deacon Adam and his lovely daughter, Vallachia." Elijah said. To us he added, "Bishop Constantain is a member of the Holy Synod."

Father's mouth fell open. "All the way from Constantinople. What an honor!"

We each bowed deeply in respect.

"At last, a man I can converse with. Please have a seat." Constantain gestured to the vacant chair beside him.

Father quickly sat.

When Elijah pulled me away, I could hear Father talking excitedly. "I have many questions for our church leaders. For one, what do you make of the Gnostic Gospels? Why are there different accounts of the Savior's Resurrection?"

"You have made Father's night," I said to Elijah.

"Yes, I imagine he has found his companion for the evening." Elijah appeared to be pleased with himself. Next, he introduced me to Lord Alexandru. "He is the head of our British Court."

I did not know what this *Court* was he kept referring to. The fact that it was important was about all I could gather.

"Lord Alexandru?" I said. "That sounds like a local name."

"Yes, I was originally from this area but that was many years ago. England is my home now." Alexandru had a kind smile.

I returned his smile. For some reason unknown to me I liked him. Elijah continued to introduce me to so many ladies and gentlemen of nobility that I could not possibly remember their names. My head was swimming by the time we finally made it to our seats at the nobles' table.

"Some of the ladies did not look pleased to meet me," I observed.

"Don't worry about them. Many are pompous and would not make suitable friends. They most likely think they are better than you, or they are jealous of any youthful beauty. They worry you might be after their wealthy husbands."

I laughed at the ridiculous notion but my laugh was cut short because across the Great Hall I spotted Teller. He was wearing his best attire, which was a dark green tunic and a dark brown chlamys fastened on the right shoulder. Both the tunic and the cloak came to just above his knees and he wore sandals that laced up his large calf muscles. He looked wonderfully familiar. I was overcome with longing for him.

Once Teller made eye contact with me, he seemed to make a decision and started marching straight for our table. “Pardon me, may I have a word with my old friend?”

Elijah did not look pleased but politely nodded his agreement.

This was a brazen thing to do. I thought something must be terribly wrong. As I stood to go so did Elijah. I followed Teller to the other side of the Great Hall.

“What is the matter?” I asked.

“You seem to be enjoying yourself.” Teller wore a stern expression and his eyes were dark.

“Oh.” I was relieved that everything seemed to be well. “Not particularly. This gown is uncomfortable. The only good thing about it will be getting out of it.”

Now he was the one who looked relieved. “I’m glad to hear that you are still you. I do not want you to get used to this … way of life.”

“Why is that?” I asked, feeling hopeful. My heart started pounding.

“Because you belong with us. You know, in the village.” Once again I did not get the answer I wanted from him. Who was *us?* Did he mean *him?*

“Well, if that is all, I suppose I should be getting back,” I sighed.

Teller frowned and looked as if he wanted to say something else but Elijah appeared. He hooked his arm in mine and proceeded to lead me away, making it clear that that was enough. Soon we were back at the noble’s table where Teller clearly did not belong.

CHAPTER 14 LUDUS 1260 AD

I could not stop myself from looking back toward Teller. I would have given anything to be with him this evening. It would have been enjoyable and normal. Instead I was miserable in this bulky gown. It was difficult to reach my chalice on the table, as the sleeves kept getting in the way. I longed for my simple linen dress.

Having to sit at the nobles' table was uncomfortable enough all by itself, even without the odd gown. The people were stiff and pretentious. Not knowing how to act caused me to yearn for my familiar friends and family. I skimmed the crowd for them. Father was fully absorbed in listening to the Bishop from the Queen of Cities. Father's eyes were bright — he looked truly happy.

Mari was harder to find. I spied her holding Samuel's hand as they took part in a circle dance. She looked beautiful with her long brown braid sparkling with pearls. She appeared to be having the time of her life.

When I found my brother in the crowd, my mouth fell open. He was dancing with a girl from the village, Sarah — at least I thought that was her name. She was one of the shoemaker's daughters. Sarah was quite a bit younger than I. Josiah appeared to be teaching her how to do the circle dance and they laughed when she would miss a step. A smile crept across my face as I watched them. They made an attractive young couple.

I scanned the multitude for Teller when a clanking of flagons slowly got people's attention and the musicians stopped playing. It was time for Lord Chastellain to address his guests. He too was wearing a crown suited for a great ruler. It was grander than Elijah's. The lord's brocade was almost solid gold. It had red trim and red diamond-patterned sleeve bands. It became apparent to me that the lord was not simply a wealthy noble who had worked his way up from the merchant class. He must be an emperor, or perhaps a king, as they were called in the west. That would make Elijah a prince. The question was, the rulers of what? Surely not Denmark? I had never heard of them before.

"It appears that all are enjoying themselves. I do hope that is the case." Lord Chastellain interrupted my thoughts.

I nervously took a gulp of the drink that had been placed in front of me. I almost spat it out. Instead I choked on the substance.

"What is the matter?" Elijah whispered.

"What is this?" I asked.

"We are serving our finest and oldest wine from our cellar tonight." Elijah wore an amused smirk.

"It's vile." It was nothing like the sweet wine and meads I was used to.

He laughed and we received disapproving glares from the nearby nobles.

When I looked up I spotted Teller in the masses. He looked as miserable as I felt. Perhaps we were the only two not enjoying ourselves despite what Chastellain had hoped.

I had stopped listening to the lord's speech. What snapped me out of my own miserable thoughts was Elijah standing as his father said, "My son has a big announcement to make." He stepped aside for Elijah.

My heart began to race as Elijah took my hand to raise me out of my seat. He lowered himself to one knee and my stomach went into knots. As quickly as if he was a magician, he presented a gold ring.

The ring was enormous and had been inlaid with an elaborate diamond C. The ring itself was in the shape of the Chastellain coat of arms.

"Lady Vallachia, will you marry me?" Elijah asked.

No, no, no, was my first thought. *Not here! Not in front of all these people! He knows I cannot refuse.* Of course, I should have suspected this was his plan all along — to leave me with no way to deny him. I glanced nervously at the crowd, who appeared to be anxiously awaiting a resounding yes in response to the proposal.

Father's words echoed through my head. *You always have a choice.* I looked directly at Teller, who was standing with his arms crossed and a deep frown on his face. *I must do something!* My knees felt weak, so I went with that and let myself fall. Elijah caught me with impossible ease and speed. He lifted me as if I weighed no more than a small child. There were gasps and murmurs from the onlookers. I closed my eyes to avoid everyone.

Elijah laid me down gently on the library divan.

I opened my eyes when I heard Father. He nudged Elijah away. "Give her some room. She will recover soon."

"What is wrong? Has she done this before?" Elijah's voice was full of concern. "Should I call for a doctor?"

"No, no. She will be fine," Father said.

Mari and Teller came running in; Father stopped Teller and let Mari by.

Mari ran to my side, asking if I was well.

I nodded yes.

"She will soon feel herself. Please give her some time," Father was saying to the two worried young men.

Teller and Elijah reluctantly left the library.

Father looked over his shoulder at the door to make sure we were alone before he said, "Well, I did not know we had an actress in the family. Hopefully, you will not be joining the theater?" Father was astute and he knew me well.

"Oh, my," I said playfully. "The deacon's daughter becoming an actress. What a scandal."

Father laughed.

"What?" Mari said. "That was a deception? I was worried."

"Thank you for your concern," I said. "You are a true friend. And yes, I am quite well." I sat up awkwardly because of all the layers I wore.

Mari punched me in the arm. "Don't do that again."

"Hopefully, she won't have to," Father said. "What are we going to do about this situation?"

"What situation? What are you talking about?" Mari looked exasperated.

"Oh, come now, Mari. You know my daughter. She simply does not want to marry the young lord," Father said.

"You do realize that any girl in the village would give her right hand to be in your place tonight —" The expression on my face caused Mari to pause. She grew thoughtful and silent.

"Aye." Father's brow furrowed. "It is interesting how that works. Elijah has chosen one of the only women who would not want him in return. People tend to want what they cannot have. For Elijah, I imagine there has not been much that he could not possess. This will make him all the more determined. I am afraid we cannot put them off much longer, as I had hoped, my dear."

I nodded in agreement and felt a new strength come over me. *I'm going to have to be as determined as Elijah.* Father had filled my head with strange ideas about having the freedom to choose my own path in life. Perhaps I had been born with this independent spirit and Father had simply fostered it. Either way, I felt myself changing into the person I was meant to become. *I must leave behind that timid girl and become a strong woman.*

Mari seemed to have an epiphany as well. "I know what it is! It is because you love someone else." Her large sparkling eyes widened even farther. "It is because of Teller, isn't it?"

CHAPTER 15 LUDUS 1260 AD

Thankfully, the tournament started the very next morning. This gave the villagers plenty to do besides talk about the gala and how it ended with a disastrous proposal. The tournament was a two-day extravaganza with not only sporting competitions for the men but separate competitions for the women as well. There were cooking contests for the best roast pig, pies, preserves and more. I would be entering my jam tarts. The women also had sewing competitions for the best clothes and blankets. For this I had nothing to offer. I could manage only the most basic mending.

Josiah was excited because this was the first year he decided to compete and he had been practicing hard for the different events. Though he was still dreamy-eyed from dancing with Sarah, he went out to practice his archery after breakfast.

"Josiah seems happy," I said to Father as we went out to watch him practice.

"Yes, I only wish that for you as well. You do know we will have to deal with the Chastellains after this whole midsummer festival is over," Father replied.

"I have been thinking about it and I am prepared to refuse Elijah."

Father looked thoughtful and concerned but nodded in understanding and agreement.

Elijah had disappeared last night after my fainting act and I was not looking forward to seeing him at the tournament. I had two days at the most before I must end this charade. This thought made my stomach flutter but I was as determined as ever.

My family and I headed to the usually vacant field where the tournament was held. The field was bustling with energy and people. Tables displayed all sorts of goods for sale.

"The archery contest is about to start. I must line up," Josiah said as he ran off with his bow and quiver.

Lord Chastellain beckoned for Father and me to join him in the elevated stands, which were shaded by fabric that had been fastened to wooden poles. Father gave me a knowing look as we headed toward him. My heart quickened.

"Please join me here in the refreshing shade, my friend," the lord said to Father. To me he added, "It is good to see you out and about. I presume you are well?"

"Yes, My Lord. I'm feeling much better, thank you," I said.

"For that I am grateful."

The lord had an odd way of saying pleasant things with his mouth while his face told a completely different story. He looked at me with doubt and something else — anger, disgust, maybe hunger? Whatever it was, it made the hair on the back of my neck stand on end. *He is ... evil,* I thought.

Samuel was seated to the right of Lord Chastellain. He stood and took my hand, kissing it. "It is good to see you again, My Lady." His words seemed more genuine than the lord's.

Lord Chastellain gave Samuel a disapproving look and gestured for him to sit down. Samuel flashed me a blithe smile and took his seat, as his lord demanded. He seemed like the type of person who was always content, without a care in the world, as if nothing ever bothered him. *That must be delightful,* I thought.

Father sat to the left of the lord. "Where is your son?" he asked.

"He is competing in this year's tournaments. He must do what he can to prove himself." With this last statement the lord looked pointedly at me.

I quickly looked away. In fact, I had to suppress a strong desire to run. Something deep inside was telling me to get out of there — that the lord was dangerous. He seemed to be in a particularly unpleasant mood.

Thankfully, the archery competition started and we could all focus our attention on that. Josiah did well, advancing into the second round. He always hit the target and almost hit a bull's-eye but Teller's dead-center shot knocked my brother out of the competition. Still, that was good for his first year. Maybe he would be able to win next year. Well, that was if Teller happened to make a bad shot, which he rarely did.

Elijah's arrow split right through Teller's center arrow. It was a tie. That required an extra round between the two of them to determine the winner. Teller's first shot landed in the center of the red dot but slightly to the right. Elijah's arrow landed dead center. Teller's final shot was a hair to the left. Elijah split his first arrow in the center of the bulls-eye with such force that it sent a loud cracking sound through the silent crowd.

"And the winner is the young Lord Chastellain," Ivan announced. He shot a glare toward his son. Ivan held Elijah's arm up and the crowd cheered.

"Well done; that was impressive. I had no idea your son was such a skilled archer," Father proclaimed to Lord Chastellain.

"Wait until you see him in the other events." the lord smirked.

Oh no, I thought. *This will not go well. How could the lord be so sure of his son? He is a pampered noble and he is half the size of some of the other men competing. Archery is one thing but Elijah would not stand a chance against Ivan, Teller and some of the other men who were used to hard manual labor. Elijah was tall and lean but not overly muscular. I did not want him to make a fool of himself, especially trying to prove himself to me. Ivan and, more recently, Teller were the reigning champions in most of the strength competitions. Teller was also one of the fastest in the tournament.*

My thoughts were interrupted by Mari who ran up to the stands where we were seated. She gave a courteous bow to Father and the lord and an urgent look to me.

Samuel quickly rose and took her hand. He placed his lips to the back of her hand for quite a time — a bit too long. "There is My Lady. I had a splendid time last night."

Mari's cheeks instantly reddened. "Thank you, My Lord, as did I." She gave him a curtsy. "Please excuse me. I must have a word with Vallachia."

Her urgency caused me to stand and ask to be excused. Mari and I hurried off arm in arm — as usual. When we were safely out of earshot, I asked, "What is the matter?"

Her cheeks were no longer red and her mouth was downturned. "I spoke to Teller this morning before the tournament. He and Elijah both overheard our conversation last night."

I gave her a questioning look, not fully understanding.

Mari continued, "They both know why you supposedly fainted last night!"

Of course. Now Elijah knows why I did not agree to his proposal and Teller knows how I feel about him. I actually felt relief. *The truth is out. I will finally find out how Teller feels about me and be able to openly refuse Elijah. The townspeople will talk about how I am not a respectable lady for wanting a boy who had not proposed and whom my father had not given me permission to marry. Oh, well, there is nothing I can do about that now.* "Good," I finally said. "This entire mess needs to end."

"What about your reputation?" Mari asked.

"I plan to refuse Elijah, whether Teller will have me or not."

"Well, that is the other problem. Teller would ask you to marry him but he has nothing to offer you. No home — no money. He said he cannot propose." Mari looked forlorn.

Two conflicting yet equally powerful emotions hit me as once. The first was joy that Teller possibly loved me. The second was a pain that stabbed my chest. *He will not ask for my hand.* "Well, I must have a talk with Teller." My voice was full of determination.

"You are serious about this? You will give up everything for nothing?"

"The way I look at it is that I *do* have everything with Teller and nothing with Elijah. I hardly know him. I would do anything for love and happiness. Wouldn't you?"

Mari looked at me incredulously. I returned her stare. We were clearly at an impasse. She searched my face and I held her gaze with determination until we both broke into a hardy laugh at our differences.

"Come. The next competition is about to start. Let us take our seats," I said.

CHAPTER 16 LUDUS 1260 AD

Samuel left his seat by the lord to sit by Mari. They were soon happily chatting away. I was thrilled for her. Samuel seemed amiable and he was entertaining company. I felt a twinge of trepidation when I thought about him having to return to Denmark. I pushed the thought aside. *Let her enjoy his company while she can.*

"All is well?" Father whispered.

"Yes, I think so."

"You look pleased."

I did not reply, as Lord Chastellain looked even more disgruntled – if that were possible. It was best to end the conversation with prying ears nearby.

The throwing contests were about to start. First was the javelin tossing. Josiah did not make it into the finals but did quite well. Elijah barely made it into the finals. I felt nervous for him. *Why do you care about him?* the voice in my head asked. I could see that there was good in Elijah. Perhaps if he could get out from under his father's influence, he would be a kind man. I considered Elijah a friend.

However, there was no need to worry about Elijah. His final javelin toss went a good three lengths farther than any of the others. Mari and I exchanged an astonished look.

"Well, who would have guessed?" Father said. "Elijah must not have been trying as hard in the first round."

Lord Chastellain did not look surprised; in fact, he had a passive expression on his face. He looked almost ... bored.

For the ball-throwing contest, Elijah did not hold back. This time he won handily. No one came close to meeting his mark.

"Have you ever tried to pick up that metal ball? It is so heavy — I would be lucky to throw it one length," Mari exclaimed.

We all chuckled — all but Chastellain, of course.

"I have never seen someone throw that far. You must be very proud of him," Father said.

The lord did not look proud, simply inert. He did not reply.

I no longer needed to worry about Elijah. Now I was concerned for Teller. He had come in a distant second and that was clearly not good enough for Ivan, as he looked furious. I felt an angry heat rising to my face. It was not as though Ivan's toss had come any closer to winning. In fact, Ivan came in fourth place! I had a strong desire to point this fact out to Ivan. *He is such an arse.* I took a couple of deep breaths to calm down.

Father patted my arm. As usual, he probably knew what I was thinking.

The final events for the day went much the same. Elijah jumped impossibly far into the sandpit. He won, even though Teller's jump had beaten the previous town record — Ivan's record.

At this point, Lord Chastellain gestured to Elijah with his palm facing down and moving his arm slowly up and down — a gesture that usually means *slow down* or *restrain yourself.*

Elijah nodded. He started out behind in the sprint but easily finished slightly ahead of Teller. He did not even look winded after the race.

I narrowed my eyes with suspicion. *What is going on? The lord and his son are clearly in collusion — again. Perhaps they are cheating, somehow?*

After the day's competitions, I sneaked away to find Teller. When I spotted him, my heart quickened. I ran to catch up with him but had to make a quick turn to avoid Elijah and the mass of people around him cheering and congratulating him. Teller was headed into the woods.

Perfect, I thought. *With all the attention on Elijah, no one will notice that I followed Teller.* Catching up to him, I slowed my pace to match his. He gave me a weak smile and we walked in silence for some time. I knew how he was feeling and did not know what to say. He was used to being the best in the village.

"Your father is not going to be too hard on you, is he?" I asked.

"Well, I'm going to avoid him for a while longer — in hopes that he will calm down." After a pause, he added, "It is all the Chastellains' fault. I wish they would go back to wherever it was they came from. They are getting in the way of everything!" His jaws clenched.

"Yes and there is something odd about them. They are ... I am not sure exactly. I mean, it appeared that Elijah was not trying at times, perhaps even holding back in the games," I tried to explain.

"How could a scrawny, spoiled lord be so good at such games?"

"Precisely my point. Something is amiss."

Teller nodded thoughtfully. "Your uncle warned me that I should ask your father for permission to marry you before someone else did. I don't even have time to get settled enough to ask you to be my bride. Not with Elijah pushing you into marriage."

I smiled and put my arm in his. That was enough of a marriage proposal for me. "No one is going to push me into anything. There must be something we can do ... let's run away. We could elope."

"Where would we go? I have nothing — no money to move to a new town."

It seemed like a plausible idea at first but it truly was a childish notion. The urge to run away from one's problems was normal but not always the best of ideas. The thought of leaving my father and brother was unbearable, not to mention Uncle Ezekiel. *Who would take care of them?* "I suppose you are right. How can we leave our families?"

"Aye, who would protect my mother and little brothers from my father?"

I stopped him from walking and looked into his eyes; they were dark and troubled. "I wish we could run away, though."

He put his arms around me and whispered, "As do I."

I wanted to stay like that forever — in his arms but eventually I pulled back. "It is not that complicated. I will refuse Elijah and that will give you more time. Meanwhile, we will know how we feel about each other. I will wait for you."

He pulled me in close and gently placed his lips on mine.

I could have gotten lost in that kiss but I felt that we were being watched. For the second time that day, the hair on the back of my neck prickled. I pulled back and looked around. "We should be getting back," I said. We had wandered quite a way into the forest.

"I will walk you home." His eyes were brighter, greener. Then they darkened. "Father will be looking for me and I can't put off confronting him for much longer. Besides, I should be there to divert his anger from my family."

I felt ill at the thought. "How will you fare?"

"Well enough. He will want me to compete tomorrow. So maybe he will be lenient with me." He made a point of looking into my eyes. "You know I would never treat you as Father treats us."

"I know." Teller was kind, unlike his father. He had always been caring and protective toward others.

"I hate my father sometimes and I have sworn that I will not be like him."

It was difficult to imagine what it would be like to hate one's father. *It must be terrible,* I thought.

We had to pass Teller's house on the way to mine. As we approached his home, we heard yelling. Teller took to his heels at a full run.

"Where is he? Where is that worthless son of mine?" Ivan shouted.

Teller burst through the door and I ran in after him.

"Here! Here I am. Leave them alone."

Teller and his father start circled each other.

"You let some puny pampered little boy beat you today. You are a disgrace!" Ivan's cheeks were red with anger and his fists were clenched.

I stood in the doorway. I wanted to grab Teller's two youngest brothers and run away with them.

"I beat all of your records today. I did better than you ever have. Does that not count for anything? Nothing I do is good enough for you!" Teller retorted.

I'd thought Ivan looked angry before but now he looked murderous. His eyes were wild — like a rampaging bull. He swung at Teller, who easily dodged the blow.

Teller came up under his father, grabbing his tunic by the neck and slamming him against the wall with his forearms pressed against his father's chest.

The entire house shook. I instinctively put my arms around Teller's two youngest brothers, covering them the best I could. I wanted to protect them in any way possible, even if it was only to block their view of the fight.

Ivan's eyes were wide. Teller threw his father to the floor. Ivan winced in pain and clutched his arm. He must have landed wrong.

Teller towered over his father. "Never! Never again. Not to me, not to them." He gestured to his mother and brothers. "You will not hurt anyone anymore." In a lower voice, he added, "It's over."

Father and son stared at each other for a long moment. Teller grabbed my arm, firmly leading me out of the house. It was almost dark and I was breaking curfew; soon Teller would be as well. We walked quickly in silence to my home. I was in shock. How different our two homes were. Mine was quiet and peaceful. It seemed that standing up to Ivan was for the best. If his father knew he could not bully Teller anymore, things might get better ... I hoped.

When we got to my door, I wrapped my arms around Teller.

"I'm sorry you had to see that," he whispered.

"Is all well, or rather, will it be?" I asked.

"Yes. It felt good. It has been a long time coming."

"I'm proud of you. That must have been the hardest thing you have ever had to do — standing up to your father like that. ... Why now?"

"I'm not entirely sure. I want things to be different. I don't want us — you and I — to live under his tyranny."

I smiled as I was truly happy for the first time in months. I kissed his cheek and headed for my door. With everything that had happened this evening, I had forgotten about being inconspicuous with Teller.

"If, by chance, things are not better, please bring your family here," I said.

"Thank you but I think all will be well." He smiled that beautiful smile, the one that had first helped me to realize I had fallen in love with him.

"I'm sure you are right. This needed to happen. Goodnight and good luck," I said.

"Goodnight."

CHAPTER 17 LUDUS 1260 AD

The next morning I felt as light as a cloud and full of energy — *Teller and I are to marry ... someday.*

"Well, it is wonderful to see you smile. Do you care to elaborate on why?" Father inquired.

"Yes, of course, Father." My face fell. "There is one matter of business we need to attend to. We must send the Chastellains a clear and final rejection letter."

"I suspected that was coming. Aye let's be done with it. After the festivities today, we will send them a letter." Yet Father looked worried.

"What is wrong? What do you think they will do?" I asked.

"Lord Chastellain is a powerful man. Let us hope that he will do nothing. They should take rejection like the gentlemen that they are." Under his breath, he added, "I pray."

This concerned me. *There is nothing they can do. Or is there?*

The first event of the day was the broadsword contest. The competitors wore metal breastplates and the goal was not to kill or mortally wound anyone. Whoever was able to hit the other's breastplate first was the winner. This lasted most of the morning, as it was a popular event, with many of the men taking part.

That afternoon the competitions would end with a ball game. We called it Ludus ball, after our town. This was fitting since Ludus also means play. There were few rules and the game was simple and chaotic. The only objective was to get the inflated pig's bladder into the opposing team's goal, which was made of two wooden fence posts stuck in the ground on either end of the field.

Father and I went to watch Josiah's fencing matches. I was relieved that the Chastellains were nowhere to be seen. However, part of me was uneasy about why they were not in attendance. It seemed unusual that they would miss the last day of festivities after being so involved in them yesterday.

Josiah won his first fencing match and lost his second to Teller. Teller went on to win the final match handily. Ivan did not participate for the first time since he had been old enough to compete. He was favoring the arm he had fallen on last night. However, he appeared content and cheered for his son. Ivan beamed as he raised his son's arm in victory.

I felt blood rush to my cheeks. *How could Ivan say such horrible things to his son last night and now proudly claim Teller because he was a winner again?* I had to fight the urge to slap Ivan across the face.

I did not fully understand Ivan. Above all else he valued being the best. This ideal did not match my own. Ivan's values were not necessarily bad, as they pushed Teller to try his hardest. It was Ivan's temper and meanness that were the problem.

Father and I cheered for my brother in the Ludus ball game. The day was an enjoyable one, except I felt terrible for Mari. She was forlorn because Samuel, like the Chastellains, was nowhere to be found.

"You do not think Samuel would return to Denmark without saying goodbye?" Mari asked.

I shrugged, as I did not have an answer. All I could do was place an arm around her shoulders to try to console her.

Father gave a young boy a coin to carry the renunciation letter to the Chastellain manor directly after the Ludus game — during which Teller had scored the most goals. Two of the players lifted Teller up on their shoulders as everyone applauded. The ball players were bruised and sore after the game, yet exhilarated. Hungry, too, I imagined, as everyone migrated to the town center for the final pig roast and feast to end this year's midsummer festival.

Everyone seemed to be in high spirits. The entire village hummed with energy and laughter. I could not have been more elated, either. I was finally on my way to having the life I'd recently realized I had always wanted — Teller and me surrounded by our children.

A scream rang out. All fell silent. I looked around to see where the terrifying sound had come from. There was a commotion not far from us. My family and I ran over to see. It was the missing farmer — he had returned and he was alive! He had stumbled into the feast and now lay on the ground. I searched for his name in my head. *Luka,* I thought. He did not look well. He had odd wounds on his neck and wrists that looked as if they had been cleaned and tended to. He was whey-faced and obviously weak.

"I escaped," he said with a labored voice. "Monsters …" He trailed off, too weak to go on.

"Get him inside," Father yelled.

Two men carried Luka into the tavern.

Sofia, the local healer, pushed her way through to Luka and sent out orders for fresh water and rags. "Give him some room!" she said as she shooed people away.

Ivan made his way closer to the ailing man. "Who did this? What happened?"

Luka's eyes rolled back in his head. He moaned.

"Leave him alone!" Sofia barked at Ivan. "He needs rest. Let me see what I can do. You can get your answers when he is better."

Ivan glared at the little old woman. He turned to the growing crowd and declared that the culprit might be near and a hunting party should head out immediately — led by him, of course.

I ran to fetch Sofia water. It was not long before a group of men headed out with whatever weapons they could find — swords, javelins, spears. A few merely had pitchforks. Teller and his father were in the lead. They headed in the direction from which Luka had come.

Father asked Josiah not to go but Josiah said he must help if he could. Father decided to see to it that the rest of the townspeople went home. We cleared the village center by telling everyone to get safely inside. We waited until everyone had gone home before we did the same.

It was well after dark and the men were still not back, I started to doze uneasily. Father coaxed me to go upstairs to bed. He said he would wait up for Josiah and the others to return. I tossed and turned in bed and woke at the slightest of sounds. I would sit up occasionally to see if Josiah was in his bed across the hall. The last I looked, he was not.

CHAPTER 18 LUDUS 1260 AD

In the hours before dawn, I woke with an eerie feeling. The hair was standing up on the back of my neck. A tall lean figure was hovering over my bed. I started to say, "Father, is that — ?" when a hand appeared over my mouth. The figure scooped me up and before I could even try to scream, we landed on the ground below my bedroom window. I was being carried through the forest so quickly that I could hardly make out the trees as they flew by.

There was enough moonlight so that I could make out my kidnapper's face. It was Lord Chastellain. I started to scream and his hand came up quickly to easily muffle it. Through the wind in my ears I heard what sounded like a faint voice. This stopped the lord and Elijah appeared from out of nowhere.

"Father, what are you doing? Let her go!"

The lord set me down gently. I tried to run but his iron grip on my arm stayed me.

"What are you going to do?" Elijah asked the question as if he knew the answer and dreaded it.

"You know very well my intentions. I'm going to turn her into one of us." The lord's tightly lipped smirk was more terrifying than his words.

Turn me into what? I thought. I could no longer suppress the panic that was taking over. I did not like the sound of it.

"Father, please, why would you do that?" Elijah was slowly stepping toward us and the lord was moving farther away with every step Elijah advanced.

"For you, of course. You want her, do you not?"

Elijah's hands were held in front of him as if surrendering. "No, no, I don't. Not when she does not want me. You read her letter and we both know she loves someone else. It is done." Elijah paused briefly, then tried another angle. "Please, we don't have time for this. We must be leaving. The hunters will find us soon. Leave the girl and the rest of the villagers to live out their human lives."

"We have time — unless you did not take care of the farmer?" the lord questioned.

"Of course I took care of him. The old lady got in the way. She is dead as well."

"Dead! You killed Sofia and Luka? Why?" I could not refrain any longer. I fell to my knees but the lord supported my weight easily. Tears filled my eyes. *What is going on? Why would Elijah hurt them?*

"You see, Father? You think turning her will make her love me. She will only hate me all the more. Let her go and we will move on. It is only a matter of time before they find us," Elijah pled.

"And watch you brood about for another hundred years or so until you are able to find another beauty like this. I don't think so. I want only your happiness, Son. That is all I have ever wanted. The way I see it, you can either kill the boy she plans to marry or turn her. Is it not better to turn her and leave the boy alone? You will thank me someday for this."

The lord did something surprising. He bit into his own wrist until blood flowed down his arm. I caught a glimpse of two long teeth. The lord had fangs like a lion's. He pulled my hair, jerking my head back. I screamed as pain spread like fire across the back of my head.

"No!" Elijah yelled.

I choked on the blood Lord Chastellain was pouring down my throat. There was a loud cracking sound as Elijah threw his body into his father's. Elijah swiftly caught me and gently lowered me to the ground. I tried to spit the blood out. My head was spinning. I looked for the lord but he was nowhere in sight. Everything went black.

PART II CHAPTER 19 LUDUS 1260 AD

When I came to, I did so slowly and everything was hazy and confused. I sat up and studied my surroundings. I was lying under a makeshift lean-to, which was shading me with leaves and branches. Elijah was sitting against the trunk of a nearby tree. He was as still as a statue, not moving to look at me.

"I'm very sorry. I did not want this for you. I tried to stop Father." With a sad smile, he added, "I did not even want this life for myself."

My last memories came flooding back and my heart began to race. There were so many questions running through my mind. In a flash, Elijah was at my side. I jumped at his sudden closeness. All I could hear was my heart pounding in my ears.

"Shhh," he said, "there is much you need to know. I will help you."

"Get away from me!" I ran out from under the lean-to and doubled over, covering my eyes. It felt like there were knives in them. I was virtually blind. An agonizing scream escaped from me and Elijah pulled me back under the lean-to.

"Please, listen to me! Let me explain and then you can go, I promise. Well, actually, once the sun has set you will be free to go," he corrected.

"You killed them," I stammered. It was all I could think about — all

I could manage to say — all that mattered. I was trapped who knew where, with the killer the village men had been looking for. The memory of the baker's blood-soaked body on the forest floor appeared in my mind. "Emil! You killed him?"

"Well, not that I suppose it matters but my father was the one who killed him." Elijah said this as if it were a normal occurrence.

I felt ill. I wrapped both arms tightly around my stomach. "Is that what you are going to do to me?"

"No." Elijah sighed. "What Father did to you is worse."

"Worse? Worse! What could possibly be worse?"

"Remember, you asked. You are in transition. Over the next day or so you will become a creature of the night, like us — Father and me."

"What does that mean? A killer — a demon?"

"Of sorts. We have been called such things. We refer to ourselves as vampires."

"What in the world is a vampire?"

"Where to start? Perhaps I should start with the worst of it. We need human blood to survive and the sun is no longer our friend. We are creatures of the night and the shadows. The sun's painful effect on the eyes fades after a couple of decades but you will always prefer the more comfortable shade and darkness."

It felt as if the earth was spinning. "You are out of your mind! How long have I been here? I have to get home!"

"You have been here since last night. I'm afraid home will no longer be safe for you or your family."

I could only take so much. The day was growing old. "Father will be worried half to death. I must go!" I tried to rise but Elijah grabbed my arm to stay me.

"That is not possible now and yes, they will be out looking for you. That is why we must move quickly, as soon as it is dark."

"Move quickly to where?"

"You are going to need to feed soon and I don't suppose you will want to do that to anyone in your village."

"I can't leave my family — my friends."

Elijah took a deep breath. "Look, what I am saying is, your old life is over. You have a new life now — an immortal one. It will be safer for everyone you care about if you leave the village. Father and I are leaving for Denmark. We have a home near Copenhagen where it is easier for us to go unnoticed."

"You mean so you can kill people more inconspicuously?"

"Please, listen to me! It takes time to learn to control your need for blood. Come to Denmark with us. We can help you adjust to this new life."

I narrowed my eyes and glared at him. *There is absolutely no way I am leaving with them.*

He tried another angle. "It was my father who killed my mother."

This did get my attention. I could not help asking, "Why?"

"He, like most new vampires, thought he could control his thirst. He knew that he would not hurt my mother or me. Now she is dead. I saw him turn into a monster and drain her of life. Father disappeared. He later said it was because he did not want to hurt me. From that point on I was raised by a handful of servants. John, my father's most faithful servant, became like a father to me."

I was captivated by the story. "How did you become ... like this?"

"My father returned eight years later, when I was of age. Like you, I did not have a choice."

Could it be true? No. I thought of his mother's large room. *That could have been her room — a long time ago.* Some of the pieces fell into place. "You were from here? Originally, I mean?"

"Yes, the manor outside of town is largely where I was raised. Father preferred that I be brought up in a safer rural area. He spent a lot of time away on business when I was growing up. This is the first time in many years that we have returned to Ludus for any length of time."

"How old are you?"

"Well, as I said, I stopped aging when I was about eighteen or so. I have been on this earth for almost seven hundred years — give or take. One tends to lose track after a handful of centuries pass."

My lips parted in amazement. "So that would be the good side to being a ... vampire — eternal youth?"

"Yes, immortality, strength and speed. We are many times stronger and faster than any human. We are well suited to this earth. We can move quickly across land, sea and air."

A hysterical laugh escaped. "You mean to tell me you can fly?"

"Yes and I will teach you, if you want me to."

It was all too much. I shook my head and fell silent for a time. I stood and slowly stepped out into the sun. Once again, my eyes felt as if they were on fire. I stepped back into the shade. *Well, I'm not going anywhere if I can't see.* I sat down, exasperated.

"What am I to do? I can't leave Father to wonder about me. It will tear him up. He will search endlessly. And Teller..." My heart started to ache. *Would I never see them again?* My thoughts strayed to Mari. She had been such a dear friend. Tears started rolling down my face and Elijah wiped one away.

"We will think of something. We will send your father a letter saying ... I'm not sure ... some story."

Some story. Father would have to be content with 'some story'. Anger surged to the surface. Slapping Elijah's hand away from my face, I stood and moved as far away from him as I could without the sun burning me.

"You are a murderer. I want nothing to do with you or your wretched father. He did this to me. I will never forgive him!" I'd hoped this would offend him but it did not.

Elijah said nothing. In fact, his expression did not so much as change. He still looked ... sad.

This calmed me a bit. "You mean to tell me that you have forgiven him for everything he did to you — to your mother?"

"It is my life, so I have grown accustomed to it over the years. Sometimes I still feel anger toward him, leading me to believe that I have not fully forgiven him. Now he has done it again — trying to control everything. Making decisions for me and making a mess of things."

I plopped back down, still as far away from him as possible. "Is there nothing to be done? There must be some way to undo this. What if I do not drink ... blood?" I swallowed hard on this last word.

"Would I go back to … normal?" I had a horrible feeling about the answer to this, yet there was still a touch of hope. That small bit of hope was all I had left.

"No. If you don't feed, you will die."

"I don't want to hurt anyone! I do not want to be a … killer." I racked my brain; there must be another way.

CHAPTER 20 LUDUS 1260 AD

"What about animal blood?" I asked.

"I have experimented with drinking animal blood," Elijah explained. "It apparently only prolongs our downfall. After several months of consuming only animal blood, I was too weak to hunt. Father saw to it that I fed properly, of course. So, my next experiment has been trying not to kill the people whom I feed from. I am getting better at it. Luka survived. The problem is that keeping humans prisoner is no better than killing them and if I let them go, then humans will discover that we exist and hunt us. We'll have to relocate more often. I have been searching for alternatives my whole life. So far, I have not found any good ones." His voice was monotone and the gray storm raged in his eyes.

"You hate what you have become, don't you?"

"At times, I do find happiness. It is not all bad." I could tell he was only trying to make me feel better.

"Then I will not feed. I would rather die than become a killer and have to live with that for all eternity." Such a life sounded like the definition of hell. *That is it. That is the best option — the only choice.* I closed my eyes and let the tears come freely. I would not even get to say goodbye to the people I loved. It was better than killing them. It had to be done. After a long while, I opened my eyes.

"Do you really mean that? You would rather die?" He looked ... impressed.

"Yes and if you do actually care about me, you will let me die."

He did not say anything. He looked disturbed.

"I'm serious, Elijah. You said you did not want this life for you, let alone me. Don't interfere with my choice."

"I wanted you to have a choice between a human life and a vampire life. Death, while you were still so young, was not one of the options I had in mind. Besides, it is not going to be easy. Your urge to feed will be too strong; it will change you."

My throat was already so dry I felt I could drink the entire Mures River and that would not be enough. I rubbed my throat, hoping this might help somehow.

"You see? This is only the beginning; your thirst is going to get a great deal worse. Let's hope you can last until dark and we can get you to a neighboring village."

"I'm not going to drink someone's blood!"

Elijah shook his head. "At sunset, you need to run with me far away from here. I have nothing here strong enough to restrain you when your thirst gets too powerful. I don't think I alone can stop you — even if I truly wanted to. If you are not going to feed, we must run far into the forest, away from any people."

"Do you promise to help me?"

"Aye," he said with reluctance. He put his arm around me and this time I let him. I needed to be comforted, as the sun was getting low in the sky. I cried into his shoulder for a long while.

When the sun was setting, I pulled myself together. "Will you take my body to my father? I want him to know what became of me and not hold out hope for my return. That is the least I can do."

Elijah nodded. "Of course."

The light was fading. It was dark enough for us to run. He clasped my hand and we sped through the forest away from Ludus. The trees were flying by in a blur. I could not help myself; it was exhilarating to be able to move at such a speed. I could duck under or jump far over fallen trees with ease.

Though I had not thought it possible, the thirst was getting worse. I felt myself slip away. A crazed new feeling rose from deep within. It was unlike anything else I had ever felt. A raging monster was taking over. I fell to my knees and screamed in pain and frustration.

"I need a drink; get me something to drink!" I yelled at Elijah. A searing pain spread through my jaw. I covered my mouth with my hand and screamed again.

He stepped away from me, shaking his head *no*. I did the most unexpected thing. I lunged to attack him. My body was out of my control. A hungry beast was in charge now. I did not know if it was anger or frustration, or if I was trying to feed from him.

In a split second, he changed into something else entirely, a creature I never could have imagined in my wildest dreams. His skin was like stone. It was gray and cracked. His face turned into that of a monster, with long fangs and glowing yellow eyes. Enormous bat-like wings unfolded behind him and he took flight swiftly and was soon safely out of my reach.

My irritation came out as a roar. It was a sound I had never made before. I desperately looked around for something, anything that might help to stop the pain that had started in my throat but now spread through my entire body. I took a deep breath though my nose and caught the faint scent of something sweet — something I needed. I ran in its direction. Out of the corner of my eye, I could see the large, dark figure in the sky following me. It was not long before the scent grew stronger. I spotted the glow of a distant light. Within a few moments, I was at the doorstep of a lone farmhouse.

Elijah, the monster, landed a couple of lengths away. "No, don't! Vallachia, these are innocent people. If you are still in there, remember you don't want this. Fight the urge!"

Urge? *Urge*! This was not an "urge" — this was a complete loss of control! I was possessed with no command over my own body. I vaguely registered what he was saying. The smell inside the small farmhouse was delectable. It was well beyond temptation. I must have it — that delicious sweetness coming from inside the home. I broke through the door. Elijah, back to a handsome young man, was at my side in a flash. I must not have looked like myself because the family inside screamed when they saw me. I lunged toward the closest person when a strong force slammed me against the wall. The noise was deafening and the small farmhouse shook.

"You don't want this; please remember!" Elijah pled. I was furious — mad with pain. I threw him across the room, slamming him into the adjacent wall. More screams came from the family.

All I knew was that he was standing in the way of what I wanted — no, what I needed! I grabbed the nearest person and sank my long teeth into his neck. Relief spread through me. The pain and the thirst slowly subsided, I could feel myself coming back. The monster inside was leaving and I was slowly returning. All that was left was a middle-aged man's body in my arms, and his terrified family watching, as I drain him of life.

"No, no, no! What have I done?" I fell to my knees and the body rolled onto the floor. Elijah grabbed my arm and we were out the door in a flash. We were running, running and I never wanted to stop. I did not think about where we were running; I was simply trying to escape the horror — the guilt. Finally, the large Chastellain manor appeared in front of us.

"Father and I are leaving — please come with us," Elijah said. "Your transition is complete. You are one of us. There are things about our world you need to know. We can help you."

"Help me? Your father did this to me! I want nothing to do with either of you. Leave me alone!" I shoved him away. I focused all my anger and sorrow into running. I could hear that Elijah did not follow. He had apparently gotten the message.

I did not stop until I reached the highest peak of the Carpathian Mountains in the northeast. This was where I would stay. Of course, after what was probably a couple of days, the guilt of leaving my family and friends searching for me was unbearable. It was time to tie up loose ends.

I no longer trusted myself around anyone now that I fully understood the power of the monster that lived inside me. There was no way of knowing how long it would be until it came back but one thing was for certain; I would have no control when it did. Leaving was the best thing to do. Elijah was right. I had no idea where to go but it should be somewhere far from the ones I loved.

I stood on the edge of a cliff and wondered if or how I could possibly fly. *Would it kill me if I jumped? Perhaps I should.* But I could not. For one, Father would never find my body. He would never know what had happened to me. And I had the feeling it would be terribly painful, yet I would still survive, somehow. So I ran southward. Moving quickly and swiftly was a thrill. I was down the mountain in no time.

CHAPTER 21 SIBIU 1260 AD

I could not think of a good story to tell my family. *What will the letter to Father say?* The only thing that came to mind was that I had decided to elope with someone — Elijah, I supposed. *We ran off into the sunset.* I sighed in disgust. *What a cliché. Besides, this does not make sense on a number of levels. Father, Mari and Teller know me better than that. They know I want to be with Teller and stay in the village; nothing could have changed my mind about that over the course of a couple nights. Not to mention, if Teller did believe this story, it would hurt him dearly. That is the last thing I want to do.*

What other story could there possibly be? Think. I told myself. *Why else would a young woman run away in the night?* I was obviously a rotten liar. In our household, there had never been a need to lie. Father was open and nonjudgmental. I never had to hide anything from him. I could always tell him the truth. In fact, he usually knew the truth before I did, as was the case with my new feelings for Teller.

Thinking about this made me long for home. I desperately wanted to return. I always knew I had been content in Ludus. Now that it was gone, I fully realized how lucky I had been — a loving father and brother, good friends and hopefully someday an engagement to the love of my life. Somehow, I needed to stop thinking of home and all I had lost.

In Ludus, the one future a girl had was to marry and hopefully become a mother and someday a grandmother. This was the only possibility for us. There were no other choices. Now that I was thrown into this new and dark world, my old world seemed that much more appealing. The future had been clear. I knew my place and my job. *What now?* The only future I could have imagined was gone. What that meant, I could not even begin to fathom. For the first time in my life, I had no idea what to expect — no more hopes — no more dreams. All that remained was emptiness. I shook my head to push away these unbearable thoughts.

A young woman could not simply run off into the woods and survive. So what explanation will I give my family? I needed something that could ease their minds and be believable. Nothing came to mind, then it hit me. *I can tell them that I decided to join a convent. That is it! It will make sense to the villagers; after all, I am the deacon's daughter. Father and Teller will think it odd, as I never mentioned it before and why would I run off without telling them? But at least this lie might be easier on Teller. It is better for him to think I left him for God rather than for another man. It will have to do.*

It was not long before I came across a town that was many times bigger than Ludus. I stopped on the outskirts. *This must be Sibiu.*

My dress was torn in a couple of places and soiled with dirt and dried blood. I could only imagine what my hair looked like. Surely it was dirty and tangled like a rat's nest. I leapt in a nearby tree, knowing it would be easy, as I had been catapulting over obstacles while I ran through the forest.

From this height I was concealed and could overlook the town. The scent of people overwhelmed me as a sharp pain pierced my throat. I watched the town as it settled down for the night. I could hear every word that the people nearest to me spoke. They banged things around. *Are they fighting with one another*? I resisted the urge to cover my ears. It took me a moment to realize that it was not *these* particular people who were loud but that my ears were oversensitive.

I could hear better than before, too well, actually. At least all the noise distracted me from thinking about the insatiable thirst.

I waited for night to fully set in. My sights were set on a manor in the center of town. The small castle was a tall, yet not very wide stone structure with only a handful of small windows. A stone wall surrounded it. The wall was slightly taller than a man. I remained hidden until the lights in the small castle went out, indicating that those inside would soon be fast asleep. The front gate was guarded by a sentry, so I quickly leapt over the wall and entered the castle through a back window.

I needed clothes, a comb and a few coins to be able to pay someone to carry a letter to Father. Of course, the letter could not be sent until tomorrow. I would need a cloak, one with a hood to be able to shade my eyes from the sun. The thought of stealing was displeasing. I promised myself that after the letter was sent home, I would find a way to support myself — though I had no idea how.

I moved through the castle without making a sound. I could hear heartbeats and breathing in some of the rooms, which I avoided. I worried about getting close to someone. *What if I lost control again? Would the beast take over if I got too near?* I prayed it would not.

In the apse of the Great Hall there was a desk, complete with an inkwell, quill and papyrus scrolls. *Good, I could write the letter there,* I thought. The place was dark, yet I could see perfectly. Finally, I found an empty bedchamber with some clothes in a chest. The dress was too short on my frame, stopping a few inches from the floor but it would have to do. From the looks of the simple dress, it must have been a spare for a maid. I found a washbasin with water and cleaned my face. The final touch was to comb my hair. This made me feel better.

I needed to dispose of my old dress. In the kitchen I found the wood stove still had hot coals, left over from the preparation of the evening meal, no doubt. I placed the ruined dress on the coals and watched it burn. *My old life — gone.*

I returned to the hall to write the letter. Thankfully, I did not need a candle to write by, as the light might have drawn attention to my presence.

. . .

My dearest Father,

I am very sorry for any worry I have caused you over the past couple of days. Please forgive me and know that I am alive and well. I have decided to join a convent. Please do not try to find me. Perhaps after I have completed my training and become a sister of the Church, you can come for a visit. Until then, please respect my choice as you always have. Tell Josiah and my friends how truly sorry I am as well. I miss you all dearly.

Your loving daughter,

Val

Tears rolled down my cheeks by the time I was done. *What a ridiculous lie. Would they believe it?* I supposed this was all I could do. Hopefully, it would bring some comfort to my father and brother. The only thing that was true was that I was indeed sorry and I missed them more than anything. *At least they will know this much.* I had to remind myself that the point of the letter was to let them know I was alive so they would stop looking for me and move on with their lives.

I rolled the letter and tied it with a piece of sinew. There were a handful of coins in the desk drawer. I took them. Back in the bedchamber, I found a small travel bag. I was putting a change of clothes in the bag when I heard loud — to me anyway — footsteps. In a flash, I was hiding in the clothes cupboard with the door open only a sliver to see out. Candle light flooded the doorway, revealing the figure of a man. If the man had been a vampire, he would have heard my pounding heart.

"Who left this door open?" the man's voice mumbled. He looked around, shut the door and walked loudly away.

He must have been a guard, doing his rounds. I ran, leaving the cupboard door and the bedchamber door open. I did not want to risk making noise by shutting them. I grabbed a leather rain cloak by the front door on my way out. This all happened in a flash and soon I was back in the woods.

The next morning I walked as slowly as possible into town. I had to be very careful not to move too quickly. *How had Elijah done it in the tournament? He had appeared to be human enough but he had indeed been refraining.*

Even with the cloak's hood over my head, I still had to squint and my eyes stung in the bright daylight. Yet the pain was tolerable. In fact, it was good, as it distracted me from the aching in my throat.

"Pardon me," I asked the first person I saw. "Is there someone who could carry a letter to Ludus?"

"What was that, little missy? You must speak up," the man hollered.

I flinched at the man's loudness. *My voice seemed to be loud enough and why was he yelling?* Then I remembered, it must be my improved hearing. The image of Elijah and his father talking so quietly that I could not hear them ran through my mind. So I repeated the question in all but a yell and the man gladly pointed me in the direction of a local trader.

It took some searching but I found a man who said he would travel through Ludus in a week or so. My heart sank. *Poor Father. It would take over a week before he would receive my letter and learn that I was alive.*

"That will have to do," I sighed. I handed him the letter and some coins. "Thank you kindly."

It was a relief when I was safely out of town and under shade; not to mention away from the delectable scent of people.

At least I did not kill anyone. I suppose that is something. Now what? Where shall I go? Perhaps a larger city is a good idea after all. The requirement to feed would return at some point. All I knew was that at dark I would run south, in the opposite direction of Lord Chastellain. I had no idea what awaited me.

CHAPTER 22 TARGOVISTE 1260 AD

I ran, speeding high into the Southern Carpathian Alps. I avoided the scent of people, changing my course if it became too strong. Avoiding the main roads, I made my own way through the forest. After only a couple of hours I topped a high peak and could not believe what I saw. Below was the largest body of water I had ever seen. The lake was nestled in a basin surrounded by tall mountains. The smooth blue water looked like glass from the Chastellain's windows. It was pristine and too refreshing to pass by.

I had grown up swimming and bathing in the Mures River. My thoughts strayed to Elijah saying that vampires were — *what was it?* — "Well suited to land, water and air." A cool swim sounded pleasant.

I emerged from the evergreens and undressed on the shore. In only my undergarments I waded up to my waist and dived headfirst into the clear lake. I moved easily through the water, too easily. Webs had formed between my fingers. I gulped in water at the sight of them. Yet I did not choke or feel the need to come up for air. It was the same as drinking water out of a cup. I turned my hands around, studying them. The same thing happened to my feet. I no longer had toes but long webbed flippers. *How can that be?*

I felt something moving on my neck. With trepidation, I slowly raised my hands to examine my throat. My heart raced as I realized there were gill-like slits on my neck, allowing me to breathe. In panic I opened my mouth. Again, there was no choking as water rushed in, just a cool drink of clear water. Once I recovered my composure, I swam with great speed out into the middle of the lake, ever downward.

This was amazing!

Once reaching the middle of the lake, I stood on the bottom and took in the strange sight. Plants swayed against my legs and brown and gray fish of different shapes and sizes swam about in random directions. They did not seem to be the least bit concerned with me. I was standing where no human had ever been — no living human anyway.

I enjoyed the lake. It was isolated and quiet, so I stayed there for three more days. I did not sleep, only dozed a couple of times. When I woke the sun had barely moved in the sky.

Being alone was not entirely unpleasant — at first. I had never been alone before and eventually it started to weigh on me. At first, I missed my family and friends. Then, I began to miss people in general. I did not want to be utterly alone for an eternity. Company would be needed in order to keep my wits about me — even though that would mean I would be a danger to them. *If I were to go to a city, there might be others like me.* I was unsure if that was a good thing or not.

I continued onward to the southeast until I came to the largest population of people I had ever seen. I knew it was Targoviste. This was the nearest city to Ludus. Father had been ordained as a deacon here. Indeed, this was the farthest he had ever traveled. He had said it was southeast of Ludus just over the mountains. Therefore, this had to be Targoviste. I never thought I would actually see this place. A large Orthodox church with towering spires was the most impressive building in town. I smiled as I walked past the church; *this must have been where Father studied.*

I inspected the dark empty streets in awe. It occurred to me that Targoviste was too close to home. Someone may come here to look for me. If a girl from Ludus wished to become a nun, the convents here would be a likely choice. I had to get even farther away.

Reluctantly, I left the beautiful city and continued to head southeast. It was not long before I came to a town much like Sibiu — larger than Ludus, yet small compared to Targoviste. I walked into a large tavern in the middle of town late that night. I received questioning looks from the locals, mostly men, in the tavern. I still had some of the money I had stolen, so I sat in the corner and ordered food and drink from the old woman working there.

"It is late for a young lady to be out by herself," the woman inquired.

I only nodded in agreement. She was working hard. I watched her try to keep up with orders. I suspected her husband or son was working feverishly to prepare the food in the back. *Perhaps they could use my help?* I thought.

I ate some, even though I was not hungry for normal food. I forced myself not to stare at the men's bare necks. I supposed that was what I really wanted … *to open that soft flesh with my teeth and let the blood run down my throat.* I shook my head to push away the terrible thought. I had hoped regular food would lessen my hunger for blood — it did not. Being in the midst of all these people made it unbearable.

Needing something to do, anything to distract me and keep me busy, I approached the old lady. "Excuse me, madam. I used to work in my uncle's tavern. It seems that you could use my help."

She looked at me with curiosity. "We do need the help. We have no children of our own." She wiped her hands on her stained apron. "Let me fetch my husband."

When she returned with an elderly man, I said, "My name is Vallachia. I'm new in town and would like to work here, if you would have me?"

The old man's gaze was critical. "Why do you want to work? Why doesn't your father, or perhaps husband, provide for you?"

These were fair questions and I had expected them. "I have no family here. I come from the north. I'm thinking about settling here."

This last bit was not entirely true but it seemed like the right thing to say. There was no way to guess what my future would hold.

"Why did you leave home?" His voice was full of accusation.

"I was not happy at home. I wanted to see what else was out there." This would have been exceptionally rare but was not entirely impossible. Besides, what else could I say? *I'm a nomadic vampire?*

"It is no secret, we could use the help. What will you work for?" the old man asked.

"Room and board would do," I stated.

The woman appeared open to the idea.

But the man eyed me for a bit longer. "Allow me to discuss this with my wife."

I nodded. They retreated to the kitchen, which was only partially portioned off from the main sitting area. I turned my back and sat down. I could still hear them perfectly even though they were out of human earshot.

"I don't know; I don't like her. She is hiding something," the old man said.

"Please, dear, she is a young woman who needs our help. She is out there all alone! We could use the help and we have the extra room upstairs." Her plea was answered with silence so the woman continued, "We do not want her to have to become a lady of the night, now do we?"

"If she is not already, wandering about by herself."

"Either way, God would want us to help her."

The man sighed, "Very well, we will give her a try."

The lady was beaming when they returned.

"My name is Anna and this is my husband, Paul. Welcome to Bucharest! This is the Dancing Stallion."

That explained the horse rearing up on its hind legs on the sign outside. I had never heard of Bucharest before.

CHAPTER 23 BUCHAREST 1260 AD

"Let's get you settled into your room." Anna led me up a narrow wooden staircase.

"Thank you," I said with genuine relief.

Anna showed me to a modest room. I did not seem to need much sleep, so I was up cleaning the kitchen for hours the next morning before Paul came down to start cooking. The place was in need of a good cleaning and there was plenty to be done. I was grateful for this, as being busy kept my insatiable thirst under control. I worked all day and into the night. I stopped to eat only when Anna was convinced that I would drop dead if I did not. I never tired. Even when the tavern was slow, I found many things to do, such as cleaning the mice nests out of the cupboards, bringing in wood, washing laundry, sweeping cobwebs and dirty floors — to name a few. It was wonderful to be so busy, as it also kept me from thinking about home or the next time I would need to feed.

Anna appreciated all the help. She complimented me frequently and made sure I was comfortable in my room. She repeatedly asked if I needed anything, which I did not.

The husband was not so easily won. Their room was not far from mine and I could hear them when I should not have been able to.

"I don't trust her. Something about her is ... not right," Paul said to Anna one night.

"Don't be silly. She is a polite, hard-working young lady. Besides, I think she has been good for business. More and more of the young men in town have been coming in and I don't think it is just for your good cooking, dear."

"Well, I think she is trouble. When she is near I feel the hair on the back of my neck stand on end."

I put the pillow over my head, trying to block out the conversation that I was not supposed to be hearing, not to mention, all the other noises of the town. The pillow only slightly muffled them.

I had often felt that same way around Lord Chastellain. He made the hair on the back of my neck tingle in warning. I had even been afraid of Elijah at times. Now I knew why. They were monsters. I thought of other times I had felt that way, like after Teller and I had kissed in the woods for the first time. It dawned on me that Elijah or perhaps his father must have followed us. That was how they knew that Teller and I had made plans to marry. I remembered them discussing Teller the night Chastellain had turned me.

Apparently, I had been able to sense that they were a danger, as Paul could sense it in me. He was right — I was trouble, trouble that was inevitably coming. It was only a matter of when. I would hold out from feeding for as long as I could.

I would often go for a walk after hours. Anna would discourage it, as she was worried about me. Little did she know that it was not I she should be concerned for but rather, the townspeople. I would reassure her that everything would be well. Eventually, so that I would not worry Anna, I would wait until their breathing was heavy with sleep before leaving through my window.

I was slowly learning to adjust to this new life — one of being furtive and constantly thirsty. The night became my favorite time. Going for walks on warm summer nights had always been enjoyable. Now that the cold did not bother me, any night was a wonderful time to be out. The fresh air was the only break I could get from the constant hunger when humans were near.

The tavern was full most evenings, since I had come to town. Many young men seemed to be attracted to the "mysterious new girl." Unfortunately, I was that girl. Some would stop me while I was serving food and try to make conversation. I tried to ignore them, or I would tell them that I was too busy to talk. Some even heckled me as I walked by. These men — or boys, rather — I ignored entirely. They wanted my attention and I was not going to give them the pleasure.

One particularly crude fellow went so far as to grab my arse one day when I walked by. I kept walking, as I did not want to lose control and hurt the man. Thankfully, Paul saw what had happened and came to the rescue.

"William," he said to the crude man, "if you cannot control yourself and act like a gentleman in my establishment, then we will have to ask you to leave ... permanently."

Paul and Anna were well liked and Paul had several friends who came to stand beside him.

"Very well, as you wish," William replied with slurred speech and a mocking bow.

I was grateful for Paul. He was a good man and I liked him despite his not liking me. I admired his courage to stand up for others. He was also insightful and intelligent.

The next morning, I was up chopping vegetables and meat for the day's cooking when Paul came down. "Thank you for yesterday — with William," I said.

"Aye, he is a bad drunk and has caused trouble before. We may have to boot him out someday," Paul replied. "You do not seem interested in any of the young men who approach you. Why is that?"

A vision of Teller came to mind. He was the reason that I did not care for any other suitors. I did not know what to say to Paul. Luckily, Anna came in, interrupting our conversation. She appeared ill. "What is the matter?" I asked, glad for the change in subject.

"It's nothing, dear. I did not sleep well, that is all. I had a horrible dream." She paused. Her eyes looked as if her mind was far away. "It was about a murderous beast. He was large with dry-gray skin, bright yellow eyes and horribly long teeth."

I frowned, as the image of Elijah flying above me came to mind. It was an exact description. Perhaps Anna was insightful as well, like her husband, yet in her own way.

Paul studied his wife with concern. "It was only a dream, my dear. Why don't you go lie down?"

"It did not feel like a dream," Anna said. When she turned to head back upstairs, she knocked a clay pot off the counter.

Forgetting my slow human pretense, I shot across the room to catch the pot before it hit the floor.

Anna did not fully see what had happened; she turned toward me. "Oh, thank you, dear. What good hands you have."

However, Paul had been staring directly at me. We looked at each other for a long moment. His eyes were wide and then they narrowed. "Yes, good indeed." He placed his hand on his wife's back and walked her out of the kitchen.

Oh no, I thought. *I will have to be leaving soon.* Living with people was difficult, to say the least. I constantly had to fight the urge to feed and having to move so slowly at all times was cumbersome. Part of me wanted to break out — to be able to move freely and quickly.

CHAPTER 24 BUCHAREST 1260 AD

I was truly fond of Paul and Anna. They were good people. I feared I would hurt them. *Perhaps I should move on.* The need to feed could overtake me at any time. *I will stay only a couple more days.* I had no idea where I would go but I had best be on my way.

Paul largely avoided me for the rest of the day, after witnessing my unnatural ability to catch the pot before it shattered on the floor. He only spoke business, such as informing me of when a guest's food was ready. This was good, as I had no answer for him as to how I was able to move so quickly. Anna came down that afternoon and seemed more herself.

After closing the tavern that night, I headed up to my room. Two sets of new dresses were neatly sprawled across the bed. They were simple and beautiful. *Anna must have gotten them for me. How kind and thoughtful.* I sighed.

Paul's voice could be heard from his room. "How can she work so tirelessly? I'm telling you, something is wrong with her, she is not … human, or she is super … human. I don't know."

"Not this again, dear. She is a blessing, like the daughter we never had. She is helping us so much. Don't you like all the help?"

"Yes, she has made our lives much easier. She is perfect — too perfect. I have the feeling she will be moving on soon. Please do not get too attached to her, Anna."

"What? Moving on!" Anna's voice rose. "Surely she would not leave us. Where could a lone girl possibly go?"

Once again, I was amazed by Paul's canniness. He somehow sensed that I had plans to leave. I did not want to hear any more. In a flash, I was out my window and walking in the clear night air. My heart felt as if it weighed twice what it should. Not only was I putting Anna and Paul in physical danger by living with them but I was also going to break Anna's heart when I left. She thought of me as a daughter. Stay and I put them in mortal peril; leave and I hurt them. No matter what I did, it was wrong.

Not for the first time, I wished I had taken Elijah's advice. A large city would be better for a vampire. We could keep our distance from humans and be more anonymous. *I cannot move from town to town, leaving behind people who care about me.* It was decided — I must head for a city. If I continued southeast I would eventually end up in Constantinople. The thought of seeing the Queen of Cities was exhilarating.

It had been almost a month since I had first fed. It was a relief that I had been able to endure this long. However, I could feel myself getting hungrier. The pain in my throat was getting harder to ignore. It was the next night when I felt that horrible beast start to stir inside. I did not know how long I had until it took complete control. I quickly excused myself from work, saying that I did not feel well and must lie down.

I hardly paused in my room before I was gone out the window. Anna would probably check on me and I would not be there. But that did not matter. I had to get away from them! I did not want to hurt them or cause an uproar in their tavern. I was going to have to be discreet this time. I did not want to be recognized. Hopefully, there would be a lone person wandering the streets.

In no time at all, I was at the other end of town. The night was still young. I could smell and hear all the humans around me. The stealthy predator inside slowly consumed me. Luckily, the monster did not want to be seen either. It instinctively wanted to protect itself by staying hidden. This time I did not fight it as much. I understood that it could not be stopped and I succumbed.

We, the monster inside and I, walked the streets, looking for the right opportunity. We spotted a man walking by himself and the monster attacked. In a flash, we were on him and eventually I felt the monster slip away as the delicious blood soothed my burning throat. Again the beast left me with a dead man in my arms.

I ran swiftly into the forest and knelt by a stream. Plunging my hands into the water I tried to wash the blood away. Tears rolled down my face. *I cannot live like this!* Again I wished for death.

I stayed by the stream for quite some time until I could gather my wits. *Should I hide the body? No, the man's family deserves to know that he is dead.* It was the least I could do for them. I left him where he lay.

Back in my room, I packed the new dresses Anna had given me and grabbed my precious cloak for day walking. I left a letter for Anna telling her goodbye and thanking her for everything, though I knew she would have to find someone to read it to her. The townspeople would soon be rallying and I did not want to be around for that, trying to play innocent. There would most likely be a meeting to discuss who could have killed a man like that and why. I had to move on before I did any more harm. With my leaving the same night as the murder, some might suspect me but I did not care. *Why should I care? They would be correct in their accusations.*

I walked out of town, ignoring people I passed and disregarding the commotion that was forming around the dead man left in the street.

"And where do you think you're go'in?" a man's voice came from behind me.

I turned to find William following me. I glared at him and kept walking.

He caught up with me and grabbed my arm. "You think a little lady such as yourself can make it on her own out there?" His mocking tone was grating.

I should have disappeared in a blink and left him standing alone in the street but something stayed me. I wanted to test him, to see how much of an arse he truly was. *Would he hurt women? If so, perhaps I could cure him of that.* I looked around quickly and could see, smell and hear that there was no one else nearby. William was most likely aware of this as well. He had followed me waiting until I was alone. *Good.* I thought.

"What do you want?" I said in a soft voice, trying to sound scared as I pretended to try to get out of his grip on my arm.

"Oh, I think you know what I want." His smile was sordid. He pressed himself against me, pushing me into the wall of a nearby building. His breath reeked of spirits. He moved one hand toward my breast and the other started pulling up my skirt.

That was the evidence I needed. Anger flooded through me. *How many women had he done this to? How many more would suffer his unwanted attention?* I grabbed his hand at my breast and twisted. His arm made a loud cracking sound and he fell to his knees with a pain-filled yell. I had meant only to hurt him enough to get his attention and make him stop, not break his arm. *Humans are so fragile!* I was still not used to this new strength. I picked him up by the neck of his tunic until his feet were dangling above the ground.

"Please, let me go," he pled.

"Would you have let me go if I had begged? You think women are simply your playthings!" I felt the pain in my jaw as the fangs formed. "I hope you think twice about how you treat women because next time you do something like this, I will do more than break your arm."

William's eyes were wide with fear.

It was an empty threat but he did not need to know that. I heard someone coming, so I dropped him and disappeared. Once William had told the townspeople what he had seen, they would know it was I who had killed the man tonight. I had to get as far away as possible by daylight.

CHAPTER 25 CONSTANTINOPLE 1260 AD

I made my way to the southeast, leaving Bucharest far behind. My thoughts raced with me. A new feeling had come over me. While I felt horrible for the man I'd left lying dead in the street, I had also done something good. Perhaps I could give back to people somehow. I knew it could never make up for what I had to take from them but it was a start. Maybe this was my way of justifying being a killer. Yet for the first time in a month, I felt a small glimmer of hope. There was a little spark of light in the darkness.

Well into the night, a couple of hours before dawn, I saw a faint glow up ahead. Stopping at the forest's edge, I surveyed the land. There were expansive fields largely of wheat sprawled out before me. The fields ended abruptly at a thirty-foot-high wall. I had heard stories of great walled cities but never could have imagined that walls could be this tall. The wall extended in either direction as far as the eye could see — even vampire eyes. Evenly spaced guard towers were situated atop of the massive wall. From the shadows of the forest's edge — concealed with my dark cloak — I watched the imperial guards and studied their patrol pattern.

As soon as the sentries were out of sight, I sped to the wall and jumped to the top. The view was overwhelming and I momentarily forgot about avoiding the sentries. The outer ring of the city was left in shambles. Only a few of the numerous buildings were occupied and in good repair. Most of the buildings were burnt ruins. Many had been torn down – most likely for firewood – leaving only the faint remnants of foundations. In some places small fields or gardens grew where there had once been a flourishing city. My heart sank into my stomach as I surveyed the destruction. Father told me stories of the devastation of the last crusade and how prosperous this city had once been. *How could Christians do this to other Christians?* I wondered.

In the distance I spotted another great wall, which rose even higher than the one I stood on.

"The Wall of Constantine," I whispered.

I heard a guard shuffle loudly toward me, so I leapt down into the city and disappeared quickly into the shadows of the ruined buildings. Within seconds I was at the city's second protective layer. I stared up at it, uncertain as to whether or not I could jump that high. The wall extended at least forty feet into the night sky. I decided it would be safest to get a running start before jumping. Thankfully, there were fewer guards on Constantine's wall. I ran full speed and jumped with all my might. I managed to catch the top of the wall with my hands. I was surprised to find that I could easily swing my legs up onto it. I scrambled to the top and looked around. Not even bothering to whisper this time, I said, "Dear Heavenly Father!"

There was a sea of rooftops, all different shapes and sizes, including round rooftops similar to the ones in Chastellain's paintings. It seemed so long ago, as if a couple of lifetimes had passed since I first set foot in his halls. *What had it been? Only a few months,* I supposed.

This was a dreary thought, so I forced myself to stop thinking of home. The city that spread out before me was breathtaking. I'd never dreamt of traveling this far and seeing such a sight.

Am I actually enjoying myself? This cannot be, after killing someone tonight! How could I possibly feel jubilant and hopeful at the sight of

Constantinople? This was the holiest of cities, the mother of Orthodoxy — the God-protected city. I shook my head in an attempt to quell my excitement. *What is wrong with me?* I chastised myself until I felt properly miserable again.

My eyes moved past the seemingly endless streets and buildings to an even more impressive sight. The city gave way to an endless expanse of water. *That much water could not possibly exist.* I had heard tales of the vast oceans but never could have imagined so much water in one place. It made the lake in the Alps look like nothing more than a tiny dewdrop. Once again, the sound of someone approaching brought me back to my current situation. This time, jumping that far down was intimidating. I hesitated for a moment, finally bailing off the wall only to discover that I landed on my feet with very little pain. Disappearing once again into the shadows, I heard sentries from atop the wall yell.

"Did you see that?"

"What is it now?"

"It was a shadow. It leapt off the wall and moved quickly, that way." The sentry pointed in my direction. I sank farther behind a wall.

"You're just see'in' things again."

With great stealth I moved deep into the city. *What am I to do?* Surely there would be other vampires in the city. I did not know what to think about this. What would they be like? Friendly? Hostile?

I wandered through the streets in awe for quite some time admiring the large buildings and unusual architecture. The sun would be up soon, so I searched for a tavern or an inn. I caught a glimpse of a moving shadow out of the corner of my eye. When I turned toward it, I saw nothing. I kept walking and soon I saw it again. Something or someone was following me. I hurried toward a building that looked to be a local establishment. As I was about to enter, a woman appeared in front of me.

"You don't want to go in there," she said casually.

I stepped back. Based on her sudden appearance she was most likely not human. Uncertain of what she would do, I wanted to give myself a head start.

"Why not?" I asked.

"Because I think you are looking for us."

I looked around and there was no one else in sight. "Who is 'us'? There is only one of you."

"Oh no, there are more. Let me take you to meet them." She took off down the street and kept talking, "My name is Rosalia. Friends sometimes call me Rose. Our coven is not too far from here."

I jogged to catch up with her. "Coven? What is a coven?" I had never heard of such a thing.

"Oh dear, you are new, aren't you?" She frowned.

"How did you find me?"

"Have you forgotten your manners? I introduced myself and the proper thing for you to do is to tell me your name in return."

"Yes, of course, my apologies. My name is Va ... Val," I stuttered. I decided that until I knew more about this strange new world, I had better not reveal too much about myself. People would think Val was short for the more common name Valeria. That would do for now.

Rosalia looked at me with suspicion. I was obviously not good at hiding things. "Well, *Val,* to answer your question — we watch over our city. When a new vampire wanders in, it gets our attention."

That was not exactly what I meant. "But how did you know I am a ... ?" I did not want to say the word because that would be admitting to something terrible. "You know."

Rosalia laughed. "It's your scent. You clearly smell unlike that of a human. Not to mention, you move too gracefully to be one of them."

I inhaled sharply. She was right. She smelled different — not sweet, as humans smelled. Not that her scent was bad, it was simply different. There was no pain in my throat and no desire to feed on her, as was the case when humans were around.

Rosalia inspected me for a moment. "The boys are going to love you. I bet you have no trouble luring them into your deadly trap." She reached out as if to pinch my cheek.

I dodged her hand.

"Be easy," she said with a smile. "I'm not going to hurt you. We look out for one another."

So far I was not overly fond of Rosalia. She seemed arrogant and contemptuous. She also appeared to like who she was, perhaps even revel in it. The thought made me ill — vampires who loved the hunt, the kill.

CHAPTER 26 CONSTANTINOPLE 1260 AD

Rosalia led me into an enormous abandoned building. We wound our way through the halls, passing one dark, empty room after another.

Now that I found another vampire, I had a burning question. "Is there anyway to … become normal again?"

"Why would anyone want to be human? And no there is not." Rosalia shook her head at my ludicrous question.

My heart felt like a boulder in my chest. *Elijah must be right — there is no way back.* I had been hoping beyond hope that there was a way to undo the vampire curse — perhaps one Elijah did not know about. My hope was slipping away as was my home and family. *Are they truly lost to me forever?*

Rosalia entered a room and stopped in front of an old bed with a rotting mattress. She easily lifted the bed with one hand; revealing a flat circular stone in the floor. With her other hand she lifted the stone cover by its round metal handle. Stairs could be seen leading downward. I peered into the dark chasm straining to see the end — I could not.

"Well, are you going to go or just stare?" she said.

After an uneasy glance at her, I cautiously started down the stairs.

Rosalia snickered at my apprehension.

We descended deep into the earth for what seemed like ages. The stairs were a smooth stone; the walls were a rough-cut rock. I was feeling more than a little uneasy in this closed space. I did not know that there could be tunnels this deep underground. I hoped that the other vampires were not hostile, as it would be difficult to escape this place.

Finally, we stopped our descent and entered a long hallway with many rooms off to either side. Smooth stone columns appeared at even intervals. In between them were elaborate carvings depicting scenes of war and of sensual naked humans and vampires. Again I was Rosalia's entertainment. She laughed at my expression; I must have looked awestruck.

At the end of the long hall was a huge round room that was lavishly furnished. The burning candles briefly hurt my eyes until they adjusted. Fine fabrics and tapestries hung from the ceiling and there were statues and beautiful pieces of furniture scattered about. Lounging on the furniture were vampires, probably a dozen or more.

In a large chair in the rear of the room sat a middle-aged man — or vampire, rather, with a powerful air about him — the leader, I presumed. He was handsome, with the darkest complexion I had ever seen. His skin was remarkably smooth, almost hairless. I had never seen anyone like him. He was so different I wanted to study him. I forced myself not to stare.

Hanging on either side of the leader were two long tapestries. They were dark green in color with images of large black spiders. As discomfiting as they were I could not help admiring the craftsmanship. The detail was intricate, as the ominous insects were well defined. *Wolf spiders,* I thought.

"Look what I found!" Rosalia announced with confidence and pride.

Everyone in the room stopped talking and turned to look at us.

"Come meet our leader," she said.

I did not move. Rosalia had to pull me by the arm. She bowed to the dark-skinned man. "This is Lord Ramdasha of the Indies and this is Val. She is new in town."

I bowed and Ramdasha stood. A large man moved to stand to the right of Ramdasha. Both stared at me with great intensity and I was not sure which one was more intimidating.

"Where are you from?" Ramdasha demanded.

I forced myself to look him in the eyes. They were dark, old and dangerous. All I knew was that I did not want him to know too much. My family must stay as far away as possible from this sinister world. "I am from Targoviste," I lied but it came out clear and steady enough.

"What is your family name?" he demanded.

This stumped me for a moment. We did not often use family names in Ludus. The only ones to do so were the Chastellains. Something inside warned me not to mention that name. Family names were only for nobles and royalty, whose status was given to them by their ancestors. I had heard some regions commonly used family names but Ludus did not.

"I do not have a family name. I am a commoner. My father was the local smithy." This was the first profession that came to mind. I also hoped he would notice that I spoke of Father in the past tense. I had a strong feeling I should protect my family, so I would tell these vampires that I had no living kin.

Ramdasha studied me.

"My Lord, by the looks of her clothes, she is indeed a simple commoner," Rosalia said.

I had the feeling Rosalia was trying to help me.

"It appears so. Who turned you?" Ramdasha's voice was deep and commanding.

In that instant, it dawned on me that his approach was unwise. The more he tried to intimidate me, the more I would resist. I knew now, without a doubt, not to trust him. I would tell him nothing. If he had been smart, he would have at least pretended to be friendly. If he had welcomed me and gained my trust, even a bit, I would have told him anything.

I shook my head. "I did not see a face. A man-like figure with wings and bright yellow eyes appeared in front of me and then I was choking on blood. I woke up alone in the forest."

Ramdasha looked disappointed, for which I was glad. He waved his hand, as if to dismiss me.

Rosalia pulled me away. "Let's find you a room." She was cheerful which was odd, as this was in stark contrast to Ramdasha's mood.

More vampires had come in since I arrived. "How many vampires are in this … coven?" I asked.

"Twenty-two. No, twenty-three now." She pointed at me. "The sun must be on the rise, as the last of the patrols have returned for the day."

"You were on patrol when you found me?" I asked.

"You catch on quickly." She smiled.

We walked back down the long hallway and when we were near the stairs leading out, she paused. "This room is unoccupied." We entered a good-sized bedroom. It, like the rest of the place, was furnished with the most modern and exotic décors.

"This is lovely; thank you." I placed my small travel bag on the desk. "There, all settled in." I chuckled at my pathetic situation — no home, very few belongings.

Rosalia shut the door. "Look, don't mind Lord Ramdasha. He is only concerned with power and control. It is good you are a commoner; you will have more freedom this way. He is only interested in influential people. So you will not be of concern to him, unless you do something to anger him."

"I will try not to do that." He was intimidating and the last thing I needed was to be on his bad side, that is assuming he had a good side.

CHAPTER 27 CONSTANTINOPLE 1260 AD

"Allow me to show you around and introduce you to some of the others," Rosalia said.

I followed her down the long hall, heading toward the large round room.

"This is the training room," she said as we entered another chamber off the main hall. The center of the room was empty and every sort of weapon imaginable lined the walls.

"What do you have to train for? Are we not strong enough as it is?"

"Strong enough by human standards but not for fighting one another. For that we must train. If you are smart, you will do the same." She must always be happy because even this she said with a smile. Part of me envied her carefree manner and part of me found it annoying.

I did not like the thought of vampire soldiers. *For what purpose, a vampire war?* Elijah's warning rang through my head: "There are things you need to know about this world."

I was growing more agitated by the minute, then Rosalia opened the door to the library. This helped lighten my souring mood. *Maybe it will not be so bad here after all.* It was not as large a collection as the Chastellains' but it was still an impressive number of books.

"We need something to occupy our time," Rosalia said. "We don't need much sleep and we don't go out much during the day, so we train and read a good deal. Allow me to show you to the common room for the less powerful vampires in the coven. The commoners' common room." She laughed at her play on words.

I could not help smiling as well. I snatched a book off the shelf before following her.

Not far from the stairway, we entered yet another room. There were a handful of vampires talking at ease. The room fell silent when we entered.

"For those of you who were not in Lord Ramdasha's chambers earlier, this is Val from Targoviste," Rose announced. "Val, this is Orrick and Aaron."

Orrick nodded a greeting.

Aaron rose, took my hands and kissed each cheek. "Welcome," he said.

I clenched the book to my chest and leaned back trying to put some space between us.

Rosalia gave him a shove. "Down, boy; that's quite enough. This is Irene and Sonia," Rosalia continued.

Irene shook my hand. "I am happy to meet you."

"I am pleased to make your acquaintance as well," I said.

Sonia nodded. I gave her a smile and she looked away shyly. She was young, too young to be a vampire. *Who would turn such a young girl?* My stomach sickened at the thought.

"You are no longer the newest member of our coven, Sonia," Orrick stated.

Sonia looked pleased.

"She came to us a couple of years ago," Orrick explained.

"How old are you?" Aaron appeared genuinely interested.

"About seventeen ... or eighteen now, I suppose," I said.

"I deduced that much. What I mean is, how long have you been a vampire?" Aaron clarified.

"Oh — a month or so," I replied.

Gasps and a couple of chuckles broke out.

"I could tell you were new but I did not realize you were that young," Rosalia said.

"How old are all of you?" My tone was more defensive than I would have liked.

"Rose is the oldest of our group. She has been a vampire for almost fifty years. And Sonia is the youngest. What, seven or eight years a vampire?" Aaron said.

Sonia nodded in agreement.

Orrick lit up. "I wager you don't even know how to fly yet."

I shook my head no. "I swam once, which was amazing. Well, it was wonderful after I stopped panicking about the gills on my neck."

This brought about a round of laughter.

"Then it is settled. We will teach Val to fly tonight. We leave at dusk." Rosalia announced.

"I have patrol duty tonight and won't be able to go." Aaron frowned. "That is too bad. I enjoy watching novices learn how to fly."

The others were excited and it was contagious. *Flying!* It sounded thrilling, wonderful and frightening. I could not wait until dusk.

They began to tell me about the way things worked around here. There were not many rules. Of course, we were to obey Ramdasha. This was usually not hard, according to them and mostly they stayed out of his way. We were to be discreet when we fed and no humans were allowed to find out about this place. This made sense. I feared for any human who ventured down here.

"Eventually, you will have to take your turn on night patrol," Aaron said.

"Do you simply look for new vampires?" I asked.

"Yes, and any other news you think might be important to the lord," Rosalia said.

"Don't worry. During the first couple of patrols, you will go with another vampire," Orrick said.

"Otherwise, if you are not on patrol, you are free," Irene added.

"It is highly recommended that you learn to fight," Orrick's tone was serious.

"Women fight as well?" I asked. The thought of learning to fight had never crossed my mind. This was not only because of my gender but also because of my father's teachings. He had always encouraged me to find another way. Father believed that violence only begets more violence.

"We are as strong as male vampires and we can learn to fight equally well," Rosalia said.

"Whom would we be fighting and why?" I asked.

Orrick sat up, looking even more serious than before but Aaron spoke up first. "Oh no, not boring politics! Can't we talk about something else?" He dramatically tossed himself into a chair.

Orrick glared at him. "You mean to tell me that what our leaders do does not concern you?"

I wanted to know more but, like magic, the cavern came alive.

"Thank goodness, we are spared from Orrick's politics," Aaron said. "We can get out of here for the night!"

I was curious about what Orrick had been going to say but it could wait. The thought of a flying lesson took precedence and for the moment I forgot my concerns about vampire wars.

CHAPTER 28 CONSTANTINOPLE 1260 AD

Rosalia, Orrick, Irene, Sonia and I sped through the city. We stayed in the shadows and avoided humans. It was fun, like a game, sniffing the humans out and hiding from them before they could spot us.

Soon we came to the city wall and easily leapt onto it.

"The Golden Horn." Rosalia gestured to the narrow channel of water on the other side of the wall. She dived gracefully head first into the water.

The rest followed and lastly I jumped feet first off the grand city wall. We emerged from the water on the Galata shore and ran quickly to the top of a hill far to the north of the city. On one side was a sheer cliff. I glanced over the edge. I had a bad feeling about this.

"In actuality, all you have to do to learn to fly is jump off a cliff. Your body will know what to do and you will take flight — as in the water, when your gills naturally formed," Rosalia lectured.

I stepped back from the cliff's edge. "Yes but I knew how to swim as a human. That was easy. I obviously could not fly as a human."

"Don't worry; we will not push you off the cliff," Sonia said.

"Yet," Orrick added with a smirk.

I took another step away from the cliff.

"First, we will try to get you off the ground, so you can get used to it," Rosalia said.

"Then you'll push me off the cliff." I was not afraid of dying; it was dying a painful death that worried me.

Rose laughed. "You see? I told you; she learns quickly."

"She had better," Orrick said.

I glared at him.

"When I was new," Rose said. "I had to become afraid or angry for my wings to come out on demand. Of course, now it is as easy as telling my legs to walk." In the next moment, Rosalia was no longer a lovely young lady but a hovering gray stone-like monster with giant bat wings. "Give it a try."

I thought of the last time I had been angry. That was at William. The thought of him touching me was infuriating but I did not feel any different. I shrugged at Rosalia.

"What worked for me is to imagine being attacked," Sonia said. Her voice was kind and soft, still that of a child's. I could not imagine her killing someone. It broke my heart to think that a vampire would turn someone so young and innocent.

Sonia also appeared as a monster, swooping through the air above me.

"Very well." I shook my head and tried to focus. "Being attacked," I said out loud but to myself. Again, nothing happened.

"Let us hurry this along, shall we?" Orrick said as he lunged toward me with his fists up, poised to attack. That succeeded. In an instant I was hovering out of his reach.

Cheers erupted from the vampires.

My legs looked terrible. I held my hands out and stared at them. They were not mine; they were ugly, gray and cracked. I panicked causing my wings to falter. This sent me plummeting to the ground with a loud thud.

"Well done. I think she is ready," Orrick said.

With that, the four of them grabbed me and easily threw me over the cliff.

"Noooooo," I yelled. The ground sped toward me as I fell in terror.

It felt much longer than only a moment or two. Time flew by. Then … time stopped. Enormous seven-foot wings extended out horizontally, suspending me in the air. I glided with ease.

"Yes!" I yelled in triumph. *This is fabulous!* That was when I heard the whoops and howls of the others. There were two massive winged creatures on either side of me, cheering me on.

"Flap your wings," Rosalia's voice said, though I could barely recognize her in this form.

I studied my wings and focused. They slowly moved up and down. I began to gain altitude rather than slowly gliding downward. *It is like learning how to walk* — or so I imagined. I had to figure out how to control different muscles, in this case, ones I did not know I had. Flapping the wings felt like flexing my shoulder blades.

The others dived and spiraled through the air with ease. I watched with a child's amazement. All I could do was focus on adjusting to the wind speed and not falling out of the sky. I wobbled with even the slightest change in air pressure or wind.

We flew through the valley, speeding over a large farm and a small farmhouse. Orrick — at least I think it was Orrick — flew low over the sheep in a pen, scaring the poor creatures. He laughed heartily as he corkscrewed through the air.

"How high can we go?" I asked.

"Let's find out," Rose said.

Up and up we went. It appeared we could fly until we tired, which was a very long time — essentially until we had to feed. Finally, we all stopped and hovered. We were many times higher than the mountaintops and far above any clouds. It was as if I could see the entire world from up here. I narrowed my eyes and strained to see as far as possible. The world seemed to curve away from us in all directions, as if the earth were round and bigger than we could ever have imagined. I laughed out loud as I thought, *The earth is spherical, just as Father believed.* I wished I could have told him he was right. It was the most beautiful sight I had ever seen.

"This is the best part." Orrick tucked his wings in and dived head first.

The others did the same. I followed more cautiously.

I never wanted to land. I would have been content to stay in the air forever. *Landing? How does one land?* My exhilaration faded and my heart began to race.

The others landed back on the cliff. I circled them to watch. Their wings were fully open, flapping hard as they slowed. They landed on their feet with ease. Their wings quickly folded up and disappeared. Once again, they looked like normal humans, fully clothed. *That is convenient,* I thought.

"Are there any tricks to landing?" I yelled down to them.

"Keep your wings fully extended and parallel to the ground rather than perpendicular," Irene yelled back.

This simply baffled me. When I tried to rotate my wings, they folded in too far and I dropped hard to the ground, rolling five times before coming to a stop.

"Ouch," I moaned as I got to my feet. It hurt but the pain quickly vanished.

Everyone roared with laughter.

"You did very well," Sonia said.

She was sincere. I already liked her.

"Aye, until that landing," Orrick said in between laughing wildly.

As incensed as I was becoming with Orrick, I could not help laughing with them.

"Come along; the sun will be on the rise soon. Let's get back," Rosalia said.

CHAPTER 29 CONSTANTINOPLE 1260 AD

After a time, I grew comfortable in Ramdasha's cavern. There was no sun to hurt my eyes, no smell of delicious human blood to make my throat ache. I did not have to constantly work to move slowly like a human. I even began to consider Rosalia's band of "commoners" my friends.

Nights were usually spent flying. I practiced moving my wings in different ways to learn what would happen when I did. I practiced taking off from the ground — as opposed to being thrown off a cliff. And, of course, I practiced landing. This was the most difficult part but I was slowly getting better. During the day I read from the supply of books in the library and spent time with Rosalia and the others. I had not seen much of Orrick, so I asked Rosalia one day about the politics of vampires and if there was anything I should know. She said that Orrick was the expert on such matters and that I should consult him.

So I sought Orrick out. Much to my dismay, he was in the large round room at the end of the hall, Ramdasha's throne room. I had gone out of my way to avoid this room and Ramdasha. My stomach fluttered as I entered. Many eyes turned my way but thankfully Ramdasha hardly gave me a glance. I wish I could have said the same for the large man to his right. He stared at me intently. I looked away and I scanned the room for Orrick. My skin crawled as I could still feel the vampire's stare. I all but ran to Orrick. Not caring that I was interrupting, I blurted, "May I have a word?"

"Now?" Orrick frowned.

"Please. … And not here." I looked around uneasily.

"Excuse me," Orrick said to the vampire he had been conversing with.

We joined our other friends in the small common room.

"This had better be good," Orrick said.

"Sorry about that. I have not seen you much lately and Roselia said you were the one to consult."

"About what?"

"About what I need to know regarding the vampire world?"

His eyes brightened but he did not smile.

He must be eager to have someone who will listen to him, I thought.

Aaron stood. "I think I'll go to the training room." He stopped in front of me, issued a half-mocking bow. "Please excuse me, My Lady."

I frowned at him and playfully pushed him away.

"To start …" Orrick gestured for me to sit in a chair across from him. "There is a group of vampires in the North. Some of them are very old. They call themselves the High Court of Elders. By and large, they are the leaders of our kind. They make the laws and ruthlessly enforce them."

"Doesn't the High Court reside in Denmark?" Irene asked.

My head started to spin. *Elijah … and the Court he always talked about.*

"That is right, Denmark. And the head of the Court is … what's his name, Lord Castain?" Sonia said.

My body went rigid at the mention of this name because I knew exactly whom she meant.

"No, Lord Chastellain." Orrick shot Sonia an irritated glower.

I inhaled sharply and then forced myself to breathe normally. *Remain calm!* I hoped the others would not notice the sudden change in me that had occurred at the mention of the name Chastellain.

Orrick continued, "The High Court is concerned that the vampire race is growing too fast and that this puts the human race in danger. Their laws state that vampires must remain hidden from humans, for the protection of both races, so they claim. We must live and feed discreetly under the High Court's laws."

Orrick's tone indicated that he was not in favor of such laws. However, they made perfect sense to me. "You do not approve of such laws restricting us." I struggled to keep my voice steady.

"Lord Ramdasha is the leader of the resistance to the High Court. He does not like laws that restrict vampires. He stands in direct opposition to the Elders. I follow Lord Ramdasha. After all, it makes sense; we are by far the more powerful race. Why should we have to be the ones to live in hiding? We should be the ones who rule this world."

I forced myself to close my mouth, which had fallen open. What Orrick was saying was appalling. I quickly pushed thoughts of Elijah out of my head and gathered my composure. "What are Ramdasha's plans for us?" I was relieved that my voice sounded casual, as if I did not truly care.

"Only the vampires closest to Lord Ramdasha know his plans," Orrick replied. "I'm not one of them. Although that is why I have been spending more time in the Great Room. I hope to move up in rank."

"If vampires don't remain anonymous, won't humans retaliate and burn our lairs?" Sonia inquired.

"There would be a war and we would win." Orrick's smile was full of malice.

I shivered and resisted the urge to slap Orrick. *That will not do any good. This is preposterous! Orrick actually believes that he is better than humans and that vampires should rule over them.*

I fought to maintain my composure. "Wouldn't Ramdasha require an army to accomplish his goal of overthrowing the High Court of Elders?" Hopefully, I sounded only half-interested, simply making conversation.

"That is *Lord* Ramdasha," Orrick corrected, "and I don't know but I am sure that is why he encourages us to train so much."

"Yet are we not to remain inconspicuous? That is one of Lord Ramdasha's decrees, is it not?" I asked.

"Yes, for now he does not want to go to war with the High Court. They swiftly and mercilessly carry out this law. I suspect that he is not ready to directly challenge the Elders. Lord Ramdasha does not want to draw too much attention from them — yet," Orrick said.

I felt ill. Having heard enough, I let it go for the time being and was glad when Rosalia changed the subject. She was looking forward to accompanying me on my first patrol of the city tonight — although I was barely listening, as she mapped out the night for us. My thoughts were of Elijah and the Elders. I was clearly on the wrong side. It was fortunate that there was a Court that worked to keep vampires under control. I should leave for them at once, though I hated the thought. The image of Lord Chastellain made my blood boil.

What am I to do? I could not stay here and support this crazed power-hungry Ramdasha. Perhaps I had some time. It appeared that Sonia might not fully support him. Maybe I could discreetly find out who else disagreed with Ramdasha and convince them to come to Denmark. I liked this idea, as any vampires I could take from Ramdasha would weaken his resistance to the High Court.

One thing I did agree with Orrick on was that I should learn to fight. It would not come amiss and it seemed that I might need it after all in this violent world in which I was now forced to live.

That night on patrol, Rosalia gave me a tour of some of the most magnificent places in the city. We waited until there was no one around, then flew to the top of a large oval-shaped arena.

"The grand Hippodrome." Then Rose's face darkened. For the first time since I'd known her she looked angry. "Or at least it used to be grand. It is in need of repair. It is still used for certain royal ceremonies and the like. I wish you could have seen this city in her prime. She used to continually buzz with many people from all over the world and her wealth was unparalleled. I was still a human but clearly remember the endless days and nights of looting. My family and I stayed hidden until the pillaging slowed. Those two-faced barbarian heretics from the West — I wish I had been a vampire then. I would have killed them all. The gold, jewels and many precious icons were looted and taken West, mostly to Venice, so I hear." She paused and took a deep breath as if to put herself at ease. She smiled in her usual carefree way. "Emperor Michael will rebuild this city to its former grandeur. Soon we will be a world power once again."

Father did not like to talk about the last dreaded Crusade. He would say only that it was "a dark time in Christian history." It had once seemed so far away and so long ago. But being here made it seem like only yesterday — the devastating effects were right in front of me — practically screaming at me. I was saddened for the city and for Rose.

"Come," she said. "Let me show you my favorite place of all." We leapt down onto the chariot track. In the middle of the long corridor stood towering obelisks.

"There were once many statues of past emperors and heroes adoring the arena. Four life-size bronze horses used to stand atop the entryway," Rosalia informed me.

The track itself was lined with full-body statues of previous champion charioteers — well, some still remained, while others had been stolen or destroyed and only their bases remained. I studied the amazing craftsmanship of one such statue. At its base it bore the name Elijah, 644–656. I quickly looked closer at the statue's face. *It is Elijah! My Elijah — I mean Elijah from Ludus. He really is as old as he said,* I thought.

Rose came back to where I was standing and eyed the statue as well. "Aye, I remember hearing stories about him. He was the best charioteer to ever compete in this arena. No one has ever come near to beating his twelve-year winning record. He never lost a race. When I was a small girl my brothers used to pretend to be Elijah and my sister and I dreamt of marrying him." She chuckled. "You would think he was a vampire."

"Yeah." I breathed.

I glanced around at all the empty stands rising high above me. I could imagine them filled with brightly clothed people. The sound of cheering and many horse's hooves pounding the ground, rang in my head. I imagined Elijah in Roman warrior's garb, rounding the sharp corner while being pulled by four lean and swift horses. As good as he was with horses, I had no doubt his would be the best. They would do anything to please him — running faster and harder than the other horses. I smiled at this vision when Rosalia interrupted my daydream.

"What is it?"

The imaginary crowd stopped roaring in my ears as I reluctantly pulled myself back to the present. "I was picturing what life was like here many years ago. I wish I could have seen it."

It was ironic that her childhood infatuation was now her coven's enemy. "How old is Ramdasha or how long has he been in power?"

"He is about as old as I am," Rose said. "He has risen to power over the past forty years."

That made sense. The Chastellains must have lived here long before that, at least for a time. I smiled at the thought that the man this statue was fashioned after was indeed a vampire and that Rosalia had no idea he was Lord Chastellain's son. Even if she had heard of Elijah, the lord's son, she had not put the two together and I was not about to make the connection for her. As far as anyone here was concerned, I knew nothing of the High Court. I still needed to find out how Rose felt about the issue.

As we exited the Hippodrome, I decided that this was as good a time as any. "What do you think? Should we have to live in hiding, or should we be allowed to rule over humans?" I tried to sound nonchalant.

"It would be nice to be free and open about what we are. The thought of spending an eternity in that cavern ..." She shook her head and looked disgusted at the thought.

"Aye," I replied, as if in agreement. That was her answer. I could count Rose out. I swallowed my disappointment.

CHAPTER 30 CONSTANTINOPLE 1260 AD

Rosalia and I stood in front of the Hagia Sophia. I had seen the large domed church from afar but up close its size was overwhelming. The painting in the Chastellain's manor had not depicted the true beauty nor the sheer mass of the building. Rose flew up to a window opening and landed on the sill.

"Wait. We cannot go in here!" I said.

She gave me a mischievous smile. "We can do whatever we want." She disappeared into the large dome.

I double checked to make sure no one was around and leapt onto the sill. I stepped onto the upper balcony just below the window and looked down to find a single person in the middle of a sea of white. The floor was like nothing I had ever seen before. It looked like an ice-covered lake — impossibly shiny and smooth. Surely it would break under my feet if I jumped down from this height.

"Well, come along," Rose yelled from far below.

"What is the floor made of?"

Rose laughed. "It's marble, like the statues in the Hippodrome."

That was impossible; stone could not be so shiny and smooth.

At my continued hesitation Rose stamped her foot on the floor. "You see, it is safe."

I leapt over the rail and used my wings to slow me so that I landed softly on the strange floor. I was still sure it would crack like a sheet of thin ice under my weight.

"You are so strange." Rosalia laughed again.

"As far as I'm concerned, floors should be made of wood or stone."

"I already told you: this *is* stone."

I still did not believe it; it was not like any stone I had seen before, not even like the marble statues.

Rose kicked off her shoes and started to glide around the smooth surface in her stockings. "Give it a try."

I took my shoes off and she grabbed my hand, pulling me forward. "Push off with your feet, like this." Soon we were gliding across the floor. She swung me around until we were both spinning in a circle. The world around us was only a blur. When we finally stopped, we were both laughing and dizzy.

My laugh was cut short by the sight high above me. Throughout the process of sliding around, we had landed by the front altar and in the high central dome above was a larger-than-life mosaic of the Virgin Mary and Baby Jesus. My first reaction was to prostrate myself on the altar and pray to them. I had not prayed since I had been turned into a demon. Blood rushed to my cheeks. *Jesus is no longer My Lord; he has forsaken me.* My stomach knotted. I studied the images before me. *Where do vampires come from? Is it possible God made us? No. The devil more like.*

"Someone is coming; we must have awakened the bishop. Let's go," Rose whispered. She quietly grabbed her shoes, jumped onto the balcony and disappeared out the window. I had gone numb. I followed her even though I did not care if I was caught.

Once outside the Hagia Sophia, Rose took one look at me and asked, "What is wrong?"

I spared her the details of my spiritual crisis and simply replied, "I wish my father had been able to see this cathedral — the holiest of all churches." Even if it could no longer be my church, it was still the Great Mother of his church.

She smiled. "We had better get to work. Let's be on our way."

As we walked through the city, she showed me many other wonderous sites, like the Emperor's palace, the public bath houses and the royal gardens, to name a few. Her immense love for this city was apparent. She was excited to show it off. When the eastern sky turned yellow, we headed back to the cavern.

After seeing so many new things my mind was racing and I was far from tired, so I headed straight for the training room. The room was busy. Vampires everywhere, dueling with swords, boxing, breaking stone columns — the usual, I imagined. I did nothing but observe for a time, as I had no idea where to start. Eventually, I headed for the swords. I picked one up and started getting a feel for its weight in my hand.

"Need a lesson?" came a deep and unfamiliar voice.

I turned to find the largest man, or vampire, I had ever seen. His dark eye's stared down at me. Up close he was even bigger than I remembered. His bulky frame was riddled with muscles. Instinctively, I stepped away. I recognized him at once from Ramdasha's Great Room. I must have looked intimidated because he tried to reassure me with a smile. Yet I was not reassured.

"Allow me to introduce myself. My name is Riddick. You look as if you could use a lesson in sword fighting."

Riddick, yes, I had heard the others speak of him. He was Ramdasha's commander in chief. No one was closer to Ramdasha than he. He had olive skin similar to Teller's. Riddick did not exactly look like Teller but there was some resemblance. Perhaps it was simply their skin and their massive forms. Still they could pass as brothers. I collected myself and said, "My name is —

"Val, from Targoviste, I know. Come."

I followed him to the dummies that had been hacked to bits, apparently with swords. He showed me how to hold the sword and swing. By the end of the day, we were fencing in duels, though I'm sure he spared me his full force and skill.

The next day was spent boxing. Riddick put one hand on my waist and grabbed my arm with the other to show me how to hold my hands in a fighting pose. I recoiled at his touch.

"Be easy," he said.

I did not like this. He was too close. I removed his hand from my waist. "Is that necessary?"

He raised his hands, palms facing me. "Very well, have it your way." But the smile he gave me sent a chill down my spine.

Later that day in our common room, Rosalia jeered, "Someone's caught the eye of the commander." She looked pointedly at me.

Aaron put on an overly dramatic display of being distraught and heartbroken. With his hands over his heart, he pretended to be dying and flung himself into a settee.

Everyone laughed at his theatrics and I could not help the smile that crept across my face.

"No, no and no. You are all wrong." Yet I knew they were right. Since the first time I had seen Riddick the day I arrived here, I did not like the way he looked at me, that piercing stare. I shivered.

"Riddick and Val! Oh, my!" Sonia mocked.

"Stop, all of you! What are we, twelve years old?" I was growing aggravated.

"I knew she would be leaving us to mingle with royalty," Irene said.

"Be sure and put in a good word for me," Orrick said.

"I'm not leaving and I'm not interested in —" I stopped short because it dawned on me that if I did get closer to Ramdasha, I might be able to find out what his plans were. I could warn Elijah and the Elders. Excusing myself, I retired to my room. I had to think. This would be dangerous. If Ramdasha found out I was spying, he would undoubtedly kill me. Yet they had no reason to suspect me. I would give it a try, a couple of weeks at the very most. There was a knock at my door and an uneasy feeling came over me.

"Riddick, what a surprise," I said.

"No, it isn't." He swiftly bypassed me, letting himself into my room.

How inconsiderate! I pushed the door open further. I did not want to be behind closed doors with him.

"What can I do for you, My Lord?"

He smiled; apparently he liked being called "My Lord." "There is something you can do for me. Foreign dignitaries will be visiting and Lord Ramdasha is planning a banquet for them. I was hoping you would accompany me."

My first reaction was to refuse but this sounded like an opportunity to find out what Ramdasha was planning. *Remember, Riddick is your way in,* I told myself. "It would be my pleasure." I returned his smile.

"It is settled," he replied.

I had hoped he would leave but he did not. Instead, he looked around the room, wandering further away from the door.

Oh no, I thought. "Who are these leaders who will be visiting?"

"They are nobles from Portugal and France."

"What is the reason for their visit?"

"Now you're getting into politics and that is nothing a woman should worry herself with."

I resisted the urge to glare at him and managed to say, "Yes, of course." *He is such an arse.* "Well, if that is all, then I will see you tomorrow for training."

"That is not all." In a flash he was close — way too close. I stepped back and bumped up against the chest behind me. He moved forward, almost precisely in step with me and bent down. His lips were headed for mine when I pushed him gently back. *How am I going to get out of this?* I decided reason was my best chance.

"Less than two months ago, I lost my entire family and my fiancé. I need … time. I don't want … this." *Whatever this was?* I thought. "Let's go slow."

He clearly did not like the rejection and he did not seem concerned that I had loved someone else. "Slow?" was all he said.

"Yes, let us get to know each other first. Besides, as vampires, we have time in plenty."

"'Get to know each other?'" he repeated, as if he had never heard of such a thing. "I am trying to get to know you."

I held his gaze — imploring him to leave me alone.

"Very well, I will see you for training tomorrow." He spun around and stormed out.

I exhaled. *Thank God he left! I don't know if I can do this. Riddick clearly wants more from me than I'm willing to give. Vampire men seem to be less gentlemanly than human men. Well, less than some human men anyway. What gall he has, bursting in here, expecting …* I shivered at the thought. *He assumed that my agreeing to be his companion for a banquet also meant that I would allow him to take me to bed.*

CHAPTER 31 CONSTANTINOPLE 1260 AD

I trained with Riddick over the next week and any other spare time was spent in the company of my new friends. This was primarily in hopes of avoiding any further advances by Riddick. I appreciated the training. Riddick was an excellent fighter and a good teacher. I was greatly improving.

Spending time with Rose's band of misfits gave me time to find out how the others felt. I knew whose side Rose was on and it was clear what Orrick believed. When I questioned Irene alone one day, she too seemed to side with Ramdasha. I was losing hope when I confronted Sonia. She could see both sides of the argument but her remaining love for humans won her over.

"I do not want a war with humans. I still have family in the city. I fear for them," Sonia said.

I empathized with her.

That left Aaron. I got my chance to talk to him one night when we were both scheduled for patrol. I found him alone on a rooftop.

"What do you think about Ramdasha and his plans to challenge the Court of Elders?" I asked.

For the first time since I had met Aaron, his face grew serious. "I can't bear Orrick sometimes and his talk of war with humans. 'We are the dominant race.'" Aaron mocked Orrick. "We are nothing but monsters. I used to try to argue with him but I quickly learned that defying Lord Ramdasha is dangerous. So I deal with Orrick by joking, I suppose. Sometimes I think about leaving but where would I go? This is my home, my beloved city."

It appeared Aaron was being sincere. I could trust him — I hoped. "I will try to find out what I can about Ramdasha's plans at the banquet and then I'm leaving for the North. I hope you and Sonia will join me."

His eyes widened. "You mean to Denmark, to Chastellains realm?"

"Yes, I plan to warn them if I find out anything useful."

"You can't simply march into Lord Chastellain's Court and claim you have information about Ramdasha."

Something told me that I could "march into the lord's Court." My thoughts strayed to Elijah. "I have to try," was all I said. I had probably said too much already. "Please consider coming with me. Ask Sonia to come as well, if you get a chance."

Aaron looked away. He was in deep thought, yet there was a glimmer of hope in his eyes. "This is a dangerous game you're playing."

"It is not a game," I replied.

THE DAY of the banquet arrived. I had had a particularly grueling training session with Riddick. He was pushing me harder as I improved.

"Thank you for working with me; I do appreciate it," I said. "You are a wonderful instructor."

He grabbed my waist and pulled me close. Apparently any amiable gesture was a signal for Riddick to advance. His mouth was on mine before I fully realized what was happening.

I let him kiss me for a moment, then firmly pushed him away. "I have to prepare myself for the banquet." I slipped out of his arms and did my best not to run away from him. *I must get out of here!* I thought. Riddick would not take no for an answer much longer.

Rosalia, Sonia, Irene and I got ready in Rosalia's room. Riddick had provided me with a brocade for the occasion. These long silky layered gowns did not seem *as* odd to me now. We laughed and joked as we took turns helping one another get ready. In the end, we all looked like royalty.

When we entered Ramdasha's Great Room, Orrick and Riddick approached. Orrick swept Rosalia out to the center of the room. They danced gracefully across the floor — a beautiful couple, though I wondered why they did not act like a couple otherwise. Many other couples were dancing together as well. I had never seen people dance face to face like this.

Riddick took my arm. "I did not think you could possibly look more beautiful but you do."

"You are too kind, My Lord." *I only have to get through tonight,* I tried to encourage myself.

The Great Room was decorated more lavishly than before. A large chandelier hung from the center of the high round ceiling. Candlelight reflected off its beautifully cut glass. The room was dazzling. Riddick led me over to the long table set aside for the leaders.

He proudly introduced me to some of the new faces. Unlike at the dance with Elijah, this time I actually paid attention. The two who stood out were Lord Mendoza of Portugal and Lord Belleaire of France. They sat to the left of Ramdasha, and Riddick and I sat to his right.

In the center of the room, I spotted Aaron and Sonia, who were mostly jesting rather than dancing. Aaron shot me a quick and knowing glance. I gave him a slight nod, then quickly looked away. I was focused on Ramdasha's conversation with the two foreign lords. Mostly niceties were exchanged.

We ate and drank. I tried the red wine that had been poured for us. I did not spit it out this time but it still tasted horrible. *Why would anyone consume this bitter drink?* I thought.

Ramdasha raised his goblet of wine in toast. "Here is to my comrades in the fight for vampire freedom."

"Hear, hear," cheered Lord Mendoza and Lord Belleaire.

"Hear, hear," Riddick added, tapping his goblet with theirs.

I followed his lead and tried to smile. I hoped it looked more sincere than it felt.

"Now we dance." Riddick stood. He grabbed me under the arm and pulled me out of my seat.

He is such a brute. Did he not know that it is proper to ask a lady to dance, not demand it? I covered up my annoyance with another smile. I did not like this spying business. I had been raised without artifice and preferred to be straightforward. *It will all be over soon,* I told myself.

It was unfortunate that I had to leave the table because it looked as if Ramdasha and his honored guests were talking more seriously. I was trying to concentrate on what they were saying but this was difficult because Riddick wrapped an arm around my waist and pressed his body to mine; with his free hand he took mine and held it up.

"What are you doing?" I protested.

"Don't tell me you have never couple danced before?"

"Of course not! This is inappropriate. Even married couples don't dance like this." I tried unsuccessfully to put some distance between us.

"You are in our world now. Look around," he whispered. His grip on my waist did not loosen.

I did look around. Most of the vampires who were dancing were in pairs gliding around gracefully. Orrick spun Rosalia around and her bright orange brocade flowed elegantly about her body. The only exception was Aaron and Sonia, who had gotten a handful of others to join in a circle dance. This type of group dancing was what I was used to.

"You see, anything is acceptable down here. We live beyond the sight of God," Riddick said.

I shivered at the thought. With a great sadness I resigned myself to this fact — we were damned. The social norms of the people above no longer pertained to us. I also stopped trying to push Riddick away.

"Come now, don't look so forlorn. It can be fun. Follow my lead."

It was all I could do to keep up with him as he moved me across the floor. For a time I forgot about trying to spy on Ramdasha.

Eventually, I began to get the sense of dancing in this manner, or at least became somewhat comfortable in following his lead. When we danced close enough to Ramdasha, I was able to catch parts of the conversation, such as Ramdasha asking how many trained fighters they each had. But Riddick swept me away and I could not hear the answer.

"Not bad for your first time, yet you seem distracted," Riddick said.

It was too difficult to get much of Ramdasha's conversation so I decided to try another angle. As flippantly as possible I asked, "Have Portugal and France decided to join Lord Ramdasha?"

"Yes, Lord Mendoza and Lord Belleaire are very influential in their respective countries."

"I can imagine." I tried to sound impressed. I needed to play up to him in order to get more information. I rubbed my fingers up and down his arm and smiled. This seemed to work. He looked thrilled. "Who else is on our side?"

"Macedonia is with us and a small coven of vampires in Bulgaria have pledged their support to Lord Ramdasha. If we can gain the support of a coven in Hungary, we may have enough to finally challenge the Court. Unfortunately, they are reluctant to undermine the High Court of the Elders."

"Hmm." I tried to look uninterested. I had so many questions. Was Ramdasha planning an all-out war and if so, when? Or was he planning a covert assassination of the Elders? *Go slowly,* I told myself. We glided in silence and I pretended to be interested only in him.

"Are they planning an attack?" I ventured.

"Yes, eventually. First we need more allies if we are to be successful against Chastellain's large army."

I almost tripped. "They have a large army?"

"Yes, they have legions of vampires ready to fight all across the

North, from England to Poland." He chuckled at the expression on my face. He twirled me around and said, "Enough about politics. Tonight is about us."

I smiled. Out of the corner of my eye, I could see that Aaron and Sonia were also trying to subtly listen to Ramdasha as they "danced."

Most likely I could not ask many more questions without raising suspicion. I had gotten all Riddick knew, or all he was willing to tell, at least. So I decided not to push my luck. We danced in silence and I pretended to be content.

When we returned to the table, I felt the monster inside stir to life. *Not tonight!* I had known it would be coming soon, any day but I had been trying to put off feeding for as long as possible. It had been over a month since I had last fed. I tried to ignore it and failed. Ignoring it only makes the beast roar louder. Soon it was screaming at me.

"You look unwell." Riddick said. The genuine concern in his voice surprised me.

"Yes," I admitted. "I have not fed in a while. I'm going to have to excuse myself."

"How long has it been?"

"Over a month."

"Why would you starve yourself like that?"

Perhaps it is because I hate killing people? I wanted to yell at him but managed to refrain. Instead I said, "You'll have to excuse me, I must go."

"I will go with you."

"No!" I softened my voice. "I will find you later."

He looked reluctant, so I added, "I promise." Then I was gone.

CHAPTER 32 CONSTANTINOPLE 1260 AD

Out into the fresh night air in hunting mode, I was relieved to learn that no one had followed me. Vampires did seem to prefer to feed alone. I had not witnessed any feedings this past month.

It was not long before I spotted my prey. A lone man was walking through an alleyway. My mouth watered and my jaw ached when I caught his scent — I felt myself slip away and lose control completely. It was not until the pain in my throat subsided that I was able to think for myself again.

I could feel a part of me die with every kill. Would I eventually become as cruel and heartless as those monsters in that hidden underground cavern, celebrating and plotting to become even more powerful? I could not let my humanity gradually disappear. I had to find a way to keep hold of it. Though I supposed life would be easier without a conscience, I could not let that happen. Somehow, I had to fight the monster inside! *But how?* It seemed hopeless, utterly impossible. Tears fell onto my gown.

I caught a glimpse of a figure standing at the end of the alley. I narrowed my eyes to see better. I recognized the handsome face at once.

"Elijah!"

I ran to him, throwing my arms around him. He was familiar, someone from home. I had not felt this happy since Teller and I had planned our future together. He seemed surprised at first, then he put his arms around me in return.

"I was beginning to think I would never be able to find you," he whispered.

I pulled away. "How *did* you find me?"

"I followed the smell of blood."

I glared at him and pushed him away. His eyes were a troubled cloud of gray, filled with worry and the usual sadness. I stepped closer. "What is wrong?"

"We must talk but not here." He clasped my hand and we took flight.

We landed in the woods, safely out of the city.

"I can't believe you are here. You came looking for me?" I asked.

"Of course," he said as if it was somehow obvious that he would come into enemy territory in search of me.

"How did you know I was in Constantinople?"

"The world of vampires is much smaller than the world of humans. We travel quickly and so does news. A beautiful new vampire wandering into Constantinople and calling herself Val is indeed news. I knew it was you and came at once. I worried you would be in trouble here. I had to come and warn you. Of all the places, how on earth did you find your way into Ramdasha's coven." He shook his head in disbelief. He ran a piece of my silk brocade between his fingers. "You appear to be doing well for yourself."

"You should not have come. You are in danger here." If Ramdasha captured Elijah, that would be the perfect leverage over Lord Chastellain.

"Yes and you will be in trouble as well if you are seen with me. Come to Denmark with me now," he pled.

"I was planning to leave for Denmark soon but I must go back for my friends first."

"There is no time. Leave with me. Your friends will follow if they can."

"No, I can't leave them. I need to go back to find out if they will come. They will not leave their city without me. They do not know you."

"I don't like the idea of you going back." Elijah's voice was stern.

"If I can get even a few to join you in the North, that will be two fewer vampires on Ramdasha's side. I need a couple of days."

Elijah looked displeased. "Two days, that is it," he said with finality. "I will wait for you in Adrianople, the largest city northwest of here. Go to the first inn you find. That is where I will be."

I nodded in agreement. It was hard to leave him but I made myself pull away.

"Vallachia." He stopped me from leaving by grabbing my arm. "Two days, or I will be back with an army."

"You had better not start a war and destroy this city for one person." I stared at him in disbelief. "Tell me you would not do that!"

"I would indeed. War is coming. It is inevitable."

We stared at each other for a moment. He was serious. There was no use in arguing and no time.

"Two days," I agreed and took flight for the city … alone.

As I flew my mind was racing. I would spend one day getting a sense of some of the other vampires. I would see if I could convince any of them to leave with me. At dusk on the following night, we would set out for Denmark.

As soon as I set foot in the long corridor, four large figures surrounded me and grabbed me. I knew straightaway my careful planning was all for naught. They swiftly placed thick metal shackles around my wrists, chaining my arms behind my back. I fought the restraints but they did not yield. One of the four men was Riddick.

"Let go of me!" I said. "Riddick, what is the meaning of this?"

With a firm grip on my right arm, he glanced briefly at me. Anger flashed through his eyes. He turned away; staring forward. "It was very foolish of you to come back here."

They marched me down the hall, taking me to Ramdasha, no doubt. Surprisingly, they turned me toward one of the doors I had never ventured beyond. It led to more stairs, twisting and leading even farther down into the earth than we already were. I began to think the stairs might never end. A relatively small room appeared in front of us, with a number of small barred cells branching off from the center room. This was what I was afraid of: a dungeon prison. In the center of the room stood Ramdasha.

"A little birdy tells me that you had a clandestine meeting with your lover tonight. And no, I don't mean Riddick." Ramdasha's voice was deep with malice.

Riddick's already stern grip on my arm grew even tighter.

I simply stared at Ramdasha. I doubted that there was a way to talk myself out of this one, so silence was best.

"Unfortunately, I don't know what you two lovebirds discussed. *Someone*" — Ramdasha indicated the man holding my left arm — "thought it would be best to come tell me what he saw in the alleyway, instead of following the spy and our enemy to see what they had to say."

The man on my left put his head down, fully abashed.

I was relieved at this news. *Elijah got away! He is safe and they don't know what we'd discussed.* I tried to think of a lie that would help but nothing came to mind. So I continued to stare at Ramdasha in silence.

"It does not matter if she speaks, as I would not believe anything that came out of her mouth. Throw her in a cell and chain her up. Her execution is set for tomorrow night." He came within an inch of my face. "You will excuse me; I must be getting back to my guests." Then he was gone.

CHAPTER 33 CONSTANTINOPLE 1260 AD

In no time, I was sitting on the cold stone floor. My wrists and ankles chained to a cell wall. I fought the restraints but they were too thick even for a vampire. The barred door in front of me was slammed shut and locked.

Riddick paused outside the cell. "I can't believe I fell under your spell. I should have known you were not a commoner. You lied to me. You said you lost your fiancé. I never would have guessed that you were betrothed to Prince Chastellain. It was all simply a show." Judging by his anger, he was honestly hurt.

"I'm not betrothed to anyone," I whispered. This statement made me sad as I was reminded of Teller.

"I see, then you are the prince's whore?"

I gritted my teeth to hold back what I wanted to say — *it would be better to be Elijah's whore than yours.* It was not wise to antagonize one's jailer. If I made him angrier — if that were possible — there was no telling what he might do. I was in no position to defend myself.

Quiet, Vallachia, I told myself. I needed to think. I slammed my head against the stone wall behind me and closed my eyes. I heard Riddick storm out of the dungeon. I was alone.

Part of me felt relieved. *Soon this miserable life would be over. I will never be able to hurt anyone again. I hope they kill me quickly. I don't fancy pain but then again, who does? The problem is that Elijah will start a war if I do not return to him.*

I have to get out of here — somehow. How did I get myself into this situation? I'm the daughter of a peaceful deacon. I never wanted to hurt anyone, let alone start a war. It is not for myself but for peace that I have to get out of here. But how? The only two who I could possibly count on are Aaron and Sonia. They do not know I'm here. By the time they discover I'm missing, it will be too late.

I banged my head on the stone wall again, this time in frustration. "Ouch," I said out loud.

As time wore on, my thoughts wandered. *What did Elijah mean by, "War is inevitable"? Is there no hope of reconciling with Ramdasha?* I had a bad feeling Elijah was right. *It might be better if the Court of the Elders attacked now, before Ramdasha's army has time to grow in strength and numbers.* This may have been a justification to make me feel better, that I would not truly be the sole cause of a war.

Father taught me that there is always an alternative to war and violence and that we must try the alternatives first. Does this apply to the world of vampires? I was not sure. *Father was always able to keep the peace in our village. He never resorted to fighting. Yet I cannot imagine trying to reason with Ramdasha. He seems to want war.* Thinking about Father made me miss him and our home all the more. I wished he were here. *He would know how to comfort me.* A tear rolled down my cheek.

I shook my head. *Think of something else so you don't go mad.* Surprisingly, Riddick came to mind. *It is interesting that he is concerned only because I rushed into the arms of another man. He is not interested, as Ramdasha is, in the fact that the man was Elijah, the son of their enemy. Riddick is simply jealous, and not angry that I am a turncoat.*

Riddick is selfish. He is in this for his own status and power. He most likely does not care which side he is on as long as he is promised power and wealth. He is a henchman — Ramdasha's muscle. It is unfortunate that the Elders do not know this. If they were to promise Riddick more power than Ramdasha offered, they could most likely buy him. If war is indeed inevitable, then he would be an asset to whichever side he is on. Listen to me — plotting political maneuvers.

Surely it was daylight by now and time was moving too slowly. I wished it would hurry up and end. The torturous waiting was the worst part, which was most likely why Ramdasha did not kill me straight away. There was nothing *to* do and nothing I *could* do to get out of this predicament. Once again, Elijah had been right. *I should not have come back. I will not even live long enough to get it through my thick head that I should listen to him. He is old and wise ... and kind.* This train of thought was disheartening as well, so I tried to think of nothing. I focused only on my breath. In, out, in. ... Soon I drifted off, more to escape this prison than because of a need to sleep.

A noise woke me. Through the darkness I could make out a large figure opening the barred door to my cell. Judging by the size, it had to be Riddick. Panic rose in my throat. Either it was execution time, or he had other plans for me first.

"What are you doing?" My voice was higher than normal.

"Shhh," was all he said. Riddick looked over his shoulder. He approached and I fought the restraints to no avail. He raised his hand toward me and I flinched away — sure that he was going to strike me. I heard keys jingle in his hands. He quickly removed the manacles from my wrists and my arms fell to the ground. He released my legs as well. I stared at him with wide eyes.

"Go!" he whispered. "They will be coming for you soon."

I could not believe it. I gave him a quick hug. "Why?" I had to ask.

"I needed some time for my anger to subside."

"What about you? Won't they know you let me go?"

"I have an alibi. Now *go* before I change my mind."

I nodded and in a flash I was headed out of the dungeon at full speed. Once in the long hallway, I heard voices up ahead. I hid behind a column, trying to hold my breath. My heart was pounding. As soon as it was clear, I headed for Sonia's room. I did not slow until I was in her room with the door shut behind me.

She had been sleeping. Startled, she sat upright in bed.

"I am out of time. I must leave. Will you come with me to Denmark?"

It took her an instant to register what I was saying. She nodded and quickly moved around the room, gathering some keepsakes in a small bag and soon we were headed to Aaron's room.

"We are leaving for the North — now!" I spoke quickly to Aaron. "Are you with us?"

Aaron was sitting at his desk. He had been writing in a large book. "Now? But I'm not ready. I would need to pack and —

"There is no time! Grab important items that are not replaceable, such as family heirlooms, if you have any."

Aaron must have sensed the urgency in my voice because he moved quickly around his room. He began to pack some clothes.

"No, you can get more clothes in Copenhagen." I grabbed Sonia's hand and then Aaron's and pulled them with me. We were able to leave the cave without being seen. We had to hide from vampires in the abandoned manor above the cavern. It was dusk and they were headed out on patrol. This also meant that Ramdasha would be on his way to the dungeon to kill me. In fact, he might already know that I was no longer there.

"Why are we hiding?" Aaron whispered.

"If Ramdasha finds me, I'm dead. And you will be too, if you are found with me."

"Follow me. I know another way." Sonia led us up some stairs and eventually into an old bedroom. She stopped in front of a dusty fireplace covered in cobwebs.

"What now?" Aaron asked.

Sonia removed a brick from the fireplace, revealing a small lever. She pulled the lever and the fireplace moved aside, unveiling a staircase leading upward. We disappeared into the fireplace, which closed behind us. This led us to the rooftop.

"We should be able to take flight from here without being seen," Sonia said.

I hoped so. Ramdasha's patrols would be heading out all over the city. After being captured once, I did not want to be caught again. We ran at full speed, taking flight off the roof.

I did not even begin to let my guard down until the city was safely behind us.

Well outside the outer city wall Sonia paused to give her city one last glance. In that short time I had grown fond of the city. It was difficult to leave. Aaron took Sonia's hand and turned her toward the west. If leaving this magnificent city was difficult for me, I could only imagine how my companions were feeling.

I searched the horizon for a large city to the northwest. We flew over small villages and a large monastery isolated high on a hill. Finally, sprawling buildings came into view. *That must be Adrianople.*

"There." I pointed to the city. "We have to meet someone."

"Who?" Aaron sounded concerned.

"Elijah."

"Who is Elijah?"

"You may know of him as the son of Lord Chastellain," I said.

"Wait! You mean to tell me you know Lord Chastellain?" Sonia said.

"You have been spying for the Court the entire time you lived in our coven?" Aaron asked.

"Not exactly and it is not your coven anymore," I said.

We landed outside of town. I gave Sonia a hug. It was clear that leaving the Queen of Cities and her remaining family behind was difficult. We proceeded to walk down the main street as humanly as possible — meaning that we walked frustratingly slow. It did not take long to find a local inn. I spotted Elijah immediately. He was sitting in the far corner keeping a watchful eye over the place. Relief flooded through me. I'd thought I would never see him again. I lost my composure once again and threw my arms around him.

"What is the matter?" Elijah asked. "You are trembling."

"I'm better now. It was a long day though."

I turned to find Sonia staring at us with her mouth open and Aaron was wide eyed.

"Let me introduce you," I said. "This is Prince Chastellain." To Elijah, I added, "This is Sonia and Aaron of Constantinople."

Sonia gathered her composure and bowed. "My Lord."

Elijah critically studied them. "Are you sure we can trust them?"

"Yes, I trust them. They do not agree with Ramdasha's plans for vampire domination."

Elijah surveyed them for a moment longer. "Let's get as many miles between us and Constantinople as we can."

We quickly left the inn and were soon flying northwest.

The night was perfect, nothing but clear skies and the stars shone bright. There were rolling green forests and occasionally glistening lakes and rivers. Autumn had fully set in as we moved north. My vampire eyes allowed me to see the shades of red and gold leaves. Being able to fly was the best part of this new life. It was the only thing that brought any enjoyment. Flying made me feel alive. While imprisoned, I had been sure I would never fly again. *Could it be that I am grateful to be alive?*

CHAPTER 34 COPENHAGEN
1260 AD

It was well into the night, yet well before dawn, when I saw a city ahead. It was much smaller than Constantinople. I could see a large castle outside of town.

"Almost there." Elijah smiled.

He must be relieved to be home, I thought.

I could not believe we were already here. *Flying is much faster than running.* We flew high over the city and headed for the castle. Elijah landed on a massive terrace on an upper level. This palace was at least five times bigger than their home outside of Ludus.

"This place is ... wonderful!" Sonia said.

Elijah took my hand and looked to the others. "Let me show you to your new rooms."

Aaron studied us for a moment. "So that is why you were not interested in Riddick?"

I did not know what he meant until I saw that he was staring at Elijah's hand in mine. I did not think twice about it before but now I felt uneasy, so I quickly dropped Elijah's hand. "We are not together."

Sonia and Aaron looked at each other with raised eyebrows — clearly not believing me.

"Who is Riddick?" Elijah's voice was deeper than usual. Something flashed through his pale blue eyes — anger, perhaps.

"Oh no. I should not have mentioned it," Aaron said under his breath.

I turned to face Elijah. "I have so much to tell you but let's get them settled in first." There I was, back in another tangle, with someone I did not love bidding for my affections. I trusted Elijah and cared for him. Yet I did not love him as I did Teller. *Will I ever be able to love again?* I had to remind myself that, although it felt like a long time ago, it had only been a hair over two months since I'd lost Teller. *I need more time.*

Elijah gave us a brief tour of some of the main rooms. The Great Hall was breathtaking and the library — spectacular. This palace put the mansion in Ludus and Ramdasha's quarters to shame.

He showed Sonia and Aaron to adjacent rooms. They seemed pleased with the place and content to retire to their new rooms. Elijah showed me to a room one floor up from theirs.

"Where is your room?" I asked.

He pointed to the door across from us.

Of course, I thought. "Where are your father's quarters?" I wanted to avoid Lord Chastellain for as long as possible.

"Down the corridor on the right." Elijah gestured. "I will let you get settled in. I need to inform Father that I am back and that you are here."

"Settled in — that won't take long. I brought nothing and have nothing." I had not even returned for my precious cloak for daytime walking. "Elijah, I have so much to tell you about Ramdasha's plans."

"Good. Let me ease Father's mind that we are well, then I will return."

I was glad he was not taking me to his father right away. The thought of seeing the lord again was unsettling, to say the least. I hated him for what he had done to me — what he had taken from me — which was everything. I nodded to Elijah and retired to my third new room in under three months. *Is this what being a vampire is like, always on the move? I hope not.*

It was not a room; a chamber might be a better word for it. It was huge, with high ceilings and a large four-poster bed. The bed had its own canopy and silk curtains draped elegantly down to the floor. High windows with heavy curtains lined the far wall — to keep out the sunlight, no doubt. Amongst the windows were tall elegantly carved wooden doors leading out onto a large balcony.

The view was wondrous. To the west, pristine faraway lakes glistened in the moonlight and not far off, lanterns in the city could be seen shining brightly. Fall was already coming to an end this far north. Some of the trees had already lost their brightly colored leaves.

To the east of the city there was nothing but water, a seemingly endless ocean. It reminded me of the waters to the south of Constantinople. I could smell the sweet seawater from here.

The sky in the east was growing brighter. Soon the sun would be up and I did not have a cloak to help protect my eyes. To have to leave the balcony and the beautiful views would be difficult. Yet I would soon have to retire inside. I was still on the balcony when a slight swish of air moved across me and Elijah appeared at my side.

"What do you think? I hope you will like it here." His voice was low and soft.

"It is beautiful. The palace, the view, everything — it is too much. You are very gracious to allow us in your home. Thank you."

"The Oresund. Magnificent, isn't it?" Elijah had been looking out over the vast waters to the east

"And the city, is that Copenhagen?" I asked.

"Aye, a wonderful place." We studied the scene a bit longer before he continued, "I had this room prepared for you. I'd hoped it would be yours someday."

"You are too kind and generous." The guilt was difficult to contend with. I did not deserve all this. The previous day and night came flooding into my memory. *Where should I start?*

"Two nights ago when you found me, I had been attending a banquet that Ramdasha held for Lord Mendoza of Portugal and Lord Belleaire of France. Ramdasha is trying to gain supporters so he will be powerful enough to challenge the High Court of Elders. Riddick said that the Portuguese and French Lords were joining Ramdasha. Ramdasha toasted them, calling them 'comrades.'"

Elijah's brow furrowed. "This is not good news. To lose the support of Portugal and France brings us one step closer to war. How many others have pledged their support to Ramdasha?"

"Riddick said that his only other supporters were in Macedonia and a small coven of vampires in Bulgaria. He also informed me that Hungary is reluctant to defy the Elders at this point. Ramdasha is still trying to convince their leaders to join him."

"How many are in Ramdasha's coven in Constantinople?"

"Twenty, now that we left."

A warm smile came over Elijah's face. "We must arrange a meeting with the Elders straightaway. It may have been fortuitous that you wandered into Constantinople after all."

The thought of seeing Lord Chastellain again made my stomach turn. It was difficult to fully grasp the idea that he was on the right side. He was fighting to keep vampires a secret and protecting humans as much as possible but in my mind he was still the enemy. I could never forgive him. "I don't want to see your father."

"I understand. My father has done horrible things. He wanted me to be happy, that is why he turned you. He ..." Elijah trailed off. "It is complicated."

I nodded; I would have to put my personal feelings aside. It was more important that the lord and the rest of the Elders knew Ramdasha's plans.

"Who is this ... Riddick?" Elijah frowned.

"He is Ramdasha's right-hand man, a skilled warrior and he is training Ramdasha's coven to fight. He is a henchman, of sorts. He cares only about personal gain and status. I started training with him and avoided his advances. As I learned more about Ramdasha's aspirations, it dawned on me that I could use him to gain information — the information I just revealed to you."

Elijah's expression remained stern. "He was enamored with you and he told you all this?"

I nodded.

"How far did you have to … take this relationship?" The hardness was back in his voice.

"I did not sleep with him, if that is what you are asking. Though it is none of your business!" I headed inside; the new day's sun was stinging my eyes.

Elijah followed. "I'm sorry; you are right. You are not promised to me but you know how I feel about you."

I sat down on the edge of the bed. Elijah sat beside me. He gently rubbed a hand down my hair.

I grabbed his hand to stop him. I had to deal with this sooner rather than later. "You know how much I loved Teller. It has been under three months since I lost him. Since I lost everything. I need … time."

Elijah's stormy eyes were raging. He nodded. "I have waited hundreds of years to find someone whom I wanted to be with for an eternity. I can wait another hundred years if I must." He gave the slightest smile. "Though I pray it does not take that long."

He was wonderful. *I don't deserve a man like Elijah anyway,* I thought. I resisted the urge to lay my head on his shoulder — to be comforted by him. I made myself move to the window instead. I peered out at the breathtaking view of the sun rising from the ocean.

"I have news of my own." He hesitated. "Our fathers have been writing to each other."

I could not believe it. News from home! My heart leapt into my throat. I turned to Elijah with wide expectant eyes.

"Your father's letters say that, while he is respecting your wish to be left alone, Teller never believed for an instant that you joined a convent." Elijah chuckled, apparently amused by my lie. "Teller has searched several convents around Ludus. He has made his way as far as Targoviste, so I hear. Since he has not found you, obviously, his suspicions that you ran off with me are becoming more predominant. Father assured Adam that we had not seen you since we left town — which was true at the time."

Of course. We all left town at the same time. It would make sense that I had disappeared with the Chastellains.

"I would not be surprised to find Teller at our doorstep someday," Elijah continued. "Some of the townspeople blame us for the murders and your kidnapping. Some even suspect us of being monsters. Others think we are innocent — two lovers who ran off together."

I sat down hard on the bed. "It would be dangerous for Teller to come here, wouldn't it?"

"I would say so. There is an average of thirty vampires who come and go from here. One lone human would be in trouble if any of them were hungry."

I shivered at the thought. "Will I ever be able to go home … even for a visit?"

"Perhaps, someday. I will help you learn to control your thirst and perhaps not to kill your prey. I've been working on it and I'm getting better."

Could that be possible? Could I learn to feed without killing? That would be inconceivably wonderful. Excitement rushed through my veins. Father's warning came to mind, *if something is too good to be true then it usually is. Don't get your hopes up,* I told myself. "You are toying with me?"

Elijah laughed. "No, I would not joke about this. It has taken me a long time but I have done it. Hopefully, you will be able to do the same, in due time. For now, I must organize a meeting of the Elders. We will call for you soon." He turned in the doorway on his way out. "You know, I did try to stop you from feeding."

I smiled. "I know." He was a true friend. He respected my choices. He also let me go when I needed to be alone. That was why I trusted him and could not stay angry with him. His father was another matter entirely.

CHAPTER 35 COPENHAGEN 1260 AD

It was indeed soon when the High Court of Elders called for me. By nightfall, a knock came at the door. I expected Elijah but instead it was a vaguely familiar vampire — judging by his scent. This was no place for humans anyway.

"Good evening, My Lady. The lord has requested your presence. Please follow me."

I eyed him intently. "Don't I know you?"

"Yes, My Lady. I have seen you before."

"I remember. You came to lunch to deliver a message to Lord Chastellain back in Ludus," I said.

"That is right. It is good to see you again, My Lady. Welcome to the family."

Family? I thought as we walked down the hall. *Is this a family?* I was skeptical.

"I don't even know your name," I said.

"My name is John. I have been with Lord Chastellain for roughly seven hundred years."

"You are the one who raised Elijah … while his father was … away?" I was not sure I should be discussing the past so openly.

"That is correct. Elijah is like a son to me. I am grateful for the immortal life the lord gave me. I do anything and everything the family requires." John spoke with pride and confidence.

This was fascinating. It was as if John lived to serve Chastellain. He actually felt blessed to have been turned into a vampire. I clearly did not share this feeling, nor did I understand John's intense loyalty to Chastellain.

John walked me to Aaron's and Sonia's rooms and requested that they attend the emergency meeting of the High Court of Elders. They agreed to follow but glanced at one another with worried expressions.

"All will be well," I tried to reassure them. Yet because of my own trepidation at seeing Chastellain again, I was not entirely sure my attempt to comfort them was convincing. "How are you liking it here so far?" I changed the subject.

"This place is spectacular," Sonia whispered.

"I will tell you after this meeting." Aaron gave me a nervous smile.

I tried to put them at ease with a smile of my own. I hoped it helped.

The Great Hall was sparsely decorated, with plenty of open floor space. The floor was the same glassy marble as the Hagia Sophia but much more colorful. Large squares of marble were placed in a white, dark green and black pattern. The ceilings were wondrously high and there was a dais that held a long row of chairs — or thrones, rather. In the center was the most elaborately decorated throne. It was made of intricately molded gold with bright red cushions. On it sat the figure of a man I had hoped never to see again — Lord Chastellain.

Elijah was seated to the right of his father. To the right of Elijah was Samuel. I quickly counted twelve Elders of the Court and there were another dozen vampires standing or sitting about the room. Many of the others looked like guards or servants. Lord Chastellain stood as we approached.

Here we go. Control your temper. Remember, he is not all bad, I tried to encourage myself.

"Welcome to Denmark, My Lady." Lord Chastellain's smile could be perceived as being warm or mocking.

How does he do that? Both pleasant and evil at the same time. I thought. My jaw tightened.

"I told my son not to fear, that we would see you again soon. I am impressed you made it out there on your own for as long as you did." Lord Chastellain kissed my hand.

I gave the slightest bow, trying my hardest to be respectful, as heat rushed to my cheeks. *Was he antagonizing me — taunting me, even?* If that was the case, he was succeeding. I said nothing out of fear that, if I spoke, it would be an insult. We stared at each other for a tense moment and after getting no response from me, he moved on to Aaron.

"My Lord." Aaron bowed deeply. "I am Aaron of Constantinople and this is Sonia." He gestured to the little girl, who was — ironically — older than I.

Lord Chastellain eyed Aaron for quite some time. It was as if he could see into Aaron's soul. Finally, the lord smiled. "Welcome, Aaron of Constantinople. Are you comfortable here thus far?"

"Yes, My Lord, thank you," Aaron said.

"Do let us know if there is anything you need." Chastellain moved to greet Sonia.

Aaron stepped closer to Sonia as well. I realized he was positioning himself to protect her if needed.

"My dear." He gently took Sonia's hands in his. "So young. Who would turn such a beautiful, innocent maiden into one of us?"

"It was ..." Sonia's voice was barely audible. "I was turned by Lord Ramdasha," she managed to get out.

Chastellain watched her patiently with a gentleness that I had never seen in him before.

Sonia went on, "He thought that young humans who were turned into vampires would be more easily led ... meaning, they would be more likely to follow him without question. He created a number of us."

Slowly, so as not to startle the young girl, the lord raised his hand to her cheek. "My sweet dear. But his plan did not work, now, did it?

You were not willing to follow him blindly, as you are here." He spoke with the compassion of a loving father.

Sonia leaned her cheek into his hand, as if gaining comfort from it. "Yes, My Lord." Her voice was more confident.

Aaron gave me a questioning look. I shrugged in response, as I had never seen this side of the lord. He seemed sincere but this was not the man I remembered and hated.

I thought of my first meeting with Ramdasha. He had been so blatantly cold and calculating that, thankfully, I had told him nothing but lies. Lord Chastellain was able to win Sonia over with a few kind words. She was openly willing to tell him the truth about how she had been turned. He even appeared to gain her allegiance, something Ramdasha had failed to do with either of us. I had a feeling that Chastellain had compassion for the young-looking girl but even if it was feigned, I could not help admiring his approach.

Perhaps he is indeed a good leader maybe even a great one. This thought filled me with hope. I was reminded of something I had read while in Constantinople. *If leaders inspired allegiance with love and compassion, then their armies would be stronger than any commanded with fear. An army driven by loyalty and respect for their leader would best an army driven by a lust for power and the fear of their leader.*

"I welcome all three of you into the Court as allies. These are the Elders," Chastellain gestured toward the long row of twelve chairs. "They are the leaders, or the respective ambassadors from our allies in the North."

Samuel stepped forward. He took my hand and kissed it. "It is a great pleasure to see you again, My Lady."

I smiled and bowed slightly in response.

The lord had returned to his throne. "You have news for us from Ramdasha's coven?"

I recounted everything to the Elders. They seemed displeased with the news of losing France and Portugal's support.

Aaron confirmed my story, as he had listened to Ramdasha and Riddick, as best he could at the banquet. Aaron added that he had overheard two of Ramdasha's guards saying that they would be escorting Ramdasha to Hungary within the next couple of days. "I can only assume that it is to try to persuade the Hungarian coven to join his cause," Aaron finished.

"We must send liaisons to Hungary at once," one of the Elders said. I recognized him as Lord Alexandru from the Chastellains' ball in Ludus.

"Perhaps I myself should go," Lord Chastellain said. "We can't afford to lose Hungary."

I had to agree; if anyone could convince the leaders in Hungary to remain loyal to the Elders, it was Lord Chastellain. "My son and I will leave at once," the lord finished.

My stomach dropped. "Aaron," I whispered, "was Riddick one of the guards accompanying Ramdasha?"

"Of course, why?"

"My Lord, if I may." I ventured to take a step toward Chastellain. "I do not think it wise that Elijah accompany you."

The lord raised an eyebrow.

Oh no, how do I explain? "You see, one of the guards who will be protecting Ramdasha does not care for ... your son, not for political reasons but for ..." *How do I say it?* "He views Elijah as a romantic rival, so to speak. Elijah's presence would only infuriate him. He may even challenge Elijah. Elijah would be a distraction from peaceful negotiations."

"A romantic rival? Explain yourself." Chastellain eyed me with disapproval.

"Well," I started slow. "This guard is Ramdasha's commander in chief. He was ... taken with me."

"I'm sure." Chastellain rubbed his fingers against his forehead.

"He is the one who gave me the information I revealed to you. He was upset when I was seen with Elijah. They captured me and Ramdasha planned to execute me but this guard, Riddick, freed me."

Elijah looked concerned, as did Aaron and Sonia. I had not told them this part.

"I see, so this man ... Riddick still cares for you and would see Elijah as a rival. Very well, Elijah will stay here and take my place at the head of the Court." Lord Chastellain's tone made it clear that this was final. He eyed me with suspicion for a moment, then exited the room.

Elijah came to my side. "You did not tell me they captured you."

"There was no need. I am safe now," I said.

"I want you to know that you can tell me anything."

"I know but you needn't worry." I tried to console him by holding his gaze.

"Well, that is it, I'm never letting you out of my sight again."

"Don't be ridiculous." My ever-growing independent spirit retorted.

CHAPTER 36 COPENHAGEN 1260 AD

Elijah was true to his word. He rarely left my side. We spent our time together training, flying or swimming. Swimming in the ocean was better than freshwater swimming. He showed me creatures that were entirely foreign. I loved watching them gracefully move through the water. Their calming effect made me forget all my worries.

Much of our time was spent training. I still needed to know how to fight, especially if war was indeed inevitable. I had a strong desire to be able to defend myself against vampires. Elijah fully agreed. The better one could fight, the safer one would be. He, like Riddick, was a good fighter and teacher. Aaron and Sonia often trained with us, as well as other vampires in the castle.

After a week's time, the lord returned from Hungary. This gave Elijah even more time, as he no longer had to fill his father's seat in the High Court. The lord reported that Hungary would remain with us. Ramdasha was obviously not pleased to see Chastellain arrive and quickly retreated. It appeared that war was postponed.

That night, Elijah came to my room. "It is time for a feeding lesson."

"But I will not have to feed for weeks," I protested.

"The longest I have been able to go without feeding was six weeks. What I have found is that if I feed every two to three weeks, I can take less blood and therefore I am less likely to kill. When I am not starved, I can more easily remain in control. It is easier to make myself stop feeding. This leaves the human weak and unconscious but alive."

This was logical. Why had I not thought of it before?

"You remember the farmer from Ludus? What was his name?"

"Luka and yes, I remember him," I snapped.

"Right. With Luka I finally learned to control my thirst. He survived. Well, that was until he escaped and I had to kill him so he would not tell the villagers about us. Once I could control myself and not kill, it dawned on me that the answer was simple. I needed to change my hunting strategy so the people did not see me. This way I could leave them alive and they would not know it was I. It has worked perfectly, this way we remain hidden and the human survives." Elijah paused to let this sink in, then continued. "It has been a week or so since you last fed and two weeks for me. So tonight I will show you how I do it and then you can practice as well."

I was skeptical. "I don't know. I can't be around all that blood while you feed. What if I lose control? I don't want to hurt anybody if I don't have to."

"If you are going to learn to control your hunger, you must start pushing yourself. If you ever want to be around humans again, you must get used to their smell and learn to control yourself."

He was undoubtedly right. Yet I had a foreboding feeling that innocent people were going to die in the process. Then again, how was that any different from what I was doing now? I must try! With a rush of excitement, I stood. "Let's go."

"It would be helpful to have one more with us."

It did not take much to persuade Sonia to come with us. She also wanted to learn how not to kill. We wandered the streets of Copenhagen. When Elijah spotted his prey, he disappeared in a flash. Sonia and I slowly followed. We were behind a row of buildings off one of the main streets. Elijah no longer resembled a handsome young man; a stony gray monster was in his place. His bright yellow eyes shone like lanterns in the night. He grabbed a woman from behind. His two-inch fangs quickly pierced her neck and she soon went limp in his steel grip. In less than half the time it normally took for a vampire to drink their fill, he released the woman and laid her down gently. He looked like a human again as he approached us.

The sweet smell of blood was intoxicating. I had to place my hand over my mouth and nose. Sonia followed my lead.

"Listen," Elijah said. "Her heart is still beating, she is merely unconscious from the loss of blood. Yet she will wake."

Sonia lost control. She lunged forward to attack the woman. I threw my body into hers. This made a loud sound like rocks slamming together. It took both Elijah and me to restrain her.

"Let's get her out of here." Elijah said. We took flight, each holding one of her arms as she struggled against us. Once the smell of blood faded, she stopped struggling and we landed.

"I'm so sorry!" she said.

"There is no need to be sorry. It takes time and practice. I could not do it at first. I doubt any vampire could." Elijah said, before carrying on with the lesson. "The key is to always approach from behind so they will not see you. That lady will not know it was a vampire who attacked her, as she never saw us. While you drink, focus on their heartbeat. When it starts to slow and they go limp, you know it is time to stop. Any more and they will not recover. To focus on the heartbeat also helps to keep the monster inside from fully taking over. It takes powerful discipline and control. Are you ready to try?"

"I will forego it." Sonia sounded feeble.

"The longer you wait, the more difficult it will be to control yourself," Elijah warned.

I was not at all confident but volunteered to go next anyway. We sped to a different part of the town. I found a man sitting on a bench alone. I had to take a moment to gather my wits about me. *Concen-*

trate; I can do this! I took a deep breath. I appeared behind him and quickly secured his shoulders. My fangs sank into his neck. The blood was delicious; I felt myself lose control; the monster was threatening to take over.

Through the blurry confusion of my bloodlust I strained to think only of my victim's heartbeat. The drumming slowed and the man went limp in my grip. The voice in my head was screaming at the monster to stop but it was out of my control. It wanted more and refused to release the man.

Through a haze, I could hear Elijah telling me to stop. Two sets of hands pulled me off. Soon I was in the air, this time being flown by Sonia and Elijah. Sonia covered her nose and mouth against the sweet smell, to help her stay in control.

When we landed, I sat in an empty street with my head down. "I would have killed him," I whispered.

"Ah, but you did not. He will survive," Elijah said.

"Only because you pulled me off." A feeling of sheer misery consumed me.

"It will get easier and you will do it on your own eventually."

We all decided that that was enough blood for one night and headed home.

We kept practicing; we went out once a week to try to feed without killing. At first, it was entirely woeful. Sonia and I each killed someone when we could not be pulled away fast enough. I was losing hope, when one night it happened! It had been a couple of months of practicing but I finally was able to control the monster inside and my friends did not have to pull me off.

"He will live!" I stretched my arms to the sky. "This is the best day of my life!" I yelled into the night.

Elijah picked me up and swung me around. The storm in his eyes had subsided; they appeared more blue than gray. "I knew you could do it!" He swung my legs up so that he was cradling me in his arms.

I wrapped my arms around his neck. "Thank you," I whispered in his ear and kissed his cheek. The starlight danced in his eyes — the usual sad storm was nowhere to be found. I was caught in his gaze and lost track of time and space.

Sonia cleared her throat. "Should I leave you two alone?"

This broke the spell. I swung my legs down and released myself from Elijah's arms. It was not until she spoke that I realized I had completely lost myself in his gaze. *What was that about?* "No, no, please don't go," I managed to say.

"What is it between you two? You are obviously taken with each other. Why do you deny it?" Sonia asked.

"Deny what? There is nothing to deny," I said.

Sonia gave me a disapproving frown and looked to Elijah for help in understanding what was going on.

"Don't look at me," Elijah said. "I don't deny anything. She knows how I feel about her."

"That is enough. This is a happy moment. Let us celebrate!" I did not like where the conversation had gone or the growing confusion I was feeling. He could virtually control me with his eyes, or at least influence me. I didn't like it. I wanted to change the subject and simply be content with this major accomplishment. I might never have to kill anyone ever again! Life as a vampire might be acceptable after all.

CHAPTER 37 COPENHAGEN 1260 AD

After only a brief knock, Sonia barged into Aaron's room back at the Chastellain castle. "She did it; she did it," Sonia sang.

Aaron looked up from his ever-present writing. "That can't be. It is not possible for any vampire to stop once they have started feeding, let alone a new vampire."

"She left the man alive and we did not have to pull her away," Elijah said.

"If you can do it, then I know I can," Aaron joked.

"I'd like to see you try," I challenged.

"Well, I might have to."

Elijah held up a jug of mead. "This calls for a celebration." He quickly poured four flagons of the honey-colored liquid. We toasted to a future of not killing. The mead tasted sweet, much better than that dry, bitter red wine everyone seemed so fond of.

We laughed and joked for quite some time. My spirits were high. *I will never kill again*, I promised myself.

"Soon you will be ready for the next phase. We will go ten days without feeding and then two weeks. Eventually, you will be able to go about three weeks. That is as far as I have pushed it anyway," Elijah said.

"I cannot wait." I was beginning to tame the beast inside. This gave me a strong feeling of power and control. I would set myself free from the monster — well, as free as possible anyway. Until tonight I had not fully realized how imprisoned I had been by the beast — helpless against it. *Not anymore.*

The excitement of the previous night finally took its toll and I needed to rest. Elijah walked me to my room and I knew he wanted me to invite him in.

"Thank you for everything. I don't know how I could ever repay you," I said.

"You know how you could repay me."

I did not like the longing in his eyes — it flustered me. "I need to ... rest." I gave him a quick kiss on his cheek. "Good night ... day, well, evening — whatever it is."

He chuckled.

I retreated into my room — quick to shut the door behind me.

Since I was feeling more in control over my feeding needs, my thoughts strayed to home. I fell fast asleep as soon as my head touched the pillow. For the first time in a long time, dreams of home flooded my sleep.

I'm sure that it had not been much more than an hour's time when I woke to a figure standing by my bed. I did not want to stop dreaming of home but this startled me awake.

"Sorry. I did not mean to scare you," Elijah said. "It is dusk and there is something I want to show you. Come with me." He took my hand and pulled me out of bed.

Feeling refreshed and ready for another adventure, I followed him to the balcony. I slept for only an hour most nights and could go for a night or two without any sleep if needed.

In an instant, we took flight from the balcony. We flew higher and higher. When we were well over the ocean, Elijah tucked his large wings in and dived straight for the water. He barely made a splash as he disappeared into the Oresund. I tried to do the same but was sure I made more of a splash. In an eye-blink, the wings were gone and I was speeding through the water after Elijah with my webbed hands and feet.

We swam for quite some time until we came to a rock face protruding up out of the water. Elijah swam deeper, until he reached the bottom of the ocean. He rolled a large boulder out of the way with ease. On the other side of the boulder was a dark cave. He gestured for me to follow. It took my eyes a moment to adjust to the pitch black. Even my extraordinary vampire sight could make out only vague rock walls all around me. I did not like the trapped feeling. I was about to turn around when my head broke the surface of the water.

My lips parted, as I surveyed where we were. A large cave stood before me. Fresh water flowed into the sea from a small waterfall on the far end. Dark green moss grew on the rocks.

"This place is magnificent. How did you ever find it?" I asked.

"I found the cave some fifty or maybe it is closer to a hundred years ago. I put the boulder in front of it to help keep it a secret, from vampires anyway. Humans could never find this place. This is where I come when I need to get away."

"And you are showing *me* your refuge?"

"Of course, I want to share everything with you."

I sighed. Once again, I had to address this issue at once.

"Why are you sad?" Elijah asked.

"Well … it is just that learning to control my feeding has led me to think of home again. I want to return. Perhaps after a couple more months of practice I can go home."

His shoulders tensed and anger brewed in his eyes. He seemed to gain control, which was good because I was about to dive back into the water to get out of there before he punched a hole in the rock wall — or, worse, attacked me. Elijah was old and wise. I was sure he had more control than that but for an instant I questioned that assumption.

He knelt down in front of where I was seated on a rock and took my hands in his. "You are one of us now. You don't belong with humans. We are your family."

"Family? Your father does not like me and I am not fond of him either."

Elijah put his head down and shook it. "He thinks you are trouble."

"Trouble?"

"He says you will break my heart. He is probably right."

The guilt settled into my stomach like a boulder. I did not want to hurt Elijah. I cared about him. Confusion overtook me. Part of me wanted to stay here forever. I could get lost in his stormy eyes and perhaps someday love him as I loved Teller. Or could I? No, I belonged with Teller and my father. And my brother! Who was taking care of them? I'd never thought I would be able to care for them again but maybe, just maybe, I could. If there was any chance at all, I had to go back.

What about Elijah, Sonia and Aaron? Well, they do not need caring for, I justified. *This is ridiculous. There are beautiful vampires coming and going from Chastellain's castle all the time. Elijah did not need me.*

"Elijah, there are plenty of noble ladies who would love your affections. Why me?"

"That is correct. I courted many women, especially when I was younger. I quickly grew tired of the selfish vampires who were only interested in me for the status and power. Do you know why we stayed in Ludus for so long?"

I shook my head *no* but I had an uneasy suspicion about the answer.

"We would usually go there for shorter periods of time, as sort of a retreat, to get away from Denmark. I saw you in the village market one day. I knew you were different. I watched you for some time. You were so kind and helpful to others. You worked without complaint and loved your father and brother so much. I knew you were the one I wanted. Granted, I did not know you would be so hard to win. I thought you would be captivated by the wealth and power, as others from my past so easily were. Of course, I was wrong and that made me want you all the more."

Elijah was truly good. The thought of hurting him made the boulder in my stomach feel even heavier. If I was to go home, I must go soon. My feelings were becoming more and more confused. Part of me wanted to kiss Elijah to stop him from hurting and part of me wanted to run away. I did not know what to do.

"If you were to return home, it would be dangerous," Elijah reasoned. "You have enemies now. Don't think Ramdasha has forgotten your betrayal. If he were to learn that you have a family, he would hunt them down in retaliation — not to mention, you would be vulnerable without our protection. You are safe here. You would be putting everyone you care about in danger if you returned. You and your family are better off if you stay away."

As reasonable as this sounded, I could not help but think that he was exaggerating the danger. *He does not want me to return to Teller. How would Ramdasha possibly find me in Ludus anyway? Then again, Elijah had found me in Constantinople.* Elijah's words rang though my mind: "The world of vampires is much smaller than the world of humans." I was more confused than ever. I needed to consider the options and not make any rash decisions. I had time, as I had only fed once without killing. I still had to make sure I could control myself before I could make the right choice about going home.

I nodded, as if in agreement. "I will stay … for now." This was the truth.

I could almost see the gray clouds in his eyes give way to the blue. He smiled and put his arm around me. Laying my head on his shoulder, I lost track of how long we sat like that.

CHAPTER 38 COPENHAGEN
1260 AD

I was more determined than ever to feed without killing, as it could mean that I would be able to return home. It was not long after my first successful feeding that Sonia succeeded as well.

I picked her small frame up and swung her around. I slightly tossed her up and she landed gracefully on her feet with a bow. Elijah and I applauded.

"You did it! Congratulations," I said.

She beamed with excitement. "Let's tell Aaron!" She ran off in a blur and we followed.

When we caught up with Sonia she was hugging Aaron's neck. "I did it; I did it," she sang.

"Did what?" came a voice behind us.

We turned to find Samuel standing in Aaron's doorway.

"I fed without killing!" Sonia announced.

"That is not possible." Samuel issued his usual carefree smile.

"Honestly. Elijah has been teaching us and Val's done it twice," Sonia said. "I knew once I saw Val do it, that I could, too. You have to try, Aaron, please! Anyone can do it with practice and we can help you."

Aaron looked at Sonia in utter disbelief. Then, as if giving in to her enthusiasm, he conceded. "Very well, I will try."

She squealed and jumped into his arms. She was so endearing. We all chuckled at the newly forming couple — or at least that's what they appeared to be.

"We can teach you as well, Samuel," Elijah said.

"You are all mad. It is not possible to control yourself while feeding."

"Let us show you that it *is* possible," I said.

He studied us for a moment to make sure we were not joking. "Very well, prove it."

"This is excellent!" I said. "Elijah's School for Vampires. Think of the possibilities. We can teach any vampires who are willing."

I was truly excited about the idea of helping vampires not to kill. How wonderful that would be! But then I remembered home. My mind was made up. As soon as I was ready, I would return.

Elijah opened more mead and we toasted. Elijah looked at Samuel as if realizing he must have come looking for him. "Is something amiss? Does Father need me?"

"No, all is well. Since when do I need a reason to want to see my dearest friend? Someone has been taking up all your time." Samuel looked pointedly at me. "I was simply missing our old carefree days as bachelors."

Elijah chuckled. "To carefree days."

We all raised our chalices, again.

My thoughts strayed. I would miss my new friends. Samuel and Aaron's blithe natures were contagious. Sonia was so sweet. I felt protective of her and of course Elijah …

Perhaps someday I could return, when I was sure my family was cared for. *What does that mean? Dead?* I did not like to think too much about the far future, or about not growing older while my family did. It was complicated but I had to make sure my father was taken care of as he aged. I had to return and try to be normal. I would regret it forever if I did not. Forever could be a long time for a vampire.

I had plans to slip away alone. It was only a matter of when. At first, I thought of returning as a nun. But that would not do because, while I had no idea how a human-vampire relationship would fare, I was returning to be with Teller. Or at least I would try to mend things between us. Hopefully he will forgive me for leaving him. I could not deceive myself about this. My chest ached with longing when I thought about him and my pulse quickened at the thought of seeing him again.

I did not know what I would tell everyone back home. I supposed the lie would have to be that I had changed my mind … *again* — like a silly fickle little girl and that the convent had not worked out. Though the ruse was not ideal, it might be believable.

I stayed with the Chastellain coven for six more months. The winter was brutal — by human standards. The world outside my balcony became a glistening frozen wasteland and there was much less sunlight but we did not mind it in the least. In fact, since the bitter cold did not bother us, this environment was ideal for vampires. Now I understood why they preferred the weather in the North.

By the spring, I was becoming quite skilled at not killing. I could go three weeks in between having to eat. I knew the time was right. I had also been keeping my distance from Elijah. We were still together a good deal but I did not allow myself to be tempted to find comfort in being close to him. No more hand holding, arms over shoulders — that type of closeness.

I spoke to no one of my plans to return home. When Elijah wanted to be closer, I would tell him I needed more time. He seemed pleased, as long as I was around and not talking of going home anymore.

I planned to take two of the most basic gowns I could find out of the large wardrobe the Chastellains had supplied my chambers with and a handful of small provisions. Even these "basic" clothes were too fancy for my poor village. They had been embroidered with thick golden necklines and gold trim, yet they would have to do. The other thing I needed was a hooded cloak for daylight walking. This was the only thing I ever asked Elijah for. Of course, it was outrageously fancy.

They had a human tailor come to the castle from Copenhagen to take my measurements for the cloak. The poor little man was escorted in and out of the castle by two guards — who had recently fed. The tailor most likely thought it was to protect the nobles and their possessions from him but the sentries were actually for his protection.

When the finished cloak arrived, it was nothing like what I had asked for, which was an inexpensive rain cloak made of common leather. Instead, it was made of silk. The hues of purple changed colors with each movement. It was the most beautiful fabric I had ever seen. The finishing touch was a gold trim. *How will I explain this regal cloak to the people of Ludus?*

Elijah draped it around my shoulders and turned me toward the full-length looking glass in my chambers.

"This is too much! I can't accept it," I said.

"You don't like it?" Elijah asked with concern.

"It is the most beautiful cloak I have ever seen but … it is too extravagant for me. A simple cloak would have sufficed." Leather was common and cheap, unlike the impossibly soft and thick foreign fabric of this cloak. "Besides, purple is the most difficult dye to make, making it the most expensive and it is illegal. It is meant only for the emperors and empresses of the Eastern Roman Empire."

Elijah laughed. "You are no longer in the East and that is not the law here. Besides, as vampires we are immune to such trifles."

What Elijah did not know was that I planned to return to the East. Yet it was highly unlikely that Emperor Michael would discover me wearing purple in Ludus.

He stood behind me, looking over my shoulder in the mirror. His hands were on my shoulders. "It suits you perfectly." His voice was full of affection.

Too much affection; the guilt was overwhelming. *How can I accept this, when my plans are to leave him?* I shrugged the cloak off and threw it on the bed.

I would need it to go out during the day as a "human" in Ludus. I would have to have it. This cloak was meant for an empress in winter, not a poor girl in the summer.

"Thank you," I finally said, swallowing my guilt.

"It is nothing."

~

THE TIME CAME — the time to return home. It was hard to think about leaving my new friends but my excitement at seeing my family and old friends outweighed my trepidations.

The final thing I had to do was leave a note. It read:

MY DEAREST FRIEND ELIJAH,

I am truly sorry to leave you but I must return home. Please understand and please do not follow me, as I am sure that would not end well for anyone. I wish you the very best in love and happiness. Do not wait for me.

Val

I LEFT this on my pillow at dusk and was gone. There was no point in trying to lie to Elijah about where I was going. He knew the only other place I wanted to be was home. I told myself that he would not be overly hurt. Certainly, he would be angry at first but he would soon move on.

In a little over an hour, I was almost home. I landed in the woods surrounding Ludus and was about to walk into the village when it dawned on me, *I can't wander home in the middle of the night on foot. I must think like a human. A young woman would not travel alone ... well, ever, let alone at night.* I bit my lower lip. *What to do?*

I would have to go to a neighboring village and hire a cart to take me to Ludus during the day. That was how people traveled and how I would have returned if I had still been human. It had been over ten months since I left home, granted it felt like a lifetime. I had not had to act like a human in quite some time. This would be a difficult adjustment — for everyone.

CHAPTER 39 LUDUS 1261 AD

I left the forest outside of Ludus and flew to a neighboring town. At first light I found a man who was willing to take me to Ludus by cart.

I opened the small travel bag I had brought and offered him a hand mirror with beautiful gold trim. "I presume there is a lady in your life who would fancy this." I was sure to raise my voice so he could hear me. I would have to get used to talking loud for humans.

He looked at the mirror with wide eyes. "Are you sure, madam? This is worth more than a ride to Ludus."

"It isn't to me."

"Well, then, let's get you to Ludus." He helped me onto the cart bench.

The ride was painfully slow and my stomach twisted with anticipation. *How would everyone react to my sudden reappearance? Would they believe my lie? Could I control my thirst, being around people again?*

Finally, we arrived at Father's doorstep in late afternoon. It was comforting to see that the village looked the same. With the hood up for protection I approached my old house. *What now? Do I knock or march right in?* It had been my home once but so much had changed. I had changed and this tiny home no longer felt like home. Apparently I had not thought of everything. I decided knocking was best.

Father stared at me for a moment as if I were an apparition.

"Father, it is I."

Another pause. "It is? I can't believe my eyes, my daughter returned to me! ... Josiah, come quickly!"

It felt like heaven when Father hugged me. Tears of joy flowed down my cheeks. *I am home! I'd thought that returning home would be impossible but here I am, in my father's arms again.*

He took my hands to lead me inside but recoiled at the touch of my cold skin. "You are freezing, my dear. Come in by the fire before you catch your death."

I did not feel cold. This was normal for vampires — our permanent temperature. Yet I did not argue as I pretended to warm my hands by the fire. Taking off the outrageous cloak, I placed it over a chair.

Father was thinner than I remembered but other than that he looked largely the same. *He must miss my cooking. Perhaps he is thinner because he has gone without my famous jam tarts.* I smiled at the thought, though it did make me feel guilty for not being able to be here to care for him.

Josiah came racing down the stairs at the urgency in Father's voice. He did not look as surprised as Father had. Unlike Father, Josiah looked very different. He stood taller than I, a good deal taller. He was not a boy anymore but a handsome young man. My heart swelled with pride.

He ran to embrace me.

"I told you she was well, Father." Josiah looked at me and added, "I knew you would return."

I gave him a warm smile and another hug.

He shivered. "You had better stay by that fire, sister, or you will catch a cold."

Lesson number one. I was going to have to refrain from hugging. I had not fully realized how much colder we were than humans.

"Where were you? Did you marry that young lord? Why didn't you write?" Josiah started in with the burning questions.

"Be easy, son; there is time. Let her tell us about her … *adventure* at her own pace. What is important is that she is safe and she is home."

"I appreciate that, Father. It is wonderful to be home! However, you have every right to know where I was, so I do not mind the questions." I wanted to get the lying over with as quickly as possible. I sat down by the fire and started reciting what I had rehearsed. At least this much I had prepared for.

"I traveled to a convent in Constantinople. I studied and worked with the Sisters of the Church. It was wonderful and peaceful at first, no worries or concerns. But in the end, I could not do it. I missed home too much." There, I said it. Hopefully, they would believe this story.

"So you are home to stay?" Josiah asked.

"Yes." I hoped.

"I thought perhaps you returned for my wedding."

"Your wedding!" I stood. "You are getting married?"

"Yes, Sarah and I will marry on midsummer's eve."

"That is … wonderful news." I gave him a brief hug this time and resisted the urge to pick him up off the ground — which, of course, as a human I would not have been able to do.

When we settled down, Josiah's face fell. "You still could have written."

The look on his face cracked my heart into two pieces. The last thing I ever wanted to do was hurt the little brother who had always been there for me. "Leaving was difficult and writing home was too painful," I said.

This was true. At first I did not know if I would ever be able to return, so putting home as far behind me as possible was best for everyone. Besides, the only thing I could have written were lies. "I am so sorry. I hope you can forgive me."

"Well, don't do that to us again," Josiah said.

I nodded in agreement. This was a difficult promise to make. I would try not to leave them again. That was the best I could do.

"My spring flower returns in the spring," Father declared. "We must have a town gathering to celebrate your safe return. Josiah, run and get Teller, will you, my dear boy? He needs to know that our Vallachia is safely back."

Josiah ran out the door.

My heart leapt up into my throat. I had to sit back down to stop myself from trembling. *Does he still want me?* I panicked as the thought occurred to me for the first time — what if he was engaged to someone else? He could have given up on me and rightfully so. *Breathe,* I told myself. *All will be well.*

As always, Father seemed to understand my thoughts and knew exactly what to say. "Don't worry, my dear. Perhaps if I am lucky, both my children will marry this summer."

My first thought was one of joy. *Teller still loves me!* Doubt crept in. *Can this work? A marriage between two different ... creatures?* There was only one way to find out. This was one of the reasons why I had come back. I smiled at Father but surely he could tell I was still nervous.

CHAPTER 40 LUDUS 1261 AD

Teller's large frame appeared in the doorway of my Father's home. He was much more muscular and a bit taller than when I had seen him last. He also looked … older. All traces of boyishness were gone. He was even more beautiful than I remembered. I was overcome with longing. I moved toward him. His bright green eyes looked as if they were filled with relief at seeing me. They quickly turned dark. I remembered those eyes. They reminded me of his father's, full of anger. This was enough to stop my approach. Terrible memories of his father's fury came flooding back.

Neither of us spoke. Josiah shifted uncomfortably.

"Where is your husband?" Teller broke the awkward silence. He looked around as if he expected to find someone else in the home.

"Husband?" I was momentarily confused. It took a split second to realize what he meant.

"She has been in a convent in Constantinople. That denotes abstinence," Father said.

Teller rounded on Adam. "Do you think I don't know that," he snapped.

I stepped forward — I hoped not too quickly — to intervene if need be. I was not about to allow anyone to hurt my father.

Teller turned to me. "Do you actually expect us to believe that rubbish? You in a convent?" His tone was mocking.

My heart raced and I could feel my cheeks flush with anger. "What is that supposed to mean? That I am not virtuous enough to become a nun!" I took a deep breath to calm myself. "Besides, if I had been married and I assume you mean to Elijah, then I would not have left town."

My family looked at me with wide eyes. I was not the same timid girl who had left here last summer. I was stronger and no one was going to push me around, not even the man I loved.

Confusion flashed through Teller's eyes, yet he managed to keep his expression stern.

It was Father who spoke. "My dear, Lord Chastellain and his son are back in Denmark. They left town at the same time you did. That is why Teller ... and others, were convinced that you had run off with the young lord. It does make sense, you see."

"They left?" I tried to sound as if this were news.

"Tell her the rest of the story." Teller spoke through clinched teeth.

Josiah and Father exchanged a wary look.

I was already growing tired of the lies. I knew what was coming and I had to pretend I did not. *It is time to find out how good of an actress I am.*

"You see, my dear," Father started slowly, "the night you left, Luka and our healer Sofia were killed."

I sat down in a chair and put my head in my hands. That horrible night swam through my head. I was truly sorry they were dead. "By whom?" I finally asked. It seemed like the thing to say.

"By your precious nobleman, lord-whatever his name is," Teller spat.

I had never seen him like this. It made me question everything. Perhaps I should not have come back. I had had enough. I stood and approached Teller. *Don't lose control,* I warned myself.

"Would you *stop* calling him mine? I knew nothing of any of this. I came back here for you. Apparently that was a mistake." I glared at Teller.

With this, his demeanor changed. He lowered his head and shook it. He turned to Father. "I'm sorry to have caused a disruption. I am glad your daughter returned to you." With that he left.

At least he had the decency to apologize to Father, I thought.

Josiah stepped forward as if to comfort me but Father stopped him. Father gave Josiah a look that said, *Give her some room.* Josiah backed off.

Yes, I wanted to be alone. How did Father always know what I needed and what was best for me? He was so wonderful. I had known it would not be easy coming home but it was more complicated than I had imagined. I grabbed my cloak and small bag and headed for my room.

It looked exactly the same, as if I had never left. I picked up the blessed patriarchal cross Father had carved for me. That seemed so long ago. I wanted to crush it into a million pieces but refrained and dropped it carelessly back on the small table. It had not protected me. God had abandoned me. I threw myself on the bed.

"Teller will come around in due time," Father was saying to Josiah.

This was horrible — I could hear everything they said. I covered my ears. I had hoped that my reunion with Teller would have gone better but what did I expect? I would have been furious if he had left me to become a bishop or a monk. I would have been even more devastated if I'd thought he had eloped with another woman.

Father was right, of course — give him time. Teller was right as well — Elijah had killed Luka and Sofia. It was strange how things had changed; now that I too had killed, I no longer judged Elijah so harshly. Of course, before I had been turned into a demon, I had hated Elijah for taking innocent lives.

A life of lies. That was what I had come back to. I was unsure if I could live like this. I would not be able to stay in the village forever anyway. After a handful of years, people would notice I was not aging. Maybe I could tell them the truth, or at least tell Father. Then he too would be outraged at the lives my kind took and the villagers would burn me at the stake if I did not flee fast enough.

Maybe after Josiah was married and I could see a couple of nieces and nephews born, then I could tell Father everything and plan to leave again but this time telling him when and why. Perhaps Father and I could live with the Chastellains. Are you out of your mind? I thought. What was I thinking — Father living with thirty vampires? That would never work. Elijah was right — I never should have returned. He was always right, yet I still had not learned to listen to him. Perhaps I never would.

Slow down, I told myself. After all, who knew what the future would hold? I would stay at least until Josiah's wedding, then take each day one by one. I was going to go mad, sitting here trying to figure out what to do. My first thought was to jump out the window. *Think like a human,* I reminded myself. So I slowly walked downstairs instead. "I need to see Mari."

"Grand idea." Father smiled. "She will be glad to see you. She always makes you feel better."

Before I walked out into the sunlight, I swung the elegant cloak over my shoulders and I lifted the hood over my head.

"Vallachia," Father added. "We are glad you're home."

I smiled, even though I was crushed inside. He must be the best father, man and person in the world. I had abandoned him without warning and still he thought only of me. He was truly selfless.

CHAPTER 41 LUDUS 1261 AD

I walked as humanly as possible until I could hear, smell and see that I was alone and then I took off in a flash. It felt good to run. The fresh air helped clear my thoughts. In no time I was at Mari's door. Her mother answered and began screaming at once — or so it sounded to my sensitive ears.

"Oh my dear, it is you! How are you? Mari! You have a guest!"

"I am very well," I spoke softly, trying to quiet her down. She essentially pulled me into the home. I had always thought of Mari's mother as loud and overbearing and had even admired her for this, as she was nothing like me. She was funny and sociable. Now she seemed doubly overbearing and I fought the urge to cover my ears. In fact, once inside, my senses overwhelmed me. The small home was full of people, as Mari had a large family. The smell hit me like a sack of stones and my throat instantly stung.

Keep yourself together! I thought.

When Mari saw me she squealed and threw her arms around my neck. She smelled delectable. I felt the slight ache of the eyetooth, which signaled the growth of ridiculously long fangs. I had to get out of here! I held my breath and as gently as possible pushed Mari away, which ended up with my picking her up by the waist and setting her down at arm's length.

"Do you mind if I borrow your daughter for a bit, ma'am? We have a good deal of catching up to do." I spoke quickly to Mari's mother.

I did not wait for an answer. I grabbed Mari by the wrist and dragged her out the door. Once outside, I bent over and took several deep breaths. This instantly cleared my head and the pain in my throat and jaws subsided.

"Are you ill?" Mari voice was full of concern.

Once back in control, I stood and smiled. "I'm fine. It is nothing that some fresh air can't cure."

Lesson number two — I was going to have to get used to being in confined places with lots of people again. It had been a long time since I'd worked for Anna and Paul in the Dancing Stallion. I had forgotten how hard and painful it could be.

Act normal, I told myself. So I put my arm in hers and we walked at a snail's pace. I thought of Elijah taking leisurely strolls with me, seemingly so long ago, pretending to be human. How frustrating it was to have to move so slowly. I smiled at the memory.

Thankfully, Mari did not seem to notice my cold arm beneath the heavy cloak.

Her large brown eyes were full of curiosity and she started right in. "Well, well. Empress Vallachia in royal purple." She ran her free hand down my arm. "I've never seen such fabric. Yet why are you wearing a winter cloak? It is warm out." She reached up to push the hood off my head.

I quickly stopped her by holding the hood in place. "No, don't! I ... can't be in the sun anymore," I blurted.

"What? You used to love the sun."

"Not anymore, it bothers my ... skin," I lied. "A reaction or something."

"I've never heard of anyone having a reaction to the sun before."

I gave her a weak smile. "It is wondrously rare."

She returned the smile. "I have so many questions. When did you get back?"

"This afternoon."

"Did you join a convent, or did you run off with that handsome rich lord?" It was obvious which of the two seemed more likely to her. "Judging by this fancy attire" — she ran her hand down the gold trim of the cloak — "I would guess the latter."

"I was at a convent in Constantinople."

"Constantinople!" Mari's month fell open. "What was it like? I'll wager it was spectacular."

I thought of all the amazing sights in the city. I described them the best I could to her and told her about the colossal buildings and walls; the mosaics and marble floors. She was intrigued, even though my descriptions did not do the city justice. It was a relief not to have to lie for once.

"Is this how they dress in Constantinople?" Mari asked.

"Yes, this is common attire there," I lied. "But that is enough about me. I came to find out what has been going on with you."

"Not much. The usual, helping Mother with all my siblings. Nothing like getting to live in the Queen of Cities." Her voice was full of envy. "Maybe I should become a nun."

I hoped she was joking and would not try to run off. It would not be safe for her. We were opposites in many ways. She wanted my life — my feigned life anyway — and I would have given anything for hers. To be normal and care for my family was all I wanted.

Mari's expression grew serious. "It was terribly hard on Teller after you left. I was very concerned about him for a while. He searched endlessly for you for about three months. He would not have given up then, except for winter setting in, making travel more difficult. He probably would have tried to get all the way to Denmark."

Tears filled my eyes. I did not want to talk about Teller. "What about you? Any suitors, engagements, or potentials?"

Mari blushed. "Well, Father wants me to marry Iuliu. You know him, the farmer's boy, outside of town. I don't want to live in the country, so Mother is helping me put off the engagement by saying that she needs my help until her younger children are older." Her cheeks reddened even more. "Samuel — you remember him, a friend of the Chastellains?"

My mouth went dry. "Yes, I remember. What about him?"

"Well, he has written to me a couple of times. I keep hoping he will come back for me. I know it is only a dream, Samuel being a nobleman and all." Mari's voice was wistful.

My mind raced. *Samuel never said anything about writing to Mari but then again, why would he? Had he said anything about me? It is not that he is a nobleman that is the problem. It is that he is a vampire! I don't wish this life on anyone, let alone Mari. Hopefully, he will leave her alone, instead of encouraging her. If I had known this, I would have at least found out what Samuel's intentions were by writing to her.*

"Are you with me?" Mari eyed me with suspicion.

"Sorry. What does Samuel say in his letters?" I tried to sound as blithe as possible.

"Well the best part is how he wishes we could be together. Mostly he tells me about life in Denmark. He lives with the Chastellains in an enormous castle. He claims that it is many times larger than their estate here. Can you imagine?"

"No." I smiled. I could see how it all sounded rosy and wondrous to someone from a small village who didn't know that this faraway romantic place was filled with deadly creatures of the night. Thankfully, it appeared that Samuel never mentioned anything about my being in Denmark. *Good man.* He minded his own business and did not interfere with others. "Does he promise to come for you?"

"No, not outright." Mari frowned.

I was relieved; she had no idea of the horror that would await her if he did come back. "Well, Iuliu seems like an amiable young man. I think living on a farm sounds like heaven."

"You would." Mari elbowed my ribs playfully.

We laughed; it appeared that neither of us had changed too much. It was enjoyable to talk with her. For a moment, I felt normal again, as if the past nightmarish months had not occurred.

~

Father arranged a feast in the tavern as a welcome-home gathering. Almost everyone showed up — except Teller. The place was packed, as the townspeople wanted to know what I knew about the Chastellains and the murders. They were disappointed when I told my story and claimed to know nothing. I was overwhelmed with their strong scent. There were too many bodies packed into too small a space. My throat burned with thirst. And they were far too loud. I had to fight the desire to cover my ears. I retired early, claiming to be ill.

The best thing to do was to stay busy. I worked tirelessly for my uncle and cooked and cleaned for my father and brother. Working in the tavern helped me to get used to the pain of being around people in confined places again. At night I would fly, sometimes for the freedom of it and sometimes to feed in neighboring villages. For the first month, I fed once a week, so I could more easily control myself in the tavern and, of course, to avoid growing so hungry that I killed the person when I did feed.

Sometimes if I grew bored at night, I would read in the Chastellains' library. The windows in the lower stories of their mansion outside of Ludus had been shuttered closed. It seemed less grandiose now that I had lived in their castle in Denmark. Many of the books had been taken back to Denmark, yet some remained. The place was abandoned and probably would be for another half century. At times, it made my heart heavy to go there, as it reminded me of Elijah and the other friends I'd left behind.

On one such night, I was reading a well-used copy of the *Iliad* for the fourth time. I loved the strange stories of the old gods and mysterious creatures. My reading was interrupted by the loud shattering of glass. It came from one of the upper stories. I could hear young children whispering outside.

"Don't throw rocks at the windows. This place is haunted and you will anger whatever is in there," a young boy whispered.

In a flash I was upstairs peering out one of the windows. Since vampires did not need light to read by, the place was completely dark. I could see five small figures hiding in the tall grass outside. One of the boys was Teller's younger brother. *Just like Teller, always getting into mischief,* I thought. A smile crossed my face. *Perhaps I should give them a little scare.*

The boys dared one another to enter the fortress.

I found the rock they had thrown by the broken window. I tossed it back to them. It landed at their feet.

"See, I told you," one of the boys said. "You angered it."

"We have to get out of here!" another boy said.

I lit a candle and held it low so my shadow reflected on the wall behind me. I moved quickly from window to window.

The boys screamed and ran away as fast as their little legs could carry them.

I bent over in laughter. *At least they will leave this place alone for a while.*

CHAPTER 42 LUDUS 1261 AD

Teller and I avoided each other, or at least did not go out of our way to see each other. It took about a month for things to settle down. The novelty of my return wore off and the gossip surrounding it died down. I too was adjusting to this new life — well, to my old life again. Although without Teller, it did not feel complete.

Perhaps I should forget about Teller. However, I knew in my heart that this would be impossible. *We cannot be together anyway?* I tried to convince myself that it was for the best. *He should stay away from me, as I would be a danger to him. And perhaps he was too much like his father after all. Maybe it was an error in judgment to love him.* Yet all this logic did not change the way I felt.

Upon leaving Uncle's tavern that evening, I caught Teller's scent before I heard him.

"May I walk you home?" he asked. He had been leaning against the wall — waiting.

As a human I would have been startled but there was no way a human could sneak up on a vampire. Teller appeared disappointed that he had not scared me, as he used to do so easily.

I was not in the mood for company. I did not know what to say to him and I didn't want to know what was on his mind. It did not matter. I could not handle any more rejection from him and if he had forgiven me then we still could not be together. So there was no point in talking.

"We should not be alone together." My voice was flat, as I walked past him.

"Fair enough. I only wanted to apologize."

"There is no need for that. I would have been furious if you had left me, no matter the reason. I probably would never have spoken to you again. Let us leave it at that. It will be easiest."

I could tell this was not what he had expected and he was not sure what to make of it. Nevertheless, he continued to walk with me in silence.

"There is one thing I would like to know, though," I said.

He looked relieved at the break in silence.

"This past year, I have often wondered about you and your father. How are things between you two?"

Teller smiled and it was a welcome sight. His eyes were the bright green I remembered from childhood, full of kindness. This made the wall I had carefully built around me crumble a bit.

"Things have been better. Father domineers over the younger boys. But he does not hit us anymore. I should have stood up to him a long time ago. He treats me with more respect. We are more like friends, rather than father and son."

"That is wonderful. I'm glad to hear it." A smile of relief crossed my lips.

"I have been working with my father, learning the trade. I am getting better at working with metal. Business has been good. With my help, Father can take on more work."

Is he telling me this to let me know he is ready to marry? That had been our plan a year ago or so and it seemed that he was getting settled and could support a family. If I had still been human, this would have been the best possible news. "I'm happy for you." But my tone was far from thrilled.

We walked in silence for a bit longer. "So, do you forgive me?" he asked.

"The question is, do you forgive me?" I corrected.

He looked thoughtful for a moment before answering, "Truthfully, I don't know. I was worried sick when you disappeared. I thought you were dead. We searched the woods for you for days. When we eventually received your letter I was … angry."

We stopped walking.

"You see, it is going to take time. Perhaps we can start over as friends?" Friendship seemed plausible, until I said it. I knew straightaway that that was not possible. I wished it were; I missed my old friend. I would have given anything to be able to go back to that. Yet we had ventured beyond friendship and there was no going back.

He put his hands on my shoulders. "I don't want to be your friend."

My entire body tingled at his touch. This overwhelming sensation unsettled me and I jerked away from him. *What was that?* I could hardly think. I wanted to touch him again to see if the odd sensation was still there. Yet I was worried that it might be too much if it were. I did not want to lose control.

"I have to … get home," I stammered. "Goodnight," I said with more emphasis. I left him standing in the street. I'm sure he was confused — so was I. I did not stop until I was in my bedroom. I tried to gather my thoughts.

What was that feeling? Hunger for blood? Lust? Longing? No, it was something different. The only thing that was clear was that I was helpless when it came to him. I would always love him.

For the first time, I thought of turning someone into a vampire. I wanted to be with Teller for eternity. I had to shake the thought away. *What am I thinking?* I did not want this for anyone, not even myself. During my transition into a vampire, Elijah had said that he wanted to give me a choice between a human life and a vampire life. Originally I'd hoped we could live out the rest of Teller's human life together. There was always something in the back of my mind that told me this would not work, for a number of reasons but I had chosen to ignore it.

I finally faced the cold hard truth that I had been avoiding — a human life together was not possible. Vampires did not age and it appeared that we were turned, not born. I had never met a vampire who had had a child after being turned, so we must not be able to give birth. All this meant that in order for us to be together, Teller would have to choose to become like me.

This past year was a blur and I had been preoccupied with trying to survive. The thought of having children never crossed my mind. Teller had been out of my life; so having a family seemed inconsequential. But now I was faced with the ugly truth. *I will never be able to have his children.* Letting this realization come to the surface caused the tears to stream down my face. I wept for the children I would never have. It was as if I were a mother who had lost all of her children. I rubbed at the pain in my heart until my chest ached.

I slept for a long time, longer than I had ever slept as a vampire. It was the only way to lessen the pain. When I did wake — though it had really only been a couple of hours — my thoughts were clearer. *I will not turn Teller. I will not take his human life away from him. If he did find out what I have become, he would be appalled. There is no way he would choose this life. I would not have. I must let him go.*

A new wave of grief hit me. *I can never be with Teller.* I let out a yell of frustration and in an instant I was out the window, flying high up in the sky.

The cool air on my face helped. It somehow dulled the pain. I did not know how I would live without Teller. I needed him. We were meant to be together. The thought of him marrying someone else crushed my heart into a million pieces. It was supposed to be me at his side — but not now. That was no longer possible. If I truly loved Teller, I should leave him alone.

CHAPTER 43 LUDUS 1261 AD

As usual, I stayed busy and tried not to think too hard about the helpless situation I was in. I spent time with my father and brother. I enjoyed their company whenever possible. We played games by the fire some nights. I cherished these times, as I did not know how long they might last.

Soon the whole village was busy getting ready for the midsummer festivities. This was welcome, as I too had plenty to do. Much time was spent making plans for Josiah's wedding. I helped father build a pergola, under which Josiah and Sarah would be married.

Teller did not seek me out, which was good, as it made it easier for me to stay away from him. He must have taken my quick retreat the other night as a rejection. I told myself it was for the best.

Occasionally, at night, I would borrow the weapons for the upcoming tournament and practice. My weapon of choice was the sword, although I was also becoming skilled with the bow and arrow. However, I missed having someone as fast and strong as a vampire to practice with.

Early one morning before the sun had risen, I was headed home when Teller was leaving his house.

"Do you not sleep?" he asked.

"Not much these days," I answered honestly.

"What were you doing?" He looked behind me as if this would give him a clue about what I was up to.

"I was... setting up for the tournament."

He stepped forward and took my hands in his. I was not as shocked by the sensation this time but it was still strong and strange. I did not want to let go. In fact, I never wanted to let go.

His brow furrowed. "Why are you so cold? Are you ill?"

I forced myself to let go of his hands. "No, I am well."

He narrowed his eyes and pursed his lips. "Did your brother mention that he asked me to be his chief groomsman at his wedding."

I was glad for the change in subject. "That is wonderful. I did not know you two were close."

"We became closer after your ... disappearance."

"Of course." *I will never live that down.*

"Will you go to the dance with me?" This came out quickly, as if Teller was unsure of how I would reply.

My heart leapt into my throat. I could not help the excitement that overcame me. Of course, I should have refused but instead I said, "Yes, I would be honored." At least I resisted the urge to throw my arms around him and kiss him.

It felt like I was walking in the clouds as I arrived home. Part of me was warning that this was not a good thing but I ignored it and allowed myself to be content — that was, until I reached my room. There was a surprise waiting for me. By the window stood a petite figure, that of someone caught between childhood and womanhood. It was Sonia.

"What are you doing here?" My voice was quiet so Father would not hear. I knew Sonia could hear me well. I gave her a long hug. It was good to see her but her face was grim.

"What is it?" I tried to give her a comforting smile.

"I am here on behalf of Lord Chastellain. He requests that you return to Denmark at once." Her formal tone was concerning.

"Why, what is wrong?" Thoughts of vampire war, or some important political maneuver raced through my mind.

"It is Elijah." Her voice was melancholy.

I felt panic arise. "What happened? Is he ill?"

"After you left, he would barely leave his room or talk to any of us. He refused to feed. Lord Chastellain … forced the issue and … well, as you can imagine, it was not pretty."

I do not believe it. Elijah was killing again. He could resist the kill better than any of us. I sat down hard on my bed. I had imagined that Elijah was moving forward with his school and teaching any willing vampires how to leave their victims unconscious but alive. What a fool I had been.

"Why must I return?" I asked.

"Our lord thinks that you will be able to help his son."

"What? How?" *Elijah must be as angry as Teller was about my leaving.*

"Do you not see how much Elijah loves you?"

"The problem is that I love someone else. Elijah knows this."

"I am here because I am loyal to our leader and because I care for you. As your friend, I'm asking you to let this human boy go and return with me. You are one of us and we must follow our leaders. Otherwise, there will be chaos for vampires and humans alike. Lord Chastellain means well."

I could feel the blood rush to my cheeks. "I don't care what Chastellain wants. He did this to me. He took everything from me. I hate him! I will not blindly obey him like a minion."

Sonia recoiled and turned her gaze to the floor.

I took a deep breath. "I'm sorry. I did not mean to hurt you. I understand the lord is concerned for his son. Please tell him that I am sorry but I cannot help him. I do not love Elijah."

"Please reconsider. Lord Chastellain wanted to come here himself. I persuaded him to allow me to come and reason with you first. If you do not return soon, he will take matters into his own hands."

"What does that mean? What would he do?"

"I have no idea but I have a bad feeling; it would not end well."

What could he do? It is not as if he could force someone to fall in love, I thought.

Sonia took both my hands in her tiny ones and gazed at me with large pleading eyes. "We miss you, too, Aaron and I. You got us out of that horrible coven and you helped us learn to live a better life. Please come home to us."

I kissed her forehead. She was sincere and kind. "I appreciate that you came instead of the lord. You are a dear friend. I'm truly sorry for Elijah, as he is a good friend as well. I wish him a swift recovery and hope he can find happiness. Please tell the lord that if I return it will be on my own terms. I have business here. I will not leave my family again. Not yet."

Sonia walked to the window. "I pray you reconsider." With a weary smile she transformed and took flight. I watched her for a while. The sun was rising. She blocked the sun from her eyes with one arm. It did not seem to bother her. She must be getting older, as the sun's painful effects were not as strong.

Having the strength of a vampire gave me a sense of independence. I was no longer going to take orders from anyone, especially Lord Chastellain. The one thing he could not take from me was my freedom of choice. If I allowed him to do that, I would have nothing left of myself.

CHAPTER 44 LUDUS 1261 AD

The day the villagers had been preparing for was here. I was excited for my brother. Today he would become a man. The festivities would start midday with Josiah's wedding, followed by the village dance. This year, the annual dance and the celebration after my brother's wedding would be one and the same. The following day the tournament would commence.

Sarah asked me to be a bridesmaid and I was thrilled to be in the wedding. Mari came over that morning to get ready. This year our dresses were unpretentious and much more comfortable.

"I'm glad Teller asked you to the dance. I knew he would come around. Next we will be attending your wedding," Mari chatted away.

I was not as sure as she was about the future. "I can only dream of my wedding." This was the truth. I tried not to be downtrodden about the fact that Teller and I could never marry. "And I'm glad Iuliu asked you to the dance. Perhaps you will find that a farm may be a good choice for you after all."

Mari glared at me. "It will not compare to last year's grand gala, where I met Samuel."

I did not reply. The sooner she forgot about Samuel, the better. I was not going to encourage or discourage her. I thought ignoring it was best. She and I also had different memories of the "grand gala." She had had a wonderful time and I had been miserable.

After a good deal of fussing, we were dressed. We both looked down into the washbasin at our reflection — we had no other looking glass. We were two beautiful young ladies full of hopes, dreams and trepidation about our futures.

The ceremony was simply lovely. I had spent most of the previous night gathering flowers from faraway fields. I covered the pergola with yellow and white daisies, as well as pink and purple flowers, of which I did not know the name. This was not only for decoration but also to shade me from the sun. I potted flowering dog rose shrubs and placed them along the aisle. Their large white blooms led the way for the bride and groom. It was the most colorful wedding Ludus had ever had — like something out of a fairy story.

To distract myself from how handsome Teller looked, I forced myself to focus on Josiah and his lovely bride. Josiah's crystal blue eyes shone bright. He looked handsome as well. He would make a great husband and father, like our father. I could tell he was ready for this big step. He had no doubts about his future. He was prepared to take on the world and he would do well. I was grateful to be a part of this ceremony. No matter how much longer I could stay, at least I had not missed my brother's wedding. I envied Josiah; he was going to have the life I wanted. I could not keep from daydreaming about my own wedding.

When it was over, everyone headed to Uncle Ezekiel's tavern for the feast and dance. My stomach fluttered as Teller took my gloved hand and wrapped his arm around mine.

"Shall we, My Lady?" he asked.

I smiled. "After you, kind sir." Being this close to him was intoxicating and where we touched there was that shock of energy between us. I kept my cloak and gloves on, hoping he would not feel my coolness. I had also hoped that the gloves would lessen the strange tingling sensation but they did not. It was like a warning to stay away and an intense attraction at the same time. Teller walked slowly so eventually we were alone; everyone else was in a hurry to get to the tavern to eat and drink their fill.

"It should have been our wedding today," he whispered.

"You did not ask me." I gave him a devilish smile.

Without warning he stopped walking and pressed his lips to mine. My senses overwhelmed me and my knees almost gave way. He held my waist to support me.

When he pulled away, his brow was furrowed. "You are cold again."

"I'm warm enough. Actually, I have never been better." I laid my head on his shoulder as we continued to the tavern. I wanted this moment to last forever. I tried not to think about how this could not last.

We all gave our well wishes to the newlyweds. As we toasted and cheered, the men picked the bride and groom up and carried them around the tavern, while the rest of us danced around them. Mari and I locked arms, starting a traditional circle dance. We sang songs from our village, songs of days long past and songs of love.

When it was over I headed home with my family, which now included Sarah. I was sad for this wondrous day to end. I did not want to say goodbye to Teller that night. I wished that he, like Sarah, was coming home with us.

It was a relief to learn that Sarah was moving into our home. This would be her first night away from her family. This arrangement made the most sense, as our home was larger and less crowded than hers and my brother did not have enough money to build his own home. I did not want to stay in my room and listen to the new couple's private life with my vampire ears, so I was out my window and flying as soon as possible. I flew high over the Carpathian Mountaintops and off into the night.

THE TOURNAMENT WAS GOING WELL — for Teller. Mari, Father and I watched from wooden benches as usual. This time I sat with my hood up, as I always did when the sun was out. It was amusing to imagine dressing as a man and beating Teller at his own games. I had been trained well by Riddick and then Elijah, so Teller would not stand a chance against me. The thought made me smile.

My brother competed in only a couple of games. He was distracted at best, giddy with love. This gave rise to many a joke amongst the men. It filled my heart with joy to see my brother so happy. I wished him this happiness for the rest of his life.

The tournament moved along seamlessly until the final round of the fencing competition. With the flick of his wrist, Teller swiftly disarmed his opponent. The problem was that the sword went flying through the air and headed straight for a small boy in the audience.

I had to act. In a flash I was gone from Father's side and I caught the blade end of the sword before it hit the boy in the head. People gasped as they surveyed the blood running down the blade and pooling on the ground. I moaned in pain and dropped the sword. I could feel my hand tingle and eventually start to itch, as it was already healing. The pain subsided as well. That was when I noticed the sharp sting in my eyes. The hood of the cloak had flown off. I had to squint and I could not see clearly. A woman stepped forward and asked to see the wound.

"Your hand must be cleaned and bandaged," she was saying as she reached for me.

I quickly pulled the hood over my head and proceeded to wrap my hand in my dress, pretending to use it as a bandage, when in actuality I was using my dress to hide the disappearing wound.

"No, no, I am scarcely hurt. I will tend to it myself." I backed away from the woman. As I did, I bumped into Teller.

"Let me have a look," he said, as he reached for my hand.

I jerked away. "No. Honestly, I am well." *I must get out of here!* Trying not to move too fast, I pushed past Father and Mari. As soon as I was out of sight, I sped home. I washed the drying blood from my dress and hand and was putting a fresh rag over my slightly scarred hand when I heard Father return. He called for me.

"Yes, Father, I am here," I answered.

He ran up the stairs. "Do you need help?"

I held up the clean fake-bandaged hand. "No, I cleansed the wound and the bleeding has stopped. It should heal quickly — I mean, nicely."

He looked relieved, then narrowed his eyes in suspicion. "That was a brave thing you did, grabbing that sword to save the boy."

"Well, I could not let him get hurt or possibly killed, now, could I?"

"Yet I was closer to the boy than you. I did not even see it coming, let alone have time to act."

"I'm younger and more agile, I suppose. Perhaps it is that you are getting old." I smiled. I was hoping to use humor to get myself out of this predicament.

He returned my smile. "Well, what matters is that you and the boy are safe. Since I'm not needed here, I had better head back. Do you feel like returning?"

"Perhaps I will rest." I thought it best to feign injury. Besides, this way I could avoid everyone's questions for a while longer about how I had been able to move so fast. "Please inform Mari and Teller that I am well."

"Of course and I will see how you are faring after the next round of games."

"Thank you, Father."

He nodded and left.

People will be talking about me. I will have to be leaving, much sooner than I would like. The problem is, how to leave? I will not disappear this time. Should I tell Father the truth? Should I tell Teller the truth? Should I let him choose between a vampire life and a human life? The selfish part of me wants more than anything to have Teller by my side forever. The other part does not wish this life on anyone, *especially Teller. He should marry and have children. That is the future I want for him. Yet maybe he could learn to feed without killing. Stop being selfish!* I chastised. *Don't try to justify turning him into a killer.* I was going to go mad sitting in my room.

CHAPTER 45 LUDUS 1261 AD

Thankfully, Father came back within the hour. "What do you say we go to the feast?" he asked.

"That sounds wonderful." I was more than happy to get out of the house and away from my helpless musings.

We walked arm in arm to the center of the village. Teller approached, bowed slightly and held out his arm to me. Father took my "good" hand and unwound it from his own offering it to Teller. It was a gesture that fathers often made when giving away their daughters in marriage. I felt tears form. I blinked them away.

"I am glad to see you are well," Teller said.

I nodded and changed the subject. "How did the rest of the games go?"

He smiled with confidence, which brought an image of Riddick and his ever-present arrogant expression to mind.

I shook my head, as if disapproving. He could be quite supercilious, as could Riddick. I could barely see this because of the way I felt about Teller. If he had not been so beautiful and if his presence had not held such power over me, perhaps I would have viewed him differently. A surprising thought crept in, *is he in any way like Riddick? No, of course not!* I quickly dismissed the thought.

Teller led me to his family's table. Ivan's piercing glare was impossible to miss. I returned his hard stare until he finally looked away; I refused to be intimidated by him. My unwillingness to back down seemed to upset Ivan even more. It was a direct challenge; he knew that he could not subdue me. This was what I assumed his problem was.

My family joined us. Josiah wasted no time in speaking his mind. Looking pointedly at Teller he said, "When will you marry my sister?"

"I'm not going to let her get away again or allow someone else the chance to ask for her hand." With this Teller stood from the table and went down on one knee.

My heart pounded in my ears. *But we can't be together.* The worry turned to joy — I let it consume me.

He held my un-bandaged hand up and said the four wonderful words I had only dreamt of hearing from him. "Will you marry me?"

I looked at Father for approval — old habits were difficult to break and a girl could not marry without her father's approval. He smiled and nodded. I knew what this meant — *The choice was mine.*

"I would love to," I said. This was not a solid *yes* but not a lie either. My mind was spinning. *What was I going to do?* Teller hugged me and we stood up together.

Father rose to his feet as well, to make the big announcement. He raised his hands and spoke loudly, to get everyone's attention, "Hear, hear!" He waited for other tables to quiet down. "My lovely daughter has agreed to marry this fine young man. I am blessed to have both my children find love and happiness. I can't wait to be a grandfather." He smiled as laughter and cheers erupted from the crowd. "May we wish them the very best!" he concluded.

With this, many congratulations followed. I smiled and looked at Teller. His eyes shone like emeralds. This was enough for me — for now. From the corner of my eye, I noticed Ivan get up from the table and walk away. *Curious,* I thought. He clearly did not approve of Teller's proposal.

I tried to concentrate on the conversation at our table but other conversations — ones not meant for my ears — kept creeping in. One young man at a table not far from ours was saying to his friend, "I don't understand. He wins all the tournament games *and* gets the prettiest girl in the village. How is one man so lucky?"

"That is the way it works. Get used to it," his friend replied.

I turned my attention back to our table but my extraordinary hearing picked up another conversation. A woman seated behind me was whispering, "She moved so quickly. It was as if she had disappeared, then reappeared in front of the boy."

"And did you see? She hardly flinched when she caught the sword," another woman replied. "Her hand was bleeding everywhere and she did not cry out in pain. I would have been frantic if my hand had been almost cut in two by a blade."

As I often did around humans, I wanted to cover my ears. These were other people's private conversations I should not be hearing. *Concentrate!* I told myself. I was better able to attend to the conversation at our table, though it appeared from other small tidbits I overheard that Teller and I were the main topic of interest in the village.

After the feast, the little boy that I had saved and his mother came up to us as we were leaving.

"I want to congratulate you on your engagement and to thank you for saving my son." The mother gave a slight bow.

"Thank you and it was nothing. I'm relieved your son was not hurt."

The mother gestured toward my bandaged hand. "Will your hand heal well?"

"Yes, I can move my fingers and there will only be a slight scar. It will be a story to tell my children." I smiled, trying to reassure her that she need not worry about me.

"I am grateful for that," she said.

As they walked away, we could hear the boy telling his mother. "She is so pretty, Mama."

Teller and I smiled at each other and headed home. We walked in silence until we were alone.

"You know you are a heavy sleeper?" Teller said.

"What do you mean?"

"You did not hear the pebbles hitting your shutters last night?"

"No." It was not that I was a heavy sleeper — I simply had not been in my room last night. I had been flying high over the mountaintops. "You were throwing rocks at my window last night?"

"I wanted to talk to you before I proposed. I knew your father would leave the decision to you, so I wanted to know what you would say first. But you were too difficult to wake. So I took a chance that you would say yes."

"You know how I feel about you. You knew I would say yes."

"Not necessarily. You can be hard to read and your behavior can be … well, erratic."

"Erratic!" I laughed. *Try being a vampire surrounded by humans,* I thought. *Erratic is the perfect word for my behavior.*

He stopped me and placed his lips squarely on mine. The same sensation went through my entire body. I placed my arms around his neck and kissed him back harder. He tightly wrapped his arms around my waist and pressed my entire body to his.

Instantly, I could feel myself losing control. His strong lightening touch was overpowering. The feeling was more than I could handle. It was beyond hunger or lust. It was a passion that brought out the monster inside. I was on fire. My eye-teeth ached. *I'm going to hurt him.*

"Stop!" I breathed. I was talking to myself more than to him. I forcefully pushed him away, almost knocking him down. "I have to go." I tried to reassure him with a smile but I had to keep my lips pressed together to conceal the long fangs. "I'll … see you tomorrow," I stuttered.

As I headed for home, I could hear him mutter, "Erratic," under his breath.

Once in the privacy of my room, I paced the small space between my bed and the window. "What am I going to do?" I whispered. I tried not to panic but my loss of control was unnerving. *Why can't I control myself with him? Perhaps vampires feel everything more intently? Love, longing, lust … hatred, everything* — I did not know for sure. *Does every new vampire feel this way or is it something ... unique between Teller and me? Whatever it is I must be careful. I do not want to hurt him.*

I also failed as a human today, though I did not regret that. I could not have lived with myself if I had let that boy die when I could have easily saved him. Obviously, I would not be able to keep up this human façade for much longer.

My voice of reason kept telling me that Teller must be told the truth. I searched for some other way. *There is no other choice,* the voice replied. I finally had to agree: *I must show Teller what I am and explain everything.* It was not a pleasant idea. I imagined he would be scared and repulsed, as I had been. He would hate what I had become and I would lose him forever. *He deserves to know,* the voice inside warned.

Things were moving too fast. If he did not love me enough to become a vampire, then I must end this whole deception and allow him to move on. This thought sent pain through my chest. I rubbed my hand over my heart. I was not sure why. Perhaps it was to try to rub the pain away. It did not help; the pain remained. *How can I bear his rejection?* It did not matter. If that was his choice, I would *have* to bear it.

The decision was made. I would tell him the truth and let him decide his own future. I must be prepared to walk away and leave him alone — forever — if need be. I lay down and tried to rest. There was some comfort in this decision. *No matter what Teller chooses, I will not have to live a lie anymore.* This entire false life would be over and we — hopefully — could move on with a new life. I could not imagine what that life would be like, which was disturbing.

I finally dozed off. When I woke, it was still a good while before the sun would be up. I thought about leaving for a quick flight but perhaps Teller would come to my window again. That would be the perfect opportunity to tell him the truth. If I was going to enact this plan, I must tell him as soon as possible. *I will not put him in danger any more.*

CHAPTER 46 LUDUS 1261 AD

Teller did not disappoint. Well before daybreak, I heard something crack against the shutter. *How could anyone sleep through that?* I thought. My heart raced. I had to hold my bandaged hand in the other to keep them from shaking.

I went to the window and signed that I would come down. I walked slowly and quietly to the back door. I took his arm in mine and led him into the woods behind my house.

"Where are we going?" he asked.

"Away from the town. There is something I have to tell you … and show you, as you will not believe me otherwise."

"Very well." He frowned. It must have been my determined and cryptic tone that concerned him.

"There is something I wanted to talk to you about as well. It is my father. He thinks … " Teller paused.

"I know. He is not happy about our engagement."

"Yes, well, you see, some people think that it was some sort of monster that killed those people last summer. Father thinks that it was the Chastellains and that they are demons of sorts. I know that sounds insane, but if you think about it, it is logical. The deaths stopped after the

Chastellains left town. Maybe they were extraordinarily strong and that was how the young lord beat me in the tournament last year. You said it yourself, that you thought it was odd how he was able to win so easily."

I nodded. "And what does this have to do with me?" I knew where this was headed but I wanted to hear exactly what Ivan was saying — and what many of the villagers would also be thinking, as the rumor spread.

"Well ..." Teller hesitated; he clearly did not want to tell me. "After the incident with the sword yesterday, Father thinks ... that you are a demon as well."

There, that was it. I would indeed have to be leaving soon. I pulled on Teller's arm to stop him from walking. We were alone in a clearing. I looked at him in silence. He was expecting me to deny it and I did not. He had to know.

Teller was becoming uncomfortable with my silence. "I told Father that that was ridiculous. One problem with his logic is that no one else has been harmed since you returned. I don't doubt that the Chastellains were responsible for those people's deaths but you are not like them."

Again I said nothing.

"Say something! Why are you not denying this serious accusation?" Teller's frustration was mounting.

I put my head down and stepped away from Teller. It would have been easy to deny Ivan's claims. Even laugh them off as being ridiculous. But this was my chance to come clean.

Teller narrowed his eyes. "Please tell me it is not true."

"I plan to tell you everything — the truth in its entirely. I want to offer you a choice — one I did not have."

"What are you saying? You are talking nonsense."

I stepped closer and looked him in the eyes. "It is not nonsense. I will show you. Though I wish it were not so, I am not human anymore."

He backed away from me. "Then what are you?"

"I swear to you, Teller, I will not hurt you. Let me show you. Please do not run. You must trust me." I reached for his hands but he pulled away.

"Have you gone mad?"

I shook my head no. *Here goes. There will be no going back after this.* I jumped straight up, transforming in an instant and hovering above him. He fell backwards and stumbled away from me. I knew what a terrifying beast I was in this form but if he was to make a decision, he must know. He ran for the village. I landed in front of him, returning to my "human" self.

I held out my hands to stop him.

He backed away.

"Please listen. I came back because I love you and because I have learned not to kill people."

"You are a murderer?" He was full of disgust.

I did not blame him — it was appalling. "It is not going to be safe for me in Ludus for much longer. My father and brother have Sarah to help out in the home, so I will be leaving soon and I want you to come with me."

He shook his head and kept backing away.

"I know this is a great deal to take in," I continued. "I would give anything to have my old life back, to marry you and raise a family but that is no longer possible."

"No! Stay away from me." Teller tried to run around me.

I quickly stepped toward him and grabbed his arm.

"Let go of me!"

"I will. I will let you go and never come back if that is what you want. But first you need to know what I am offering you. You can become like me and we can be together forever, or I will leave and let you live out your human life here. The choice is yours."

He had been struggling in my grasp but stopped. He must have seen in my eyes that I was sincere and that I would not hurt him.

"I will never become a killer!" he spat.

"I don't kill anymore and I can teach you to do the same, to control your thirst."

"Thirst for what?"

"We are vampires and we need human blood to survive."

"Vam-what?" He glared at me. Which made him look more like his father. "Let me go!"

"Is that your choice, then? If so, I will leave you alone and never return." I could hardly force the words out.

"Yes! That is my choice." He spoke through clenched teeth.

He might as well have stabbed me with a knife. I let go and wrapped my arms around my stomach. What had I expected? I did not want this life, either. Would I have chosen it to be with him? *I don't know; maybe.* The pain was overwhelming and I barely registered the sound of far-off swishing. The noise grew louder; it must be coming from large wings. This thought pulled me from my heartache. *A vampire!*

I scanned the sky. Teller had reached the edge of the clearing and a large winged figure was landing in front of him. In a flash, I was by Teller's side.

Teller started at my sudden appearance. "I said, leave me —

But I was not looking at Teller. I was staring at the old man who had appeared in front of us. If trouble found me in Ludus, I had thought, it would be Ramdasha's doing. If he'd found out I had family here, he would take revenge against me. But I was wrong; trouble came in the form of an alleged ally.

I stepped in front of Teller. "Get back!"

"Well, well. What have we here?" Chastellain said. "I could not help hearing raised voices. A lovers' quarrel already? What a shame."

"What do you want?" I demanded.

Chastellain lost his smirk. "You know what I want. I sent orders for you to return. And yet here you are."

"I am not a soldier in your army, one you can command," I said.

"You think not? Then what *are* you?" He stepped forward.

I pushed Teller back a step. I'm sure it was a rhetorical question but either way I did not have an answer. "Let the boy go. I will return with you after I tell my family goodbye."

"I don't think so. You see, I told my son that there were two options: we could turn you, or we could kill the boy. I decided to turn you. That did not work, as you came running right back here. So you leave me no other choice. It is time for the alternative."

"No, please! I'll do anything; just leave Teller alone. In any case, he does not want me — or this life. I will leave with you and never come back."

"Oh, now that the ones you care about are threatened, you will obey me. You see, I need to know I can trust you. You have disobeyed me once, a blatant act of treason. Why should I believe you?"

"Please, Chastellain, I beg you!"

"That is *Lord* Chastellain to you!" he boomed.

I flinched away and in a flash he grabbed Teller. The loud sound of boulders colliding rang out, as I threw my body into the lord's. Teller was thrown to the ground. When I spun around, I saw that the lord was standing behind Teller. Chastellain had one hand on Teller's jaw and one on the back of his head. He slightly lifted Teller off the ground. Teller clawed uselessly at the lord's hands around his head.

I stepped forward but as I did, I heard a terrible sound, that of bones cracking. A shock of pain pierced my neck and ran down my spine. I stumbled and almost dropped to my knees. Teller's body went limp in Chastellain's hands.

A scream was stuck in my throat. I ran to catch Teller as he fell to the ground. I did not care what Chastellain had planned for me. Let him kill me too if he must. Part of me wished he would kill me.

"That is the price for treason, my dear." Chastellain's voice was as calm as the night.

With that I felt the air swoosh around me as he took flight. I did not look at him. I knew he was gone.

"No, no, no!" I let out a scream. I rocked Teller's body and wept. My sobs were cut short as I barely made out the faint sound of a heartbeat. *He is not dead ... just dying.* His spine had been broken. There was no doubt he would die unless I turned him. *Perhaps there is still time. Would he want me to turn him to save him? I do not know. Would I have wanted that?* I didn't know the answer to that either. But there was no time — a decision must be made. "I cannot lose you like this — not if I can help it," whispered in his ear.

I felt my fangs grow on command. I hadn't known vampires could do that. They always formed automatically with feeding but it seemed I could also make them grow when needed, like now. I placed the point of one razor-sharp tooth on my wrist and ran it lengthwise down my arm. Blood flowed from the cut. I held Teller's head back with one arm so his mouth fell open and with my bleeding arm held over his head, I let my blood run into his mouth. I did not know how much he needed but soon my arm stopped bleeding and the pain was replaced with an inching sensation as my arm healed. *I hope that is enough.*

I held his torso upright to make sure the blood would trickle down into his stomach. *Please, please let this work!* I prayed through my tears. It was not long before I heard his heartbeat strengthen. *It is working!* Relief flooded through me, then apprehension sneaked in. *He will despise me for turning him.*

The sun was on the rise at this point. I picked Teller up and walked into the forest, even farther away from the village. I found a north-facing overhang that would shelter us from the sun. I had nothing to do but wait for him to wake. That left plenty of time to think, which I was beginning to see as a bad thing. Perhaps I was prone to thinking too much and it got me into trouble.

CHAPTER 47 LUDUS 1261 AD

The first thing that crept into my mind was an intense hatred for Chastellain. I never had liked him, even when I was a human. My initial hatred had waned a bit over the past year. It had been tempered by his political goals to keep vampires in check. He worked to keep them, or us rather, from running amok and taking over the world. At one point I'd even thought of him as a good leader. I could no longer see any of that. He was a wretched man who desired only power and control. I would not give him either. This renewed hatred was much stronger than before. I would never forgive him.

Father's teachings rang like a warning in my head. *Not to forgive is a sin. To hold hatred in the heart only destroys one's soul.*

"Never, you hear me. Never!" I shouted at the voice of wisdom in my head. I hoped Chastellain was still within earshot but I knew he was long gone. *He leaves others behind to clean up after him. Coward,* I thought.

Chastellain's logic — if it could be called logic — is sheer nonsense. Did he think that by killing Teller, I would go running back to his son and fall in love? That made no sense! Did he think I would gladly become an obedient servant in his court because Teller was gone? I will never do either!

I could all but hear father's voice. *Never say never, my dear.*

Never could be a long time — especially for a vampire.

After pondering such vengeful thoughts for far too long, I began to see that I would have to learn not to dwell on this hatred, or Chastellain would be controlling me. He would win. I turned my thoughts from my loathing of Chastellain to what I would say to Teller when he woke.

There was so much he needed to know and he probably would not allow me much time to explain. He would be panicked and angry, as I had been. *So what is most important for him to know? I will try to convince him to leave the village. We must run far from here, until he has fed and his transition is complete. That is about all that could be done. Then I will have plenty of time to explain things in more detail. In fact, we will have an eternity together.* A faint smile crossed my lips. *If he is not too angry with me for turning him.*

I did not know where we would go, it did not matter.

My thoughts turned toward the physical pain I had felt when Chastellain had broken Teller's neck. It had been brief but intense. *What caused it? It was not as if Chastellain could have hurt me from that far away. Perhaps it was similar to how I felt when Teller touched me. Could I also feel his pain?*

He had the ability to overwhelm my senses with a kiss. No one else had ever done that, not that I had a large frame of reference. Riddick definitely had not. When he had kissed me, my only thoughts had been of getting away. Elijah and I had never kissed but his touch was not shocking like Teller's. If I were being honest with myself, I would admit that Elijah's touch was pleasant and comforting. I even missed him at times, yet it was not the same as with Teller.

Teller was resting peacefully as if in a deep sleep — a sleep from which he could not be awakened. I wrapped my fingers around his. No warmth. He was already as cold as I. The now-familiar tingling sensation spread up my arm until it radiated through my body.

We must have some kind of connection. Could it be that as a human my senses were strong enough to feel his presence this way? I don't know. I will have to find out if other vampires have such strong reactions.

The day wore on. As the sun set, I was filled with dread. He would not be trapped here by the sun. He could run off and I did not know if I could stop him when the new monster inside took control. My stomach twisted at the thought.

I was beginning to think he might never wake, when a low moan escaped his lips. His head and arm gave a slight jerk.

I sat still and let him wake gradually, though I wanted to tell him everything he needed to know. *Go slowly,* I told myself.

"Vallachia? Is that you?" He sat up slowly.

"Yes, I'm here. It is only the two of us." I spoke softly. *Give him time to let all the horrible memories come flooding back,* I thought.

He put his head in his hands, as if it hurt. He rubbed the back of his neck. I would have been surprised if it did not hurt. His breathing grew deeper and faster. He looked at me with wide eyes, jumping to his feet he said, "What is going on?"

"There is so much you need to know. Please give me time to explain. I will tell you everything. No more lies. I swear it!"

He backed away from me. I could not read his expression at first; it was entirely unfamiliar. It must have been one of fear.

"I will not hurt you, I promise. In fact, I saved you — in a way."

He studied me with intensity. He seemed to decide that I most likely would not hurt him.

I remained seated with my arms wrapped around my legs. I was perfectly still so I would not startle him.

He tilted his head to the side. "Well?"

"You are in transition. After you feed, you will be like me, a vampire."

"What does that mean? I have never heard of such a creature!"

"It means a number of things. It's most important to understand that you are a danger to humans. You will need to feed on human blood. At first it will be difficult to control your thirst."

He raised his hand to his throat and made a slight choking sound.

"Yes," I continued. "Please run with me away from the village so you do not hurt anyone in Ludus. We need to get as far away from here as possible!"

He seemed distracted; I had lost his attention at the end of my little rehearsed speech. He was deep in thought — putting the pieces together, no doubt. His green eyes darkened with anger.

"Chastellain was here for you. You *were* with ... what's his name, the lord's son, the entire time you were gone. You lied to me!" There was no more fear in his eyes, only anger — pure anger.

Of all the things to worry about, is this what most concerned him? "Not the entire time. I had to lie to everyone. The villagers would have tried to kill me. Also, humans are not meant to know about us. Don't you understand? I love you, only you! I risked everything to return to you."

His tense shoulders relaxed.

"What is important is that we get you out of here. We need to get far away from the village until you have fed. Then we can discuss this matter. I will tell you everything!"

"Feed? You mean on a person? And you did this to me, made me into a cannibal?"

"I had no other choice. You were dying. I could not lose you like that. I have learned to control my thirst. I do not kill people." Under my breath, I added, "Not anymore."

"I don't believe this. This can't be happening. It is all a terrible dream. I will wake soon to my perfect life and ... He trailed off.

"I wish it were a dream. Every day I wish for my old life back. I would give anything to be your wife and have your children. That will not happen now." A tear ran down my cheek. *We must leave now!* the voice in my head screamed. I slowly stood. "Please run with me, away from our village!"

He stepped toward me and reached for the tear on my cheek.

I gently took his hand instead and in a flash we were running. There would be time for tears later. Teller could lose control at any moment. He had no idea how hard it was about to get. Neither did I, for that matter.

We had not been running long when he pulled his hand out of mine. He stopped and so did I. I did not like what I saw. He was clearly not himself. He had a wild look in his eyes. The demon was taking over.

"No, not yet. We are not far enough away." My heart pounded. I reached for his arm but he narrowly evaded my grasp and started running back toward the village. I took flight and landed in front of him.

"Stop!" I yelled and braced for the impact. With the familiar loud crack, I was thrown to the side and he was gone.

I made the biggest mistake of my life — I sat on the ground for a moment too long. A feeling of dismay overtook me, as I realized that he was headed for the nearest people and I would not be able to stop him from killing someone in the village. Elijah had not been able to stop me and he'd been well trained in vampire combat.

My blood turned to ice when it dawned on me that the first house Teller would come to was mine. He was headed back directly from where we entered the forest and that would lead him straight to my house. My family was in grave danger!

CHAPTER 48 LUDUS 1261 AD

I shook my head, *No, no. Get up, now!* the voice of reason demanded. In a blink I was flying after Teller. I forced my wings to move faster than ever before. Even so, time seemed to slow. It was like a bad dream in which I was running with all my might but couldn't get anywhere. There was no way to reach home fast enough. In actuality, I arrived at our doorstep quickly but not quickly enough. Father had most likely fallen asleep in the living room chair — waiting up for me. His limp body was in Teller's arms.

I grabbed Teller by the back of the neck and threw him against the wall. Father was covered in blood. I listened for a heartbeat but heard none. He was dead, all because I was too late, because I had created the monster who killed him.

Taking Father in my arms, I screamed, "No! Please, no."

The commotion woke my brother and his wife. I hardly noticed the shuffle upstairs.

Sarah's screams rang out and my brother was at my side.

"Dear God, what happened?" Josiah said.

All I could do was shake my head. The painful knot in my throat would not let any words pass. My most dreaded childhood nightmare had come to fruition. Teller was indeed the death of my father and it was my fault. As a child I could not have imagined such terrible creatures as vampires so I turned us into wolves. Now that I knew the dream had told the future, my thoughts turned to the third mysterious wolf from the nightmare — the one who was the death of Josiah. *My brother is in danger!* I knew that if I stayed in his life, he too would be killed by one of my kind. I had to get as far away from him as possible. The only way to protect him was to keep my kind away from him.

A glance around told me that Teller was gone. *Good,* I thought.

Not long after, half the village was in our living room.

I vaguely registered Ivan speaking. He was demanding to know what I knew about this. "Did you see the killer?"

No response. I simply could not form words.

"Answer me, girl!" Ivan spat.

I slowly shook my head no. I wanted to punch him in the face. I wasn't entirely sure why. Perhaps I thought it would make me feel better.

"What *did* you see, then?" Ivan asked.

"Leave her alone! None of us saw what happened," Josiah said.

Ivan turned to the mass of people gathered in our tiny living area. "All able-bodied men, come with me. The sooner we start the hunt, the more likely it is we can catch the culprit."

Good luck with that, I secretly scoffed. *They will not be able to find Teller.*

Some of the older men from the village carried my father's body out on a makeshift stretcher. They would clean the body and prepare it for a funeral tomorrow. The women went to work as well. They mopped up the blood and picked up the broken candles from where I had thrown Teller against the wall.

These people are wonderful. They care for one another and do what must be done without question or complaint. I will miss this place, I thought.

I do not remember much about the next morning. All was a haze. Mari practically had to dress me for the service. "I did not get to say goodbye," I whispered.

Mari put her arm over my shoulder. "Shhh," was all she said.

~

FATHER'S BODY was placed on a wooden table in the middle of the meadow outside of town. He had been wrapped in a white blanket. Wooden benches had been placed around the table.

Uncle Ezekiel sat with his arm around me. I wore the heavy cloak for protection from the sun. He appeared not to be able to feel my coldness through the thick fabric. I had never seen him cry before. In fact, I had never seen him upset. Yet at his brother's passing, his eyes were filled with pain and his face was wet with tears. This broke my heart twice over; I did not think the pain could get any worse ... but it did.

Father had always been the one to speak at funerals, so I had no idea who would speak at his. It was surprising when Josiah moved to stand by father's body. He looked solemn yet determined. ...

"ADAM WAS NOT ONLY a father to Vallachia and me but he was a father to this town as well. He was our spiritual leader. He cared for us all and loved us. It was with love and grace that he led us and guided us. I wish I could thank him for all the things he taught me. I know that I can never be as good, as intelligent, or as selfless as my father but I must do my best to fill his shoes. I hope we can all take a piece of him with us and continue his legacy. He was the standard for which I will strive and hopefully, I can make him proud by being half the man he ... was ..."

AT THIS POINT Josiah choked on unwelcome tears and could not go on. Both Sarah and I went to his side and helped him to sit down. Thankfully, Clamius, the oldest and wisest town leader, stepped up to add a few words about our father. I remember only bits and pieces. My mind was a fog.

"Our dear Adam was taken from us too soon … He is in a better place, as he now resides with God. Let us all say a prayer for his soul … I beg of you, Lord, please take Adam with open arms into heaven. Amen."

I was proud of my brother. I did not like to speak in front of crowds. He was brave and did what had to be done. He said what needed to be said about our amazing father.

After the service, Ivan pushed through the crowd to get to me. I assumed he wanted to give me his condolences but instead he said, "Have you seen Teller?"

"No." I had not seen Teller that day and I did not care where he was. I refrained from adding, *What a surprise you did not find him last night with your hunting party.*

Ivan's eyes narrowed with suspicion, then turned to Ezekiel to offer his condolences. Ivan clearly suspected my involvement. He did not bother with pretend sympathy. I had to give him credit for that; Ivan may be many things but he was not a hypocrite. However, if he suspected my involvement in this tragedy, it meant that I must be leaving soon. I would have to say goodbye and leave at dusk, before Ivan tried to have me burned at the stake for being a witch.

Back home, our house was abuzz. Neighbors brought food. Mari was cleaning the kitchen. I sat in Father's chair, surrounding myself with his scent for the last time. I hoped this village would never change and that the people here would always take care of one another like this.

Eventually people trickled out, heading home to tend to their own families.

"I should go but I will be back tomorrow," Mari said.

"Please wait. I have something to tell you … once everyone has gone," I said.

She nodded and went to work folding clothes. Perhaps she was like me in that life was easier if she was busy. Finally, Mari, Sarah and Josiah were all who remained.

"Gather around," I said.

This they did. Kneeling in front of Sarah, I put my ear to her stomach. She started at the odd gesture and tried to back away but could not. My steel arm was secure around her waist. I listened hard. The faintest of sounds could be heard — a tiny little heartbeat, as I had hoped. I chuckled at the concerned expression on Sarah's face.

"A new life." I stood. "You two will soon be parents."

CHAPTER 49 LUDUS 1261 AD

Sarah's face lit up.

"How could you possibly know that?" Josiah asked.

"Trust me, little brother. I know. It is the perfect gift for Father," I said.

Josiah took Sarah's hands and gave her a warm smile.

"You will make wonderful parents," I said.

Mari gave Sarah a congratulatory embrace.

I hugged my brother. "You will be an even better father than ours," I whispered.

"That is not possible." He shook his head in sorrow. "What will I do when I need him — when I need his advice?"

"Father is not gone. He will always look out for us. He is in here." I placed my hand over his heart. I don't know where this wisdom came from but as soon as I said it, I knew it was true. "Father will still guide you."

"I can always ask you for advice." Josiah said.

I frowned and shook my head.

"What do you mean? You will not be here?" Worry flashed through his eyes.

"I wanted you all together because I have to say goodbye," I said.

"What! You're leaving … again?" Mari said.

"Please know that I would not leave you if I did not have to."

"For how long? And where will you go?" Mari asked.

"I am leaving for good this time and I can't tell you where."

"Why not?" Josiah's voice was stern.

"Because I do not know where I will go. You must trust me when I say that people are in danger while I am around. I have to leave to keep you and this town safe. Know that I did not do this to Father and I would never hurt any of you. But that is why I must leave — to keep you safe."

"I cannot bear to lose you and Father." Josiah's voice cracked.

"I am sorry it has to be this way." Tears formed in my eyes. I wrapped my arms around him one last time. "Take good care of Sarah. She is the start of your new family. They are what matters. This town needs a deacon. There is no one better suited than you for the job. I am proud of you." I turned to leave.

"Are you cursed, perhaps with the kiss of death?" Sarah asked. "My mother used to tell me stories of the death kiss when I was a child,"

"Something like that." *Close enough*, I thought.

Mari's eye's widened. "Are you a … witch? Is that how you knew Sarah is with child?"

I almost laughed. "No. I am not a witch."

Mari's shoulders relaxed. She took me at my word. "Is there anything we can say to make you change your mind?" Her eye's filled with moisture.

"I must leave not only for your sake but for mine, as well. I am also in danger the longer I stay. I will write this time, I promise. Please do not worry about me. I will be fine. I can take care of myself." With that, I grabbed my precious cloak and a bag containing two dresses.

I paused in the doorway not wanting to step over the threshold. With a brief nod to my family I forced myself out into the night. It was good that they did not try to stop me, because I might have stayed. They must have sensed that I had no other choice.

I could hear Mari crying all over again. What a horrible day! Tears were running down my cheeks as well. Walking out that door was the hardest thing I had ever done.

I disappeared into the woods, ran and took flight when I was sure not to be seen. I could not help but look back. Once high above Ludus, I glanced around for signs of Teller. I was not surprised when I found none.

One small part of me wanted to try to catch Teller's scent in order to track him. But the greater part wanted nothing to do with him. I knew that if I were to find him, all I would see was Father's blood-stained body. I could not think past my grief. I did not know when or if I would see him again. When I thought of the future — his or mine — I saw nothing. I did not know where he would end up and I had no idea where I was going. There were no plans, no dreams and nothing to hope for. All had been lost.

For no particular reason I flew west. Of course, Constantinople must be avoided at all costs, though it would have been enjoyable to see the beautiful city again.

There was no chance in hell that I was going to Denmark. I would not give Lord Chastellain the pleasure of showing up on his doorstep, even though I would have liked to see Sonia and Aaron. If I were being honest with myself — which I was not — I would have admitted that it would be nice to see Elijah, as well. I quickly dismissed any thoughts of my friends in Denmark. Like everything else, they too were lost to me.

I did not know where I would end up but it would be farther west than I had ever gone before. I must start a new life. Perhaps I would find a new coven, one loyal to the Court of Elders. This was not for Chastellain's benefit but for my own. Vampires must remain discreet and hidden from humans. I would search for those of my kind who also believed this way. I knew which side I was on. It was merely a coincidence that Chastellain was on the same side. I could not help that.

It was still well before dawn when I caught sight of many distant lanterns. As far as they spanned, I knew it must be a large city. I landed outside of town. As normally — or as humanly — as possible, I headed for the lights. The sun was threatening to rise when I came across a man and a woman out for a stroll.

"Pardon me," I said. "Would you be so kind as to tell me where I am?"

"My young dear, are you lost?" The woman placed her gloved hand over her chest in exclamation.

I opened my mouth to answer and realized I did not know if I was lost — which must mean that I was, though be it intentional. "Of sorts," I managed.

"Well, you are lucky because you have arrived in the finest city ever built — London!" the man exclaimed.

PART III CHAPTER 50 LONDON 1261 AD

After becoming familiar with the city for a couple of nights, I decided that London was agreeable and might even make a good home. It was not nearly as developed as Constantinople. London was simple — I liked it. There seemed to be a lot of cloud cover, which was also suitable.

I knew it would not be long before the vampires of London found me. On the third day, I wandered into a tavern to escape the sun that finally decided to shine. I sat in the back of the dining area and avoided the curious stares. A man marched up and sat across the table from me uninvited. His was dressed better than the other men in this place.

"Well, well, what have we here? I presume that you must be new in town."

I leaned forward to get a better smell. This confirmed my suspicions; he was not human.

The thought of giving a false name had crossed my mind but that would not work for long. I knew the leader of the English coven from my time in Denmark and from the gala in Ludus. If, or when, we met, Lord Alexandru would recognize me at once. "Yes sir, my name is Vallachia. I was hoping to make London my new home."

"Pardon me; where are my manners?" He stood, took my hand and touched his lips to it. "My name is Hector. I know that name — Vallachia — from somewhere. It is not a common name."

I shrugged. "I have never been to London before."

"Well, I must take you to meet Lord Alexandru. He insists on meeting new vampires who enter his realm."

I stood. "I suppose you should, kind sir."

Hector raised his eyebrows, not expecting me to come so willingly.

"There is not much for me here, except some relief from the daylight. Surely I can find that with Lord Alexandru as well."

Hector gave a slight bow and we were off.

Lord Alexandru lived in a modest castle outside of London. His throne room was beautifully appointed with the latest décor. Recognizing me at once, he stood from his high seat.

"Ah, yes, the beautiful young Val …"

"Vallachia, My Lord." I bowed.

"Yes, yes, of course, the lovely Vallachia." He kissed my cheeks. "To what do we owe the honor?"

"You know her, My Lord?" Hector sounded surprised.

"Yes, of course. She is a friend to the Court. Our paths have crossed several times." Alexandru turned to me. "In fact, are you not engaged to the young Lord Chastellain?"

"No, My Lord, we were never betrothed." It was not difficult to imagine where he had gotten this impression. The first time I'd met Alexandru, Elijah had proposed to me, then in Denmark, we were always together.

"Oh, that is a pity. I had hoped to receive a wedding invitation soon. I love weddings, especially royal ones. Come, have some wine."

One thing I remembered about Lord Alexandru was that he coveted his wine almost as if it were a religious ritual. He gestured for me to take the seat next to his throne. Wine was poured. Alexandru inhaled the aroma and swirled his goblet. "Did you come with news from Copenhagen?"

"No, My Lord. I have no news. I am here because I had hoped to settle in London."

"That is marvelous. Of course, you are welcome, my dear." He frowned. "Why did you leave Denmark? I thought it was your new home."

Obviously, Alexandru had no idea I had left Denmark to return to Ludus. *What do I tell him? Why had I left? It is complicated. I cannot tell him it is because I loathed Lord Chastellain, as I wanted to be a part of his Court.*

I pretended to take a sip of wine. The smell was displeasing. It was the well-aged bitter wine that the wealthy often enjoyed. I placed the gold goblet back on the table without touching the substance. "I needed to get out on my own. I'm a relatively new vampire. I wanted to find my own way. Yet I want to remain in the North to fight against Ramdasha when the time comes." This was the truth, though not the entire truth.

Alexandru seemed to be satisfied with this answer. "Well, then, welcome. We will see to it that you are properly settled." He turned to Hector. "Send word to Lord Chastellain straightaway. Tell him the lovely Vallachia is safely in our company."

My heart sank. "Please, My Lord, must you tell him I am here?"

"Of course. Things have never been more unstable for the Court of Elders. Vampire populations are on the rise. We need to know where our allies are at all times."

"Yes, of course, My Lord." After all, who could argue with that?

Hector showed me to a rather small room not much bigger than my room in Ludus. It contained two even smaller beds.

"Why are there two beds?" I frowned.

"One is for you and the other is for your roommate. You see, the palace is quite crowded. We have begun construction on a new and much larger castle. However, for now, we must make do," Hector replied.

"Roommate?" I had never shared a room before.

"Yes, her name is Mary."

My stomach turned at the thought of sharing such a tiny space with someone I did not know. *I suppose that is one way to get to know someone*. When Hector was gone, I stretched out on one of the beds. I did not like it that Chastellain would soon know I was here. I feared he would come for me and demand that I return to Denmark. Blood rushed to my cheeks at the thought. I daydreamed of killing him if he did come for me. *Perhaps if I chopped his head off — surely that would kill a vampire?* I wondered if that was what it would take for him to leave me alone — death?

In my mind I saw Father's disappointed face. He had taught me better than that. I could almost hear his voice. *If you were to harm Chastellain, then you would be no better than he.* Tears fell. I knew this to be true but I hated Chastellain more than anything.

CHAPTER 51 LONDON 1261 AD

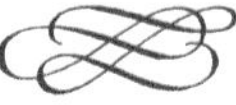

It was not long before Mary came barging into the room, interrupting my reverie.

"So it is true. They told me I had a new roommate." Mary's voice indicated her displeasure. "I had grown accustomed to privacy."

My mouth fell open at the site of her. I had never seen a woman like her. For starters, she had short brown hair, like a man's! In some places, it was against the law for women to cut their hair. The Bible says our hair is our glory. On top of that, she wore men's breeches! There was no doubt that, from a distance, she could be mistaken for a man.

I tried to compose myself by closing my mouth and clearing my throat. "Hello, my name is Vallachia," I managed to get out.

"I'm — "

"Mary, I know. I love that name."

"And your name is ... unique."

I could not help rudely staring at her. She was so ... different.

"You are on my bed."

I slowly moved to the other bed. There was no point in getting off to a bad start with her. I could imagine that not getting along with a roommate could make life difficult. After all, she had been here first and I did not care which bed was mine.

Mary threw herself down on her bed.

I watched her and said nothing.

"Out with it," Mary said.

"I am sorry! I don't mean to stare but I have never seen a woman with short hair or dressed the way you are."

"Not all of us are classic beauties such as yourself," she retorted.

"I do not think that is it. Besides, you have a very pretty face." This was true but I had to admit her hair was appalling.

She frowned, as if that were not a compliment. "Since I am stronger than human men, I have found that behaving like a man gets me further."

I did not understand. "How so?" One thing was for sure, I was completely fascinated by her.

"Men treat men differently from the way they do women. I can be seen on the streets at night and people don't think I am a helpless girl; or worse, assume I'm a prostitute. Men who think the latter usually do not survive. However, dressed like this, I'm largely ignored. I like it that way. It keeps unsavory vampire men from bidding for my affections as well. On top of all that, it is more comfortable. I can move with ease. I never intend to wear a dress again."

"That makes sense." Thwarting unwanted advances did sound nice, though I was far from wanting to cut off my hair. However, I had to admit that wearing breeches did offer some advantages. "Where are you from?" I asked.

Her spirits seemed to lighten. "I'm from a small town outside of London. And you?"

"Denmark," I lied. If vampires knew about Ludus they could easily find my family and I wanted to keep this world as far away from them as possible.

Mary bolted upright. "I've heard about you. You're the regal beauty who is to marry Lord Chastellain's son … what's his name?"

"Elijah." I said through gritted teeth. "and why would you think we are engaged?"

"I've heard the stories from Denmark about what a perfect couple you are and how much you love each other," she mocked, indicating her disapproval of gushy romance. Her eyes widened. "What are you doing here?"

"I needed a fresh start."

This was the truth and she seemed to understand. Perhaps she had even felt the same way at one time or another. This outsider's perspective on my relationship with Elijah was painful. *I suppose we had been close once — too close. Had I falsely encouraged him?* The now familiar guilty stone settled into my stomach. *I do care about him. I would still be killing if it were not for him. He was always kind to me.* I shook my head. *Forget about him! Forget about all men.* By "all men" I meant Teller.

SETTLING into a new life in London was going as well as could be expected. As the months passed, I began to let my guard down. Chastellain did not come for me or even write, except in his response to Lord Alexandru's news that I was living in London. Lord Chastellain said to send me his condolences regarding the loss of my father. The fact that he had the gall to mention Father was infuriating. This also indicated that he had remained in Ludus long enough to learn of Father's death.

I immediately sent a letter home to my brother. He needed to know that I was faring well and getting settled into a new home and a new life. I hoped it would help him not to worry about me. I did not tell him where I was, so he would not be able to write back. Though I desperately wanted news from home, I did not want anyone trying to follow me. I thought perhaps Ivan might want to find me to try to get answers about his son's whereabouts. It would not be safe for anyone to look for me, so I gave no clue as to where I was.

Much of my time was spent with Mary. Curiosity got the best of me, I simply had to find out what it was like to dress like a man. "May I borrow a pair of your breeches?"

Mary's brown eyes shone. "You are going to love them! They give you much more freedom to move. We will have to get you some that fit." She tossed me a pair.

I pulled them on. They were entirely too short.

Mary was right. I had not realized how lucky men were. Breeches did not get tangled around my legs or other obstacles when I passed by. After a couple of days of wearing breeches, I had all but forgotten about my dresses.

"Soon you will cut your hair short, too." Mary laughed.

"I think not!" I replied.

"It would be a shame to ruin such beautiful golden locks."

I could not tell if she was mocking or envious.

Mary fetched a man's hat from her small collection. "Here, try this." She combed my hair back, pulling it up into a tight bun and placed the hat on my head.

I laughed at the sight of myself in the modest looking glass over the washbasin. I shook my head. It felt free and airy without even a braid down my back. I was not sure if I liked it.

"Trust me; not having your hair in your face all the time is wonderful."

Again, Mary was correct; it was pleasant not to have to flick hair out of my face all the time.

These were major improvements for my training. I could fight better in breeches and with the hair out of my face. Despite disapproving looks from the other vampires, or from humans we passed in the street, I enjoyed this new appearance.

CHAPTER 52 LONDON 1261 AD

At sunset, Mary and I would usually head out into the city. We sat on the rooftop of a tall building in order to admire London from high up. The view was spectacular. The River Thames glistened as it wound its way through the land. The soft glow of candles, lamps and household lanterns made the town look like a sea of stars mimicking the sky above. Soon most of these lights would be extinguished as the town slept and the stars in the nearly cloudless sky would appear even brighter.

I had better feed fairly soon, I thought. "While I was in Denmark with Elijah, he taught me to feed without killing."

Mary furrowed her brow. "You are lying."

"It is true. I have not killed anyone since I was ... very new. Come; I will prove it to you."

Below, a man walked alone — never a good idea with a thirsty vampire around. I jumped off the roof and landed noiselessly behind him. Before he could turn, I grabbed his head to stop him from seeing who I was and sank my teeth in his neck. The taste was sweet and delicious. Then his heartbeat slowed, I released him and gently lowered him to the ground.

"It will take him some time to recover but he will survive. He also did not see me. He will have no idea what happened to him."

Mary's mouth hung open in amazement. She kept her distance from the smell of blood. "How did you make yourself stop?"

"It takes much practice and someone to pull you off at first. One must also be motivated to not kill."

"You know other vampires who can do this as well?" She was still skeptical.

"Yes. I can teach you if you would like."

"I don't imagine I could ever do that."

"Will you try?"

Mary hesitated. "I suppose."

"It would be easier if we had a third vampire to help me pull you off. I may not be strong enough to do it alone."

Mary looked thoughtful for a moment. Her eyes brightened. "I know just the one. Elizabeth despises the killing. She is new and this would give her real hope. I worry about her. She hates being a vampire. I fear she may try to take her own life, which for us is not easy."

I could empathize with Elizabeth. "Wonderful! There is no time to waste."

Mary's eyes sparkled with hope.

We went straight back to the castle to find Elizabeth. I had seen her around. She, like Sonia, had been turned when she was young — too young. In fact, Elizabeth's small frame reminded me of Sonia and made me miss Sonia all the more.

Elizabeth did not believe Mary when she told her that I had fed without killing. "It is true. I saw it with my own eyes," Mary said.

"I can teach you and Mary to do the same."

Elizabeth only frowned — not daring to believe in such a wonderful possibility.

I went on to explain how the key was to feed regularly at first to help keep the craving and the monster under control. By the time I finished, Elizabeth's eyes had a light in them that had not been there before.

"It is hard work but it can be done, I promise," I said.

Elizabeth was still reluctant but agreed to help me teach Mary.

We tried that night and of course we had to pull Mary off the woman she was feeding from. We practiced a couple of times per week. Elizabeth eventually decided that she too would try. Thankfully, we did not kill anyone but after a couple of months, they were growing discouraged.

"Please, don't give up. It takes time to learn to control the beast inside. You will acquire the ability," I said.

"How long did it take you?" Elizabeth asked.

"About two months. For Sonia it was a bit longer. It took Elijah years but then again he was doing this on his own."

I worried that they would give up. *Maybe I am doing something wrong. If only Elijah were here to help. He would know what to do.*

Thankfully, the following week, Mary succeeded in feeding and we did not have to pull her off. This gave Elizabeth the confidence she needed. It proved that it could be done. She too was eventually able to feed without killing.

Elizabeth threw her arms around me. "I can't believe it! I did it. I owe you my life, as you have made it worth living again."

I returned her hug and gently set her down. "I never doubted you. The pleasure is all mine. One thing we can do is find others who are willing to learn to feed as we do."

"That is it!" Mary's smile broadened. "Imagine the possibilities."

Word spread quickly around Alexandru's castle about what we were capable of doing. There were plenty of willing vampires and we worked with each of them. Some remained skeptical and some were — unfortunately — not interested. I tried not to concern myself with them and concentrated on the vampires who were motivated not to kill. It was time consuming, which was a good thing. It filled the emptiness of losing my family … twice and it gave my life purpose.

Things were going as well as could be expected, as I had little time to dwell on my past. When I did think of Father, the image of him and my mother together once again, standing hand-in-hand, would come to mind. This allowed me to feel joy for my father. *He has been reunited with his beloved wife.* Life was … good.

CHAPTER 53 LONDON 1262 AD

I came to London in the summer and it was not until the next spring of 1262 that someone from Denmark came for me. Never in my wildest dreams would I have guessed who.

I had hoped Sonia and Aaron would come to visit. If they did not, I would have to visit them someday, perhaps when I was not so busy teaching vampires to feed properly. That was what we called it, feeding properly. I still wanted to avoid Lord Chastellain at all costs. I had even secretly hoped Elijah would visit, though I tried not to think about him and I still worried that the lord himself would come for me one day. I was wrong — none of them came.

One beautiful spring night, Mary, Elizabeth and I had left the castle. Our man-like way of dressing had influenced Elizabeth as well. We looked like three men from a distance; well, perhaps two men and a boy, as Elizabeth was quite small. Elizabeth and I even had our long hair tucked under men's hats. This was a strong deterrent for male vampires. I enjoyed the lack of attention from them. Most men assumed I was engaged to Elijah, or they were appalled by my masculine appearance. Either way, it worked for me. I was not interested in any of them. Mary and Elizabeth felt the same way.

As we walked an empty street, I noticed a young woman in a fancy gown. She moved confidently toward us. She was graceful — a bit too graceful. A gentle breeze brushed against my face and I was able to catch her scent. This confirmed my suspicion, she was not human. "Do you know her?" I whispered to my companions.

"No," Mary said.

The strange woman lifted her head and from under her headdress her face came into focus. My jaw dropped. "Mari…" I rubbed my eyes because I was sure they were tricking me.

"Surprise!" Mari's laugh rang out through the night.

Which was no doubt caused by my wide-eyed, open-mouthed expression. "Mari, what … how?" I tried to say.

She laughed again. Hardly missing a beat, she put her arms around me in a fierce hug.

I was in shock but eventually returned the gesture. When she pulled away, I managed to say, "You look wonderful! How did this … happen?"

She stepped back and eyed me with disproval. "And you look … different." She struggled to remain polite.

"What are you doing here?" I asked. We obviously had some catching up to do.

"I was on my way to Alexandru's castle to find you. I have something for you." She handed me a beautifully sealed parchment. I knew straightaway what it was — a wedding invitation. *But whose?* I quickly broke the seal unrolled the letter. The pieces fell into place as I read …

Your presence is requested at the wedding of Lord Samuel of Denmark and his bride-to-be, Mari of Ludus.

"I can't believe it. He came back for you. And he … turned you …" I whispered.

Mari simply beamed and all I could feel was delight for her. I picked her up and spun her around. "Congratulations!" Then I remembered my manners. "Oh, I am sorry. Mari, here are *Mary* and Elizabeth."

"It is a pleasure to meet you!" Mari proceeded to kiss each of their cheeks.

"I like her," Elizabeth whispered.

"Well, she does have a fine name," Mary admitted. "We will head out and let you two talk." Mary had to pull Elizabeth away.

After they were gone, I could not contain the many questions racing through my mind. I started with what I could piece together. "Samuel came back for you?"

"I was elated when he returned."

"How much did he tell you about vampires? Did he give you a choice about becoming like him?"

"A choice of sorts, I suppose. He told me what he was and I did not believe him or even understand what he was saying. He asked me if I wanted to be with him forever, which of course I did. Then he asked if I trusted him. I said I did. The next thing I knew, he was bleeding and I was helpless to get away from him. The last thing I remembered was the taste of blood."

"That is terrible." Samuel had not truly given her a choice.

"Aye, it was a nightmare in the beginning. I regretted the decision and hated myself. It took much convincing but we were able to pull Elijah out of his dark ravine. He finally agreed to help us learn to feed without killing. Things have gotten better since then. I would have found you sooner but I am just now coming to terms with everything."

"I am glad you are here, even though this is not a life I would have wanted for you. I tried to protect you from all this."

She nodded. "I know but things are excellent now. I have never been happier and I love the life I have in Denmark." If her words had not convinced me that she was telling the truth, then her eyes certainly did. They glistened like stars in a clear night's sky.

I smiled. "It is selfish of me but I am grateful that you will be my friend for many lifetimes."

Mari gave me another hug. "About the wedding, you will come?"

"I would not miss it for the world."

"That is wonderful because there is no one else besides you who could possibly be my chief bridesmaid."

"It would be my pleasure."

Mari's jubilance was contagious. My spirits had not been this high since before my father's death.

"It is settled ... but you will not dress like that, I hope?" Mari frowned with exaggerated disapproval.

CHAPTER 54 LONDON 1262 AD

"Of course I will not dress like a man for your wedding." I laughed.

Mari looked genuinely relieved. Then her expression turned serious. "What about you?" She hesitated. "Did you come to London alone? Teller is not with you?"

My heart sank at the mention of Teller. "No, I came alone. I have no idea where he is. Did he come back to Ludus?"

"No and his father ran himself ragged looking for him."

Although I had never cared for Ivan, this news did make me feel terrible for him. I would not wish that on anyone. To have a son disappear without a clue — that was simply tragic. Maybe I should write to him and tell him some partial truth so that he could stop looking and begin to move on.

Mari studied me. "Samuel told me only that Lord Chastellain turned you and that after you learned to control your thirst, you returned home. Although I asked, Elijah would never tell me more. In fact, he does not speak to anyone about you. No one knows what happened the night ... you know ..."

I did know what she meant — the night Father was killed. I did not want to relive it, all the heartache and pain. I had lost both

Father and Teller that night. Then I had to leave my brother. I told her how I could not be with Teller without showing him who I was. "So I did and of course he rejected me, or the creature I had become ..."

Mari could not believe that Chastellain tried to kill Teller.

"Lord Chastellain seems so ... levelheaded. Surely he would not do something such as that," Mari said.

I finished my story and Mari said nothing for a time.

"Teller killed your father. I'm so sorry." She paused. "Well, that explains a great deal, like why you did not come back to Denmark. I will not be able to look at Lord Chastellain in the same way."

Good, I thought. All this talk of that horrible night was rekindling the coals of hatred in my heart.

Mari's face brightened. "You should come back to Denmark with me. Sonia and Aaron would be delighted to see you and who knows? Perhaps you and Elijah can ... you know." She did not seem to have the right words.

Now she was playing matchmaker. I glared at her.

"Or not." She paused. "Just imagine how perfect it would be, two dearest friends marrying two dear friends. I'm sure if you came back, Elijah would forgive you."

It occurred to me then how young at heart Mari was. *Had that extra year of being a vampire hardened me that much?* I did not know if I believed in love anymore.

"Forgive me for what? Loving someone else? Rejecting him at least twice? That is pretty unforgivable, don't you think?"

"Not if you were to choose him."

'Choose him'. She made it sound simple. I had not fully admitted this to myself yet, but Teller was out there somewhere and I had not given up on him. I gestured to my clothing. "Can't you see that I am intentionally not wanting any male attention?"

"Aye, I am sure that is an effective strategy." She eyed my clothes with raised eyebrows. "A better strategy would be to commit yourself to someone. That also stops potential suitors and you don't have to dress like that."

"You should try it," I teased. "It is wonderful. Breeches give you much more freedom."

"Freedom to do what?" Her voice sounded appalled.

"Run, fly, fight, things vampires do…"

"Elijah says I should learn to defend myself. He says that this world is different and more dangerous than the human world. Samuel does not force the issue, so I don't know what I think about learning to fight. I have not gotten used to the idea. I'm still trying to master the ability to fly."

"Elijah is right, you know. We in the North have enemies."

"I know — Ram-whatever. If you come back with me, you can teach me to fight."

She was obviously trying to tempt me into returning to Denmark. "Honestly, I abhor Lord Chastellain. The thought of seeing him again makes me ill."

"You will have to see him at my wedding — the one you promised to attend."

"This is my home, Mari." My voice was stern.

"Very well, come back with me to help me prepare for the wedding. I need you there."

I frowned. "There are plenty of servants in the Chastellain Court to help you."

"But they are not my dearest friend from childhood," Mari sang.

Her large brown eyes plead her case. *How could I refuse that?* "Very well but only until the wedding. Stay with us for the day and we will leave for Copenhagen at dusk tomorrow. That way I can let everyone know where I will be."

With a squeal, she gave a quick jump of excitement.

"Just until the wedding!" I reminded her.

"I know. I know."

We spent the rest of the night flying. I took her to my favorite overlook, which was far from the city.

Having Mari back in my life and all this talk of home had me thinking. "Have you ever felt …" I was unsure how to say it. "I don't know, different when you encountered a certain person?"

She pressed her lips together in concentration. She had no idea what I was trying to say. Neither did I.

"After I was turned, when Teller and I would touch, it was like a shock went through me. It was a pleasant sensation — like an intense tingling," I tried to explain. "It felt … wonderful, too wonderful, actually… " I trailed off. "I have never had such a sensation with anyone else. And there was a brief moment when I may have felt his physical pain."

Mari was thoughtful for a moment. "That is strange."

"Aye — strange," I said.

"I always knew, even when we were young, that you two had some connection. It was like you were meant to be together."

My stomach turned. I knew Mari was right. Teller and I were destined to be together. I should have found him right away. There was no telling where he was. For the first time in almost a year, I allowed myself to admit that I longed for him. Surely he would find me.

CHAPTER 55 LONDON 1262 AD

At dawn, we returned to Lord Alexandru's castle. I introduced Mari to the lord. She had a wedding invitation for him as well, which he gladly received. I packed a couple of things and reluctantly put a gown on at Mari's behest.

When I told Mary and Elizabeth that we would be leaving for Denmark at dusk, Mary rolled over in her bed, turning her back to us, saying nothing. I looked at Elizabeth for an explanation of this odd behavior. She shrugged indicating that she did not know what was wrong with Mary.

"Mary, I will be back in three months' time, after Mari's wedding."

"I don't care," she said.

I shook my head at Elizabeth and only received another unknowing shrug.

"I promise to return and … I know, why don't you two come with us?"

"Go away," Mary said.

"What is wrong with you, Mary?"

"Nothing, I'm perfectly well."

"I can see that," I said with sarcasm. I did not know why this upset me but it did. I hooked my arm in Mari's and we were gone.

~

As we drew closer to Denmark, my trepidation grew. I dreaded having to be cordial to Chastellain and ... *how would Elijah receive me?* There was no predicting his reaction to my return. I did not know if it was better for him to remain angry with me or not. *It would be for the best if he left me alone. Or would it be better if he forgave me? At least then we could be friends again. I missed his friendship but it was never as simple as friendship on his end. What if he still wants more and I cannot give it to him.* I tried to concentrate on how wonderful it would be to see Sonia and Aaron.

When we arrived, Mari led me straight to the Great Hall.

"No, not now. I don't want to see Lord Chastellain — not yet," I pled with Mari.

"Come; he needs to know you are here and Samuel will most likely be in the Great Hall at this time." She gave me a reassuring smile.

I took a deep breath. *Very well, control your temper. Do this for Mari,* I told myself. Mari opened the grand doors and virtually dragged me into the hall. I spotted the lord at once. Instantly, my heart beat faster and my cheeks warmed with anger. I stopped Mari as we walked.

"I cannot do this," I whispered.

Samuel's voice proclaimed with great pride that his lady had returned.

This distracted Mari and I slipped out of her grip. I turned to leave. Unfortunately, Lord Chastellain was blocking my exit. He took my hand before I could pull away.

"My dear lady, it is about time you returned to the Court." The lord's sarcastic smirk caused my shoulders to tense. He gently kissed my hand.

I glared at him. "It is only temporary, My Lord, until the wedding. Then I will return to England."

"We shall see about that. Meanwhile, welcome home."

His over-confidence made my blood boil. *Aye, we shall see,* I thought. I bowed slightly. Sidestepping him I exited the hall. I had to get away from him in order to stop myself from slapping his face.

Attacking the leader of the High Court of Elders would be a foolish thing to do. The more he tried to control me, the more defiant I became. I was determined that he would not keep me here.

I heard Mari and Samuel's joyful reunion back in the Great Hall as I headed toward Sonia's and Aaron's rooms. I hugged each of them in turn. Sonia had tears of joy in her eyes.

"I'm not back for good, only until the wedding." I did not want them to think I was moving back here.

Sonia pouted.

They wanted to know about London. I told them about my work — teaching vampires not to kill when they fed. That brought us to Elijah.

"Where is he?" I asked. He had not been at his father's side in the Great Hall.

Sonia and Aaron exchanged a knowing look.

"I have not seen Elijah in days," Sonia said. "No one knows where he disappears to at times."

I knew where he was. "Please excuse me." I stood to leave, feeling an urgent need to see Elijah. They looked at me with curiosity. I hugged each of them again. "It is wonderful to see you both!" Then I was gone.

I flew low over the Oresund. I liked to reach down and feel the cool water. I did not think Elijah would like others to find his refuge, so I made certain no one followed me. I dived into the water. Soon I was in his cave. It was exactly as I remembered — roomy, with a beautiful green mossy waterfall. He had brought more provisions to the cave over the past year. There were blankets, pillows, a chair and books. This was most likely because of the increased time he apparently spent here since I had left. I slowly emerged from the water.

He looked up at me from his book as if I were a specter. Slamming the book closed he quickly stood. "Is it really you?" He wrapped his arms around me.

CHAPTER 56 COPENHAGEN 1262 AD

I did not hug Elijah back. A horrible thought had occurred to me over the past year. Perhaps Elijah had sent his father to kill Teller, or at least knew about the plot. I usually pushed the thought away because I did not want to believe Elijah would do that to me. I had to know the truth. Part of me did not believe Elijah was capable of such evil. He was nothing like his father. Or was he? I pushed him firmly away.

He looked into my troubled eyes and took my hands in his. "I am sorry to hear about your father. He was a great man."

I stared at him. I had to know what role he'd played in the attempted murder of Teller.

When I did not speak he asked, "What is wrong?"

"What do you know about the night my father died?" My voice was full of accusation.

His eyes widened in surprise, most likely at my hard tone. "I know nothing of that night. Father informed me that Adam had died. It was your father who used to send news from Ludus but since his death, we have not heard anything."

I stared intently into his smoky blue eyes, trying to discern the truth. It appeared that he did not know anything.

"What happened that night?" Elijah asked.

"How do you think your father knew about my father's death?" I answered his question with another.

He looked thoughtful.

"What do you know of your father's visit to Ludus?"

"What visit? When?" His brow was lined with concern.

I studied him; it was becoming obvious that he'd had nothing to do with it. "Did you know the lord sent for me, demanding I return here at once?"

"I told him not to and that it would not succeed in getting you back. Clearly, he did not listen to me." He shook his head. "That is not a surprise."

"Well, when I did not return as he requested, what do you think your father did?"

His eyes widened. "My father killed Adam?"

"Not exactly. Indirectly, I suppose."

He shook his head again, this time indicating that he was confused.

"You knew nothing about your father's plans?"

"No." His voice was stern. He put his hands on my upper arms. "What happened?"

Elijah's eyes were the usual sad storm but they were sincere. This convinced me that he had nothing to do with Teller's attempted murder. My resolve faded, as did my anger at the thought that he had known about or encouraged his father's plan to get rid of Teller.

"I'm sorry," I wrapped my arms around him. "I had to be sure I could trust you." I proceeded to tell him the story of his father's visit and my father's death.

Elijah sat down in his chair as I paced. He put his head in his hands. "I told Father to leave you alone. He thinks he knows what is best for me but he never listens to what I want … or what you want, for that matter. I knew you wished to be left alone. I asked him to honor that as I had."

How could I have doubted Elijah? He is not his father. Deep down, I had known that. He was selfless and kind. He was willing to leave me alone for as long as I needed. That was why he had never come for me in London. He had indeed been honoring my wish. I placed my hand on his shoulder. He stood and took my hand.

"I'm sorry he did that to you. That was why you went to London instead of returning here? To avoid my father?"

I nodded yes.

"But you are back." He voice was soft and tender.

He has already forgiven me for leaving him ... for Teller. How could that be? I pulled my hand out of his. "Only until Mari and Samuel's wedding. Then I will return to London." My voice was flat, as if this were a rehearsed line.

"Well, luckily, that is months away. That is plenty of time for me to convince you to change your mind."

"I will not stay and besides, shouldn't you be angry with me?"

"For what — leaving?"

"Yes," I said.

He gave me his beautiful crooked smile. I could not help smiling back. I'd missed that smile more than I had realized. The gray storm had cleared from his eyes. They looked bluer than they had moments ago.

"Let's get out of here," he said. Then he did something unexpected. He picked me up and threw me into the water.

"What ... ?" I said when my head broke the surface. But he dived in next to me. He splashed me. I splashed back but it was too late — he was already underwater. He grabbed my foot and pulled me under.

We headed back to the castle. When we landed on his balcony, he took my hand in his. After collecting Sonia and Aaron we headed to the Great Hall.

"You found him," Sonia declared.

"Of course. He tells her where he hides and not the rest of us." Aaron pretended to be bitter.

"Come. Let's get Samuel and Mari. We have much to celebrate," Elijah said.

"And it seems he is not going to tell us where he disappears to," Sonia said.

We gathered in Elijah's chambers. Elijah poured the wine. It still tasted horrible but I drank some anyway.

"Here's to Samuel and Mari and to Vallachia returning home," Elijah said.

Aaron added, "Hear, hear."

Our goblets rang out as they collided.

"Back for now," I amended Elijah's toast. "Here is to being with old friends." This prompted another round of clinking metal goblets.

It was not long before the conversation turned to politics.

"Our informant in Bursa sends news that the vampire population is growing out of control in parts of Southern Europe. Humans are calling it Tarantism," Samuel was saying.

"What does that mean?" I asked.

"People are being bitten and at times going crazy. They say they are 'dancing' wildly in the streets. Most likely this madness is caused by a loss of blood. Of course many humans are dying because of this 'madness.' They blame the bite of the wolf spider for the chaos and deaths."

"What is a wolf spider?" Mari asked.

"We often refer to them as tarantulas," I said. "Ramdasha had large green tapestries that contained sinister-looking spiders hanging in his cavern. The spiders were tarantulas — his symbol."

"Do you think he is responsible for the growing vampire populations?" Aaron asked.

"Most likely," Elijah answered.

"This is getting depressing," Sonia said.

Elijah changed the subject. "Father has finally agreed to learn to feed without killing. Who will help me teach him?" He was looking at me, though he asked the question to everyone in the room.

"I would rather die," I said.

"This is for the good of humanity. You would not turn your back on a fellow vampire who is trying to do good."

I glared at Elijah. He was trying to make me feel guilty and he was succeeding.

"I will help," Samuel offered with his usual carefree manner.

We continued to talk and drink for hours.

"I need to rest. Where will I be staying?" I asked Elijah.

He stood. "In *your* room, of course." He took my hand and led me out.

"Surely it is not that difficult to find. I can manage. After all, my room is just across the hall."

My sarcastic tone did not deter him from walking me to the door. The others retired as well.

"Good day," I said to them. This term had replaced "goodnight" a long time ago because if we did sleep it was usually during the day.

Elijah gave me a kiss on the forehead. "I have sorely missed you. You have no idea how wonderful it is to see you."

"I have to admit, it is good to see … everyone." I put my head down at the sorrow his kind words caused — words I could not fully return. I swiftly retreated to my old bedchambers and shut the door. The large room was exactly as I had left it, except without the letter on the pillow, the letter that must have terribly hurt Elijah.

I tried to push the guilt out. *He is kind and good … and handsome.* I shook my head. *Think of something else.* It was strange to be back in this huge, fancy room. It made me miss my small, humble quarters back in London. They were cozy, at least. I was used to having a roommate. This room felt cold and lonely. Still, I lay down and fell fast asleep.

CHAPTER 57 COPENHAGEN
1262 AD

There was much to do to get ready for the noble wedding. My time was spent with my friends. I avoided Elijah's father whenever possible, though they told me his training was going well.

"Soon he will be able to feed like us," Elijah reported.

The lord is a strange character. I thought. *How could he ruthlessly kill Teller, then want to learn to feed without killing? He does fight to protect humans and keep vampires from taking over the world, yet he could kill humans so easily when it served his purpose. He was a true conundrum.*

The night of the wedding arrived. Sonia, Mari and I bathed in expensive oils. It took us hours to get Mari ready. Sonia was an artist with hair. She curled and pinned Mari's hair up perfectly, letting the curls hang beautifully around her face. We tended to prefer the latest fashions of the East. Mari said she wanted to look like an Empress on her wedding day. She wore a white silk brocade with thick gold trim. The final touch was a jeweled headpiece with strands of pearls hanging down around her face. She was exquisite. She looked like an empress indeed. It was clear that she had no doubts. She was ready for marriage.

"You are the most beautiful bride to ever walk the earth." I gave her a hug.

As the chief bridesmaid, I entered the Great Hall first to start the ceremony. Elijah was waiting for me. As the chief groomsman, he held out his arm for me to take. We walked down the aisle side by side. Aaron and Sonia followed.

"I wish this were our wedding," he whispered.

I frowned. Teller had once said that same thing to me at my brother's wedding. Pushing the sudden sadness away, I gave Elijah a weak smile.

Despite his handsome crooked smile, his eyes were more gray than blue. I had learned to read the color of his eyes. When they appeared blue it meant he was happy. They had been blue these past months. Today they were iron gray. This broke my heart twice over, first for Teller, then again for Elijah.

Thankfully, Mari entered the Great Hall, distracting me from my reverie. She was breathtaking. The soon-to-be newlyweds were beaming. This raised my spirits. *It will be difficult to leave, yet I can visit from time to time.*

After the perfect ceremony, the dancing began. Elijah held his arm out with a slight bow. I answered with a curtsy. There was no one else I would rather dance with tonight. Besides, dancing with Elijah kept others away. Some men had been watching me. I stayed close to Elijah and did not give them the chance to ask me to dance.

I wished it were possible to fall in love with Elijah, the way I had been with Teller. Maybe I still loved Teller and that was the problem.

Elijah gave a heartfelt speech to his closest friend and his new bride. I wished them the best as well, although my speech was much shorter than Elijah's, as I did not like speaking in front of people. Samuel thanked Elijah and me for introducing him to Mari. That seemed so long ago, back when Mari and I had both been human and we'd had no idea the two men we were with were ancient and dangerous creatures of the night.

After an entire night and day, the festivities came to an end. The newlyweds were nowhere to be seen at that point. They had long since slipped away. As chief groomsman and bridesmaid, Elijah and I had the duty of seeing all the guests off.

It was a relief to retire to my room. I could not wait to get this gown off. I missed my trusty breeches back in London. I slept for the usual hour. At dusk I would be leaving. I crossed the hall to Elijah's room and knocked — no answer. I opened the door but the room was empty. I found him in his cave.

"You are leaving, aren't you?" he said as soon as my head broke the surface of the water.

I nodded. "It is not like last time, though. I need you all. I will visit and you all can visit me as well."

"At least you came to say goodbye in person this time and I won't learn that you are gone by some ridiculous note."

I stepped toward him. "Elijah, I am sorry. I still need time to figure out what it is I want. I have friends in England as well."

"You mean you still love Teller and hope he will find you."

How could he possibly have known that, when I had barely admitted it to myself? "I still do not want to be around your father." This was all I could think to say and it was true. I did not know how I felt about Teller. "Come visit me in London."

He stood and took my hands. The storm was raging in his gray eyes, any trace of blue was gone. This made my heart ache for him. He leaned down to kiss me. I put my hand over his heart to stop him.

"I'm sorry; I can't," I breathed.

I dived into the water. I had to get out of there before my resolve vanished entirely. As usual, Elijah did not follow; he would give me the room and the time I needed. I returned to say goodbye to the others, promising them I would visit and encouraging them to do the same. They said they would.

"Thank you for coming," Mari said. "I know it was hard on you to see Lord Chastellain."

"I am glad you found happiness." I tightly wrapped my arms around her.

At dusk, I flew east. I wanted to visit home first. Though I had written to my brother many times, I had not received any word from home, as they did not know where I was. It had been a year since I left. I had to see how he was faring. I would only observe from the shadows. I did not want to disrupt their lives — again.

I landed in a tree outside my childhood home. The memories of my father's death came flooding back. *This might be too painful. Perhaps I should not have come.*

A baby cried for its mother inside the dark home. Sarah rose and a lamp was lit. She reached into a tiny bassinet by the bed and lifted a beautiful baby from it. She sat in a nearby chair and fed the hungry infant.

A tear of joy ran down my cheek and relief flooded through me. *The baby is healthy.*

CHAPTER 58 LUDUS 1262 AD

The next day was Sunday. I watched as the villagers gathered for church. Sitting in the shade on the opposite side of the wall from where my brother gave his oration, I listened to every word. Josiah sounded like Father. I beamed with pride. I could not have created and delivered such a beautiful liturgy. It was fortunate that the townspeople had him. They did not know how lucky they were. It was a comfort to learn that there was someone to fill Father's important role as the village peacekeeper.

"He who receives the precious blood — the blood of our Lord Jesus Christ, preserve his body and soul unto everlasting life." Josiah delivered the Divine Liturgy.

How many times I had heard those exact words from Father. Now they had an entirely new meaning.

I wished that Teller and I were attending the oration with our firstborn child as well. That was the life we were meant to have, the life I longed for. It was lost forever. Now I had an absurd life, one I never would have dreamt possible.

I had to see my brother. He must know how proud I was of him. He was about eighteen and a full-grown man. It might be helpful for him to see that I was well — well, physically anyway.

I waited in the shadows until everyone had left the church. One of Teller's little brothers closely resembled Teller at that age. Just when I thought my heart could not ache any more, I felt it break entirely in two. *Where is Teller? Should I try to find him?*

That seemed impossible. I did not know where to start. He could be anywhere. The best thing would be for him to find me. For that, I needed to stay put and visible, to vampires anyway. I must stay in London. In vampire circles, it would be easy to find me. It was no secret where I was. *So why has he not found me? Maybe he does not care about me.*

Elijah had been right, I supposed. Of course he was; he was always right. I should have known this by now. I still loved Teller and I was waiting for him. There was no other reason for keeping Elijah at arm's length if not for a distant hope that Teller and I could be together. Otherwise, I would allow myself to become lost in Elijah's stormy eyes. All this thinking was making my stomach ache.

Josiah was the last to leave the church. I covered my head with the trusty hood before stepping out into the sun. "Josiah," I called.

Josiah turned and stared at me for a moment. "I can't believe it!"

"That was a wonderful oration," I said. "Father would be proud."

"How did you ... but you were not in church?" Josiah asked.

I gave him a quick hug; hopefully, he would not notice my cool temperature even though it was a warm day. "It gives me much joy to see you."

"Where did you come from?" He looked around for the answer to this question.

"It does not matter. I had to tell you how proud I am of you and how happy I am for you."

"You must come meet your niece!" The excitement brightened his eyes.

"I would love to. Please know that I can't stay. I only wanted you to see that I am well."

"Where have you been?"

"That does not matter either."

"You are rather cryptic. What happened to you? I have so many questions. Do you know where Mari is?"

Cryptic. That was the perfect word for my life. "Mari is well — very well indeed. Please tell her mother I said so."

I stopped my brother as we approached home. I put my hands on his shoulders gently, being extra careful not to hurt him and looked him in the eyes. "It is not safe for anyone from here to try to find us. Please trust me. We stay away to protect the ones we love."

Josiah returned my intense stare with a nod of understanding.

I simply could not resist. "Has there been any word of Teller this past year?"

"No. Most assume he must be with you as well," Josiah answered.

I put my head down and shook it no, trying hard to swallow the knot that had formed in my throat.

Josiah put his hand on my shoulder. "I'm sorry."

We entered my old home, which was no longer mine and never would be again. Sarah looked up in surprise as we entered. She held a tiny sleeping baby in her arms. She smiled and nodded a greeting.

"Hello, Sarah. Motherhood is treating you well. You look wonderful."

"Thank you," she said with a shy smile and gazed down at her baby. She stood and brought the baby to me. She placed the tiny bundle gently into my arms, supporting her fragile head. "Meet little Vallachia."

I did not even try to hold back the tears that formed in my eyes. This was as close as I would get to having my own children. "She is lovely." I held her as lightly as possible to my chest.

"We hope she will be as beautiful as you," Sarah said.

"Oh no, I'm sure she will be much prettier."

It was difficult to leave but I had to before anyone else from the village spotted me. There would be so many questions that I could not answer. My brother walked me out at dusk.

"So you have been ordained as a deacon?"

"Aye, I spent the majority of the past year studying at the great cathedral in Targoviste. It takes most young men roughly two years to complete the training. Some of them could barely read. Since I was already well educated and had read the Bible many times over, I quickly became a star pupil. I devoured any religious text I could get my hands on. Bishop Justinian did not want me to leave. He tried hard to convince me to stay and become a bishop. But under no circumstances would I leave Sarah. So they finally ordained me as a deacon and I returned as soon as possible. It was difficult to miss the birth of little Vallachia but I am here now and able to provide for them."

The wonderful story made me smile. I could not have been happier for my brother. "Don't worry; you will have many more children to see born." I paused for a moment. "I'm delighted for you. I needed to return to see if you were faring well and now that I know you are, I can leave with peace in my heart."

"I wish I could say the same for you, big sister." He frowned. "Don't get me wrong, you look lovely as always but not ... happy."

"This is not the life I wanted. I wish to be with the people I love. Please, know that I am very sorry for that. Yet I will visit when I can." I gave him a hug until he shivered.

"You're freezing."

"I'm warm enough, little brother."

Ivan exited his home and spotted us. "Hey!" Ivan marched toward us.

Oh no. I turned to leave — headed for the forest.

"Wait!" he demanded. He caught up to us and seized my arm.

"You are going to want to let go of me." I turned to face Ivan.

Josiah came to my defense. "She does not know where Teller is."

"Then she's lying." Ivan tightened his grip on my arm. "She is a liar! Where is my son?"

"I don't know, Ivan. I'm very sorry he is gone. I would find him if I could." I tried to soothe him.

"You know what happened to him! Where is he?" He tried to yank me back toward the village but I held my ground. As strong as he was, he could not move me.

"Let go of her. She knows nothing," Josiah demanded.

"Ivan, for your sake, please listen to my brother. I don't want to hurt you."

Ivan chuckled. He was used to bullying people. There were not many men in the village who could best him.

I grabbed his hand that held my arm and put pressure between his thumb and fingers, the weakest part of the hand. The pain cut his chuckle short and he had to release me. I threw his hand back at him and turned to leave.

Ivan grasped my shoulders from behind. "You won't get away that easily."

My training took over. I raised my arms and grabbed his head and neck. I threw my upper body forward pulling him over the top of me. He landed hard on his back with a moan. I tried to be as gentle as possible. When training with vampires, I could be more forceful but I did not want to kill or even hurt Ivan.

I looked at my brother. "I'm sorry you had to see that. I have to go."

With wide eyes Josiah nodded. "Goodbye, big sister."

In a flash I was gone, taking flight as soon as I was alone. Josiah was like our father. He was loving, supportive and understanding. He did not demand anything of me and he trusted me to make my own decisions. I was lucky to have him in my life at all, even if it was only briefly.

CHAPTER 59 LONDON 1262 AD

I arrived in London late into the night, I circled Lord Alexandru's small castle once and landed on a balcony. I found Mary and Elizabeth in the Great Hall. Elizabeth was glad to see me. She jumped to her feet and hugged me. Holding her off the ground, I returned the gesture. "It is good to see you." I whispered.

I started toward Mary. She crossed her arms and glared at me. This stopped my approach. "It is good to see you too, Mary."

"So you did come back?" Mary posed this as a question.

"I promised you I would."

"And you are alone. Where is your *prince*?"

"What is wrong with you? What did I ever do to you?"

"Nothing," she snapped and walked away.

I looked to Elizabeth for help.

She frowned and followed Mary out of the hall.

I was about to follow when Lord Alexandru approached.

"I was beginning to worry," he said. "We arrived back from the wedding yesterday. Where did you go?" He kissed my cheeks in greeting.

"I had to make a quick stop," I said.

"Well, I am glad you are back safely."

"Thank you, My Lord. It is good to be back." *Or was it?* I thought as I wondered about Mary's strange behavior. *What had come over her?* I would try to get to the bottom of this but first I needed to feed. It had been a bit too long and I did not want to lose control. I headed out instead.

As I laid my barely breathing victim down on the street, I caught a glimpse of two figures. They moved quickly in the shadows. I took a deep breath; their odor confirmed that they were vampires. I did not entirely recognize their scent. They slowly approached.

"Is it she?" one of them asked his companion.

Something told me they were not friendly. I quickly slid the knife from its sheath under my gown.

"Yes, that is she. Tall, long blond hair, remarkably beautiful."

"Finally. We have been following the scent of blood for far too long in this wretched city," the other man said.

As they moved closer Orrick's face came into view. I did not recognize the other man. *A new recruit of Ramdasha's*, I guessed.

I backed away. "What do you want?"

"We've been looking for you," Orrick said.

I continued to back away with every step they advanced. "Why?"

"To take you back to Ramdasha. As you may recall, he has some unfinished business with you. He does not care if you return dead or alive," Orrick said.

"And you just now found me? It took you long enough," I taunted.

"She is a feisty one," the unfamiliar man said to Orrick. "It is too bad she has to die. Such a pretty face is hard to find."

I attacked first, charging the closest one. He blocked my knife blow with his sword. I spun around, throwing my elbow into his face, knocking him back. This time, I did not restrain my full strength. I spun again, throwing my knife into Orrick's chest. He dropped to the ground. I lunged for Orrick's sword as it fell from his hand.

The other vampire charged and I blocked his swing with my new weapon, Orrick's sword. While we exchanged blows, Orrick slowly pulled the knife from his chest as he moaned in pain. I took my opportunity — the man attacking me swung low. I let his sword hit my hip because this left his head unguarded. I swung hard for his neck as the pain from his blow exploded across my thigh. I fell to my knees as his head rolled away from his body. I quickly turned as Orrick came at me with my knife that had been in his chest. Blood spilled down the front of his tunic.

With one swing I easily knocked the knife from his hand. He continued to charge. I rolled backward, kicking him off me. This sent another shock of pain through my injured hip. He flew over me. I jumped to my feet, pointing his own sword at his chest. He put his hands up in surrender.

"Turn around," I demanded.

This he did.

"Any quick movement will cost you your head as well," I threatened.

He must have believed me because he marched to the castle without so much as a protest.

We burst into the Great Hall. Lord Alexandru stood at once and gestured for his guards. In a flash, we were surrounded. I let Orrick's sword drop, as they took control of the prisoner. I put my hand on my thigh and ventured to look at my wound for the first time. It was the deepest cut I had ever had. The bleeding had stopped and it tingled, which meant it was healing.

Hector appeared at my side. "Are you harmed?"

"A little." I was surprised my voice came out steady. I trembled inside.

"What is going on?" Alexandru demanded.

"This man and his accomplice attacked me."

"And where is the accomplice?"

"He is dead," I answered.

Hector's mouth fell open. "You managed to kill a vampire?"

I nodded and bent down to seize a piece of fabric that had been sewn to Orrick's overcoat. I ripped the armband off.

"They are Ramdasha's men." I held up the dark-green fabric with the black tarantula embroidered on it.

Alexandru gracefully unsheathed his sword and placed it at Orrick's neck.

"What are you doing here?"

Orrick said nothing.

So I answered. "They said they were here for me. Apparently, Ramdasha is still seething because I escaped from him. He sent these two men to find me. He wants me dead."

Alexandru pressed his sword into Orrick's neck until blood appeared. "Is this true?"

Orrick nodded.

"Take him to the dungeon. Send word to Lord Chastellain. The Court will have to decide what to do with him," Alexandru said.

Two guards dragged Orrick away while a third led them out.

"Well done," Alexandru said.

I bowed. "If you will excuse me, My Lord, I must get cleaned up." I headed for my room. Mary and Elizabeth were there. This time, when Mary saw me, she did not look angry, only worried.

"My God, are you injured?" Mary jumped to her feet.

I was a bloody ruin, although most of the blood was not mine. I nodded and took off my soiled dress. I washed as much of the blood off my face and hands as I could in the washbasin and put on a short tunic. I lay on my bed. The pain in my hip was almost gone but I felt tired.

"What happened?"

I told them the story as Mary gently inspected my thigh.

"It is healing well," she said.

It was nice to see her smile. I closed my eyes.

"Let her rest," Elizabeth said. "You can tell her when she wakes."

Tell me what? I pondered as I drifted off.

CHAPTER 60 LONDON 1262 AD

I woke to a man staring down at me. Startled, I sat straight up in bed. He placed his hands on my shoulders. "Be easy. It is only I," Elijah said.

I threw my arms around his neck. "How did you get here so quickly?" I whispered. It felt good to have him hold me; he was becoming the definition of comfort. He rested his head on my shoulder. I could feel how worried he was about me.

"You have been asleep for a while. I presume it took an hour to get the message from Alexandru that you had been attacked and I left at once."

That meant I had been asleep for almost two hours — more than I had slept at one time since I was human. *I must have needed the sleep to heal,* I thought.

"How are you feeling?" He pushed me away gently and looked into my eyes.

"Very well." I spoke the truth: my hip no longer hurt. I became conscious of my bare legs. I seized a blanket and covered them.

He put his hand on my thigh. "I saw the scar. Is it better?"

I took his hand and held it — to remove it from my hip. I did not like the sensation when he touched me there. Not because it hurt but because it made me feel … odd. I did not have a name for it in my innocence. I was also embarrassed that he had seen my bare legs and thigh. My body was always well covered.

That was how Mary found us, sitting close on my bed, hand in hand. Her face turned to a scowl when she saw Elijah. "I should have known." She slammed the door as she left.

"Who was that?" Elijah asked.

"My roommate, Mary." I threw myself back down on the bed in frustration. "I don't know what is wrong with her. Ever since I left for Denmark, she has been behaving strangely. I don't understand. I did nothing to upset her — at least nothing I can think of. She apparently does not like you for some reason, yet she does not even know you."

Elijah smiled down at me with his wonderful crooked smile. "I forget sometimes how young you are. You have been on this earth, what, nineteen, maybe twenty years at the most? You are still very innocent."

I pushed myself away from him, sitting against the wall. "What are you talking about? I'm not ignorant."

"You are very intelligent, yes but still … young. You see, Mary is in love with you."

"What? Is … that possible?"

He laughed at my opened-mouthed expression.

I had no immediate frame of reference for this; I had to scan my memory. I remembered the Bible verse stating that a man lying with another man was a sin. I shook my head. This couldn't be true. I jumped to my feet and instantly became conscious of my long bare legs again. I grabbed a pair of breeches.

"Don't worry." Elijah gave a devious smile. "It is nothing I have not seen before."

I still did not like the longing look in his eyes. I glared at him.

"Why do you have men's clothes?" he asked.

"They are more comfortable," I said.

"I hope you will not be cutting your hair short as well, like Mary's."

"I just might because you said that."

"Well, even that would not work to keep me away from you."

"I should talk with Mary," I changed the subject.

"Tell her to get in line. I found you first." He smiled.

I shook my head and left. I found Mary in Elizabeth's room. When I entered, Elizabeth stood.

"How are you feeling?" she asked.

"All better." I smiled.

"That is wonderful news ..." Elizabeth fidgeted with discomfort. "Well, then, I will let you two talk." She hurried out.

When Mary looked at me, her face was stained with tears. *Oh, no!* I thought, *Elijah was right.* It was wondrously annoying how he was always right. I suppose if I lived to be hundreds of years old, I too, would be right more often.

I sat beside Mary. "What is the matter?"

"If you have not guessed by now, then forget it!"

"I did not have any idea. Elijah" — she cringed away from me at the mention of his name — "told me that he thinks you are in love with me. But I did not think that was possible. Is it true?"

A tear ran down her cheek. I had never seen her cry. In fact, there was a time when I had thought she was not capable. She'd seemed too strong for that. I had no idea what to do. I placed my arm over her shoulder.

With that she put her hands on my waist and pulled me closer. She pressed her lips to mine.

Startled, I pushed her away.

She stared at me. Waiting for a response ... an answer.

"I'm sorry, Mary. You are a good friend, I care about you but ... "

"But not like that," she finished my sentence. Her voice was flat

I shook my head *no.* "The truth is that I gave my heart away a long time ago. I hope that he will find me one day."

"You mean you're not in love with the prince?" Mary looked hopeful.

"Not exactly. If I could let go of this boy from my childhood, then ... it does not matter because I have not let him go. It is complicated." I hated this situation. It was forcing me to think about my feelings. I did not want to admit this to myself, let alone anyone else.

Mary lay down on Elizabeth's bed. "I should have known that you would never want to be with me."

With a heavy heart, I said, "I am sorry. I greatly value your friendship. I hope this will not change things between us."

"Leave me alone." She buried her head in the pillow.

My heart sank even further. I did not want to lose her as a friend. I slowly stood and looked back one last time before I left.

Elizabeth was waiting in the hall outside her room. "How is she faring?"

"She needs a good friend like you." I put my hand on Elizabeth's shoulder.

She nodded in understanding.

Hector rounded the corner and spotted us. "There you are, My Lady. The last of the Elders have arrived. There is a meeting in the Great Hall. Your presence is requested." He looked to Elizabeth. "In fact, we should all be there."

"Thank you, Hector." To Elizabeth I added, "Tell Mary. I will see you in the Great Hall."

CHAPTER 61 LONDON 1262 AD

Once surrounded by the large crowd in the Great Hall, I felt embarrassed about my breeches and simple tunic. Everyone was dressed to the hilt. Elijah stood to the right of his father and on his father's left stood Lord Alexandru. The Chastellains each wore large golden crowns that sparkled with brightly colored stones. They were draped in red robes with gold trim. This was excessive, even for Lord Chastellain. It must have been to make their role as the head of the Court incontestable.

King Chastellain and his prince, I thought. Elijah did look the part of a proper noble who would one day be king — if his father had not been immortal. *I must be mad for not loving him.* I shook my head to push the annoying thought away.

Lord Chastellain was taken aback when he spotted me. He had never seen me dressed in men's clothes. This put him at a loss for words, which I thoroughly enjoyed. I gave him a confident smirk.

The lord shook his head. "My dear Lady, would you be so kind as to tell the Court what happened to you last night?"

I nodded and went on to tell them about the two men who had attacked me.

"This is the first time Ramdasha's men have traveled this far north and attacked one of us," Chastellain declared. "This goes beyond a small act of defiance. This is a declaration of war."

I did not like the sound of this. *It seems ... unwarranted.* "My Lord, if I may." I bowed to him. I was not smart enough to know when to keep my mouth shut but I was smart enough to know that small gestures of respect went a long way with the lord. In fact, such decorum was required.

He looked pleased and gestured for me to continue.

"This was most likely an act of personal revenge for my betrayal and escape from Constantinople, not an act of outright defiance toward the High Court of Elders."

"Ramdasha knows how important you are to us." He glanced at his son. "He might as well have attacked one of the Elders." In a loud, deep voice that made it clear my time to speak was over — and made me flinch — he boomed, "Bring forth the prisoner."

Two guards appeared, dragging Orrick between them. Chastellain towered over the prisoner, who was forced to his knees in front of him. "What do you have to say for yourself?"

Orrick stared up at the lord — no answer.

In one swift motion, Elijah stepped forward and issued a deafening blow to Orrick. There was a loud crack and Orrick's head was thrown violently to the side. Blood trickled out of his mouth.

I stepped forward to ... to do what? Was I going to defend the man who would have killed me if he could have? I stopped myself. It must have been a natural instinct to protect the defenseless.

Orrick put his head down. "We came only for the girl. Under Lord Ramdasha's rule, she was to be put to death. We came to carry out his orders," he muttered.

Elijah wound his fists into Orrick's tunic and proceeded to lift him so his knees no longer touched the ground.

"Ramdasha has no jurisdiction here and he too must follow the rule of the High Court of Elders. You, and your lord, are traitors."

Elijah's voice was dark and dangerous. I could clearly see his father in him. I took a step back. *Who is this man? Did I truly know Elijah?* I was not sure.

He threw Orrick to the ground and drew his sword, placing it to Orrick's neck. "Do you have anything else to tell us?" Elijah demanded.

Orrick put his shaking hands up. "No, no, My Lord."

"Then you are of no further use." Elijah raised his sword.

I looked away.

"Wait," I heard Lord Chastellain say. "Perhaps he still has a purpose. The Court must decide the prisoner's fate."

Elijah gave a hard stare to his father and reluctantly put his sword back in its sheath. Instantly, two guards stepped forward to take control of the prisoner.

"Perhaps we should send him back to Ramdasha with a message and without his right hand," Alexandru suggested.

This sparked much debate amongst the Elders.

Finally, Lord Chastellain announced the decision to the crowd. "From this day forth anyone wearing this symbol" — he held up the green armband I had taken from Orrick — "is to be killed or taken prisoner and brought to me. The attacker is to be beheaded and his head sent to Ramdasha as a warning."

Orrick's shoulders slumped at the news of his impending death.

"This is what happens to people who defy the High Court of Elders," Lord Chastellain concluded.

There were cheers from the audience. The lord nodded to Elijah. With one smooth motion Elijah severed Orrick's head from his shoulders. It happened so quickly that I did not have time to look away. With his free hand, Elijah gracefully caught the head by the hair and held it up to the crowd, which produced more cheers.

How barbaric, I thought. *Yet it was I who had beheaded the other attacker. How is that any better?* This fact complicated my moral judgment of Elijah killing Orrick.

Lord Chastellain went on to describe new sanctions and rules. Combat training was to be greatly increased and was made mandatory. When vampires traveled outside of coven lairs, it was to be done in pairs at the very least, if not in groups and we were to be armed at all times.

This all seems logical, I thought. *I understand Ramdasha's desire for revenge. I too had such thoughts. Unlike me, Ramdasha's anger had festered over the past year while mine had waned. Instead of letting it go, he wasted time and manpower trying to hunt me down. This was not a shrewd political move on his part. But then again, who am I? I was a poor deacon's daughter, not a political leader.*

Still, to risk further angering the Court in order to get revenge on one person is asinine. He must have thought his men would succeed in killing me. The Court would not have known what to make of my disappearance. I shivered at the thought. *Ramdasha will attack when his forces are strong enough. Perhaps he is ready for war and he's provoking the Court.*

Between Mary and the beheading, I was frustrated and wanted to take action. I slipped out of the Great Hall and headed to the training room. The Elders were clearing everyone out for a private meeting anyway.

One thing was for sure; Ramdasha's vengeful nature meant that he would not take kindly to receiving the head of one of his men. I thought of Rosalia for the first time in a long time. She too would be heartbroken and angry to learn that we had killed Orrick. I could see the cycle of hatred spiraling out of control. Once in motion, this cycle would be difficult to stop. There would be more attacks and most likely, as Elijah had predicted, war. I needed to be prepared to fight. While I could obviously defend myself, I needed to keep improving. My life depended on it.

CHAPTER 62 LONDON 1262 AD

I took my frustration out on a dummy, cutting it to pieces with a broadsword when my blow was blocked. I followed the sword that was interlocked with mine to find Elijah smiling at me. I relaxed. He slid his sword down mine. With the slightest movement of his wrist, he hooked his sword under my hand guard and flicked my weapon away. The sword clanked loudly as it came to rest on the stone floor.

He pointed his weapon at my chest. "Never let your guard down."

"But it is only you."

He lowered his sword and stepped close.

I was in no mood to get lost in his wonderful — sad eyes. I was confused about him. There was clearly another side to him and I did not know if I liked it. I stepped back and looked away, in order to reduce the power that his gaze had on me.

"That was quite a show you put on in the Great Hall." I posed it as a question.

"Come. Let's get out of here." He looked around at the others who were also training. "So we can talk."

I followed him out of the training room. We strolled down a

deserted street, our swords hung at our sides. We did not leave them behind as we previously might have.

"You understand that I had to kill the prisoner?" he asked.

I shrugged, as I was not at all sure that Elijah had had to kill Orrick.

He stepped in front of me and placed his hands on my shoulders to keep me from avoiding his gaze. "He tried to kill you. Don't tell me you feel sorry for him."

I frowned.

His sly crooked smile crossed his lips. "Did you not take one of their heads as well?"

"Yes but I was defending myself and he was far from defenseless." There was a scar on my hip to prove it.

Elijah nodded. "My father is the ruler of the vampire world. If I am to be seen as a worthy successor, if something were to happen to my father, then I must be willing to take action. I have to protect my people. If we are to remain in power, we must punish treason swiftly and harshly."

I shook my head. "But you did it so easily."

"Aye, the fact that it was you he attacked made it all the easier. I have in the past and will in the future, if needed, kill to keep the peace and keep our kind underground. I fight this war every day."

"That sounds like hell." I said. *No wonder Elijah is sad most of the time.*

My thoughts strayed to Ramdasha, *He will stop at nothing. However, there must be a better way to lead people than severe punishment. Father believed that good leaders used love and compassion to guide others.* I felt a spark of hope ignite inside me — a new purpose.

"Besides, what kind of man would I be if I did not defend you?" The passionate look in his eyes was unsettling.

"It is not your job to defend me, Elijah. I can take care of myself."

"Thankfully, you can, or you would not be here. Even so, it is my job to protect you. I want to protect you."

How can I argue with that? My defenses lowered. I put my arm in his as we walked. "Maybe it is our job to protect each other and the

Elders." I paused. "I knew him, you know. His name was Orrick. His beloved, back in Constantinople, will be all the more angry at the Court. The fight will be personal for her now. By sending Orrick's head to them, we are only continuing the cycle of violence and anger. There must be a better way!" I could feel the spark grow inside me. *I am on to something, perhaps a better way to lead.*

Elijah's eyes narrowed and he nodded in agreement but he too appeared not to know what that "better way" might be.

"What did the Elders discuss after everyone left?" I asked.

"Mostly the same. They are debating about whether to attack Ramdasha now, before he is able to gain more power, or wait for him to start a war."

"What did they decide?"

"The Court is divided. Some do not think he will ever be able to gain enough supporters to succeed in an all-out war against us. Others want our armies to set out at once. The debate is more heated now that he has attacked one of us on our lands."

"What do you think we should do?" I asked.

"I think we should attack sooner rather than later."

I nodded. Elijah was probably right — of course he was; he was always right — even though I did not like the thought of attacking first. "When will you return to Denmark?"

"I'm not going back without you. If you will not come with me, then I will stay here — as much as I can anyway."

I took my arm from his and narrowed my eyes at him. Since I had admitted to Mary how I felt about Teller — which forced me to fully admit it to myself — I had to be honest with Elijah, too. I did not want to lose his friendship but I had to take that chance, as it would not be fair to lead him on.

"Elijah, I have to … talk to you about something. I care about you, you know that but I … hope that Teller will come for me one day."

He pressed his lips together. The grey storm raged in his eyes. "I know. Where is he?"

"I have no idea and I do not know where to begin to look for him."

"So you are going to wait for him?"

I nodded. The pain in Elijah's eyes cut deeper than my enemy's sword. "I don't expect you to be able to be my friend and I definitely don't want you to wait for me. But I would be grateful for your friendship."

He took my forearm in his hand. "To friendship."

I clasped his forearm in return. It was a gesture often made when making a bargain. I smiled with relief.

"You know, I like you in breeches." A glint of humor crossed his face.

I glowered at him.

"Honestly," he said. "If it helps you to better defend yourself, then I hope you always wear them. ... Besides, they will deter potential suitors when I am away."

I punched him in the arm, hard enough to knock a human down but he hardly swayed.

He laughed. "I know — just friends."

CHAPTER 63 LONDON 1262 AD

Elijah stayed true to his word and remained in London. He slept in the royal guest quarters. Mary moved into Elizabeth's room – undoubtedly to avoid me – so I had a room to myself again, which I did not particularly like. I missed Mary's company.

It had been months since Orrick's attack, when Elijah, Elizabeth and I were training a new recruit not to kill. His name was Chadwick. Elizabeth and I pulled Chadwick off a human when out of the corner of my eye, I saw Elijah draw his sword. I surveyed our whereabouts and quickly ascertained that we were surrounded by nine vampires. They slowly closed in on us. A burly figure appeared to be leading the way.

"Well, well. I should have guessed I would find you with your *prince*." The large figure said the word "prince" as if it left a bad taste in his mouth.

"Do you know him?" Elijah whispered.

I nodded but kept my eyes on the ominous figure. "Riddick, don't do this. If you kill us, or even attack us, you will start a war – a war you cannot win."

My words stopped his approach.

He must know that I am right. Killing Lord Chastellain's son would bring down the full wrath of the North on Ramdasha.

"I have my orders and, besides, it will be a pleasure to kill the prince. If you surrender Val, I may be able to persuade Ramdasha to be lenient with you."

I remembered my theory about Riddick; he did not care about politics. He was hoping to somehow get me back.

"Why don't you do the wise thing and join the High Court of Elders?" I asked.

Elijah widened his eyes, as if to say, *Are you mad?*

Maybe I was.

Riddick chuckled. "And what would I get in return? You, perhaps?" His expression was mocking, hungry and dangerous all at once.

I shivered.

Elijah stepped forward.

I threw my arm across Elijah's chest to stay him.

"I am not a prize to be won, Riddick. The Elders are more powerful than Ramdasha will ever be. If you fought for us, we could offer you power and riches beyond any you could gain in Constantinople."

Elijah narrowed his eyes but what I said appealed to Riddick; he had a greedy glint in his eye. He paused for quite some time, then shook his head. With the wave of his hand, his fighters attacked.

As a man lunged toward me and our swords collided, I noticed that Riddick did not move to attack. He stood back. Soon there were two men assailing me. It was all I could do to block their blows. I did not have a chance to issue a kill shot; I was only on defense. The sound of swords colliding was all that could be heard.

One of my attackers got close enough to issue a blow to my jaw with his fist. I fell to the ground and raised my sword over my head to block the blow to my neck. This left my torso exposed and the second man raised his sword with both hands to stab me. A knife, from who knows where, found his neck. He dropped his sword and fell to the ground.

This surprised my other attacker and I was able to thrust his sword away and plunge mine deep into his chest. My thoughts went to Elijah and Elizabeth. Elijah was defending himself against three men. I threw a knife from my leg scabbard into one of their backs. When I turned, I saw Riddick pulling the knife out of my attacker's neck and with the knife he finished the job by cutting the man's head off.

What is happening? I thought.

Riddick looked at me and nodded; he turned to fight off one of Elizabeth's attackers. I moved to Elijah. He had killed another of his assailants and was fighting one on one with the last. He had it under control, so I went to the man who had my knife in his back and placed my sword to his throat.

"Will you pledge your support to the High Court of Elders?" I asked.

His eyes were glossy with pain. "Never," he muttered. He swung his sword upward toward me but with the slightest movement of my arm, my sword went through his neck, leaving his body headless. It was frightening how easy and natural this was becoming. At least he was faithful to his cause until the end; I had to give him credit for that.

I looked for Elijah and saw a man coming up behind him as he fought off his last attacker.

"Look out!" I yelled.

In a flash, I threw my body into the man attacking Elijah from behind. We landed on the ground together. He punched me in the face, throwing me off him. This sent a fresh round of pain through my already aching jaw, causing me to drop my sword.

He thrust his sword down toward me and I rolled out of the way as the blow hit the ground where my head had been. When I looked up to see where he was, an impact from behind caused him to fall to the ground. I jumped to my feet and saw that the blow had come from Riddick — again. Elijah had finished off the last of his attackers. He charged after Riddick.

"Stop!" I ran to stand between Elijah and Riddick.

"What are you doing?" Elijah voice was incredulous.

"He's helping us. He saved me."

Riddick threw his sword down and put his arms up in surrender.

Elijah relaxed his shoulders a bit and we both assessed the scene. Elizabeth stood with a man lying at her feet. He was not moving. Her arm was badly injured. I ripped a piece of cloth from the sleeve of my tunic. She flinched and moaned with pain as I wrapped the cloth around the large open wound on her arm.

Elijah was tending to Chadwick, the new recruit. He did not look to be faring well. Elizabeth and I joined Elijah by Chadwick. I tried to bind some of his wounds to stop the bleeding but soon we heard Chadwick's heart stop beating. I stood and buried my head in Elijah's chest. He wrapped his arms around my shoulders.

"He was too young; he had not been trained to fight. This is my fault," I moaned.

"No, it is not your fault," Elijah whispered. He tapped me on the back to get my attention. I looked to his face and followed his gaze. He stared at Riddick, who was down on one knee in front of us.

CHAPTER 64 LONDON 1262 AD

"I'm sorry for your loss," Riddick said. "From this day forward, I pledge myself to the service of the High Court of Elders, My Lord."

I'm sure my mouth was hanging open. Elijah and I looked at each other. I gave him a shrug, indicating that I had no idea what to do. Elijah stood even taller and stepped away from me.

"Unfortunately, your fate is not up to me. However, we will speak on your behalf to the Court. After all, you did save us."

Riddick bowed his head as a sign of respect. I'm sure my mouth was still agape in amazement.

A moan of pain came from one of Riddick's men. "Take him prisoner," Elijah said. Elizabeth pointed her sword at the wounded vampire. He slowly got to his feet, holding his hands up.

There was one order of business to attend to before leaving the battle scene — the human whom Chadwick had fed from. He was still alive and would wake only to find himself in the middle of this massacre. I picked him up. "We should get him out of here." The blood from the wound on his neck smelled sweet and it made my throat ache. I held my breath the best I could.

Elijah moved to pick Chadwick's body up, as he would be buried in the cemetery outside Lord Alexandru's castle. However, Riddick offered to carry him. Elijah reluctantly let him. I laid the human in the grass of a small hill several hundred lengths away from the fight. We headed back to the castle.

We took Chadwick to the dungeon, where his body would be prepared for burial. I kissed Chadwick's forehead.

"I'm sorry, Chadwick," I whispered. Elizabeth put her hand on my shoulder. I placed my arm carefully around her, being conscious of her wounded arm. "How are you faring?"

"Hopefully, I look better than you." She gave me a weak smile.

I tried to smile back but a sharp pain reminded me of my wounded jaw. I gently placed my hand to my cheek. *Ouch.* It was swollen; my face felt as if it were twice as large as it ought to be. Surely there was a well-developed bruise covering most of my cheek from the blows it received.

"Let us get the politics over with," Elijah sounded tired. With that we marched the prisoner, and Riddick — who willingly went with us — to the Great Hall. Once again, guards surrounded us when we entered the hall, only this time there were more. Security had been increased since the first attack.

"My dear, what on earth has happened now?" Lord Alexandru appeared at my side.

"Send for my father," Elijah demanded.

Alexandru nodded to Hector, who was off at once. "Is everyone well?"

"The three of us will be fine, My Lord," I said, indicating Elijah, Elizabeth and myself. "Chadwick did not survive."

"And did these men attack you?" Alexandru asked.

"No, this man saved us." I gestured to Riddick.

Alexandru eyed Riddick. "Send them to the holding chambers to await Lord Chastellain and the rest of the Court."

Riddick was reluctant — not wanting to be locked up. I gave him a reassuring nod and he went willingly with the other prisoner. Elijah, Elizabeth and I went to clean ourselves and to heal.

Mary had been in her and Elizabeth's room. She tended to Elizabeth's wounds straightaway. "You are trouble, aren't you?" Mary chastised me.

"I'm beginning to think so." My voice was full of despair.

Elijah clasped my arm and gestured with his head for me to leave with him. I looked to Elizabeth as if for approval. I had to know that she was well or would be soon.

She nodded for me to go.

Elijah and I headed to my room alone. He sat on Mary's old bed. I started pacing.

"Tell me about this Riddick fellow," he asked.

"He is a wretched man — rude, uncouth, selfish." I smiled at Elijah, well my swollen cheek only allowed for a half smile. "And those are the pleasant things I can think to say about him."

He took my hand to stop my nervous pacing. I sat on my bed across from him.

He gently rubbed his thumb down my injured cheek. "How are you faring?"

I put my head down and shook it. What was bothering me was on the surface, about to break free. I removed his hand from my face and held it. I looked into his eyes. "We can't lose you. As the heir to the throne of the Court, you are too important. You being with me tonight put you in danger."

"I'm no more important than anyone else," he protested. "Besides, you saved me tonight."

I put my head down again; it was not until Elijah had been in real danger that I fully realized how much he meant to me.

"I can't lose you." I amended my previous statement.

He moved to sit beside me and put his arm around me. "Now we are making progress," he whispered.

I laid my head on his shoulder.

"Someday you will be mine."

We sat like that for some time.

"We should get some rest before Father arrives," he said.

CHAPTER 65 LONDON 1262 AD

I woke to my jaw tingling and itching. I had to rub it to try to make the uncomfortable sensation stop. Elijah was smiling at me from Mary's bed. "It looks better."

I moved to the looking glass at our washbasin. My cheek was a ghastly yellow color but no longer swollen. The bruise was mostly healed.

Being more clearheaded after the brief rest, it dawned on me to ask, "Why do you think Riddick saved us?"

"I'm not sure. His motives are likely to spy on us … or he is here for you. I don't know which reason is worse."

Elijah left to wash and change in his chambers.

We met in the Great Hall. It was not long after we arrived that Elijah's father and his entourage surged in.

Lord Chastellain went straight to Elijah wrapping his arms around him. "How are you?" he whispered.

"I'm well, Father."

I had never seen the lord in this state. He was not one to show affection. An all out embrace was not something I thought he was capable of. He loved his son more than anything. This lessened my hatred of the lord, even if only a bit. *Why couldn't things be simple?* If people were either good or evil and nothing in between, then at least it would be easier to truly loathe someone.

Lord Chastellain shot me a hard stare. It said that he thought I was nothing but trouble.

I did not disagree. I felt responsible for putting everyone in danger and for Chadwick's death. I had chosen to help Elijah rather than Chadwick. I should have gone to Chadwick instead, knowing he would not be able to defend himself. I was also the reason we were under attack in the first place.

"Now tell me — what of these prisoners?" the lord demanded.

Elijah motioned for me to speak, as the story was mine to tell. Once again I found myself explaining the situation to the Court.

"One of the prisoners is named Riddick. He is ... was Ramdasha's right-hand man. The other captive I do not know." I proceeded to tell them how Riddick had been the one to free me from Ramdasha's clutches and how he had fought *with* us, even killing Ramdasha's men.

"What do you know of this man ... Riddick?" Chastellain asked.

"He is self-serving. He only cares about power and status, not politics as such."

"So you believe he is not here as a spy for Ramdasha but rather to gain power."

"I am not sure, My Lord but he is an asset to whichever side he is on. He is an excellent fighter and trainer. If we can buy his loyalty, then this will greatly harm Ramdasha."

Chastellain rubbed his forehead with his thumb and pointer finger. "A hired assassin — that is risky."

I nodded in agreement. It was definitely a risk to trust Riddick but it was a risk I was willing to take after what I had seen tonight. He had saved me at least twice over and it was my turn to try to save him.

"Bring forth the prisoners," Chastellain boomed.

I jumped. I didn't know if I would ever get used to his commanding voice.

In no time, Riddick and the other man were on their knees with heads bowed in front of Lord Chastellain. Elijah and I stood on either side of his father.

The lord opened his mouth to speak but I spoke first. "Riddick?"

He looked up at me.

"Why did you save us tonight?"

"Because I want to pledge my loyalty to the High Court of Elders." He spoke with confidence and slowly turned his gaze to Lord Chastellain.

Chastellain studied Riddick for a long moment, then turned to the other man. "And what do you have to say for yourself?"

"I too pledge my loyalty to the High Court of Elders."

"How can we be sure that you are not here as spies for Ramdasha?" Chastellain demanded.

Yet it was I who spoke up. "My Lord, it is highly unlikely that Ramdasha would sacrifice so many of his best men in order to get spies into the Court. He could have done that with far fewer of his own casualties and I doubt he would send Riddick to spy. He needs Riddick to train his army."

The lord narrowed his eyes. I was speaking too much for his liking. He turned to Riddick. "Why did Ramdasha send you?"

"He sent nine of his best men to kill the Lady Vallachia after the first two imbeciles failed. The Lady of the Court is correct. We were not sent as spies, only assassins. What Ramdasha did not know was that I never wanted her dead. He does not know that it was I who had set her free from his dungeon. I did not want to come on this mission but he sent me because I am his best and he thought I would succeed."

Elijah and his father exchanged raised eyebrows. Riddick knew he had said enough about me and that it was not entirely helping his case. He tried another approach. "I have intelligence that would be of use to you. I know Ramdasha's plans. I can help train your armies as well. Ramdasha's forces were greatly damaged tonight. He lost many of his top men."

Lord Chastellain seemed to be satisfied with this, so Riddick and the other prisoner were sworn in as new allies to the High Court of Elders. I was glad to at least begin to repay Riddick for saving me — twice.

"My son, it is time for you to return to Denmark," Chastellain said.

Elijah looked at me with concern.

"I will return with you," I said.

Elijah let out a sigh of relief. I knew that he wanted to protect me but I felt the same way. I wanted to protect him and in order to accomplish this, I needed to be with him.

"Please, My Lord, I wish to serve you in Denmark as well." Riddick bowed to his new ruler.

Chastellain narrowed his eyes and once again studied Riddick. "Because it is the seat of power for the vampire world, or because Lady Vallachia is returning with us?"

"Because it is the seat of power, My Lord." This was the smart thing to say and it was undoubtedly true, or at least part of his reason for wanting to be in Denmark.

"Very well. It will be better for me to keep an eye on you until I know I can trust you," Lord Chastellain replied.

"Thank you, My Lord," Riddick said.

The lord moved in close to Riddick and whispered in his ear, "You will do well to leave her alone."

The threat was clear. The lord was acting like a jealous lover, a role I found appalling. On the other hand, I hoped Riddick would leave me alone, as he was equally disgusting.

"Of course, My Lord," Riddick said.

"The other new recruit will stay here under the lordship of Alexandru," Chastellain announced.

Alexandru did not look pleased, so the lord continued, "It will be better to separate them and you will watch over him until he has proven his loyalty."

Lord Alexandru nodded agreement.

I headed to my room to gather a handful of belongings to take to Denmark. When I left my room, Lord Chastellain was waiting like a statue for me outside my door.

"What does this Riddick fellow mean to you?"

This rekindled my anger for him. He was always trying to control my love life. "I assure you, My Lord, he means nothing to me." I tried to get away from him but he kept stride with me.

"You seemed eager to save him?"

"It was the least I could do because of all he has done for me. If it were not for him, your son and I would be dead."

"Regardless, you too will do well to stay away from him."

"That is not a problem, My Lord." I stopped myself from adding that this was not for his sake or even Elijah's but because I had no interest in Riddick, besides his ability to help the Court. "Now if you will excuse me, I must say goodbye to my friends."

ELIZABETH HAD JUST WOKEN from her healing sleep. Her arm looked to be better.

Mary turned her back to me.

"I am leaving for Denmark for a while. I will return as soon as I can. Mary, if you would like your room back in the meantime, please feel free."

She ignored me.

Will she ever be my friend again? I thought.

Elizabeth gave me a hug.

"Be careful and take care of yourself," I whispered. *She should be safe without me around.*

"You too. Goodbye." Elizabeth smiled.

"Goodbye, Mary," I said.

She looked at me briefly, then turned away, saying nothing.

I had to keep trying to regain her friendship.

CHAPTER 66 COPENHAGEN 1262 AD

It was pleasant to be back in Denmark. Mari, Sonia and Aaron were all faring well. They were concerned about Elijah and me. They were also very curious about this large and intimidating new recruit we had brought with us.

Riddick soon took over as the new combat trainer in Copenhagen. He was serious about his new role and was helping the vampires in Chastellain's Court to become better warriors. At night he would teach us flight warfare. This was new to us and would be very helpful if we ever had to fight against Ramdasha's army — whom Riddick had already trained in this method of warfare.

One night I had stayed late in the training arena to practice hand-to-hand combat — this was my weakest area of fighting — when Riddick walked in. I tried to ignore him but he would not have it. He stepped in front of me, grabbed my fist, mid-punch and held it.

"Finally, I caught you. You are a hard one to find alone," Riddick said.

I twisted my fist from his hand and stepped away. "There is a good reason for that."

"You would not avoid me, would you?"

I glared at him and turned to leave. "Yes, I would."

He appeared in front of me. "Why? It is not as if you are spoken for."

"What would give you that impression?"

"There has been no engagement announcement for the prince."

"Maybe there has."

"No, that kind of news would travel fast in our world. What's the matter? He won't marry you?" His tone was mocking.

He was infuriating. I sidestepped him and headed for the door. "That is none of your business. You need to leave me alone."

"That's right — because we are forbidden to see each other in private."

"No, it is because I am not interested in your advances."

"You can't tell me that a forbidden love affair does not sound appealing."

I stopped and my mouth fell open. He was not deterred in the least by the lord's warning, as I had hoped. In fact, it made me all the more desirable in his twisted mind. I decided to try reason.

"Riddick, listen to me. I do appreciate your training and all you have done for me. However, you are in a very delicate position here. You need to prove your loyalty to the Court, not anger them. The lord can be cruel. If he thought for even an instant that you had pursued me, he would have you killed — believe me, he has done it before." Hopefully this would appeal to Riddick's self-serving side. Surely he was motivated to save his own head.

"As you wish, I will back off … for the time being." He gave me a mischievous smile.

I shook my head and tried once again to leave.

"What is it between you and Elijah?" He sounded genuinely curious.

"I already told you: it is no concern of yours."

"Then you are his mistress?"

At least he used the word "mistress" instead of "whore," which had been his word of choice when I had been locked up in Ramdasha's dungeon. Surely that was the rumor about us. That should have bothered me but it did not. Let people think that, especially when it came to men such as Riddick. I did not reply. I certainly was not going to tell him that I was waiting for someone, that I did not know where he was and that I would try to find him if it was possible.

Riddick watched me intently. Whatever he saw in my face, it caused him to drop the subject.

RIDDICK ROSE through the military ranks and was soon in good standing with the Court. He and Elijah often trained together. In order to best each other, they pushed each other to their limits. It was a friendly competition of sorts. Well, mostly friendly; sometimes it seemed they truly were trying to kill each other.

I was constantly after Mari to train. She hated it and was not very skilled. Getting her to come to the training arena was like trying to forge cold iron. Even when I did get her there it was a battle.

"Try to hit me, Mari" I said.

"But I don't want to hit you."

I sighed. "Very well. Block my attack." I was barely able to stop my fist before it hit her face. "Mari, this is important!"

"I don't see why. I am a woman. Why should I have to learn to fight?"

"You are married to a powerful man, a high member of the Court, remember? We have enemies and they are as strong and as fast as you. It is only a matter of time before the Court is attacked. You must be at least prepared to defend yourself," I pled.

Samuel appeared at her side, dipped her down in his arms and kissed her. This made me blush and look away. I had to admit they were wonderful together.

"She is a lover, not a fighter." Samuel twirled her around, then disappeared — back to his training.

Mari laughed with delight. I was happy for her, yet I could not help feeling annoyed with Samuel. He was encouraging and perhaps even requiring her defenselessness. *What if she is attacked? Would he not want her to be able to fight back? I suppose he thinks he will always be there to save her. He had better be,* I thought. This was a dangerous world we lived in and Mari did not seem to fully comprehend that.

I gave up on her — for the time being — and trained with the others.

That evening Elijah came to my room, his brow creased with worry.

"What is it?" I asked.

Once behind closed doors in my chamber, he said, "Father is sending me on a diplomatic mission to the Orient. There is a coven of new vampires there. He wants to gain their support and he is sending me to meet with them."

"That sounds ... interesting. I have never been east of Constantinople."

He took my hands. "Will you come with me?"

"Of course." It was the protectiveness I had developed for Elijah that prompted me to say yes. There was no way of knowing if these vampires would be friendly or not. I wanted to make sure he was safe.

"Samuel and Riddick will be going with us. Father does not want me to go without guards."

Now it was my brow that creased. *What is Riddick's level of commitment to protecting Elijah? Will he defend Elijah if needed?* He had saved me in the past but not Elijah — at least not directly. It would personally benefit Riddick to have Elijah out of his way.

CHAPTER 67 MIDDLE EAST
1262 AD

We traveled southeast through the night until we reached lands that were so desolate it was difficult to imagine that anything could survive in such harshness. Early on the first morning, we headed straight for the first inn we could find. Even with my hood up the sun was impossibly bright.

How do people — or vampires — live here? I wondered. Stepping into the dark inn was like waking from a bad dream — instant relief. It took a moment for my eyes to stop stinging.

The innkeeper yelled a greeting.

I instinctively covered my ears. "I forgot how loud they are." I spoke to my companions in what would have been no more than a whisper to a human.

Elijah and Samuel chuckled.

"Annoying, isn't it?" Riddick said.

The only room available was one large room containing six beds. Elijah quickly assigned us beds. He claimed the one next to me and put Riddick as far away as possible — no doubt that was intentional.

Even Elijah and Samuel seemed relieved to be out of the relentless sun. They were older and could handle sunlight better but the desert sun here was merciless. So there was nothing to do but wait until dark.

This gave me time to think, which usually meant trouble. It dawned on me that we knew very little about Riddick. We trained together almost daily but we made little time for small talk. Otherwise, I was avoiding him or thwarting his advances. Yet I was curious about him and being in a safe environment, I could finally ask him about his life before Denmark.

"How old are you, Riddick?" I sat on my bed with my arms wrapped around my legs.

He looked thoughtful for a moment. "Forty years a vampire, give or take."

"How old were you when you were turned?"

"Close to twenty."

"Did Ramdasha turn you?"

"No." Riddick snapped.

Elijah looked at Riddick with interest and Samuel sat up in his bed.

"Were you born in Constantinople?"

"No." Riddick laid down turning his back to us.

Apparently, he did not want to talk about himself, or at least his past. This was surprising, as he seemed like the type who would relish the attention and the chance to tell his story. That he did not, made me all the more curious.

"Did I say something offensive?" I mouthed to Elijah.

He shrugged and looked at Riddick's back with curiosity.

I turned my attention to Samuel. I was fired up — or perhaps bored. "Samuel, you do realize you are putting Mari in danger by encouraging her not to train?"

"She is not like you, Val."

Since the conversation had turned away from him, Riddick turned to face us.

"I understand that but she needs to at least learn to defend herself."

"I don't like it. It is ... unnatural — ladies wearing breeches and fighting like men. If it is not my job to protect her, then what good am I? It is not as if we can have children and I could fulfill my role as provider. If we abandon all traditions, then there would be nothing left. There would be no point." Samuel add softly, as if to himself, "I would be useless."

I had never seen this side of Samuel — serious, even melancholy. My initial irritation with Samuel faded and my heart went out to him.

"Unnatural: this is a good word for us. There is nothing natural about us. No one should have the speed and strength that we do. I too would give anything for my human life back. To be a mother and a wife." I paused, trying to hold back the tears. "But that is not the world we live in, Samuel. What if the Court was attacked and you were not there?"

"That is wonderful, Val. Now I will be worried half to death until we get back."

"Good," I whispered.

"Very well, your point is made. I will work with her upon our return."

"Thank you." I smiled. "I worry about Mari. She and Elijah are all that I have left of my home."

Riddick sat up looking interested. "Are you from Targoviste as well?" he asked Elijah.

Elijah looked confused.

"Oh," I said. "That was a lie. I told Ramdasha I was from Targoviste in order to protect my family."

"We are from a village nestled in the heart of the Carpathian Mountains. It is called Ludus," Elijah corrected.

Riddick nodded. "Well, it was clever of you not to tell Ramdasha the truth."

I worried about Riddick knowing where my family was. *Hopefully, we can trust him.*

"All this talk is depressing. I'm going down for a drink," Riddick said.

"I could use one as well, thanks to Val." Samuel shot me a mocking scowl. "Maybe more than one."

I gave him a weak smile, though I felt — well, Riddick had said it — depressed.

When they were gone, Elijah motioned for me to sit by him on his bed. I did. He put his arm around me and I laid my head on his chest. Being close to him was consoling and my mood lightened.

"You certainly know how to clear a room," Elijah said.

I chuckled. "Emotional conversation is an effective way to get rid of men."

He was quiet, so I raised my head to study his expression. There was a tear running down his cheek. I had never seen him cry. There was the frequent sadness in his eyes but never tears. This caused a stabbing pain in my heart. I gently wiped away the tear. I wanted to kiss him, and not for the first time. I wished I could do something … anything to take his pain away.

"What is wrong?" I whispered.

"I'm sorry. If only I had not fallen in love with you, if only I had had the strength to leave you alone, you could have had a wonderful human life. I took that from you."

"No, Elijah, your father took that from me. He made that choice for us."

"But he turned you for me. When I first saw you in the village, I wished that somehow I could be … human. That I could give you everything you wanted … everything I wanted. I was envious of Teller. He could have given you a family and a normal life — far away from this dangerous world."

I did not know what to say. I understood what he meant. When I'd returned to Ludus for Teller, I'd had some deluded belief that a human-vampire romance could work, that I could somehow be more human if I were with Teller.

"I understand Samuel's point," Elijah continued. "If we abandon all human traditions, then we have nothing left of our humanity. Vampire women do not need men to provide for them and protect them."

I laid my head on his chest.

"Seven hundred years and I am still … here. What is the point of this wretched life?" His voice was utterly hopeless.

It took all my strength not press my lips to his, instead I said, "That is not true. Mari needs Samuel. Vampire women still need to be loved. We can look out for one another. Perhaps we need to let go of human ways of thinking. If we accepted this life for what it is — maybe we could see the point of it."

"You are wise for your years."

I laid my head on his chest. His heartbeat was loud, almost too loud. "I need you. I would be lost without you."

He ran his fingers through my hair. "And I you."

"How did we get here? Two people with everything and yet … nothing. I mean, strength, power, wealth, eternal youth — do you know how many humans would give anything to be where we are? Yet all we want is a normal life … with a family and children. Is immortality wasted on us?" I said.

"No. You are right. We need to let go of human hopes and dreams. Perhaps then we can be content. We are exactly the type of immortals who should lead our kind. We are doing good by protecting mankind from vampires like Ramdasha."

"You see, there *is* a point to this life," I said.

Elijah kissed my forehead. We were still and silent until we fell asleep. Samuel and Riddick's noisy return startled me and I moved quickly away from Elijah.

"Sorry, My Lord," Samuel said. "We should have knocked."

Riddick glared at me and turned his back to us.

"You needn't apologize, Samuel," Elijah replied.

I moved back to my bed and was soon listening to their heavy breathing. I rolled over and looked at Elijah. He was awake, too. It must have been a quick hour, as we had slept enough.

"Come. Let them sleep. Besides, I could do with a drink as well." We left silently for the common room below.

CHAPTER 68 MIDDLE EAST 1262 AD

Elijah persuaded the innkeeper — with a heavy bag of coins — to allow him to rummage through the wine cellar. This consisted of several racks of wine in a dirt-walled basement.

"I still don't understand why people drink the old bitter wines." I blew dust off a flagon of wine.

"It is an acquired taste. You will learn to like it." He handed me a flagon. "This is a mead you may find suitable." He scanned the shelves. "This one, however, is a dry wine. It will do for me."

The innkeeper insisted that we eat. We accepted in order to keep a human appearance, though neither of us ate much. Human food was only for enjoyment. It was not required. I supposed we were not in the mood for fun.

Elijah picked up a deck of cards. "Do you play?"

"No."

"I'll teach you." He shuffled the deck expertly.

It was not long before Riddick and Samuel joined us. As the day wore on, local villagers came and went from the tavern. Our table was soon full of empty flagons and I had had enough sweet mead for a lifetime. *So this is what boredom is like,* I thought. It was all I could do to stop myself from cleaning the filthy tavern.

However, we were all in better spirits. I grew tired of losing at cards, so I watched Elijah play to see how he was winning.

A couple of local men asked to join us. Elijah welcomed them to our table.

"Where are you from?" one man asked.

"Denmark," Elijah answered.

The man's eye's widened. "You are a long way from home. What are you doing in these parts?"

"We are on a diplomatic mission for Lord Chastellain of Denmark."

I raised my eyebrows at Elijah. I had not expected him to tell these men the truth.

"Aye, nobles. I should have guessed as much. Is this your lady?" The man's eyes wandered all over me.

"Yes," Elijah replied without hesitation.

"It is just that I have never seen a lady wearing breeches before." The man shifted uncomfortably under Elijah's warning stare.

"It is the latest fashion in Denmark." Elijah smiled. "In all the North, actually." Samuel and I laughed; even Riddick smiled and shook his head.

"Well, she is a beauty anyway. You don't see the likes of her around these parts."

"Thank you." Elijah put his arm around me.

I leaned in closer, making it clear that I was spoken for. I hoped this would allow us to get out of here without a confrontation — meaning that we would not have to hurt anyone.

Riddick's jaw muscles flexed and he looked away from us.

"How long will you be staying?" another local asked.

"We will leave at dusk," Elijah said.

"Oh no, it is far too dangerous. You can't travel at night, especially with a lady." The man was genuinely concerned.

Riddick rolled his eyes and Samuel chuckled. We must seem like arrogant arses to these humans.

"Honestly, it is not safe out there at night. There have been cases of madness overtaking people at night." The man spoke with earnest.

This got our attention.

"What kind of madness?" Elijah asked.

"Folks callin' it Tarantism. It comes from the bite of a tarantula. Some people have even died." The man was clearly enjoying the fact that he had our attention.

"Do these bites occur only at night?" Samuel asked.

"Usually," the man answered.

Elijah and Samuel exchanged knowing looks.

"This sounds familiar," Samuel said under his breath. His mouth barely moved and the human did not seem to notice that he had said anything.

As the afternoon turned to evening, the tavern filled with more locals. One played a lute and another a drum. They sang local songs.

The music was different. It lighted my mood. "You see? This life is not entirely terrible," I whispered to Elijah.

He smiled.

We overheard two girls who had been watching us. "Maybe they are royalty, a foreign ruler and his wife?" one girl said.

"No, they are too young. A prince and princess, maybe," the other girl said.

"Vampires appear impossibly beautiful and graceful to humans," Elijah said. "We most likely look like something from a fairy story."

"Not to mention we look nothing like them. If only they knew what we truly are and how dangerous and deadly we can be." It was a relief to see that Elijah was feeling better. I'm sure it had something to do with the fifteen flagons of wine they had drunk today.

Elijah looked out the window at the setting sun. "It is time." Only vampires could have heard him. He settled our tab with the innkeeper paying him all too well.

Despite protests from some of the locals, we left.

"Don't worry; we are the most frightening things out here." Riddick reassured them on his way out. Once in the fresh air, Riddick took a deep breath and rubbed his throat.

"How are you faring?" I asked.

"I forget how hard it can be to be surrounded by humans."

Samuel slapped Riddick on the shoulder. "How right you are. Let's get out of here."

We took flight as soon as possible and continued to head southeast. The cool night air cleared my head. In no time we were over a vast ocean. It looked too inviting to ignore. I shot higher up into the sky, then tucked my wings in tight. Head first I spiraled straight for the water at full speed. It was a thrill. The others followed.

CHAPTER 69 INDIA 1262 AD

It was not long before we came to land. The earth below was lush and green, like home. Yet it was nothing like home. The trees and plants were strange, unlike anything I had ever seen before. The air was hot and heavy with dew.

"This is India?" I asked.

"Yes, we should be nearly there. Look for the lights of a city," Elijah said.

We came to a populated area but there were few lights. They did not have lanterns hanging outside homes and businesses as was common in Europe. There were many modest homes with only an occasional candle or oil lamp burning.

"This is it," Elijah said. We landed outside of the town. Many of the structures on the outskirts of town were barely glorified lean-tos. Many had rags or old blankets hanging from windows or doorways. The homes toward the center of town were more permanent structures, yet still rather modest.

"This is nothing like Constantinople, or even Copenhagen, for that matter." The disgust in Riddick's voice made it clear that he was not impressed.

"It is simple. I like it." I studied every detail of my new surroundings with awe. The trees, the plants and the homes were all so different and beautiful.

"How are we going to find this vampire coven?" Samuel asked.

"Maybe we should split up," Riddick suggested.

"No, we must stay together." Elijah voice was commanding. "We don't know if they are hostile. Perhaps Ramdasha has already gotten to them. We will have to smell them out. They have a scout looking for us. We will find them soon enough."

Not long before dawn, a figure stepped out of the shadows heading straight for us. Elijah and I reached for each other protectively. Hand in hand with Elijah, I looked to see if the others saw the approaching vampire. Riddick appeared at my right and Samuel was on Elijah's left.

Elijah inhaled deeply to make sure he was a vampire. "We are from the High Court of the Elders. We are here to speak to Shantanu."

The man was close enough for us to make out his bright smile. His face was candid and full of life. "Welcome to India! I am Shantanu. We have been expecting you." He clasped Elijah's forearm and shook it. "You must be Lord Chasteen's son." He could not properly pronounce Chastellain.

Shantanu had the largest brown eyes I had ever seen. His skin was the same beautiful bronze as Ramdasha's. In fact, he reminded me of Ramdasha at first but his features were kind and gentle. I liked him at once and soon the resemblance to Ramdasha was lost. I was fascinated by him.

"Yes, please call me Elijah."

"Ejah, it is wonderful to meet you," Shantanu said.

Elijah smiled.

For a moment I was taken back by how radiant Elijah was. His eyes were alight, more blue than grey. It was rare to see him so open.

Riddick was standing so close that I could feel his body against mine. I put my hand on his chest to gently push him away.

"All is well." I tried to reassure him.

"I present to you Lady Vallachia, Riddick and Samuel." Elijah gestured to each of us.

Shantanu greeted me first. "What is custom?" He took my hand and kissed it. "Yes?"

"Yes, that is our custom. It is a pleasure to meet you," I said.

He welcomed Samuel and Riddick. Riddick was reluctant to shake hands.

"Come. The sun will be on the rise soon," Shantanu said.

We followed Shantanu out of town. Samuel and Elijah walked with our host ahead of us.

"He looks like Ramdasha," Riddick whispered. His shoulders were tense and he his eyes were alert.

"But he is not. Shantanu is Indian like Ramdasha and that is where their similarities end."

"I hope you're right."

We ran through the jungle for some time, until we came to a clearing. Water rushed noisily over a rock ledge at the far end of a small pond. At night the lush green vegetation looked iridescent to my vampire eyes. I ran a hand over some of the strange plants.

"This place is wonderful," I said.

Shantanu motioned us to follow him. He disappeared behind the waterfall. Hidden behind the wall of water was a small cave opening, which led to a larger area. Inside were six vampires sitting at their leisure and … I smelled a human. I raised a questioning eyebrow to Elijah.

He gave me an unknowing shrug.

A lovely woman approached.

"This is my wife, Kailash," Shantanu said.

The woman bowed a greeting. If I thought her husband was beautiful, then she was spectacular. She had extraordinarily large eyes and thick, dark hair running down her back. Her skin was like a smooth-cut jasper stone — dark and flawless.

A new emotion overtook me, a strange feeling. *What was it?* The word came to me — envy. I was envious of these people. Our insipid skin must appear sickly to them. They were smaller in stature compared to us. Samuel and I were almost a head taller than any of these vampires. Elijah and Riddick must have looked like giants to them. Riddick was at least three times the size of any one of them.

The pale giants from the North — I smiled at the thought.

Shantanu introduced us to the others. They had names I could not pronounce, let alone remember.

"My wife and I lived in Constantinople many years ago for quite some time. She speaks better Greek than I. We will act as translators for you," Shantanu explained.

"When did you live in the West?" I asked

"Shortly before the French and Venetians ransacked the city. There were many of us Easterners trading in the region. It was a very lucrative business. After the city was all but destroyed my wife and I decided that it was time to return home." With a wave of Shantanu's hand, two vampires disappeared to the back of the cave.

They returned with a small girl. She was the loveliest child I had ever seen. Perhaps about eight years old and ... human. The vampires remained protectively on either side of her. Her sweet smell was strong. I glanced at Elijah with wide eyes but turned quickly to Riddick as he brushed past me toward the girl. I knew the look on his face, it made my blood run cold. He was not Riddick but a hungry monster.

CHAPTER 70 INDIA 1262 AD

I jumped in front of Riddick and pushed against his chest with all my strength. "Riddick, don't!"

He was intent only on the human girl.

My feet slid on the cave floor as he pushed me toward the human. "Riddick, look at me!" I seized his jaw to try to force his attention away from the girl. "Please, Riddick, look at me."

For a moment his gaze fell on my face and I could see him struggling with the monster inside.

"You need to get out of here. Go!" I gave him a hard shove.

He barely moved. He shook his head and tried to attend to what I was saying.

Elijah had moved to stand directly behind Riddick. I did not understand why.

"Get him out of here," Elijah said to Samuel.

Samuel grabbed Riddick's arm and they disappeared from the cave.

I exhaled in relief. When I turned back to the coven, they had formed a circle around the child, who hid behind Kailash.

Why is she here? I wondered. *How can she survive with vampires?* I took a step forward and knelt down to appear less intimidating. "Do not fear; we will not hurt you." I spoke in the softest voice I could muster.

She barely peeked out from behind Kailash's sari.

Kailash translated what I had said to the small girl. "This is Lavanya. Her name means beauty and grace."

"Then it is the perfect name. It is a pleasure to meet you." I held my hand out to the small girl.

Lavanya studied me with large brown eyes, then quickly buried her head in Kailash's clothing again. She spoke but I could not understand her.

I looked to Kailash to interpret.

"I'm sorry; she does not speak Greek." Kailash spoke with a heavy accent but otherwise perfect Greek. "She asked if you are the — how do you say — queen of the ice — no, the Snow Queen, that is it."

I chuckled and gave Kailash a confused look.

"You see, we have local legends about the Great Snow Queen of the North with her long golden hair. I often fill Lavanya's head with such nonsense before bed." Kailash did something that shocked me. She gently ran her fingers through my hair and held a strand in her hand. "I had almost forgotten that hair could truly be this color, it is so rare, even in Constantinople." She was in awe.

It was a surprise to learn that she was envious of me, just as I was of her. What was it with people — always wanting to be something they were not?

Little Lavanya spoke again and Kailash interpreted, "She wants to know if she can touch your hair as well."

I leaned forward letting my hair fall around my face.

With caution she petted my head with her tiny hand.

Kailash laughed at the girl's comment. "She says your hair is like soft wheat."

I laughed and slowly rose. It felt odd to stand to my full height because I towered over them. I stepped back to stand by Elijah; at least he was taller than I — this felt normal, comfortable.

He gave me a warm smile.

"Lavanya is my great-niece," Shantanu explained. "Her parents died of a sickness that overcame our village. There was no one left to care for her, so we do our best here. As you saw with your friend" — he gestured to where Riddick had stood — "it is dangerous for her. She requires constant protection. She is the last of my human kin." There was sadness in his eyes. Shantanu changed the subject. "Is Lady Valsha your wife?"

I was sure that when we tried to say their strange names it came out equally as bad.

"Someday, if I'm lucky," Elijah answered. He gave me a mischievous smile. "Vallachia is a member of the Court of Elders."

That brought us to business. They seated us on cushions on the floor of the cave. We exchanged pleasantries and told them about our travels. As the sun rose, several more vampires joined us. This coven numbered ten in all.

Two men stood when Riddick and Samuel entered and two others took little Lavanya to a room somewhere in the back of the cave.

Riddick looked relieved when he saw me.

He is overly protective of me. I realized. *He does not trust these new vampires and feared I was in danger while he was away.*

Riddick put his hands up in a non-threatening gesture. "I'm fine. I won't try to hurt anyone." He bowed his head to Shantanu. "Please accept my apologies."

Shantanu nodded. "We all know how hard it can be."

"I am sorry, My Lord; it had been too long since I last fed. It won't happen again," Riddick said. He took a seat beside me.

"I'm glad I did not have to break your neck," Elijah said.

I gave Elijah a hard glare. *Would he have killed Riddick if I had not been able to distract him long enough for Samuel to get him out of the cave?*

"I'm relieved you did not have to go to such an extreme," Riddick said.

"I could not pull Riddick off the human by myself." Samuel frowned.

"You keep talking about feeding without killing, as if it were possible," Riddick sneered.

I put my hand on top of Riddick's. "We can teach you." We stared at each other for a moment. I could almost feel him melt. This was not the same lion who had recently tried to kill a small girl. He was now a lamb. I did not fully realize the power I had over him until that point. I looked away, removing my hand but I could feel that his stare remained.

"Maybe I should have broken his neck," Elijah whispered to Samuel.

I gave Elijah another look of disapproval but they were both smiling. It was a joke, though be it a poor one, so I let it go.

"You could teach him?" Shantanu's eyes sparkled with a new light. "You mean you could teach us as well — to feed without killing?"

"My dear, you know it is not possible to stop feeding once we have started," Kailash said.

"The three of us" — Elijah gestured to Samuel, me and himself — "have not killed in a long time. It is difficult to learn to control the hunger but it can be done with time and practice."

Shantanu and Kailash looked at each other with wide eyes.

"It is true. We can teach you too," I said.

"We don't have that kind of time, Vallachia," Elijah said.

This time I put my hand over Elijah's. "Please, this is important. We need only to get them started — simply show them what to do, then we can head back. It will help them control themselves around Lavanya if they feed more often. The child will be safer with them. We must help if we can."

Elijah eyes narrowed and his forehead was creased. "Very well, we can stay one extra night. Then it will be up to them to finish the training themselves. Father will be worried. We can't stay any longer or he will come looking for us. We don't want that."

No, we do not, I thought. Lord Chastellain would be in a fury and anyone in his way would feel his wrath.

"Thank you." I smiled.

Elijah shook his head with a resigned sigh.

Shantanu took Kailash's hand and gave her a broad smile. "Do you think it is possible? We may not have to kill anymore?"

"Let us hope so, my dear." Kailash's eyes had a new light in them as well.

CHAPTER 71 INDIA 1262 AD

"Well then, we have a lot to do in the next couple of days. So let's proceed." Elijah went on to discuss the reason we were here, which was to gain the support of Shantanu's coven for the Court of Elders. Elijah explained the Court's laws, a task that did not take long, as there was only one important law — that vampires remain discreet and hidden from humans.

"We need humans to survive. If they thrive, so do we," Elijah said. "We do not want humans to live in terror and try to hunt us. This would lead to a war with humans — one they could not win. Surviving humans would be imprisoned, as food for us."

"That would be terrible," Kailash exclaimed. "We care about the people in our town. It pains us to have to kill."

I was growing more fond of her by the moment.

Elijah nodded before continuing, "We enforce this law throughout all of Europe. Vampires who openly reveal who they are to humans are dealt with swiftly." The meaning was clear. "However, in Southern Europe, there is growing resistance to the Court. A coven of twenty vampires —

"Actually, twenty-five, My Lord," Riddick corrected.

"Wonderful, make that twenty-five vampires, led by Ramdasha."

Elijah rubbed his forehead, a gesture I had seen his father perform many times, usually when he was concerned or frustrated. "Their hope is to overthrow the Court."

"Why?" Shantanu asked.

Elijah gestured for Riddick to explain.

"Well," Riddick began slowly. "Lord Ramdasha wants power — mostly. He and his followers believe that vampires should not have to live in hiding. They think that they are the dominant race and that humans should serve vampires."

"That is madness," Kailash said. "We need humans and they do *not* need us."

"That is the problem in Ramdasha's logic," Elijah said.

I smiled with pride as I watched Elijah. Without his father around, he was able to become a true leader. He was gifted at diplomacy.

Elijah went on to explain that if their coven pledged its fealty to the Court, they would have the protection of the Elders in return and might be called upon to fight with us if the need arose.

Shantanu and Kailash exchanged a concerned look.

"How strong is this Ramdasha?" Shantanu asked.

"He has gained supporters across most of Southern Europe. Portugal, France, some of the Holy Roman Empire and recently a small coven in Hungary." This was some of the latest new with which Riddick had been able to enlighten us. It appeared that Hungary was falling to Ramdasha, as well as a coven outside of Rome.

Shantanu frowned. "We would not join Ramdasha but the idea of being called to fight is not appealing."

"I understand. Take some time to talk with your coven about the matter. We will leave you alone to discuss the proposition. When we return, we will start proper feeding lessons." Elijah stood and bowed in respect.

Shantanu and Kailash stood and returned the bow.

Elijah gestured for us to follow him out of the cave.

We ran to the shade of a big tree not too far from the cave. I could barely see when we reached the welcome shadows of the forest. It took a long moment for my eyes to stop burning. This strange new world was even more wonderous in the daylight. Along the shore of the pond, little Lavanya was playing under the watchful eye of a woman sitting under a makeshift tent for shade. It was a joy to watch the happy child laugh and dance about. I wondered if she was able to play with other children. *Most likely not,* I thought. It was not a bad life for a child, yet still not the ideal.

Samuel tried to convince Elijah to allow him to return by himself at dusk instead of staying another day and night to train the coven. He must have been worried about Mari and anxious to return.

"That way I can tell your father that you will be a day later than expected," Samuel said.

"No. Father would be more upset if you left me. It is better that we stay together. He should not worry too much if we are a day late," Elijah said.

Samuel pursed his lips.

"Elijah, may I have a word with you?" I asked.

"You two can't contain yourselves for one day?" Samuel laughed.

"Very funny, Samuel." I punched him in the arm.

There was mostly thick forest behind us. Under the shade of the trees we were able to wander off alone. I was taking in the beautiful foliage. Some of the plants had leaves larger than my head. They were a deep green, very unlike the trees and shrubs back in Europe.

"Out with it already," Elijah said.

"Were you going to kill Riddick back there?" I asked.

"No, I was going to … disable him for a time."

"Oh." I felt my anger slip away. "We can heal from a broken neck?"

"Yes. He would have recovered after an hour or so. It would have allowed us time to get him out of there. Of course, he would have had a dreadful headache." Elijah smiled as if he liked the idea. He stopped me by putting his hands on my shoulders. His gaze was intense. "You must learn to trust me."

"I know. I'm sorry. I do trust you." My resolve faded.

Elijah's smoky blue eyes were filled with affection. "You were wonderful in there."

"You were not bad yourself."

"But you are the tamer of wild beasts, the way you stopped Riddick. You also were able to win them over from the start. You have a certain … power over people … including me." He frowned.

"I don't have control over others. I simply care about them. That is all that is needed. If people know you care about them, they are more willing to cooperate."

He brushed a strand of hair out of my face. "You continue to astonish me. How did you get to be so wise at such a young age?"

"My father's teachings, I suppose."

"You are your father's daughter. That is one of the reasons why I love you."

My heart jumped into my throat. It felt as if it were stuck there. He had never said he loved me so directly before. I should have been happy but I was not. My only thought was, *but I belong with Teller.*

He leaned his head forward as if to kiss me.

I put my forehead on his chest to avoid the kiss.

"You should not love me," I whispered.

"I know. Sometimes I wish I didn't."

CHAPTER 72 INDIA 1262 AD

I had to get some distance from Elijah. This journey had been too much already. It drew us too close — not to mention Riddick. He was getting too close as well. *Yes, some distance would be good.* I couldn't keep hurting Elijah like this and I couldn't give myself to him.

"I will go back to London for a while when we return," I said.

"Very well," Elijah's voice was flat. "We should get back to the others." He was not pleased but he did not argue.

Shortly after we returned to Riddick and Samuel, Shantanu beckoned for us to join them back in their cave. He was all smiles.

"That did not take long," Elijah said.

"My men showed great bravery. We agree that the right thing to do is defend humans as best we can from our kind. It is the least we can do for them. We are at your service, My Lord." Shantanu bowed, then took Elijah's forearm.

"Excellent choice. In return the Court is also at your service." Elijah shook his forearm. It was a gesture that was as good as any written contract — maybe even better.

After our customary brief rest, Elijah when straight into his often-repeated teachings on how to feed without killing. Most of the vampires in this coven were skeptical.

As the sun sank in the sky, Kailash as well as three others headed out with Elijah and me to the neighboring city to begin feeding lessons. The rest of the coven chose to stay with Riddick and Samuel for beginner defensive training. Shantanu remained behind to act as a translator.

The city was larger than the one near their cave. We hid in the shadows for quite some time and could not find anyone alone.

"It is our culture," Kailash explained. "We rarely venture out alone, especially women. As you can imagine, this makes feeding more difficult."

"Yes, I see," Elijah frowned.

The plan was for Elijah to show them how he could stop feeding before the human heart stopped. I spotted a couple leaving a home. I looked at Elijah. "Together?"

He nodded and in a flash we were behind the couple. Elijah sank his teeth into the man and I the woman. I had fed recently, so I did not take as much blood from the woman as he did from the man. As soon as she went limp in my arms, I released her, even though her heartbeat was still strong. I did this so she would be unconscious and would not see us.

Elijah fed a moment longer. He laid the man down gently beside the woman. The others had formed a half circle around us.

"Listen. You can hear their heartbeats," Elijah said. "They will awaken soon. They will be weak, of course but in a couple of days they will be right as rain. With practice and regular feeding you can do it as well."

They were wide-eyes and speechless.

Elijah continued. "Let us leave at once to find someone for one of you to practice on. Vallachia and I will pull you off. This way, after we are gone, you will know what to do and you can all practice until you are able to control yourselves."

"It is true; they did it!" Kailash breathed heavy with excitement. Her brow furrowed. "What does this 'right as rain' mean?"

~

THE NEXT DAY was spent in the cave. Some of the men trained with Riddick. Lavanya and her great-aunt taught me to play their favorite games. When the sun was setting, I was reluctant to leave. I liked this coven. The members were affable and their way of life was wonderfully different. From the sky, I turned back one last time to wave goodbye.

"Thank God we are out of there," Riddick said.

"Yes, I can't wait to be home," Samuel agreed.

This was not at all how I felt.

When we arrived back at Lord Chastellain's Great Hall, the lord's shoulders dropped in relief when he saw us. "I was beginning to worry." Then it was straight to business. "What news do you bring?"

"Thanks to Lady Vallachia, it was a monumental success." Elijah wore a proud smile.

The lord's grey eyes widened as they turned to me.

"Honestly, My Lord, I did not do anything. They were extraordinarily gracious and they pledged their fealty to the Court."

Lord Chastellain looked to his son for confirmation.

"Don't be so modest, Vallachia. Father, she had them under her spell from the beginning."

"He is exaggerating, My Lord. They simply liked my hair."

The lord laughed. "Your hair?"

I don't recall ever hearing him laugh and I could not help smiling. "Apparently, most of them had never seen blond hair before," I answered.

"We may have to send you on diplomatic missions more often," the lord said.

"I am at the service of the Court, My Lord. However, I plan to return to London."

The lord glanced to Elijah, whose jaw was clenched. "Very well, we will call you to service when you are needed."

With a bow Samuel and I exited. We both wanted to find Mari. Of course, she was alive and well. I briefly told her goodbye so she and

Samuel could be alone. I found Riddick waiting for me outside my room. *Oh no.* I frowned.

"Don't worry. I'm here because Elijah sent me. He has to attend a meeting. He asked me to tell you that he is rather busy. He hopes to be free by dusk so that we can escort you back to London."

"Thank you." I stepped into my room.

"You know, it makes sense."

I paused and tilted my head at Riddick.

"What Elijah told Shantanu's coven. I never looked at it from another perspective. I had always been told that the Court wants to suppress vampires. Yet I never truly felt suppressed so it did not matter to me who was in power and I had never thought much about what would happen if we did rule over humans. ... We would ruin everything, wouldn't we?"

I gave him a playful smile. "Don't tell me you are actually becoming one of us."

Riddick was deep in thought, as if he were struggling with himself.

"Look, the world is not black and white. Good and bad are not always clear. There is only gray." Surely my words did not help to clarify his beliefs.

"Well either way, I'm glad I'm here," Riddick said.

"I'm glad you're here, too." With that, I disappeared into my room and shut the door. I wanted to make it clear that that was where it ended. We were only friends. *Why didn't I do that with Elijah?* I pushed this annoying thought out of my head and packed a couple of belongings for my return to London.

PART IV CHAPTER 73 LUDUS
1284 AD

I did not think that being friends with Elijah would be possible but thankfully it was. We grew more distant physically but closer otherwise. We laughed and joked with each other as equals and friends. He stayed in London whenever possible and when he was called to Denmark, I would usually return with him. This allowed me to see Mari and my other friends often. We fell into this pattern of companionship, which soon felt natural.

It took Mary almost a year before she befriended me again, despite my attempts to talk to her and include her. Finally, she came around. It was about this time that I noticed she and Elizabeth had grown closer. I wondered if they would be lovers someday. *Maybe they already were; who knew?* I was not one to pry, as it was none of my concern. If they were a couple, they would tell me in their own time.

As the years passed I was sent on several diplomatic missions for the Court. With the success of these missions, the Elders appointed me their lead emissary. I enjoyed traveling and meeting new people and vampires. Some covens were more forthcoming, while others more reluctant but Elijah and I were usually able to win them over in the end.

Riddick unofficially appointed himself my personal bodyguard. He and Samuel always accompanied Elijah and me on our missions. Sometimes Mary was recruited to accompany us when we visited new covens, as she was one of our best fighters. She became the head of military training for Lord Alexandru's coven. Riddick, of course, became the head of military operations in Denmark. Riddick, Samuel and Mary were our "strong arms." Luckily, they were not needed very often on our usually peaceful errands. But Lord Chastellain was careful to make sure his son was well guarded.

We came across one particularly unfriendly coven while in Rus. The members were suspicious of us from the beginning. They appeared not to know much about the growing vampire trouble in Europe. There were only eight of them. Apparently, they thought that number was enough to overtake us. The leader thought we were there to take over his territory. This was about as much as we could gather, as they did not allow for much talk. In the end, we annihilated all of them. This was by far our least successful mission. I had to admit that killing the entire coven was not upsetting, as we saved many human lives.

India was as far as we traveled to the east. The farthest south that we ventured was Egypt. This spanned a good portion of the known world. A relatively large coven of vampires in Alexandria decided that they wanted nothing to do with our conflict in the North. They agreed to stay neutral. Two of the vampires from that coven returned with us to learn how to feed without killing. Egypt was hot and the sun too intense. We were more than grateful to leave for home.

My eyes and ears were always alert for any sign of Teller but no one seemed to have heard of him. Throughout my travels, I'd hoped we would find him. The world of vampires was much smaller than that of humans. Yet we never found any sign of him.

I visited Ludus at least once a year. Usually, I did not disrupt my brother's life. Instead, I observed him and his growing family from the shadows. I wrote to him often. Yet I had to watch over them as much as I could to make sure they were doing well. Little Vallachia grew quickly and soon she had a baby sister. They were healthy and beautiful. As it would end up Josiah had seven children altogether. One child died of a mysterious fever. His four lovely girls and two strong boys grew to be healthy adults. Not surprisingly, Josiah's oldest boy was named Adam.

At my request, the Chastellains had a new church built in Ludus. I wanted a simple replacement for the small run-down church where my brother ministered. Chastellain would not have it. The new church was the largest, most exotic building in town. It was much too grand and not at all what I thought a place of worship should be. In the narthex was a bust of Father; it was placed on a shelf in a recess in the wall. The building was also dedicated to Father. He would not have wanted any of this.

I watched from a distance as little Vallachia became best friends with Teller's youngest brother. The two young neighbors played together. They climbed trees and swam together; they shared all the activities that Teller and I had enjoyed at that age. As the years passed, they fell in love. Though he was five years older than she, he waited until she was of age before asking Josiah for her hand. My brother agreed to the engagement when she was sixteen.

From the shadows high up in a tree, I watched as my brother walked little Vallachia to the pergola and conducted the service. I tried to hold back the tears throughout the ceremony. When it was over, my tears fell on Elijah's shoulder; I was not entirely sure why. My thoughts had been about Teller. His little brother was a striking resemblance.

Perhaps since Teller and I were not able to be together, somehow this new couple was taking our place. Teller and I had been destined for each other at one time and since that had not come to fruition, this beautiful young couple would carry on the lineage that we could not.

Elijah said nothing. He was simply at my side, as always. He was the most wonderfully supportive person. I was exceptionally lucky to have his friendship.

Many years later our entourage was headed back to Denmark after a mission. As we flew over the Carpathian Alps, I broke off from the drove. They followed. I wanted to pay a quick homage to my father.

"So this is where you were raised?" Mary eyed the simple houses with disapproval, clearly unimpressed.

We entered the grand church.

"This was your father?" Riddick studied the bust.

"Yes. Lord Chastellain insisted on all this but it is excessive," I said.

Elijah turned his head to the front doors of the church. "Someone is coming."

I ran to one of the windows and saw my brother on the front steps. "It is Josiah. Should we leave through a side door?"

"Why don't we say hello?" Elijah said.

This was much to my surprise. My brother was almost forty. He had not seen me in over a decade. It would be painfully obvious that I was not aging.

Josiah was startled to see five heavily armed people in his church.

"Hello, Josiah," I said.

CHAPTER 74 LUDUS 1284 AD

It took Josiah a moment to get his bearings. We embraced. "My big sister. I can't believe it!" His eyes were full of questions. "You look exactly as you did the last time I saw you. How can that be?"

"It is better not to know, trust me." I reassured him with a smile.

Elijah stepped forward and shook Josiah's hand in greeting. "It is wonderful to see you again, Deacon."

Elijah had not shown himself to Josiah since 1260, when Elijah and his father had lived in Ludus, pretending to be humans.

Josiah did not recognize him at first. "Aren't you the young lord?"

"Elijah."

"That's right." He looked between Elijah and me for a moment, putting the pieces of my mysterious life together. "So you have been living in Denmark all this time?"

"Partially. I travel between London and Denmark quite often," I said.

His mouth fell open. "You have been as far as London?"

Josiah was still very handsome; his graying hair made him look like the distinguished gentleman that he was.

"Let me introduce you to my companions. You remember Samuel? He is Mari's husband."

"Greetings, Deacon. It is a pleasure to see you again." Samuel shook Josiah's hand.

"Mari, yes, how is she?" my brother asked.

"She is faring wonderfully. She does not like to travel much. Actually, it is difficult to get her out of the castle."

"Castle?" My brother shook his head in disbelief. This was a lot to comprehend.

"This is Riddick." Riddick took my brother's hand and my brother flinched in pain.

"Easy!" I whispered, giving Riddick a hard look.

"Sorry," Riddick said under his breath. He quickly loosened his grip on my brother's hand.

"And this is Mary," I continued.

Josiah gaped at her short hair.

"It is a pleasure to meet the family of our Lady Vallachia." Mary bowed her head.

Josiah studied us for a moment. He seemed not to know where to start with all his questions. "Why dress as if you were going to war?"

"Don't ask too many questions that we cannot answer, little brother. The question is, what are you doing up so early?"

"I come here early to prepare the orations. It is the best time. It is quiet and I can be alone."

"Then we won't keep you. We should be off," I said.

"But you have only just arrived. Sarah and your nieces and nephews will want to see you."

"We don't belong here." I gestured to my companions. "I'm sorry. It is for the best if you do not tell anyone about our visit — just reassure Mari's mother that she is safe and well."

He nodded and I gave him another hug.

"I'm glad to see you look happier," he whispered.

"Take good care of that wonderful family of yours," Elijah said.

"And you take good care of my only sister," Josiah said.

"Always," Elijah replied. They eyed each other with understanding, though I'm not sure I fully understood.

My companions headed for the side door. I took my brother's hands to get his attention.

He tried to warm my hands by rubbing them. "You are all freezing."

"Never fear; we don't feel cold, honestly. It is for everyone's benefit that we live our lives away from here. So please don't tell anyone you saw us."

"I know. I don't understand but I know you are doing what is best for everyone. You know I will tell Sarah. She will respect your wishes to remain away and hidden."

I nodded. As I reached the door, I looked back. "I am sorry it has to be this way. I love you very much."

His smile was warm and understanding. Then we were gone, like a late spring snow — swift and mysterious.

It was not long after this encounter that I received a letter from my brother. Now that he knew where I was, he could finally write. Our father had written to the lord, so it was easy for him to figure out where to send the letter. The letter was addressed:

Lady Vallachia
In the care of Lord Chastellain
Chastellain Manor
Copenhagen, Denmark

IT READ:

MY DEAREST SISTER,

It is good to be able to write you in return. It was wonderful to see that you are doing well and I'm delighted that you are not alone. Your enigmatic and rare appearances leave me with so many questions. You never seem to want to tell me much but I must try to get answers. Did you marry the young lord? Do you have children? If so, please bring them to visit their cousins. Please tell me why you must stay away!

Your loving brother

My eye's filled with tears. I envisioned a world where I visited my brother with my own children in tow. I pictured them playing merrily with my nieces and nephews. In my mind's eye, I watched as they grew up together. It was almost more than I could bear. I still wanted that life more than anything. My brother deserved to know the truth. *I can trust him. He will keep our secret.*

CHAPTER 75 COPENHAGEN
1284 AD

It took a great deal of convincing but Elijah eventually relented to my visiting Josiah alone. "I will leave at dusk and be back before dawn," I pleaded.

"What if something happens to you? I promised your brother I would always look after you," Elijah said.

"And you will look after me by coming for me if I do not return. But I will come back immediately, so that won't be necessary. It has been quiet for many years. I will be safe."

Elijah's brow was furrowed and the grey storm raged in his eyes. I was grateful for how much he worried about me. One thing was for sure — I was not alone. This warmed my heart.

"Only until dawn and if you are not back by then, you know what will happen."

"I know, an army will come looking for me. Don't worry; I won't come to harm." I tried to reassure him with a smile.

He shook his head in disapproval. As always, in the end, Elijah was willing to give me what I wanted.

~

I WATCHED my brother and his wife sleep peacefully. Sarah looked quite old. The loss of her sixth child seemed to have taken a lot out of her. Part of me knew I should leave and not disturb their peaceful life. Instead I woke Josiah by shaking his shoulder. He woke with a start.

"It is I — Vallachia," I whispered. "I came to speak with you — to answer your questions."

From his bedroom door, I beckoned for him to follow me. I did not want to disturb Sarah. We strolled along the empty streets of Ludus.

I held up the letter he had written. "I decided that the time was right to tell you the truth. I will tell you everything, if you promise not to expose us."

"Expose us? What are you talking about?" Josiah asked.

"You see, I live in a different world from yours. One of our rules — our main law, if you will — is that we do not tell humans about us."

"Humans? Val, what are you talking about?"

"Do I have your word?"

"Yes." He seemed to want to know the truth. He appeared … eager.

He must be relieved to finally get some answers. Unfortunately, the truth could be hard to accept. "You see, my friends and I are no longer human. We are … creatures of the night. We call ourselves vampires."

He clearly did not know what to make of this. He looked thoughtful for a moment, trying to find some frame of reference for what I was saying. It was not surprising when he referred to his chief reference, the Bible. "You mean you are demons?"

"In a way. Some of us fit that description well. I would like to think that my friends and our followers are better than that, as we no longer have to kill humans to survive."

"Kill humans?"

I watched as his mind swirled with the past. Our early adulthood was flooding back to him. I remained silent to allow him time to ask the questions as they came to him.

"So it was the Chastellains who killed those people when we were young."

I nodded.

"And you have killed people?"

Again I nodded.

His shoulders sank in disappointment.

"At first I did not want to live. Life did get better once I learned to feed without killing. We are immortal and we are extraordinarily fast and strong."

I swiftly bent over and picked up a fist-sized rock. With my human pretenses dropped, I'm sure the movement was so fast that the rock seemed to magically appear. I held it out so he could see it. Wrapping my fingers around it, I crushed the rock into hundreds of tiny pebbles. They slipped through my fingers as they fell to the ground.

His mouth hung open.

I gave him a mischievous smile. "Do you know what? We can fly. That is how we travel so quickly."

He looked at me as if I had gone completely mad.

"There is, however, a high price for all this power. For one, we do not reproduce. I suppose that is not needed when one does not age. The worst part is that we have to have human blood to survive."

He looked thoughtful for a moment. "What exactly happened to Father?"

I put my head down and took a deep breath as that horrible night came rushing back. I told him the story of turning Teller and how that had led to our terrible loss. "I blame myself and Lord Chastellain for Father's death. Teller had no control. He should not be blamed."

"The lord sounds like a wretched man — er, vampire. Yet you have forgiven him, as you now serve him?"

"It is ... complicated. He can be cruel and no, I have not forgiven him. I don't know if I ever will but he is the leader of our kind and he fights to keep vampires hidden from humans. I follow him and we work hard to keep vampires from taking over the world."

Josiah looked down at my ever-present sword. "You are a warrior?"

"Yes and an emissary for Lord Chastellain's High Court of Elders."

He was thoughtful for some time. "Even in this insane and violent world you live in, you are able to work toward peace?"

"We do our best. It is important that the Court of Elders remain in power. If they were to fall, it would be the end of a free human race."

He smiled. "Father would be proud of you."

I put my arm in Josiah's. "We are both doing our best. There is no doubt Father would be proud of you." We walked in silence for a time. "I have to be getting back. Elijah will be worried if I do not return by sun-up."

"After all that fuss when we were young, you end up marrying the young lord anyway."

I shook my head no. He seemed to sense it was a painful topic and dropped it.

"If you can truly fly, then I want to see it."

"That is not a good idea. In order to fly we must transform into ... monsters."

Now he was doubly curious. "I must see what you have become, this *vampire*."

"As long as you don't blame me for your future nightmares."

I gave him one last hug.

"Thank you for telling me the truth," he said.

"The truth is hard to accept but you deserve to know. Thank you for keeping our secret." I backed away at least fifteen paces. I jumped high in the air; my massive wings unfolded and moved with a loud swishing sound to keep me hovering in the air.

Josiah backed into a tree, his mouth was agape.

"Goodbye." I waved, as I rose high into the night sky.

CHAPTER 76 COPENHAGEN 1291 AD

It was about seven years after revealing my true nature to my brother that I received a letter from Ludus but this time it was not from my brother. It was from Sarah and I knew before I opened it that it was not good news. Josiah was not faring well. He had been overtaken by a sickness and was not expected to live much longer. This time Mari decided to return to the village for the first time since she was young. She had been much better about letting her old life go than I had been.

Of course, Elijah accompanied us as well. Once the villagers had settled down for the night, we approached my old house.

"It amazes me that this place has hardly changed — except for that massive church in the middle of town." Mari declared.

Sarah answered our knock at the door. "You received my letter!" She greeted me with a hug. She did not seem surprised at how young we appeared or at how heavily armed we were. "How did you get here so quickly?"

Of all the oddities about us, that was what surprised her the most. My brother must have told her about us, at least in part.

Sarah did not wait for an answer. Sarah was no longer a shy girl.

She had grown into a strong woman. "Well, I am grateful you are here because Josiah wants to say goodbye."

My heart sank into my stomach.

Sarah's solemn expression matched her tone. She looked much older than the last time I saw her — like a grandmother. Of course, she was a grandmother many times over and I had to remind myself that a simple human life was difficult as well — not difficult in the same way our life was, yet she'd had her share of tough times. A life of hard work and child rearing had taken its toll.

She led us upstairs to their room — my father's old room. I was aghast at how much Josiah had aged. His skin was grey and hung lose on his gaunt cheeks.

Sarah sat on the bed. "Sweetheart, there is someone here to see you."

Josiah opened his eyes and did not seem to recognize me at first. His eyes were full of pain. He had to struggle to try to think past the agony. My heart sank even farther. I frowned at Elijah and Mari.

Josiah slowly raised his hand for me to take. I did and I knelt down at my brother's side. My tears fell, as I put his hand to my cheek.

"I'm glad you could make it. I wanted to say a final goodbye. I'm sorry we were unable to have a lifetime together. Now that you are here, I am ready to meet my Maker." His voice was weak.

"No. What did the healer say? Surely you will get better."

Josiah shook his head. "I can't endure the pain any longer. I needed to see you, to know you are well. Now I wish for God to take me."

"Our healer gives him herbs for the pain. They helped to soothe him in the beginning but they no longer seem to make a difference," Sarah explained.

I nodded, accepting that whatever sickness he had was fatal and I did not want to see him in such pain a moment longer. I stood and my brother's eyes closed.

"Goodbye, my brother. I love you." I kissed his forehead and turned to the others. "He needs to rest." With that, I left the room.

"Will you and your children have enough money without Josiah?" I asked.

"You mustn't worry about us, Vallachia. Our youngest boy is studying in Targoviste. He will take over as deacon and we helped Adam buy a farm. Our youngest girl is to be married this spring. Her future husband will be able to provide for her, so we will make do."

I knew how unreliable farming could be in supporting a family. In spite of Sarah's reassurance, I worried for them.

Elijah handed her a leather sack filled with gold coins. This would have been more money than she had ever seen before. "Please take this. It will make things easier while your son is away. Write to us if you ever need anything. We will take care of you and your family," Elijah offered.

She nodded. "Thank you. God bless you."

We took our leave.

Once in the forest outside of the village, Elijah paused and wrapped his arms tightly around me.

"I can't stand for him to suffer like that. I hope he is gone soon," I whispered in his ear.

"Do you want me to end his pain?"

I pulled back and looked at him. It was what Josiah wanted. He deserved to be with God — not in misery. I nodded.

Elijah looked grave; he clearly did not want to do it. "You two head home. I will catch up with you shortly."

Mari nodded and clasped my hand. She had to pull me away.

Elijah later told me that it was quick and painless. Josiah barely fought Elijah as the pillow suffocated him. Maybe he suffered a couple of moments at most, then his pain was over forever. I was relieved, as this was better than days or even weeks of that kind of suffering. *What if it had gone on for months?* I thought. I was pleased that he had lived a relatively long and contented human life. That was all anyone could hope for.

CHAPTER 77 COPENHAGEN 1291 AD

As usual, the best thing for me to do was to stay busy after my brother's death. It is difficult to watch the ones you love grow old and die but for an immortal it was even more difficult. Maybe it was the guilt, as we were immune to the things that killed most humans. I too should be on my deathbed. Maybe it was the frustration of having so much power yet being unable to do anything to save the ones we loved. It also could have been thoughts of the afterlife that crept into our minds when people we cared about died.

I had no doubt that my brother was once again blissful and healthy because he was with his God. He was now immortal as well. But who was *our* God? What happened to us when we died, or rather, when we were killed, as we did not die of natural causes? I did not like to ponder such thoughts, so I tried hard not to think of such foreboding things.

Nevertheless, such thoughts were impossible to fully keep away. Where did vampires come from and what happened to us when we died? I had asked most everyone such questions and no one knew for certain. Was it possible God made us or were we truly the spawns of Satan himself? The latter seemed more plausible.

There was a glimmer of hope, now that my closest kin were gone.

Perhaps I could let go of the past, Ludus and the human life I had lost. This mostly meant that I hoped to be able to let go of Teller. Then perhaps I could marry Elijah and we could finally be happy. On the other hand, the thought of not being with Teller someday was unbearable.

Between our missions to gain and keep supporters for the High Court and training new vampires to feed properly, I stayed busy. The news of our being able to feed without killing spread and vampires would travel from far away to seek us out. This added to our allies in the North. We had large numbers of vampires from across the known world ready to fight for the Elders.

However, Ramdasha's numbers grew as well. We increasingly heard rumors of Tarantism in southern lands. It was not until 1346 that the war with Ramdasha went from being a cold war to a hot one. Across all of Southern Europe, vampires were becoming an epidemic. Plagues spread through cities and cases of "tarantula bites" caused mass madness and death on a large scale. The tarantula was what most humans blamed the plague on. We knew better. Ramdasha's vampires were responsible for the devastation. This was their first attempt to openly defy the Court. They were attempting to take over the human race.

It was in 1346 that our missions became less diplomatic in nature. We were sent out to destroy the enemies of the Elders. Eliminating the traitors to the Court became a fulltime task. Wherever there were plagues or stories of Tarantism was where we traveled. At times, we would find chaos in the streets. One such occasion was in the town of Lucera. When we arrived with our small, yet elite, army of thirty vampires, the terrified townspeople were running in the streets. People with blood streaming from their necks were fleeing. There were a handful of vampires causing this mess.

"This is disgusting," I whispered to Elijah as we surveyed the horrid scene.

"Capture them alive," Elijah commanded. He beckoned us forward with a hand gesture.

It was not long before we had four of them in captivity. The fifth vampire tried to attack Elijah but Riddick ran his sword through the assailant's neck. With a powerful kick to the back of the knees from Riddick, the remaining four were forced to kneel in front of Elijah.

"Do you know who I am?" Elijah's voice was dark.

One vampire ventured to shake his head *no*.

"I am Prince Elijah, the son of Lord Chastellain."

The name sparked recognition in the vampire prisoners. One of them writhed.

"Are you aware that we have laws?" Elijah continued.

"Yes, My Lord," one of the vampires murmured. He was most likely the ringleader.

This was the wrong answer; it would have been wiser for the prisoner to play ignorant. Elijah eye's flashed with fury. He grabbed the man by the tunic and yelled. "What, then, is our most important law? The unbreakable law?"

The man was too scared to answer. Elijah threw him down. He pointed his sword at the others. "Anyone else?"

"To remain hidden," another man squeaked.

"Does this" — Elijah gestured to a couple of bodies in the street — "look discreet to you?"

One of the vampires shook her head no.

"No!" Elijah yelled, causing the kneeling vampires to jump. "Do you know what the penalty is for needlessly slaughtering humans and revealing yourselves to them?"

This time, Elijah did not wait for an answer. He swiftly severed the head of the man who had remained on the ground where Elijah had thrown him. He picked the head up and displayed it to the others — giving them a good look at their leader. With the point made, the head was dropped in a bag that Riddick held open.

It was painful to see Elijah like this. Thankfully, this was not his usual self. All I had to do was look around to remind myself why he was doing this, why he was being so harsh. These men had to be stopped at any cost.

One of the men threw himself at Elijah's feet.

In an instant, Riddick's sword was between Elijah and the man, ready to stop the man if needed.

"Please, My Lord, kill me. I can't live like this. I beg of you, please kill me!" His eyes were full of pain and self-loathing.

Elijah was more in control — calmer. He bent down to get close to the man. "Death would be too easy for you." He stood. "Take them prisoner."

I knew this meant that Lord Chastellain would most likely kill them after questioning them about Ramdasha. The man at Elijah's feet wept. He truly did want to die. I knew how he felt. In the beginning, having to kill to survive had made me wish for death as well.

We returned to Denmark with our prisoners. Lord Chastellain collected the heads of traitors to be skewered on poles that lined the path to his castle — his trophies. This was much to my disliking — it was barbaric. It did, however, send a message to the enemies of the High Court of Elders. The road to the castle was lined with perhaps one hundred heads. The oldest ones were white skulls with slightly elongated eyeteeth. I couldn't imagine what this would look like to a human stumbling upon this place. It was no longer the welcome palace of old.

Lord Chastellain and I were often at odds. I had never been good at keeping my mouth shut. As the years passed, any ability to hold my tongue was lost. My place on the Court was to the left of the lord, Elijah to his right. Riddick usually stood to my left. To the right of Elijah was Samuel. We were the lord's chief emissaries and warriors — not to mention that Elijah was his son and I his son's beloved. Therefore, the lord tolerated more defiance from me than he did from others. He still had to remind me of my place at times.

With more vampires rising against us, Lord Chastellain became increasingly cruel. It was my belief that showing mercy would gain us more allies. The Court needed to be fair and kind whenever possible. I was constantly trying to keep the lord from going too far. I did not want him to become a brutal tyrant but rather the just lord I knew he could be. I was a constant bane that reminded him of the good leader he was or should be.

CHAPTER 78 COPENHAGEN 1346 AD

Lord Chastellain questioned the three remaining prisoners from Lucera. They did not seem to know anything about Ramdasha — at least anything they were willing to tell us. So they were sentenced to death. I spoke up for the man who had wished to die.

"Did you say your name is Victor?" I asked.

"Yes, My Lady." He kept his head down.

I bent down and gently lifted his head so that I could see into his eyes.

"Please, let them kill me," he pled.

"I have a better idea for you."

"Vallachia, what on earth are you doing?" Lord Chastellain demanded.

"Victor is different, My Lord." I turned to Victor. "Did you know that we feed without killing?"

Victor's eyes opened wide in surprise. "No, My Lady. Surely that is not possible."

I kept my hand under his chin to keep him from putting his head down. "It is possible and we can teach you. If we spare your life, will you pledge yourself to the service of the High Court?"

"Yes, My Lady," he whispered.

"No." Lord Chastellain said. "It is too late. The sentence has been given. He will die like the others."

"My Lord, please, we need supporters. The Court must be merciful if it is going to continue to lead our kind."

The lord's jaw muscles tightened and he glared at me.

Yes, I was a burr under his skin, a painful one and I liked it.

"Very well," the lord smirked. "You will be responsible for him and you must personally kill the other two."

Chastellain must have thought I would not do this. He knew how much I hated the beheadings. I swung around, drawing my sword at the same time. It went through one neck and then the other with one smooth motion. The blade hardly slowed as it severed flesh and bone. The prisoner's heads made a dreadful sound as they hit the floor. This was followed by the even louder thud of their bodies.

There was no point in making them suffer any longer. They were already dead, at my hand or someone else's. "Are you satisfied, My Lord?"

His smile widened. "Yes."

This way we both "won" — sort of. I proved my willingness to take orders and he let Victor live.

I seized Victor under his arm and forced him to stand. "Come," I whispered. I did not want to give the lord time to change his mind.

I had to find Victor living quarters and someone to keep an eye on him until I was sure I could trust him. Finding a room was increasingly difficult, as there were at least one hundred vampires coming and going from the premises at all times. The positive side to this was that it made it impractical for Ramdasha to attack us directly.

I knocked on one of the doors in the lower-level housing. A vampire answered.

"Excuse me, do you have a roommate?" I asked.

"Yes, My Lady but the room across the way has an opening."

"Thank you."

To the man who answered the door across the hall, I explained that Victor was his new roommate and that he was to watch after him.

I put my hand on Victor's shoulder. "Clean up and have a rest. We will be back at dusk to start your training on how to feed without killing."

"Yes, My Lady," Victor said.

I did not like the formal address, even though most everyone around here used it. "Please, my name is Vallachia."

"Yes, My Lady."

"No, what I'm saying is, call me Vallachia, or even Val, for that matter."

"Of course, My ... Val ... Vallachia."

I shook my head — it was a start. With my hand still on his shoulder I looked him in the eyes. "Don't let me down. This life can be worth living. Let us show you that it is not all bad."

"Thank you, My —

I shook my finger at him, stopping his words. "I'll see you at dusk."

If he could not say "My Lady," apparently he could not speak. He nodded in agreement.

As I left, I overheard Victor's new roommate, "Aye, she is a splendid specimen, isn't she? Don't go getting any ideas, she has the eye of the prince and there is no getting close to her."

I had murdered two of Victor's companions; I doubted he thought I was "splendid".

Elijah was waiting like a statue at my door. "It always amazes me how you are able to handle my father. At first I used to worry that you would push him too far."

"And now?" I asked.

"I understand that you know what you are doing. You have him just where you want him."

"Not exactly. It is usually a compromise."

He brushed my hair back over my shoulder. "How are you faring?"

It was the first time I had officially executed anyone. I had killed in the heat of battle but execute unarmed vampires — no. I did not answer.

He wrapped his arms around me. It was not until that moment that I realized it had indeed bothered me. *How does he know when I need him?* He had known that I was upset before I had. I put my arms around his waist and buried my head in his chest. The only thing I knew at that moment was that I would be lost without him.

"Come. I have a surprise for you," Elijah whispered.

I frowned.

He reached back and opened my door. I was skeptical about where this was going.

CHAPTER 79 COPENHAGEN 1346 AD

With trepidation I entered my bedchambers and was greeted with a chorus, "Surprise!" Our friends were waiting for us.

Mari handed me a goblet of red wine — which I now loved, the older and dryer the better. "Elijah told us you had a particularly wretched day at work."

I gladly took the goblet. "Is that what you would call it?"

Mari did not like politics or to hear too much about what we did in the field. I did not blame her, as it was either boring or bloody. "Today there is to be no talk of work. We are going to have fun."

Sonia wrapped her little arms around me. "We will start by playing your favorite card game."

"And drinking a vast amount of wine!" I held my chalice up to toast.

"To the High Court of Elders!" Samuel said.

The clanking of our chalices rang out.

Riddick dealt the cards. "Ladies have first draw."

"Wonderful. Since I'm the oldest I will go first," Mari said.

"Wait a minute," I put my hand over hers to stop her. "I'm older than you."

"No, I'm older. I lived as a human for a year longer than you. So I was older when I was turned. You are actually a year younger." Mari gave me a devious smile.

"That is not the way it works," I said. "I'm older because I have been a vampire longer than you."

Mari and I looked to Elijah and Samuel to settle the dispute.

"You are both the same age and you are both old as hell," Elijah said.

Samuel and Aaron thought this was comical. I had to laugh as well but I still punched Elijah in the shoulder.

"Look who is talking, Elijah. You're older than anyone else here," Mari pouted. She did not appreciate being called old.

"It doesn't matter," Sonia said. "I am older than either of you two ladies, so I will draw first."

She was indeed older than Mari or me, though she did not look it, so she started the game.

This was how the day went — the perfect distraction from work. When I felt the need to rest, I headed to my bed. Mari and Sonia joined me.

"The boys should leave so we can get some sleep," I said. "We have to start training Victor at dusk."

"Who is Victor?" Mari inquired.

"Don't ask," I said.

Mari laid her head on a pillow and looked as sleepy as I felt.

Riddick jumped into the middle of us. "I will stay here and look after the ladies."

"Not a chance in hell, my friend," Samuel said. He pulled Riddick's arm as I pushed my foot into Riddick's back. It took all my force and Samuel's to get him off us. The men left the room, laughing and dragging Riddick with them.

I usually did not pry but I knew Sonia and Aaron were close. The time seemed right to ask. "Are you and Aaron together?"

Sonia's cheeks flushed.

Is she embarrassed or sad? I wondered.

"We have been a couple for quite some time."

"Sonia, that is wonderful! I can't believe you did not tell us. Are you planning to marry?" I asked.

A tear rolled down her cheek and I was sorry I had asked. Sitting up, I gave Mari a concerned look.

"Do you want to talk about it? It may help," I offered.

Sonia shook her head no. Mari reached across my waist and took Sonia's hand. "We are here for you."

Sonia was silent for a while. "It is because of how I look."

I glanced at Mari to see if she understood and Mari shrugged.

"What are you talking about, Sonia? You are winsome as can be," I said.

"That is the problem. I'm not beautiful like you two. I know Aaron loves me for who I am and not for how I look but others would not understand."

"There is nothing wrong with how you look," Mari said.

"I'm not a woman. I'm a little girl. What man would want this?" She gestured to her small, thin body with disgust. She had been turned before her body had developed womanly curves. She was a hundred-seven-year-old woman frozen inside a child's body.

"It is a different world we live in. Surely vampires will understand that you are not a young girl," Mari said.

"Aaron asked me to marry him but I refused."

"Why, don't you love him?" Mari asked.

"More than anything. I never hoped to have a man. I thought I would be alone my entire life. Aaron is so wonderful; I'm lucky to have him. I said no to his proposal because I don't want others to think he is ... unwholesome. I know that this is not the case but that is why we have decided to keep our love a secret. Most vampire men would be drawn to someone who has reached full womanhood. But Aaron loves *me*, not this body. Yet we can never marry or be open about the true nature of our relationship. No one would understand."

There was an aching in my chest for Sonia. She should never have been turned so young. All she wanted was a woman's body that would never develop.

I did not know what to say at first. "I'm sorry. Perhaps with time, things will change. Our kind may become more open."

"We understand and we are delighted for you and Aaron," Mari said.

Sonia wiped a tear from her face and closed her eyes.

We were all tired. I lay down, putting my arm around Sonia.

Before dozing off, Mari whispered, "I am older."

I gave her a swift kick.

I woke to Mari pushing my leg off her. Sonia had her arm around me. I gently moved it. I felt bad for Sonia. She was fully mature in all her mannerisms and we did not think of her as a child. She was too strong and too wise for that. Being a woman in a child's body would be terrible.

My friends had helped ease the pain of the difficult night. Elijah knew the perfect medicine for me. In these hard times, we needed our friends more than ever. The sun was setting off the end of my balcony. I bolted upright. "We have to go."

Despite the lord's increasingly harsh punishments, the Court continued to lose ground. The mass killings of humans spread slowly north. Elijah's small, but effective, branch of our army had earned the title, "Vampire Killers."

At a meeting of the Elders, it was decided that we must attack Ramdasha. There was no longer any debate amongst the Elders about Ramdasha's defiance of the Court. He was clearly behind the spread of Tarantism and this was not acceptable. He was also encroaching on our territory — the North. Ramdasha must be destroyed. He was shrewd and had managed to remain out of our grasp. Since Riddick and I knew where he lived, we were to lead an army to his cavern in Constantinople.

Elizabeth and Mary came from London. The castle was bursting with life. Our allies from all around were gathering. Since there were no open rooms, Mary and Elizabeth stayed with me. I was glad to have the company. We were catching up when a knock came at my door.

"Come in," I said.

Elijah entered. "I'm sorry to break up the reunion." He greeted Mary and Elizabeth. "It is good to see you both."

Mary was much more cordial to Elijah now — well, as cordial as Mary ever was to anyone.

"Val, may I have a word?" Elijah's eyes were stone grey with worry.

Oh no, I thought. "Of course." I jumped up. We headed across the hall to his room. "What is it?"

"You are not going to like it but I want you to sit this one out."

My eye's widened. "Why?" He was right; I did not like it in the least. If Riddick had appointed himself to guard me, then I had done the same with Elijah. I had to go — to protect him.

"I have a bad feeling about this. Please, for me, stay here with Mari. Make sure she is safe."

I narrowed my eyes. "Is that an order, My Lord?"

"No, of course not. I would never order you to do anything."

"Good. I am going."

"You are so stubborn." He gritted his teeth.

He was truly concerned so I softened my demeanor. If he was worried then I should be too. I took his hands in mine. "Listen, all will be well as long as we are together."

CHAPTER 80 CONSTANTINOPLE 1346 AD

At dusk we left for Constantinople with our army of Vampire Killers. We landed outside the city and remained hidden.

"His patrols will most likely spot us as soon as we pass the great city walls," Riddick said.

I nodded in agreement. "We will have to move as quickly as possible to his cavern. We can't all go." Originally, the plan had been to have our entire army bombard the cavern but that did not seem like the wisest way to attack.

"What are you suggesting?" Elijah asked.

"We should come in from Galata, just north of the city," I said. "It is a quick swim across the Golden Horn. That way we have only one shorter wall to overcome rather than the two larger land walls. We can stay under cover of water so the sentries will not spot us. This will also place us closer to Ramdasha. Riddick and I should go in first and report back."

"No. Not a chance in hell," Elijah said.

"It has been over eighty years since we have been here. Much will have changed. Someone should scout it out first," I argued.

"Val is right, we cannot go in blind," Samuel said.

"Then I will go with you," Elijah said.

"I don't think that is wise," Riddick said. "Sending our top three commanding officers alone into what is likely to be the most heavily guarded and most dangerous place is not the greatest of ideas."

"Very well, you and Aaron will go," Elijah said.

I glared at Elijah; was he indicating that Aaron's life was not as important as mine?

"Aaron lived in Ramdasha's coven as well. He knows the area. Remember, your job is only to make a quick assessment and report back immediately," Elijah commanded.

We moved quietly north around the large city wall and down into Galata. We had a couple of hours before sun-up.

"How much time do you need?" Elijah asked.

"Give us ten minutes," Riddick said.

I reached for Riddick's forearm as he passed by. "Be careful. In and out — do you understand?"

He smirked. "Don't worry, this is what I live for." Excitement danced in his dark eyes.

I nodded. The next minutes were the longest of my life. It would have been better to be with Riddick and Aaron — at least I would have known what was going on. Not knowing was much worse.

I relentlessly paced until Mary grabbed me by the shoulders. "Will you stop?"

I sat down hard next to Elijah. "I'm sorry but what if Ramdasha captures them ... ?" Ramdasha would show no mercy. He was vengeful and Riddick had betrayed him in the worst way. Aaron had also abandoned him, for that matter. If something happened to Aaron ... poor Sonia! I started biting my fingernails, which I had never done before.

Elijah pulled my hand away from my mouth. "Don't fret. All will be well."

"I'm not so sure about that." Riddick stepped from the trees.

I exhaled with relief when I saw Aaron behind him. We jumped to our feet.

"The abandoned building that covered the entrance to the cavern has been restored. It is now a fully functioning inn, crawling with humans," Riddick explained.

"Humans? Are you sure?" Elijah asked.

Riddick nodded yes.

"Is there any other way in?" I asked.

"Not that I'm aware of." Riddick looked at Aaron posing the question to him.

"You were Ramdasha's second in command. If you don't know of any other way in, then I definitely don't know of another entrance," Aaron said.

"Do you think he is still there?" Elijah asked.

"It is impossible to tell, he may have moved on," Riddick said.

"If he were still here, the place would have to be heavily guarded and not by humans because he knows that we are familiar with this place," I said.

Elijah looked thoughtful for a moment. "That may be the case, or humans may be the perfect cover. This is the only place we know to look for Ramdasha. We have to find out what is here. Let us send a small group into the inn to inspect the room that leads to the cavern."

After much debate, it was decided that Riddick and I would ask to rent the room where the entrance had been hidden. Elijah, Samuel, Aaron, Mary and Elizabeth would come in behind us and wait in the common area until we were in the room.

We swam the Golden Horn to the city wall and waited for a sentry to pass out of sight. Flying over the wall, we sped to the inn in a blur.

Even with the looming danger it was wonderful to be back in the city. The Roman emperors had been hard at work restoring some of the inner buildings.

Once outside the inn, I left my broadsword with Elijah. I felt naked without it. At least knives were still hidden under my clothes. Riddick and I went to the front desk. All I could smell were humans — no trace of vampires. Then again, humans smelled much stronger than vampires. Their scent could be the ideal cover.

"How may I help you, sir?" the innkeeper asked.

"We would like to rent a room. Not just any room though. You see, we would like the same room where we celebrated our wedding night." Riddick placed his arm around my waist and pulled me close.

Not bad, I thought. *That will explain why we want that particular room but why would a couple stay in an inn on their wedding night? Still, the lie would most likely succeed. How did Riddick think of such good stories so quickly?*

"Of course, sir. Which room was it?"

"We don't remember exactly. We were ... preoccupied at the time, as you can imagine." Riddick winked at the man. I elbowed him in the ribs. "I can show you which room it was."

"Very well, sir." The innkeeper grabbed a set of jingling keys and we led the way. I motioned to Elijah to follow us with the slightest glance and head nod.

When we approached the door, Riddick swung me up in his arms. "This is it."

His ear was close enough that I could easily whisper without the human being able to hear. "You are enjoying this, aren't you?"

"Completely." Riddick gave me a wicked smile.

"You are in luck, sir, as the room is unoccupied." The innkeeper proceeded to open the door.

I swung myself out of Riddick's arms and cautiously entered the room. Riddick was only inches behind me. The room was modern and well decorated; it was barely recognizable. This made it doubly odd to be back here.

There was no trace of vampire scent. We let our guard down. I looked for any sign of the old entrance in the floor.

"Ah yes. Many fond memories in this room," Riddick paid the man well and quickly shut the door.

"I don't see the entrance. It has been covered by the new floor." Now that the innkeeper was gone, I opened the door so the others would be able to find us easily. "A wedding night in an inn?" I questioned.

Riddick shrugged. "Who knows? Perhaps it will become a custom. Newlyweds want to be alone, so they should take a trip after their wedding. I think I'll call it a honeymoon."

I laughed. "You are mad; such a trip will never become a custom."

"You have to admit it does make sense," Riddick said.

In no time the room was full of seven vampires. Elijah swiftly tossed me my sword, which I was relieved to have. We stood the bed against the wall in order to better search the floor.

"It should be here." Riddick pointed to a spot on the floor where the old bed would have covered the entrance to the cave.

"Aaron, retrieve the others. Show them how to find us. You all can come in through the window." Elijah turned to Riddick. "Break the floor."

Aaron quickly opened the shutters and disappeared out the window.

"Are you sure we should continue?" Riddick asked. "This door has not been used in ages. Most likely they are no longer here."

"If Ramdasha is no longer here, we need to know for sure so we can focus our resources elsewhere. It could be that they have a new entrance. Either way, we must find out. That is why we are here," Elijah said.

Riddick nodded. "Let us proceed." He swung his ax in his hand gracefully once for show, then he brought it down hard on the stone slabs. The floor cracked apart. With one more blow from the blunt end of his ax, the stone floor was in pieces. We quickly removed the rubble, revealing the round iron handle attached to the heavy stone lid leading to the staircase. With one arm, Riddick lifted the lid weighing as much as three grown men put together.

The rest of us readied ourselves — all swords were drawn. Our army was close behind. As leaders, we were the front line. Leaders had to be willing to risk their own lives if they expected others to follow them. Kings and Emperors alike, the good ones anyway, led their armies into battle. They fought blow for blow with their infantry. Therefore, it was our duty to be the first to descend the stairs into enemy territory.

The air that came from the staircase was musty. It was impossible to tell what or who might be down there. These stairs had not been used in a long time, as they were laden with cobwebs. It was difficult to imagine that there had been a time when I had called this place home, even briefly.

With one last glance, Riddick descended the stairs. I started to follow but Elijah took my arm to stay me. Elijah moved ahead of me. He beckoned for Samuel to follow.

"Wait here for the rest of the troops to arrive," Elijah whispered to Mary and Elizabeth. "We will call for you and the others if needed."

I gave Elijah a questioning look.

"Something is telling me that they should stay behind," he whispered in answer to my unspoken question.

This seemed contrary to logic. I would have felt better with our soldiers directly behind us. Yet I did not question him further. I trusted him.

We descended deep underground. There was no clear indication of vampires. Riddick had to brush away the thick cobwebs as he moved downward. The air grew thicker with each step. It was as if we were being buried alive — each breath was like inhaling dank earth.

When Riddick stepped on the bottom stair before the long hallway, we heard stone scraping against stone. I looked down to find the last stair collapsing under Riddick's weight. The sound of a flame coming to life could be heard. We briefly looked at one another with wide eyes before proceeding. An explosion came from the stairs behind us. We were blown down the long hallway.

Rocks of all shapes and sizes, as well as a heavy dust, fell around us. When I tried to move, my back screamed in pain. I shook my head to get the dust and debris off. As I slowly rolled over, it dawned on me that I could not hear. It was as if the entire world had gone silent. Elijah picked me up and I screamed in pain when he touched my back. He had blood coming from his ears and half his face was cut and bleeding. I tried to touch his face but found it hurt too badly to raise my arm. He kicked a door in and placed me gently on a bed. *My old bed,* I thought vaguely as my world turned black. *No, no, I can't; Elijah is hurt.* These were my last fighting thoughts before I remembered nothing.

CHAPTER 81 CONSTANTINOPLE 1346 AD

I woke with a start — gasping for breath. There was not enough air — heavy dirt was crushing me. *It was a nightmare.* I sat up and winced at the discomfort in my back. *No. It was not entirely a nightmare.* Wherever I was it was dark, but there was enough air to breathe, though be it dank and putrid. At least I was not buried under piles of earth. I threw my arms out in panic and my hand found Elijah's chest.

He slowly opened his eyes. Only faint scars could be seen on his face.

"Thank God, you are safe!" I threw myself on top of him, wrapping my arms around his neck.

Being careful of my back he gently wrapped his arms around me.

"What happened?" I did not let go of him.

"It was a trap. The good news is that Ramdasha and his men are not here."

"And the bad news?" Yet I did not truly want to know.

"We are entombed down here. It was an explosive powder that most likely collapsed the entire staircase."

"Explosive powder? Oh no!" Samuel would have received the brunt of the blast. I pulled away from Elijah.

"Samuel will heal," Elijah read my mind, as only he could. "All of us are safe … for now."

I had the urge to kiss him but instead I laid my head on his chest. We lay like that, me curled on top of him, listening to his heartbeat, for a long moment. I thought he might have fallen back asleep.

"Come. We must relieve Riddick," Elijah said.

I sat up. "Relieve Riddick?"

He placed both hands on my hips and lifted me off him. When he grabbed me, it sent a strange feeling through me. It was pleasant, yet confusing. I still had no idea what real intimacy was. I had to shake my head to clear it.

He went through a nearby chest. "You need some new clothes."

I looked down to find that my tunic was in tatters. With a slight tug I pulled my clothing off. There was barely anything left of the back of my tunic. What fabric remained was covered in dried blood.

"Put this on." Elijah threw me a dress.

It was one of the dresses Anna, the keeper of the Dancing Stallion tavern in Bucharest, had given me so long ago. It was musty and worn but otherwise wearable. A crooked smile crossed my face. I must have gotten the expression from Elijah. "This was mine … once." Being topless in front of Elijah was not even a concern.

I pulled the dress over my head when Elijah sat down behind me. He ran his graceful fingers across the bare skin on my back. "You are going to have some good scars back here. They will match the scar on your hip. You were burned badly and some of the debris cut you in several places."

I turned around and ran my hand across his scarred cheek. There was only one really notable scar. The rest were only thin scratches that could barely be seen. Again I wanted to kiss him. This was the moment I fully admitted to myself that I loved him. I had for a long time. It took a life-or-death situation for me to admit it but I did truly love him. I was lost in his stormy smoke-filled eyes until he brought me back to our situation.

"Come. There is much work to be done."

I closed my eyes to break his spell over me and finished pulling on my dress.

Out in the hallway, Riddick was working hard to remove the endless rubble. I put my hand on his shoulder to stay him. He looked relieved to see me.

"Get some rest," I whispered.

He looked exhausted and did not argue. He retired to my old room. Elijah and I went to work removing debris. It was not long before Samuel came out of an adjacent room.

I hugged him gently. "How are you healing?"

"Well enough."

I moved to examine his back. A sharp inhale escaped my lips. Samuel's skin was red and swollen from the healing burns and there were random fresh scars across his back from flying debris. "Is that what my back looks like?"

"Your back is not quite that bad." Elijah put a hand on Samuel's shoulder. "I'm terribly sorry, old friend but you took the worst of it."

"I will be thoroughly healed within an hour," Samuel snapped. He jerked his shirt down.

"Thankfully, you are alive and safe." I gave him another quick hug.

"It is fortunate that we all survived and that the rest of the army was not directly behind us. They would have been annihilated. This was the perfect trap. Ramdasha knew we would come here eventually and he could have eliminated the majority of our best men and trapped the military leaders down here, without risking any of his own men," Elijah said.

"He is intelligent," I sneered.

"But how did he do it?" Samuel asked.

"With this." Elijah gestured to what was left of a wooden barrel. He ran his hand along a piece of the wood and revealed the black powder that was smeared on his finger.

Samuel did the same. Sniffing the substance he wrinkled his nose in disgust. "What is it?"

"Explosive powder. It comes from the Orient, I believe. I have heard tales of its power. Yet I have never seen it or fully understood what it is capable of until now."

"So there is no other way out?" Samuel surveyed the scene and focused on the overwhelming pile of rubble blocking our exit.

"No. That is why this is the perfect trap. Only one way in or out," Elijah said.

"Do you think our men are removing the rubble from the top?" Samuel asked.

"Possibly, unless they think we are dead and they returned home," I said.

"Either way, Father would want to know for sure if we were dead. He will come to retrieve our bodies if nothing else. So we may be able to get out before we starve to death down here."

"I heard that we do not actually starve to death — rather, we mummify until someone gives us blood," Samuel said.

I frowned. It sounded as if death would be better than becoming a mummy.

"Let's hope we don't find out." Elijah said. "If they are digging from the top, then we can help by removing rubble from this end for as long as we can. We must try to get out of here, so that this is not a complete waste. We have learned two important things: Ramdasha is no longer here and he has better weapons than ours. We must get this information to Father."

Samuel constructed two makeshift wheelbarrows. We went to work digging ourselves out. We moved tons of stone tirelessly, filling nearby rooms with the rubble, leaving the main hall clear. Room after room was filled and stair after stair was uncovered. The stairway was no longer a thin passageway that fit the frame of the average man but was hollowed out to over twice the size it had once been.

Samuel was fascinated with how the explosion had worked. He removed the bottom step that had collapsed under Riddick's weight. "Look at this." Samuel beckoned us over. "A large piece of flint was placed under this heavy step. With the spark from the step moving across the flint it must have caught something, a rope, perhaps." He pointed to a long thin black line. "These burn marks run all along the walls to hidden compartments containing the barrels full of black powder."

Elijah scratched his head in wonder. "Perhaps the ropes had been soaked in a highly flammable substance."

"Most likely an oil of sorts," Samuel said.

"One thing is for sure: we are headed for a new type of warfare," I said.

Elijah and I exchanged a worried look.

Though it seemed like an eternity, it must have been only a handful of days before we heard the distant scraping of stone and faint voices.

"We are here!" Riddick yelled.

I heard movement and more voices.

"Elijah!" a faint but familiar voice called.

"Yes, Father, I am here. We are alive."

I collapsed into Elijah and we slid down the wall of the staircase.

"We are going to get out of here," he whispered in my ear.

"Thank God," I breathed. Exhaustion was a luxury I could not afford ... until now. I felt faint, as if I might fall asleep on the spot. My lungs ached for fresh air.

"Get them out of there," we could hear Lord Chastellain command.

It did not take long before a hand broke through the remaining rocks and sweet air escaped in with it. I took a deep breath, savoring every bit as it filled my lungs.

The first one through was Lord Chastellain. He wrapped his arms around Elijah.

"I'm unharmed, Father," Elijah whispered.

Chastellain did something I had not anticipated, he embraced me. "I'm glad you are alive."

I pulled back and looked at him with wide eyes. Usually he appeared not to like me in the least. In fact, I thought he despised me. *Or is it I who hated him?* I was confused and grateful and relieved all at once. "I'm glad you came for us," I managed.

Elijah gave us a warm smile.

"We have to get out of here. Victor has brought it to our attention that parts of the ceiling are threatening to collapse. He thinks that the explosion and the removal of the debris makes this tunnel very likely to fall in on itself."

That was the lord I remembered — always straight to business.

Victor carried in a large log and shoved it between the ceiling and one of the steps.

"Victor has done this all along the stairs in order to shore up the passage," the lord explained.

"These logs will not hold for long," Victor said.

Behind us, dust fell from the ceiling. This was followed by a loud crashing sound as dirt and stone fell to the stairs. Below us, the roof was caving in.

Elijah took my hand. "Everyone out!"

We ran. Riddick was the last one to lift himself out of the staircase and into the hotel room. He was followed by a waft of dust and a loud cracking sound as another section of the tunnel collapsed permanently behind him. I pulled him the rest of the way out and wrapped my arms around him.

"We escaped," he whispered.

The window in the room had been opened up to make a larger entryway. There were now mountains of rubble, as well as a large hole in the street where the staircase was completely buried. It looked as if a war had occurred here since we had last seen it.

Mary and Elizabeth each greeted me with a hug. Mary turned to Elijah and did the same.

My mouth fell open. Mary used to hate Elijah and I had never seen her show affection toward a man.

"We would be dead if you had not ordered us to stay behind. You are more prescient than I would have guessed. I'm grateful for your leadership," Mary said.

There is nothing like almost dying to bring people together. I smiled at Mary.

We turned our gaze to the collapsed street. Elijah put his hand in mine. "I'm glad that place is gone. Let's go home."

CHAPTER 82 EUROPE 1352 AD

Over the next seven years we worked endlessly to find Ramdasha. Now it was a personal mission for Lord Chastellain. Ramdasha was cunning enough to remain one step ahead and just out of reach. He stayed hidden and trusted only those closest to him. The lord sent out several calls for Ramdasha to meet us in battle. The calls went unanswered. He was a coward and he was … unfortunately, cunning.

We increasingly had to fight in the North to eliminate the growing vampire epidemic, or what the humans call the plague. Either way, "Black Death" was a fitting name for it. Elijah's single army of Vampire Killers could no longer keep up. Riddick was given his own well-trained men to lead. He did not like the idea of leaving us but we were able to convince him that he was our best military leader and he must help us defend the North by spreading out. By 1352, Samuel was given his own army to lead as well. We often had to fight on many different fronts across the North.

I was devastated when the vampire plague hit London. This was my city. Every night we launched counterattacks from Lord Alexandru's new larger castle outside the city. We fought the rogue vampires wreaking havoc in the streets. Usually these vampires were new and untrained. They did not stand a chance against us. Their only advantage was that they had numbers.

Dawn would bring about countless bodies of both vampires and humans to dispose of. Elijah, Mary, Elizabeth and I would help with cleanup by placing the bodies in mass graves.

"Where are they coming from?" I asked on the morning of one such burial.

"Someone is turning humans into vampires at a rapid rate," Elijah replied.

"We have to find out who," Elizabeth said.

A human man noticed Elizabeth. "Hey! You there, get that child out of here. He should not have to see this."

Elizabeth glared at the man.

"No one should have to see this, sir," I said.

We continued our work, ignoring his disapproving glower.

I could only imagine what we looked like to the humans around us. Elizabeth and Mary with their short hair. My hair was worn back in a single thick braid that hung down to my waist. We wore tight, flexible breeches for fighting and metal breastplates. All garments were black for stealthy night movement. We were also heavily armed with swords and knives hanging from our belts. Clearly, we were not typical human women.

To see Elizabeth, a noticeably young girl, who looked like a boy, in such attire must have seemed even stranger. There was nothing we could do about that; the humans needed us and they did not even know it.

After another week of this nightmare, we stumbled upon an underground tavern that reeked of vampires.

"This may be it," Elijah said. "This could be where the culprit is hiding."

Our men surrounded the building after receiving a hand signal from Elijah. "Try to take the leader alive," he whispered. In a flash, Elijah kicked in the door to the brothel and I was immediately behind him. With one swing of his broadsword, he severed the heads of two guards who stood on either side of the door. Several vampires charged us. They were clearly trying to protect a man sitting in a chair in the center of the room. Our troops filed in behind us and we made quick work of them. Elijah put the leader in heavy iron shackles from which not even a vampire could escape.

"Take him to Lord Alexandru's dungeon to await questioning," Elijah ordered.

The man pled for us not to kill him as two of our soldiers dragged him away. We searched the place for clues linking this man to Ramdasha or for any letters or written orders that might tell us where Ramdasha was. We found nothing.

The man who was the leader of this coven admitted to knowing Ramdasha. It was Ramdasha who had sent him to London. He claimed that Ramdasha did not stay in any one place for long.

"I have no idea where Ramdasha is, as he has certainly moved on since last I saw him," the prisoner said.

"Where were the last known whereabouts of Ramdasha?" Lord Chastellain demanded.

Blood trickled out of the prisoner's mouth and one eye was swollen shut, thanks to the Court's interrogation. "Athens, My Lord. That is where I last saw him. Please, don't kill me. I am telling you the truth — everything I know, I swear it! He took up residence in a villa not far from town."

Once it was apparent that the prisoner knew no more, Elijah and his father exchanged a knowing nod and this time it was the lord who executed the prisoner. Chastellain's rage was out of control. He wanted his enemies to be struck down — at his own hand, if need be.

With their leader dead, we were able to clean up the last of the new vampires and stop the Black Death in London. The Court Elders agreed that we had to try to find Ramdasha in Athens. The lord called Riddick and Samuel back to Copenhagen. Riddick had been fighting in France and Samuel had been destroying new vampires in the northern regions of the Holy Roman Empire.

"All of our best fighters are to head to Athens at once," Lord Chastellain instructed. "After Constantinople, we can be assured that it will be dangerous. There is no way to know what our enemy has in store for us."

It did not take us long to spot the lone walled villa outside of Athens. Our combined armies of about one hundred vampires landed in the forest outside the city. Elijah motioned for us to stay hidden as he stepped out in front of a horse-drawn cart traveling along the road.

The horse started and so did the farmer driving the cart. He pulled back on the reins and the horse reared up on its hide legs.

"Do not fear. I mean you no harm." Elijah slowly approached with his arms out, as if surrendering. He gently took the horse's reins and ran his hand down the animal's long nose. As the horse calmed, so did the farmer. In fact, the horse closed its eyes, enjoying the soft touch. Elijah had always been extraordinarily gifted with horses.

"I need to know what you can tell me about that villa up ahead." Elijah's voice was soft and cordial.

It seemed to work, as the man spoke freely about the mysterious place. "Aye, it belongs to a lord. Can't quite recall his name. He is foreign — I believe. That place has been abandoned for a long time. There are many rumors flying around about it. You see, some folks think the place is haunted. I have heard tales of dark figures moving about the place at night, although I myself have never seen such nonsense. Still, I recommend you don't go poking around there all by yourself, young man."

"Thank you, kind sir. You take care as well." Elijah released the horse's bridle and stepped aside.

"Do you need a ride, sonny?"

"Thank you for the offer but I can manage."

The farmer look at Elijah with curiosity. "Suit yourself."

We emerged out onto the road once the man was gone.

"It appears that vampires may still be lurking about in the villa. Gather what large stones you can. We attack now, before Ramdasha hears word of our arrival," Elijah ordered.

The stones were to be used to trigger any explosives Ramdasha would certainly have in place around the estate. Once we had surrounded the manor's large walls, the stones were thrown over into the yard. Loud explosions instantly sounded off. Covering my ears, I hit the ground. Horrible memories of being trapped deep beneath the earth came flooding back. I fought back the panic inside.

Elijah pulled me to my feet. "What is wrong?" His eyes were full of concern.

I shook my head. "I'm fine." Yet I struggled to breathe.

He jumped effortlessly to the top of the tall stone wall. We followed his lead. The scene was nightmarish. The entire grounds were blackened; trees and shrubs were on fire as well as parts of the villa itself. The instant destruction of explosives was a fascinating and terrifying thing. We watched intently for any sign of movement inside and saw none.

"They must have abandoned the place already," I said.

"It would appear that way," Elijah frowned. "Samuel keep your men on the wall to make sure no one escapes. Riddick, take your men in from the top and we will enter at ground level."

Riddick nodded and took flight, gesturing for his soldiers to follow. Elijah did the same.

My heart was pounding in my ears. The ground level would be the most likely place for explosives. We threw stones into rooms before we entered. Thankfully, there were no more explosions.

When we entered the kitchen, I said, "Look at this." I pointed to two cups of half-drunk hot cider.

Elijah picked up one of the cups. "It is still warm."

We looked at each other with wide eyes. "We just missed them!" we said in unison.

"They must have spied us coming and fled," I added.

Elijah disappeared in a flash. I followed him.

He yelled to Samuel out the front door, "They can't be far; they must have left recently. Try to catch their scent and follow them."

Riddick appeared in front of us. "What is it?"

Elijah spoke quickly. "We've barely missed them. Go with Samuel;

you are our best tracker. We will stay and look for any more clues they may have left behind."

Riddick nodded and took flight. His best men were close behind him.

We continued to search the villa. We found a brazier filled with hot coals. Remnants of scrolls could still be seen. They were all but destroyed and no longer legible. We continued to search and found nothing.

It was not long before Samuel returned with an update. "We lost their scent not far out over the ocean. They must have dived into the water and we can no longer track them. Riddick is still searching the area. He sent smaller groups of men out in different directions to increase our chances of finding Ramdasha."

Elijah nodded and did something uncharacteristic. He yelled in frustration and kicked the brazier over, causing me to jump.

"We almost had them." Elijah spoke through gritted teeth.

I understood his frustration. I too wanted to end this boundless search for Ramdasha more than anything.

We used the villa as a base and continued to search for Ramdasha and his men for several more days. Once it became clear that he would be impossible to find from here, as he was long gone, we destroyed what was left of the villa. This was in hopes of finding any hidden chambers or the like. It was a fruitless endeavor and we eventually headed north once again. This time we moved slowly, fighting the Black Plague — Tarantism. There was plenty of vampire destruction to tend to along the way.

EPILOGUE

With my left thumb in my right palm, I would often rub the faint scar that remained. This barely visible white line was all that was left of the day Teller had proposed to me, so long ago. It was all I had left of him — of us. A constant reminder of our love that was now lost. He was out there somewhere. It was a wide world, after all.

The End of Book One
Help others find this book by leaving a review on Amazon.
Sign up to Lynne's email list at www.lynnehill.com to get a free eBook. Plus, never miss a new release.

OF PRINCES AND DRAGONS

Book 2 in the Lords and Commoners series

It isn't easy being a vampire amongst humans…

But Teller must keep up the front if he is to achieve his dream of becoming royalty…

A prince … an Emperor … or maybe even a God.

Enough is never enough for Teller.

He must have more, more wealth, more power, more …

All in the name of winning Vallachia back.

But will he ever have enough to satisfy her?

Or is it himself who is insatiable?

Something … or someone must stop him.

The vampire battle to end all battles is coming.

Who will Teller side with?

Get your next adventure today!

WHAT CRITICS ARE SAYING about book 2...

"I cannot wait to read the next one. It's fast paced reading about an unfamiliar world. It seems like it could be real!"

— Mbhutches

"KEEPS you on your toes waiting for what will happen next! Great characters and history!"

— Miller

ALSO BY LYNNE HILL

The Lords and Commoners Series

Of Lords and Commoners Book 1

Of Princes and Dragons Book 2

Of Gods and Goddesses Book 3

A Gods and Goddesses Novelette

A Woman's World Series

A Woman's World Book 1

Lost Powers Book 2

A Collision of Worlds Book 3

NOTES TO THE READER

This book is a work of fiction. It is not meant to be an accurate depiction of the places and times discussed in this book. Possibly one of the largest known historical inaccuracies is that the main characters travel across medieval Europe and yet they can understand and communicate with the foreign people they meet. This would not have been the case, as often times neighboring villages in medieval Europe would have had different dialects making communication difficult. For ease of telling the story this fact was ignored.

The Julian calendar would have been used at this time. Again, to make the story flow better for the modern reader the Gregorian calendar was used. Since the story does not have a narrator it would have been difficult to translate the dates for a modern reader.

ACKNOWLEDGMENTS

This book would not exist without all the help from my family and friends. Many thanks to my professional editors and preliminary readers; they all helped to make this book *much* more than it originally was! My editors, Eliza Dee, Leslie Safford, Marcia Kwiecinski and Colleen Kenney (I know that is a lot) helped to improve my writing many times over. I am grateful for all their education and insight. Thanks so much to my fellow writers. Their lessons in creative writing have saved me and made me into the writer I am today. A special thanks must go out to my parents. It is a cliché but they are my biggest fans. I'm very thankful that they have always believed in me. They are forever supporting my decisions no matter how much they change or how far out they may be. I thank my son and husband for their sacrifices.

A very dear friend and "sister" absolutely demands her own acknowledgements here. She helped to push me to do better in the best way possible. Her enthusiasm and hard work on this project have been paramount. Thank you all very much!

ABOUT THE AUTHOR

Lynne Hill is the author of the *Lords and Commoners* series and the *Woman's World* series. She made the short list for the Chanticleer Book Awards and was awarded a 5 Star Reader's Favorite Award. She was born in Colorado and raised in a small town of eight hundred people. Lynne holds a Doctorate of Psychology in criminology and justice studies. She is an advocate for Restorative Justice, a theme that is incorporated into her novels. Her extensive travels overseas and her work as an American Peace Corps Volunteer in Jordan helped inspire her writing.

Find out more at www.lynnehill.com and sign up to her email list to get a free eBook. Plus, never miss a new release.

www.ingramcontent.com/pod-product-compliance
Lightning Source LLC
Chambersburg PA
CBHW030627310726
48979CB00003B/912

* 9 7 8 1 7 3 6 7 2 4 9 5 8 *